Also available from Kasey Michaels and HQN Books

Stuck in Shangri-La

Shall We Dance?

The Butler Did It

And watch for
Everything's Coming Up Rosie,
on sale September 2006.

KASEY MICHAELS

A Gentleman
by Any Other Name

HQN™

ISBN 0-373-77100-2

A GENTLEMAN BY ANY OTHER NAME

Copyright © 2006 by Kathryn Seidick

This edition published by arrangement with Harlequin Books S.A.

® and TM are trademarks of the publisher. Trademarks indicated with ® are registered in the United States Patent and Trademark Office, the Canadian Trade Marks Office and in other countries.

www.HQNBooks.com

Printed in U.S.A.

Dear Reader,

In the twelfth century Thomas à Becket was assassinated at Canterbury on the alleged orders of his friend King Henry II. Legend has it that Henry ordered Thomas's body burned and the bones scattered. It is possible the remains, buried in the cathedral at Canterbury, were found and destroyed during the Reformation. Then again, the monks may have hidden the body, even interred the bones in another man's grave.

Perhaps this is why Ainsley Becket, a student of history, among his other, varied and not always laudable pursuits, found a small, secret satisfaction in coming to Kent in 1798, bearing the name A. Becket. For he, too, had been "murdered" by his best friend, and he had relocated himself to a place where he would not easily be found.

With him, Ainsley had brought his children, those of his heart, and Cassandra, the infant his beloved Isabella had borne him. His children. His redemption, his promise, his reason for drawing breath, his hostages to fortune.

Over the ensuing years the second oldest, Courtland, became Ainsley's strength, his rock. Morgan, the fiery one, had been orphaned when her sailor father, name unknown, buttoned his pants and got up from the lice-ridden bed of her prostitute mother, who had sold her to Ainsley the day she was born.

Then there was Eleanor, Ainsley's sea sprite, his delicate flower, his conscience. Spencer, the wild one, was Ainsley's potential heartbreak, with Fanny and Rian hotly contending for the same honors.

And lastly, there was the oldest, Chance, the boy Ainsley had rescued from a Port-au-Prince pub. Old enough to remember his beginnings, Chance had spent all of his thirty years trying to forget.

I invite you to come along with me as we meet Chance and all of the Beckets of Romney Marsh.

Enjoy,

Kasey Michaels

To Michael Robert Seidick.
Welcome to the world!

CHAPTER ONE

London, 1811

CHANCE BECKET SAT IN the formal drawing room of his Georgian house located in Upper Brook Street, not two blocks from Hyde Park, unaware of his expensive, fashionable surroundings.

No, not unaware. Uncaring.

How could he not care? Wasn't this what he wanted, what he'd always wanted? What he worked for, what he longed for…what he had achieved almost entirely on his own?

Perhaps that was the rub. He had done nothing entirely on his own. His extensive education had been a gift from his father, Ainsley Becket, *the* mysterious, reclusive and very wealthy Becket of Romney Marsh.

This house? This house had been a gift from his late father-in-law. Even the furnishings, the fine silk sofa he slouched in now, had come to him along with his wife, Beatrice.

Chance sipped from the wineglass that had moments earlier dangled from his fingertips, nearly spilling onto the fine Aubusson carpet.

He was a sham, a farce, living no more than the shallow dream of a reality that had fallen far short of all his youthful expectations. Gentlemen were born, not constructed out of whole cloth. All he'd achieved was the pretty shell; there was nothing pretty inside.

And yet, this was all he had, all he could ever hope to have, which was why Alice had to be rescued from him before she became as shallow and unfeeling as himself.

"Mr. Becket, sir? There is still one more waiting on you downstairs. Perhaps you are fatigued. Shall I send her off? Or do you wish to see her?"

Chance blinked away his self-pitying thoughts as he looked at his butler. "Forgive me, Gibbons, I'm afraid I was woolgathering. What a thoroughly depressing afternoon this has been. But there's another woman? I had thought that profane Billingsgate drab was the last of them."

"Oh, no, sir, there's still the one more, and I apologize again that Mrs. Gibbons still feels too poorly to have handled this chore herself and you've had to take the trouble. She'd be up and about if she could be, sir, but her nose is still running a treat and—"

"The last applicant, Gibbons, if you will. Concentrate, please. Time is running short if I am to have someone for Alice before we leave."

"Oh, yes, sir. This last is younger than the rest, sir, and with a civil tongue in her head, if I may say so."

"Please, Gibbons, don't raise my hopes. And please don't apologize yet again for your wife's illness. I'm sure she didn't take to her bed with that putrid cold you keep telling me about simply to thwart me in my hour of need."

"Yes, sir. I'm sorry, sir. That is—"

Chance waved the butler to silence and stood up, heading for the drinks table, for interviewing potential nannies had turned out to be thirsty work. "We'll make this quick, shall we? I promised Miss Alice I'd join her for her evening tea, although I have been informed I am not to be the guest of honor, as that distinction is reserved, as always, for her stuffed rabbit."

"Buttercup. Yes, sir." Gibbons bowed. "We shouldn't wish to keep Miss Alice waiting. Although this establishment will be a cold and dreary place without her, sir, if I may be so bold."

"Our only sunshine, gone. Yes, Gibbons, I am aware of the sacrifice. But it is Miss Alice we must consider. London is no place for a motherless child."

"Very good, sir," the butler said, bowing yet again before leaving the room.

Chance took up his position in front of the fireplace, placing his filled wineglass on the mantel as he stood, hands clasped behind him, awaiting what was sure to be another disappointment. *Buttercup*. Yes, of course. A good father would have known that.

"Mr. Becket, sir," Gibbons announced from the doorway. "Miss Carruthers."

"Mr. Becket," the woman Chance now knew as Miss Carruthers said, sweeping into the room with all the grace of a duchess and the wardrobe of a miller's daughter dressed up for Sunday services. A woefully unsuccessful miller. But then, if the woman had a full purse, she would not be hiring herself out as a nanny.

"Miss Carruthers," Chance said, indicating with a

slight sweep of his arm that she should take up her seat on the sofa to the right of the fireplace, while he, bringing his wineglass with him, retook his own seat. "You have come in answer to my advertisement?"

"Apparently so, Mr. Becket." Her tone was neutral, her diction reassuringly untainted by Piccadilly, her words not quite as subservient as he might have liked. And her perfect posture would put a military man to shame.

He watched, rather nonplussed, as Miss Carruthers stripped off her gloves, noting her long, tapering fingers, her neatly trimmed nails and the fine mending on the thumb of the left glove. She then removed her aged straw bonnet to place it beside her on the sofa, revealing a thick head of warm blond hair she'd mercilessly scraped back from her forehead and into a high, thick and rather lopsided bun.

Her skin was quite nice, pale but with hints of color, and her nose was delightfully straight above a full, wide mouth and a determined chin. He felt a stir of interest, which surprised him.

Miss Carruthers was down on her luck, most obviously, but she had pride and possibly breeding—definitely more than he could claim, but then, most anyone did. Best of all, she was clean and, if his luck was to have turned all the way for the better, would be desperate enough for a decent wage to give up the delights of London for the mist and damp of Romney Marsh.

In any event, at least Alice wouldn't take one look at the creature and run screaming for her nursery.

Chance didn't realize he'd been staring until Miss

Carruthers raised her chin and looked at him with a most incredible pair of long green eyes framed by brows too low and straight to be considered in vogue. "Forgive me, Miss Carruthers. Have you been waiting long? Would you care for a glass of lemonade?"

Julia Carruthers frowned, wondering if she should accept—and take a step toward insinuating herself—or refuse, keeping the distance she was quite certain master and servant maintained. But, dear, she was thirsty. "Thank you, sir, I appreciate your offer. Have there been many other applicants?"

"None worth considering, no. I'm afraid you're the last," Chance said as he moved to the drinks table. A pitcher of lemonade was always kept there for Alice.

He bent over, opening the double doors beneath the tabletop, and Julia watched as he retrieved a lovely glass goblet, taking note of Chance Becket's tall, well-formed frame. That and the black mourning band pinned to his sleeve above his left elbow.

She'd expected a woman, a mother, not this young, handsome society gentleman. She'd been prepared for a woman. She'd dressed for a suspicious woman with a husband or grown sons in the house.

Now she felt an absolute drab, all angles and third-best finery and with her hair pulled back so tight a headache had been throbbing at her temples for the entirety of the three hours she had been cooling her heels in Mr. Becket's ground-floor sitting room. She'd spent that time as the very last of a steadily decreasing number of other applicants, some of whom had given her pause as she wondered if they all could have been the same species as herself. So her hopes had climbed. But now she worried.

Julia took the offered glass, happy to discover that Becket's household was one that could support the frivolous expense of ice. How wonderful it would be to have her days of scraping for any bit of luxury behind her, even if that meant she had to ride herd on a passel of thoroughly spoiled children.

"Thank you, sir," she said, dropping her gaze to her lap to pretend she hadn't seen the assessing look in Chance Becket's green eyes.

Not at all like her own eyes, which her father had told her reminded him of the color of spring grass. Chance Becket's eyes were the dark green of a stormy sea at twilight, so green they were nearly black, and decidedly intelligent.

Julia's nervousness increased, which was never a good thing, for being nervous made her angry with herself, and she often said things or did things she wouldn't say or do if she felt more in charge of the situation. She knew this because her father had pointed this failing out to her on several occasions, mildly informing her that she could, now and then, become somewhat pertinacious.

What she knew now was that she was acutely *aware* of the man sitting across from her and that he made her very nervous. Why was he just sitting there? Why didn't he say something? Was she supposed to say something? Describe her qualifications? Drink more lemonade, so that he could be assured she didn't approach eating and drinking like a cow at the trough? What?

She dared to look into those eyes once more. "I can only hope I am the last applicant it will be necessary for you to interview, Mr. Becket, and that you will engage my services."

There. That had sounded fine, hadn't it? She'd said enough, and just enough. It was his turn now. Julia went back to looking at him. He really did fascinate her. Perhaps in the way of the snake and the mongoose? Hopefully not.

The man had strong features that didn't seem completely English. His unfashionably long hair, combed back and tied in a thin black grosgrain ribbon at his nape, seemed darker close to his head, as if the sun had teased gold into each strand only as it grew. Not an English blonde. In fact, with his strong nose and well-defined lips, with his high cheekbones, he could almost be of Italian descent. A Roman in his ancestral past perhaps? A warrior Roman who'd conquered some fair English maiden?

And she should stop being fanciful. She had no time to be fanciful. She raised her hand, politely coughed into her fist, hoping he'd speak again before they both froze here, mute, into eternity.

Chance struggled to come up with a reasonable question, one that had nothing to do with asking her why such a strikingly handsome woman as herself would wish to be nanny in someone else's household. A woman like this should be wed, with children of her own.

"I've yet to see your letters of recommendation, Miss Carruthers," he said at last, reminding himself that he was in charge here, after all.

"As to that," Julia began, then sighed. "I have none, sir, as I am new to London. In truth, I have never worked as a nanny, although I believe I am qualified. I most thoroughly enjoy children, and my education has not been lacking."

Never been employed as a nanny? That seemed fair, in some twisted way, as he'd never before employed a nanny. It might be better if neither of them knew how they should go on and just muddled along together. With Alice in charge, of course—he'd learned that much, at least, in the past six months. "And that slight accent? Do I hear a bit of Kent in your speech, Miss Carruthers?"

Julia smiled. "I didn't think it was obvious, Mr. Becket. But, yes, I was raised in the village of Hawkhurst. My father, now deceased, was vicar of a small church there, although he came originally from Wimbledon."

"Hawkhurst, you say. Very near the beginnings of the Marsh," Chance said, his tone now flat. "Then I would suppose you have no great wish to go back?"

Julia frowned. "If you are asking if I would enter your employment here in London just to leave it so that I might return to Kent? No, sir, I would not do that. There is nothing for me there now that my father is gone."

"Ah, the classic story," Chance said, suddenly more comfortable. "The dear child of an adored father, cut adrift and near penniless when the man died, was taken to his final reward on the wings of angels. Surely, Miss Carruthers, you could have come up with better than that? You're sounding very much like one of the penny press novels my late wife devoured along with her sugared treats."

Julia stood up, her gloves falling to the floor. She bent to retrieve them, knowing that were she a man, she would then employ one of them to slap this man's face and challenge him to a duel. If she were a man.

As a woman, however, there was only retreat, but she would do her pertinacious best that it would not be ignominious, and hang the consequences. "I believe we're through, Mr. Becket. You enjoy your amusement at my expense, and I will show myself out."

Chance came to his feet, holding out his arm as if to block her escape. Prickly thing, wasn't she? And he was desperate. "A thousand apologies, Miss Carruthers, my remarks were entirely uncalled-for, as well as rude. My only excuse is that it has been a rather trying day." He spread his hands, palms up. "If you had references..."

Julia took a breath, reminded herself of the slimness of her purse. And knew that didn't matter. "I do not, sir. I have only my word and my name, which clearly are not sufficient here in sophisticated and extremely impolite London. Again, sir, good day to you."

Physically tackling her probably wouldn't work. *Damn,* Chance swore to himself. The one prospect who seemed even marginally acceptable, and he'd bungled things badly. Worse, he'd somehow allowed her the upper hand, it would seem, because now he was all but groveling, as if *she* would be doing *him* some marvelous favor if he hired her. Confounding woman! "I wish you would reconsider. And I do apologize again."

Julia hesitated. She really did need the money she would earn. It would be nice to know she had a roof over her head when the sun set tonight, one she did not have to pay for out of her meager funds. She turned, took another look at Chance Becket. His eyes really were the color of a storm-tossed sea…which should have less than nothing to do with her decision. "I…um, that is—"

"Papa? Buttercup is very hungry."

Both Chance and Julia swiftly turned their heads toward the doorway.

"Alice," Chance said abruptly, "you were to remain upstairs."

The child's bottom lip came forward in a pout. "I've been upstairs forever, Papa."

Julia was entranced. From her lovely dark blond curls to the tips of her white satin slippers, the child could have modeled for one of Botticelli's angels. Clearly she was her father's child but redone in a delightfully soft and feminine form. "She's precious and the very image of you, Mr. Becket," Julia said quietly. "How your heart must swell each time you look at her. How old is she?"

Chance answered before he could think too much about the surprising comment or the question. "Alice is five. Her mother's been gone for six months, and I'm afraid I've allowed her to run a little wild. She should be in the nursery."

"She should be where she's happy to be," Julia said, smiling at the child. "And clearly she wishes to be with you."

Chance ran a hand over his hair, then impatiently

pushed at a lock that escaped the ribbon. "I should introduce you."

"Yes, thank you, but I think Alice and I can get to know each other on our own," Julia said, already walking toward the child. She went down on her knees a few feet away from Alice and said, "Hello. I'm Julia and I'm very pleased to meet you, Alice. Is that Buttercup? She's very pretty."

Alice looked at the yellow rabbit tucked under her arm. "He's a boy." She held out the toy. "See? Papa and I tied a blue ribbon around his neck. Isn't he a boy, Papa?"

Chance walked across the room to stand beside his daughter, one hand on her shoulder. *Mine,* his gesture announced without words, although he didn't consciously realize what he was doing. *Treat her well or prepare to deal with me.* "This week, yes, Buttercup is a boy. Where is your nurse, young lady?"

Alice shrugged. "She's napping, Papa. She's always napping."

"When she isn't nipping," Chance growled quietly, and Julia looked up at him, seeing her opportunity and immediately seizing it.

"I could take up my duties today, Mr. Becket. At this very moment."

"Really, Miss Carruthers?" Chance leaned down to kiss his daughter's head. He should have thought to produce Alice earlier, for she seemed to be his trump card. "Run along upstairs, poppet. I'll come join you very soon."

But Alice was looking at Julia, who was still on her

knees on the carpet. "You're pretty. Mama was pretty. Would you like to come to tea?"

"I don't know, sweetheart. We'll have to ask your papa." Julia got to her feet and looked at Chance. Waited. Then he smiled, and her heart skipped a beat.

"So we're quite settled then, Miss Carruthers?"

"Yes, Mr. Becket, I suppose we are. Quite settled."

The woman was transformed when she smiled, Chance realized, going from pretty enough to very nearly beautiful. If only he didn't think she might be smiling because she had bested him in some unspoken contest between them. "We'll discuss your wages at another time. But I must warn you, Miss Carruthers, we are not remaining in London above another two days."

"We're not?" Julia asked, her heart doing another quiet flip as Alice slipped her small hand into hers. "You have a country residence, sir?"

"I do. But we travel to Romney Marsh, to my father's estate, where you and Alice will remain while I return to London and my duties at the War Office. Are you still so anxious to be in my employ, knowing you'll once more be stuck in the back of beyond?"

Julia squeezed Alice's hand. "I can think of nothing I would enjoy more, Mr. Becket, than being Alice's nanny, no matter where that takes me. But I will say that London, I find, holds very little appeal. I much prefer the countryside."

"And I wish you joy of it, Miss Carruthers. I'm sure my family will welcome both you and Alice to Becket Hall with open arms."

"And you, sir?" Julia dared to ask, because Alice

had accepted her and she knew her battle was already won. "You don't enjoy Kent?"

The woman was entirely too insightful for his comfort. It was time for him to be done with this. "Wind and marsh and sea and mist. And sheep. More sheep than people, except for the people who are mostly sheep themselves." Suddenly he wished to be alone. "No, Miss Carruthers, I do not enjoy Kent. Now, if you'll excuse me, I have important matters to attend to while you and Alice have your tea."

"Papa, you *promised*," Alice said, letting go of Julia's hand to scamper after him as he turned to leave the room.

Chance was instantly contrite, guilty. "I did, didn't I, poppet. All right. You take Julia upstairs and show her the nursery, and I will be there…momentarily."

Alice turned back to Julia once her father had disappeared down the hallway. "It's all right, Julia. Papa forgets, that's all. Mrs. Jenkins says he doesn't care about me, but that's not true. He's sad with Mama gone." Then the child smiled. "But soon we'll visit all my aunts and uncles and my grandpapa and we'll all be so happy."

"You're a very wise little girl." Julia held out her hand and Alice took it. "Tell me, do we like Mrs. Jenkins?"

The little girl sniffed, gave a toss of her golden curls. "No, Julia, we do not like Mrs. Jenkins at all. She snores and she smells when she breathes. I'm so glad she'd rather poke a stick in her eye than go to live at Becket Hall. And now Buttercup and I have you, and she can go away." Alice looked up at Julia. "Why would anyone want to poke a stick in her eye?"

"A good question, as I nearly did just that a few moments ago with your papa," Julia said as they headed up the stairs, three whole flights, to the top of the house. "Oh, isn't this pretty," she said as they stepped into a large room with too few windows. "Aren't you a lucky little girl."

Alice became very serious. "No, I'm a motherless child and can never be happy again," she said, clearly parroting someone else's words.

"Mrs. Jenkins said that?"

Alice nodded, holding Buttercup close. "She is very put out that I am not dressed head to toe in black because Papa said I shouldn't. And when I laugh she tells me I'm unnatural. What is that? Unnatural?"

"It's nonsense, that's what it is, and nothing to worry your pretty little head about," Julia said, looking around the room, ready to slay dragons for this child. Or at the very least pop open one of the small, high windows and stuff Mrs. Jenkins out of it, onto the flagway below. "Ah, and here comes our tea, I believe."

Alice scrambled into one of the chairs set around a low table, stuffing Buttercup into another one as a lace-capped maid carried in a large tray.

The maid stopped, wide-eyed. "Who are you?"

Julia took the tray before the maid dropped it. "I'm Julia Carruthers, Miss Alice's new nurse…nanny. And you are…?"

"Bettyann. Good afternoon and welcome to you," the girl said, dropping into a quick curtsy before casting her gaze toward the slightly ajar door on the far wall. "Will Mrs. Jenkins be leaving soon then, miss? She will, won't she?"

"In there, is she?" Julia asked, following Bettyann's nervous gaze, realizing that the uneven sounds she had been hearing were not that of wind in the eaves but rather deep snores coming from the other room. Anything less than cannon fire was not going to rouse Mrs. Jenkins. Certainly not Alice slipping out of the nursery, as she'd done only minutes ago. "Is this usual for Mrs. Jenkins?"

"Yes, miss. She mostly stays in there, and then Miss Alice flits about the house, getting underfoot—not that any of us minds, you understand. Will she be leaving then, miss?"

"Before the cat can lick its ear," Julia said, feeling rather powerful in her new position. "I will be accompanying Miss Alice to...to Becket Hall."

"Oh, very good, miss, very good. Miss Alice? You'll want to eat while your porridge is warm. There's plenty, miss, and more bowls in that cabinet over there. I'll fetch you one."

"Fetch two, please, Bettyann, as Mr. Becket will be joining us."

"Oh, no, miss. He just went out. I saw him myself as he went. Mr. Gibbons said a messenger came and Mr. Becket told him everything was settled here and he had to go to the War Office to attend to something. Something very important, because Mr. Becket is very important."

"Papa's gone? But he *promised*."

Bettyann's features softened as she looked at the child. "He'll be back, sweetings. And now you have Miss Carruthers." The maid looked apprehensively at Julia. "You will stay?"

"My bags are stored with the landlord at the White Horse in Fetter Lane. If it would be possible for someone to fetch them?" Julia asked, already searching in the pocket of her gown for her purse. Her still very slim purse.

"Mr. Gibbons will send one of the footmen directly, miss. But I don't know where to put you, begging your pardon. And Mrs. Gibbons is abed with a putrid cough these past two weeks. I suppose Mr. Gibbons might know. Oh dear, oh dear. This is all so above me."

Before Bettyann suffered an apoplexy, Julia said, "Just have the bags taken to Mrs. Jenkins's room, if you will."

"But Mrs. Jenkins—"

"Will be gone," Julia said, handing the maid a few coins.

"Before the cat can lick its ear. You said that. Oh, miss, won't that be a treat," Bettyann said, grinning, showing the space where one of her bottom teeth had once resided. "And Mr. Becket says you are to do this?"

"Mr. Becket has engaged my services, yes," Julia answered, believing she'd ducked the full truth quite smoothly.

"Come sit down and eat, Julia," Alice said around a mouthful of porridge. "Buttercup wants to tell you all about his trip to the moon last night and all the lovely cheese he brought back with him. He flew there on a *huge* bird named Simon."

"A bit of a dreamer, Miss Alice is, miss," Bettyann said, smiling.

"And what is childhood for if not dreams," Julia answered, motioning for Bettyann to be on her way. "Once you've spoken to this Mr. Gibbons, please come back and escort Miss Alice and Buttercup down to the drawing room and stay with her while I speak with Mrs. Jenkins."

"Going to be a bit of a row, is there, miss?"

"Not if I find what I think I'm going to find behind that door, no," Julia said, wondering what had gotten into her that she felt so brave. But when she sat down across from Alice, she knew. A motherless child, as she had been a motherless child. They were going to get on together so well.

The father, however, could prove to be more of a problem. But then, as her own father had often told her, it was better to begin as one planned to go on. Although he also had sighed more than once over her rather headstrong manner.

Still, everything about her new position was wonderful. A sweet child to care for. A return to Kent, to her beloved slice of England. She'd only been in London for less than a day and already she knew that the journey had been a horrible mistake. If not for the notice in the newspaper left on a bench by a traveler, she would have already been on another coach, heading back to Rye, even more perilously close to poverty than she had been and with no prospects.

She had decided to seek her future in London for a reason. The newspaper had been left on the bench for a reason. She had seen Mr. Becket's advertisement for a reason. Little Miss Alice had come downstairs for a reason.

Julia was not by nature a superstitious sort. Nor did

she put much stock in Dame Fate. She truly believed a person made her own luck. But even she had to believe that this time there may have been a reason.

As for Mr. Becket himself? She would make sure that her good luck also became his good luck. She would become, in the next hour or two, indispensable to the man. She would begin as she planned to go on.

"Hmm, what lovely porridge," Julia said to Alice and picked up her spoon.

CHAPTER TWO

CHANCE LEANED BACK ON the squabs of his town coach, muttered an automatic curse as Billy jerked the reins and the horses lurched forward. Even after all these years, he thought, Billy made a much better powder monkey than he did a coachman.

Then Chance frowned, returning his mind to the just-completed meeting with Sir Henry Cabot, one of the chief assistants at the War Office.

"How good of you to present yourself so promptly, Mr. Becket. We were afraid we might have missed you, that you'd already gone on your way." He'd put down his pen that he had been holding poised over a sheet of thick vellum. "As long as you insist upon leaving us to travel to Romney Marsh, the minister has decided that you should linger there for a fortnight, perhaps even a month, if you were to discover anything of note."

"Anything of note about what, sir?" Chance had asked as Sir Henry had dipped his pen and begun writing once more. "I had only planned to escort my daughter to Becket Hall and then almost immediately return here."

"Yes, yes, Becket, but the minister says you're to be in no rush. He's spoken to Lord Greenley in the Naval

Office and together they've decided you might as well make yourself useful," Sir Henry had said, frowning over what he'd written and then sanding the page.

"Useful, sir?" With Sir Henry, Chance knew his contribution to any conversation was to say a word or two occasionally, except when he simply nodded his agreement with some statement.

Sir Henry had held a thick stick of wax over the candle flame, then pressed the War Office seal onto the page. "There, done. Useful, yes, that is what I said. You did reside in the area for some years, am I correct? You know about the freetrading."

Chance frowned. "Very little, sir. I didn't actually...spend much time at Becket Hall."

"Really? I wouldn't have either, had I been you. Horribly rural. Well, nevertheless, nobody would suspect you of anything, as you'll simply be visiting with your family—and with your daughter along, as well. All will seem perfectly normal, with you above suspicion."

"Suspicion of what, sir?" Chance had asked this question already fairly certain he knew the answer. And Sir Henry hadn't disappointed him.

"You're to nose about quietly, Becket, speak to the Preventative Waterguard stationed up and down the coast, as well as the volunteers, dragoons and Customs officials. See what you can ferret out on your own, as well. Smuggling is everywhere on the coast, but lately we're hearing very disturbing news from Romney Marsh. We're bloody hell losing a fortune in revenue, not to even think about the secrets that could be flitting back and forth between the Marsh and Paris. We are at war, and those bumpkin idiots are ferrying Frenchmen to our shores. Traitors, that's what they are, the lot of them."

"They're men who can't feed their families on what their own country pays them for wool, so they take the wool to France, almost within moments of it being sheared off the sheep's back, then bring back a few casks of tea or brandy to sell here. This is nothing new, Sir Henry, the Marshmen have been freebooting for centuries. War with France won't stop them."

"Becket, when I require a lecture on the matter, I will apply for one. This latest bit we've heard is much more than the actions of a few malcontents. There's talk of a very large, well-organized gang operating from the Marsh. Your mission is to personally speak to our representatives and make them aware that *we* are aware of their ineptitude in not capturing and putting a stop to these troublemakers."

"And to capture a few of them myself, so you can parade them here to be hanged in chains as a warning to their compatriots, I suppose?" Chance had asked the man, not at all happy about this turn of events.

"A young, strong, strapping fellow like yourself? The idea isn't outside the realm of possibility. But I believe you're being facetious now, Becket, and we surely don't wish you to put yourself in any personal danger," Sir Henry had said, handing over the paper plus another he'd pulled from a drawer. "You may use these in any way you deem necessary, one from the War Office, one from the Naval Office. They explain your mission and give you our full authority to go where you want, when you want. We're counting on you, son. Some arrogant bastard has gone so far as to deliver casks of French brandy to the residence of Her Royal Highness, the Princess of Wales."

And she'd drunk it with her ladies-in-waiting, Chance knew, shaking his head now as the coach slowly moved through the afternoon traffic. Wisely he'd refrained from sharing that particular knowledge with his lordship. And now he was on his way back to Upper Brook Street, planning a departure for Becket Hall in the morning, before anyone could press more demands on him.

Which brought Chance back to the most recent addition to his small traveling company, the amazingly forceful Miss Julia Carruthers. Would she be ready to travel?

Chance smiled wryly. The woman would probably be ready to travel in an instant. All she'd have to do is slide a leg over her broomstick.

Still, anyone was better than Mrs. Jenkins. How could Beatrice have countenanced such an unsuitable woman? Worse, how had he not noticed that the woman was totally unacceptable?

The answer to both questions, of course, was that neither he nor Beatrice had paid all that much attention to Alice. Children were kept in the nursery, out of sight, often out of mind. Indeed, Alice had been rarely in London with them, and they had been even more rarely in the country with her. In the circle of society in which he and Beatrice moved, that was natural, that *was* accepted.

And wrong. So very wrong.

The months after Beatrice's short illness and death, even though he'd sent for Alice, Chance had been too busy at the War Office to spend any real time with the child.

No, that was a lie. He could have found time for his daughter; he simply hadn't.

And yet, Alice seemed to worship him, which was more than embarrassing. He'd almost rather she hated him or was indifferent to him.

Alice needed stability. She needed a good home and people who loved her. Besides, in that gaggle at Becket Hall, one small child could hardly make much of a difference. She'd simply be absorbed, taken up the way Ainsley Becket had taken up Chance, had taken up all of them.

And then he, Chance Becket, would be free to return to London and get on with this dreary business that was supposedly the ordinary, civilized life he had always wanted.

The coach drew to a halt, and Chance opened the door before jumping down lightly to the flagway without waiting for the groom to let down the stairs. "Be prepared to travel to Becket Hall at six tomorrow morning, Billy," he called up to the coachman. "Both coaches. And Jacmel, as well."

Ignoring Billy's heartfelt "Huzzah!", Chance climbed the few steps to his front door two at a time and entered without waiting for the footman, who should have already been there opening the door for him.

The entire ground-floor foyer, in fact, was empty; nobody there to meet him, greet his guests or even protect his home. These things had always taken care of themselves, his life moving along without a ripple. How was he to know that it was the ailing Mrs. Gibbons who held the ship steady and not his butler?

He stripped off his hat, gloves and the greatcoat he'd worn to protect him from the damp mist of a London evening and headed up the stairs. Toward the noise he could hear. Voices, raised.

"Here, here," he reprimanded when he saw half his staff—what had to be half his staff—gathered around the closed doors to the drawing room. "What's all this about?"

"Oh, Mr. Becket, sir," Gibbons said, pushing his way through the small crowd of maids and footmen—and one young girl wearing an overly large white apron and holding what looked to be a half-plucked pigeon. "It's Mrs. Jenkins, sir, and Miss Carruthers with her, poor thing. She's not going quietly."

"Not going where?" Chance asked, then stopped, flabbergasted at his own stupidity. He'd hired Julia Carruthers. Obviously, as Mrs. Jenkins had refused to relocate herself to Becket Hall. It was all perfectly logical, to a point, with only one minor yet rather important detail overlooked. He hadn't told Mrs. Jenkins to take herself off, had he?

But these had been his decisions, damn it all to hell, even if he hadn't as yet quite gotten around to explaining them to Mrs. Jenkins before leaving for the War Office. Now there were two nannies in the household, and one of them had become instantly superfluous. Gibbons had referred to Miss Carruthers as the "poor thing." God. Had the older woman attacked her unwary replacement?

"Where is Alice?" he asked Gibbons. "And unless you want your head on a pike and your carcass pickled, tell me my daughter isn't in there."

Gibbons flinched. "Oh, no, sir. Bettyann's got her all right and tight up in the nursery. It'd been the other way round, with Bettyann and Miss Alice down here, but then Mrs. Jenkins comes running down the stairs—the *front* stairs, sir!—screeching for you at the top of her lungs, and Miss Carruthers right behind her. So Bettyann— she's a good one, sir—she snatches up Miss Alice and takes her off, and... Oh, sir, you really shouldn't have left things up in the air, sir, begging your pardon."

"How can a man believe himself competent to help manage the war effort when he cannot so much as maneuver his way in his own household? No, Gibbons, don't answer, it isn't necessary. Everyone, take yourselves back to wherever you belong. Not you, Gibbons. You have someone pack up Mrs. Jenkins's things and have them at the servants' entrance in ten minutes."

"Yes, sir," Gibbons said, bowing. "And Miss Carruthers's cases are already sitting in the kitchens ever since Richards fetched them from the White Horse. Shall I have them taken up to the nursery?"

"Whatever you think is right, Gibbons. I believe I'm quite done with managing domestic matters," Chance said, then squared his shoulders and headed for the double doors...and the commotion going on behind them.

He spied Mrs. Jenkins the moment he pushed open the doors, the rather large woman standing in the middle of his drawing room, her fists jammed onto her hips as she stared across the room.

"And *I* say I stay right here until the bugger brings himself home! Then we'll see, missy."

Chance took three steps into the room, at last seeing Julia Carruthers as she sat, with her exceptional posture, in a chair near the front windows, looking as calm and placid and as regal as the queen on her throne. Vicars' daughters obviously must be made of stern stuff!

"Shall we be forced to go through this again? I smelled the gin, Mrs. Jenkins," Julia said, not noticing Chance's presence, as she was wisely keeping her gaze solidly on Mrs. Jenkins, who looked more than ready— and able—to launch herself toward her. "You are, madam, a disgrace and an abomination, and so Mr. Becket will be told when he at last deigns to bring himself home and take care and command of his own household."

Insults from both women, Chance realized. First a bugger, and then, clearly, a total failure at managing his household. Standing still and waiting for more damning revelations really didn't appeal, so he said, "Ladies? At long last, the bugger's home. May I ask what's going on here?"

Julia Carruthers, he noticed, was intelligent enough to keep her mouth firmly shut, but he wasn't quite so fortunate with Mrs. Jenkins.

"There you are!" she said, turning on him. "This… this *girl* dared to turn me off, tell me to leave. I'll not be listening to the likes of her, let me tell you! Your lady wife took me on just afore she died, Lord rest her, and I've been doing my job just as I aught and I won't be—"

"Your belongings and a five-pound note will be outside the servants' entrance in ten minutes, Mrs. Jenkins. I would suggest that you be there to gather them up or else remain here and explain to me why I shouldn't personally toss your gin-soaked self onto the flagway. An action, by the way, from which I would derive great pleasure and satisfaction."

He couldn't quite suppress a smile as the shocked woman opened and closed her mouth several times before picking up her skirts and running from the room.

Julia could no longer contain herself. "You're going to give that terrible woman five pounds? She doesn't deserve a bent penny. In any event, I was handling the matter."

"I beg your pardon?" Chance slowly turned to look at Miss Carruthers, who had risen from her chair and was now walking across the room toward him with some determination, her arms folded beneath her bosom. Lord, but the girl was in a fury.

Julia knew the words *I beg your pardon* had sounded, in tone, much more like *This is none of your business, you cheeky twit.* But she'd just spent nearly an hour with Mrs. Jenkins, a woman with absolutely no redeeming qualities. She was, quite simply, too tired, too hungry and much too angry to stop herself.

"We'll dispense with the small fortune you plan to gift the creature with, Mr. Becket, and concentrate on the woman. You *knew* that dreadful person was all but a *sot* and yet you kept her on?" She pushed one arm up straight and pointed toward the ceiling. "May I remind you in case the fact has slipped your mind—that's your *child* up there, Mr. Becket."

Chance was stung into explaining himself. "I would

have one of the maids bring Alice to me when I wished to see her. I didn't really know much about Mrs. Jenkins. Not until last week, when I informed the woman we'd be leaving for Becket Hall and she would remain there with Alice and I realized that she was totally—oh, the devil with it! Who are you to question me?"

Julia's anger left her as self-preservation raised its not very noble but definitely necessary head. "I'm sorry, sir. I shouldn't have taken it upon myself to dismiss Mrs. Jenkins. And I have no right to badger you about your…your arrangements concerning Alice. In my defense, I can only say that it has been a long day. A very long day."

As it had been for him. "And about to become longer, Miss Carruthers," Chance said wearily, "for we leave for Becket Hall at six tomorrow morning, a very convenient leave-taking or else I would replace you. However, you, madam, having routed Mrs. Jenkins, are now in charge of preparing my daughter for the journey. Oh, one thing more. May I say how gratified I am to see that Alice now has a tiger to defend her, although I would remind you that she needs no defense from *me*. And now, if you don't mind, I believe your place is in the nursery, while mine is here, getting myself dedicatedly drunk."

"Yes, sir. Forgive me, sir. Good evening to you, sir," Julia said, curtsying to the man when she'd really much rather be boxing his ears. She then quickly swept past him and into the hallway, where Gibbons, with a slight nod of his head and shifting of his eyes, directed her toward the back of the house and the servant stairs.

CHAPTER THREE

THE JOURNEY BEGAN AS did many journeys in England—amid a damp drizzle and accompanied by considerable fog.

Julia had roused Alice at five, only long enough to direct the child to the water closet and then wash her face and hands before pushing her reluctant limbs into a short blue gown Julia considered suitable for travel and a fur-trimmed blue coat with matching bonnet. She then carried the child down three flights of stairs and hoisted the once-again-sleeping princess into the traveling coach and wrapped her in a coach blanket.

Six o'clock of the morning, indeed! Did the man possess no sense at all?

"Watch her, please, Bettyann," Julia asked of the housemaid who had followed behind Julia carrying Buttercup and a small portmanteau Julia had filled with items she considered necessary for a child's comfort inside the coach. "I'll only be a minute."

Julia paused a moment to look at the fog that all but obscured the street. At home there was nearly always a morning mist, but it was white and smelled like fresh grass and the sea. Here the fog was yellow, dirty. She believed she could actually taste it. "Why did I ever think I would care for London?" she asked herself, then hiked up her skirts with more of an eye toward speed than decorum and headed up the steps once more, for she'd left her bonnet, gloves and pelisse in the nursery.

"Here now," Chance Becket said warningly, grabbing at her shoulders as she all but cannoned into him, her gaze directed on the steps. "There's no need for such a rush, is there?"

Julia looked up at the man, struck yet again by his fine good looks and, this morning, the hint of real humor in his eyes. He was dressed for travel, a gray many-caped greatcoat hanging from his broad shoulders, the snow-white foam of his neck cloth visible at his throat, and he wore a matching gray curly-brimmed beaver hat.

Tall, handsome, his smile almost boyish even while the sparkle in his eyes told her he was far from a boy. Julia sent up a short prayer that she wouldn't disgrace herself by swallowing her own tongue, drat the man.

"You said six o'clock, sir," she reminded him, doing her best to ignore the heat of his hands that could be felt through the thin stuff of her gown.

"Ah, so this is not Miss Julia Carruthers, is it? You only look like the woman. The Julia Carruthers I met yesterday would not only have snapped her fingers at my reasonable request but also told me she'd be ready to travel when she was ready to travel and not a moment before. I do believe I like this Julia Carruthers much more."

"You have considered the fact that a five-year-old child travels with you, haven't you, sir? That a long day and fresh horseflesh along the way could get you to the coast by very late this evening, but that such a punishing pace could be harmful to this child?"

"To Alice, Miss Carruthers. I do remember my child's name," Chance said, bristling. If he only had time to replace this infuriating woman, he would be a happy man. Ainsley would love her belligerent spirit, though. Since Chance was all but dumping Alice into his adopted father's lap, he might as well sweeten the pot…a thought that, rather than warm him, sent a chill straight to the bone. "She'll be fine."

"Of course, sir. You wouldn't have it any other way," Julia said, then rolled her eyes the moment she was past him and on her way up to the nursery again, and hang the fact that she'd opted for the main staircase. "Idiot," she grumbled, hiking her skirts once more before she began the climb.

She halted on the second-floor landing as Gibbons directed two footmen who were carrying baggage on their shoulders toward the servant stairs, then looked down the front staircase, assured herself she was alone.

Wetting her lips, and with one more quick glance over her shoulder, she then gave in to what her father had termed her most besetting sin. She tiptoed down the hallway, into the bedchamber that had to belong to Chance Becket.

She didn't know precisely why she wanted to see the chamber, unless she hoped to glimpse something of the man there. And if that was the case, she was instantly disappointed.

The man lived like a Spartan, the large chamber

nearly devoid of any ornamentation save a few nonde-
script paintings on the walls. His brushes and many
personal items were, of course, already on their way
downstairs to the traveling coach, but there was something so empty, so impersonal about the room, that Julia
wrapped her arms around her as if to fight off a chill.

"Lost your way, Miss Carruthers?"

Chance didn't know whether to be angry or amused
when she jumped, gave out a small startled squeal before turning about to face him, her eyes wide in her
ashen face.

"I…I thought only to be certain that all of the baggage has been removed. And…and it has." She lowered
her head and took a step forward, but he stepped to his
right, blocking her way. "Excuse me, sir."

"You're very efficient, Miss Carruthers," Chance
said, deciding, yes, he'd much rather be amused. "I vow,
I've discovered a rare diamond and taken her into my
employ. Has my valet packed up my tooth powder, or
haven't you inspected my dressing room as yet? Oh, and
the drawers? Have you checked them. You know, the
drawers containing my most personal items of clothing?"

Julia gave it up and just sighed. "Oh, all right, so I
was poking my nose where it doesn't belong and you
caught me out at it. You're delighted to have caught me,
and I'm sorry you did. I merely wanted to see if there
was something I could learn about you that might help
me in understanding…" She took a breath and said
what she had thought. "How do you live without
things?"

Chance's humor was rapidly dissipating now. "Excuse me?"

"Things, sir. Personal things. My father had a collection of shaving brushes with decorated handles he was fond of and an entire rack of strangely shaped pipes he'd collected. They're gone now, of necessity sold, but he always kept them in his chamber where he could see them. And some shells he'd gathered and a small portrait of his sister and…and you have nothing. The maids must be quite pleased, as dusting your few bits of uncluttered furniture couldn't take but a moment."

Chance looked about his fairly cavernous bedchamber as if he'd never seen it before this moment. It was a bedchamber, somewhere to sleep. Beatrice had overseen the decoration of the rest of the house but had left his chamber relatively untouched. And so had he. Clearly Julia Carruthers seemed to think this unnatural.

"There are the paintings," he pointed out, stung into defending himself.

"Yes, there are. Trees and grass and hills. And a pond. Where are they located?"

What a ridiculous question. Why didn't he have an answer? He'd been living with these paintings for over six years. Chance coughed into his fist. "Located? I don't know. My late wife was raised in Devonshire. That seems as good a place as any for trees and hills and ponds, don't you think?"

"Having lived my life next door to Romney Marsh, where hills and trees are both at a premium, I confess I really couldn't say. You've nothing of Romney Marsh or the sea here, do you, even though you were raised there?"

This conversation had gone on long enough. "I lived there, Miss Carruthers. There's a difference. And only from an age not much younger than you are now, with the majority of my time being spent away at school. There, are you quite satisfied now? Or is there anything else you'd wish to know about or poke at before we're able to be on our way?" He made a point of pulling his timepiece from his waistcoat pocket and opening it.

In for a penny, in for a pound, Julia decided, knowing she couldn't be much more embarrassed than she already was at being discovered in her employer's bedchamber. And thankfully it was much too late for him to fling a five-pound note at her and send her on her way. "The portrait over the mantel in the drawing room. Your wife, sir? Alice looks very little like her, although that may change as she grows."

"My question was meant as an insult, Miss Carruthers, not an invitation. But since you probably know that and asked your question anyway, I can tell you we meant for another portrait, Alice posing with her, but Beatrice never seemed to find the time to— We're done here, Miss Carruthers," Chance snapped out tightly, then turned on his heel and left the chamber.

Julia lingered a few moments longer—just until she could hear his heels on the marble stairs over the rapid beating of her own heart—then raced to the nursery to snatch up the remainder of her belongings.

When she returned, breathless, to the street, it was to see she'd been correct, that her new employer had chosen to ride out of London on the large red horse she'd earlier seen saddled and tied to the second coach.

Which was just as well. She really wasn't ready to face the man again and probably wouldn't be for some time. She could only hope that he would have forgiven her inexcusable behavior before their first stop along the road. During which time, she promised herself, she would practice dedicating herself to being subservient and uninterested and totally uncurious about anyone or anything other than performing her assigned duties without bothering the man again. Cross her heart and hope to spit.

"So much for setting impossible goals," Julia muttered not three hours later as she held Alice's head while the child was sick into the ugly but efficient chamber pot that Julia had found beneath her seat in the coach. They'd stopped along the way, but only briefly, to change horses.

"I don't like coaches," Alice said a few moments later as Julia wiped the child's mouth with a handkerchief. "I want it to stop. I want it to stop now, please, Julia."

"And stop it will, I promise." Julia eased Alice back against the velvet squabs and returned to her own seat, which was no mean feat, as the roadway below them must have been attacked by a tribe of wild men with picks and shovels intent on destroying it, and she was half bounced onto the floor twice.

Thinking words she could not say within Alice's hearing, she then opened the small square door high above the rear-facing seat. Pressing her cheek against the coach wall, she could see the legs of the coach driver and the groom riding up beside him. "You, coachman!" she called out. "Stop the coach!"

"Can't do that, missy. We're behind-times as it is."

"I *said,* stop this coach! Miss Alice is ill!"

"Oh, blimey," the groom said nervously. "Billy, Mr. Becket won't like that."

"And yet Mr. Becket isn't down here, holding a pot for Miss Alice to be sick in!" Julia shouted. "If you're going to be frightened of anyone, *Billy,* it should be me, as soon as I can get my hands on you! Are you *aiming* for every hole in the road?"

There was no answer from Billy or the groom, but Julia could feel the coach slowing, its bumps and jiggles, if anything, becoming even more pronounced. But at last the coach stopped.

"I'm going to be sick again, Julia," Alice said, almost apologizing.

Julia scrambled to the child, opening the off door as she did so, and pulled Alice rather unceremoniously toward the opening. Holding her by the shoulders, she said, "Just let it all go onto the ground, sweetheart. I'll hold you tight and you just be sick, all right?"

Alice's answer was a rather guttural, heaving noise, followed closely by a few startled male curses…which was when Julia realized that Chance Becket had dismounted and come to see why the coach had stopped.

"God's teeth, woman, you could give a man a little warning!"

"Or I could wish little Alice's aim were better," Julia muttered, but very quietly.

Alice had more than emptied her small belly now, and Julia once more eased her against the seat, handing her a clean handkerchief. "Stay here, sweetheart, and don't cry. I'll handle—speak to your papa."

Grabbing the brass pot with one hand, Julia kicked down the coach steps and made her way, pot first, out of the coach and onto the ground. She spied the coachman, a small, painfully thin man of indeterminate years who, she had noticed, walked with the same rolling motion of a seaman more used to ships than dry land. If he were to apply to her for her opinion on his choice of employment, she would be more than pleased to tell him leaving the sea for a coachman's seat had not been an inspired one.

"Billy," Chance said. "You have a reason for stopping, I'll assume?"

"I'll answer that, Mr. Becket. Deal with this, *Billy,* and go to sleep tonight blessing your guardian angel that I haven't dumped its contents over your head," she said, biting out the words, all but tossing the pot at the coachman, who was suddenly looking a little green himself.

"Why is Alice ill?"

Julia had to unclench her teeth before she could answer what had to be one of the most ignorant questions ever posed by a man. "The pitching of the coach, Mr. Becket. A child's stomach isn't always up to three full hours of such motion. And my stomach has expressed a similar wish as Miss Alice's, so if you'll excuse me?"

Chance stepped back as Julia looked rather wildly toward the line of trees, then all but bolted into them until he could no longer see the blue of her cloak.

"This is why women are not welcome aboard ship," he said in disgust to Billy, who heartily nodded his agreement, then went off to deal with the contents of the pot.

"Papa?"

Alice. He'd forgotten Alice. There had to be a special hell for fathers such as he. "Alice, poppet," he said, climbing into the coach, leaving the door open behind him, as the interior smelled far from fresh. His daughter looked rather pale and somehow smaller than he remembered her, as if she'd shrunk in both size and age, as she hugged her stuffed rabbit to her chest. "How are you feeling now?"

Alice sniffled, her bottom lip trembling. "I want to go home, Papa. Buttercup doesn't like coaches. Coaches have too many bounces."

How could he have been so oblivious? Good weather, fine teams, a brisk pace and Becket Hall by ten that night. He'd been thoroughly enjoying himself up on Jacmel. And all without a single thought to his daughter's comfort. He most certainly hadn't thought about Miss Carruthers's comfort…although he hadn't been able to completely put the infuriating woman out of his mind.

"I'm afraid we can't return to London, poppet," he said, cudgeling his brain for some explanation the child might understand. Being rid of her would not have been a good starting point for that explanation. "But I promise that the coachman will drive much more carefully so there aren't so many bumps. And tonight you'll sleep in your own bed at Becket Hall."

"You can't possibly mean that. Not now. You really intend to drive all the way to the coast with this child?"

Ah, and here she was again, the woman who either didn't know or didn't care about her proper place. "Yes, Miss Carruthers, I still intend exactly that—and last night sent a message to Becket Hall *saying* exactly that," Chance said, exiting the coach to stand on the ground beside her. Her pale complexion had gone positively ashen. "You look like hell."

"Compliments are always so welcome, especially when one is considering death to be a viable alternative to one's current condition," Julia said, looking back down the roadway, longing for her portmanteau and her tooth powder. "We've so outstripped the second coach? Alice's clothes are in that coach."

"The coachman knows the way. Or are you worried that my daughter's cases might disappear forever, Miss Carruthers?"

"No, those worries are for my own cases," Julia said almost to herself. Then she took a deep breath, let it out slowly. "I refuse to allow Alice to travel this way. There, I've said it."

"And meant it, too," Chance added, looking back over his shoulder. Alice's small head had disappeared from sight below the opened window. "Very well. Do you believe we can agree on Maidstone?"

"We'll stop there for the night?"

"We will stop there for the night, yes. But for now we must push on. Agreed?"

"Grudgingly, yes," Julia said, then squared her shoulders and climbed into the coach. She carefully eased the now-sleeping Alice aside so that she could sit on the front-facing seat—the rear-facing seat had been an unfortunate choice for her stomach—then pulled the child half onto her lap.

Looking out the opened window, she said, "She'll

need a bath, fresh clothing and a good night's rest, Mr. Becket. She's a small child and fragile and should be handled accordingly."

Chance nodded, knowing the woman was right, hating himself for being so selfish. "You've made your point, Miss Carruthers. No need to drive it home with a hammer."

"No need but definitely a strong desire," Julia muttered as the man slapped his hat back on his head and returned to his mount. Moments later the coach lurched forward once more, never reaching the killing pace set earlier. She then spent the next hour stroking the sleeping Alice's curls and looking out the off window while ordering her stomach to behave.

"Coming into Maidstone ahead!"

Julia blinked herself awake at the sound of the groom's shout and looked out the off window yet again, happy to see the beginnings of civilization once more.

Within an hour she and Alice were settled in a lovely large room at one of the many inns along the water. Alice had been washed, slipped into a night rail, had gingerly nibbled on buttered bread and milky tea and was once again sound asleep, now between sweet-smelling sheets.

And Julia was hungry. This surprised her, but she trusted her stomach to know best, so she washed her face and hands, frowned at her no-longer-neat hair, tucked Buttercup into the bed beside Alice, locked the door behind her and took herself downstairs to search out the common room.

"Not in there, Miss Carruthers. Lord knows the grief

you could come to if you were to encounter my coachman again while you're still of a mind to boil him in oil," she heard Chance Becket say just as she was about to step across the threshold into a low-ceilinged room sparsely peopled with farmers and travelers. "I've arranged for a private dining room."

She turned about to see that he had changed out of his hacking clothes and into a finely tailored dark blue jacket over fawn pantaloons. His hair, damp and even more darkly blond, had been freshly combed and clubbed at his nape. He looked fresh and alert and entirely too handsome to be smiling at her, to even know her name. "It was not the coachman who ordered us to all but *fly* to the coast. And I doubt, sir, that it is customary for the nanny to break bread with the employer."

Chance laughed, doubtful that anything so mundane as convention ever gave this woman much pause. If it did, she wouldn't have taken a step out of her chamber before doing something with that thick mop of hair that looked as if she'd spent the day scrubbing floors. "Perhaps you require a chaperone?"

"Oh, don't be silly. I'm a plain, aged old maid of nearly one and twenty. Nobody cares," Julia said, absentmindedly pushing a stray lock of straight blond hair behind her ear as she felt her cheeks begin to flush. Why on earth had she told him her age? "Where, sir, is the private dining room? I'm starved."

He gestured toward the hallway leading away from the small square foyer, and Julia had no choice but to precede him down the hall.

"In here," Chance said, stepping ahead of her and

pushing back the door that was already ajar. "Shall I leave it open—to ease an old maid's sensibilities, I mean?"

Julia blinked rapidly, for she was suddenly so stupidly missish that she actually believed she might cry. "Now you're being facetious. I'm the nanny, a simple domestic servant. Just do sit down, sir, so that I may."

"You are many things, Miss Carruthers," Chance said as they sat down on either side of the narrow wooden table, "but I am afraid that the role of servant is not one of them, at least not by nature. Tell me, have you ever considered the occupation of despot? I do believe you'd excel at it."

Julia picked up a still-warm roll, ripped it into three pieces, then reached for a knife and the butter pot. It was time for a change of subject. "How long will you remain at Becket Hall before returning to London, sir? I had thought you had planned only to deliver us there, but the amount of luggage you've ordered brought with you seems to contradict that thought."

"Oh, don't pretty it all up with fine words, Miss Carruthers," Chance said, using his fork to skewer a fat slab of pink ham and put it on his plate. "You poked about in my bedchamber, tallying up bits of luggage the way a headmaster counts noses. And you're alarmed that I might actually remain at Becket Hall above a day, because nothing would make you happier than seeing the last of me. Oh, and I am a horrible parent to Alice. Correct?"

Julia chewed on a piece of roll, swallowed, then smiled. "Correct, Mr. Becket. Except for that last little bit. I don't think you are a horrible parent, because Alice seems to love you, and children are the very best judges of people. After dogs, I suppose. But you're not very attentive or perceptive when it comes to your child, are you? Most of your gender aren't, leaving such things to the females. My father, I believe, was an exception, as he was forced to raise me alone."

Chance leaned back on his chair, rather amused about her reference to dogs. "So following that thought—and having known you now for nearly four and twenty hours—I can conclude that it's the mothers, then, who for the most part teach their children about tact and thinking before speaking and refraining from invading another's privacy and the art of showing respect—that sort of thing?"

Julia lowered her gaze to her plate to find that she'd loaded it with ham and cheese from the platter in the middle of the table. Yet suddenly she had lost her appetite.

"Come, come now, Miss Carruthers. Consider this a necessarily delayed interview as to your qualifications to ride herd on my daughter, as the first was rather slapdash, to say the least. I begin to worry that, raised entirely by your father, as you say you were, you are not the one to help mold Alice to be a respectful, conformable child."

Clearly the man was now driving home his own point with the head of a hammer. She was being reminded just who she was—and who she was not. And the pity of it was, she could not afford to push him any further, unless she wanted to be left here, in Maidstone, to fend for herself. "I'm her nanny, sir, her nurse, and not her tutor or her governess. I believe you can safely leave her teachings to others. I'm here to…to hold the chamber pot."

"Quite," Chance said, liking this woman better when she wasn't keeping herself in check. He'd had seven years of society women, of women never saying what they meant, what they felt—if, indeed, they felt anything. Miss Carruthers was more like his sisters, none of whom suffered fools gladly.

Which, he realized, would make *him* the current fool, wouldn't it? "Very well, we'll dispense with the interview now. Perhaps you'd like to hear more about Becket Hall? After all, you will be living there."

"For how long, sir?" Julia asked, her curiosity overcoming both her uncomfortably real nervousness and her temper.

"For you, Miss Carruthers? For as long as you can stomach the place, I imagine. For Alice, until she is grown and ready for her season. I don't wish for her to grow up in London, and my own estate is manned only by a skeleton staff, which is why I've arranged for her to be with the family. I'll visit her, of course."

"Really? And how long has it been since you've visited Becket Hall, sir? Alice has told me she's never been there."

Chance shifted in his chair. "She was taken there as an infant. Once. My wife didn't care for…for the area."

Julia had her own thoughts on what the man's wife hadn't cared for, but she'd begun to understand that saying what she thought wasn't as accepted by society gentlemen as it had been by her father. Was his family horribly rustic, that his fine society wife couldn't like them? If so, Julia knew she already liked them, sight unseen. "Romney Marsh can sometimes seem like a separate country, not part of England at all."

Chance's mind went back to his conversation with the War Office minister's assistant. "I'll agree that many of the inhabitants don't seem to believe they are a part of the war going on with France."

Julia nodded. "The Owlers. You are referring to them, aren't you? But they smuggle to survive, Mr. Becket."

"I understand their reasons, Miss Carruthers, and even sympathize, if that statement doesn't startle you overmuch," Chance told her. "We only wish they could understand our concerns. Besides the lost revenue, spies and information have been traded back and forth across the Channel with the unwitting help of the Owlers, as you call them. That has to stop."

Julia bristled. She knew the history of smuggling along the Kent and Sussex coastlines. She'd daily drunk tea left as a gift after the smugglers had used her father's church to store their haul before moving it inland. "Then the government has to do more than *say* it understands. Have the king raise the price paid for wool, sir. That would be my suggestion."

Chance smiled, knowing he was speaking with a woman who'd been raised believing smuggling was nothing more or less than a fact of life. "Don't bite off my head, Miss Carruthers. It's my solution, as well, but I am here to tell you that a similar suggestion has already been offered and refused. And for good reason. We're already strapped financing a war, remember?"

Julia shrugged, holding back a smile. How she adored a lively conversation, even a lively argument. "Better a war than an insurrection, sir. Or don't you think it will come to that? My father worried that one day we will suffer France's fate if we don't learn the lessons of their revolution."

Chance downed his mug of ale, good country ale made with Kent hops. "'To write this act of independence we must have a white man's skin for parchment, his skull for an inkwell, his blood for ink and a bayonet as pen.'"

Julia blinked, taken aback by the bloodthirsty statement. "I beg your pardon?"

"I was quoting Boisrond-Tonnerre, Miss Carruthers, not making a statement of my own. The words were said by Tonnerre, who served as one of Jean-Jacques Dessalines' lieutenants, back in 1804. That's when Haiti declared its independence after a fight begun by François Touissant, a slave whose master made the colossal blunder of allowing him to read about the so-glorious French Revolution. In other words, I am agreeing with your father, such an event is possible. And, yes, oppression makes such insurrections more than possible. Are you familiar with the history of Haiti, Miss Carruthers?"

Julia shook her head, interested and not a little impressed at Chance Becket's so-smooth pronunciation of such tongue-twisting French names. "I'm sorry, I'm not. It's an island? Is sugar grown there?"

Chance wished back his words. "Another time, Miss Carruthers. I was only thinking that there has already been one instance of a people copying the methods of the French Revolution. Indeed, we do not want another, most especially not here. Let me tell you about Becket Hall. Shall we walk?"

"I really should go upstairs to check on Miss Alice," Julia said, getting to her feet.

"I'll have a maid sent up to sit with her. Alice has no problem with strangers."

Julia still believed she should return to Alice's chamber, but she did long to hear about Becket Hall and the Becket family, as well as more about Haiti, of all places. "Very well," she said, handing over the key to the chamber. "But wait, I'll do it. I should go fetch my bonnet anyway."

"Not if you have any pity for me, Miss Carruthers. The thing is close to an abomination, you know. Even that ridiculous bun is less offensive to the eyes."

Julia went to raise a hand to her hair but caught herself in time. "One would assume you, too, were a motherless child, Mr. Becket, as that was quite an untactful remark."

Chance did not smile. "Wait for me here, Miss Carruthers, doing your best to keep any opinions to yourself."

Julia gave herself another short, pithy sermon on the benefits of knowing her place while also taking the time to munch on another slice of ham and tuck a roll into the pocket of her gown before her employer returned and led her out onto the street.

He turned to the left and then guided her around the side of the large building, down a gravel pathway to a bench that overlooked the River Medway. Or the River Wen. Julia only knew that Maidstone had been built on the banks of both waterways. Until the horrible mail coach ride to London that now seemed two lifetimes ago, she had never strayed more than a few miles from Hawkhurst, except for occasional trips to Rye with her father.

She sat, raising her face to the sun while she listened to the flow of water through the wheel of the mill on the opposite shore, the song of birds overhead…and concentrated on not thinking about the man sitting beside her. And there were flowers; flowers everywhere. Maidstone had been touted as the Garden of England, and now she knew why. "I still can't smell the Channel, but we will tomorrow. How near is Becket Hall to the water?"

"All but too near when the tide comes in during a winter storm," Chance said, a mental portrait of Becket Hall forming in his mind. "My father loves the sea."

"And you don't?"

This woman turned his every spoken word into a question about *him*. How did she do that? "I've sailed. Now, you'll be with Alice at most times, but I know my family. They're extremely informal and they'll wish to include both of you in their day-to-day lives, so you'd best be prepared for that."

Julia could sense tension building in the man, from his posture to the tone of his voice. "You disapprove?"

"It's not up to me to approve or disapprove. Only to explain. My father, Ainsley Becket, is still a rather young man. We're not his children by blood, you see, except for Cassandra. In truth, I only refer to Ainsley as my father when I'm in society, because that's easier than constant explanations. Ainsley never leaves the Marsh, you understand, and has never been to London. In any event, Ainsley was a man of business in the islands for many years and simply acquired the rest of us from time to time."

Julia was absolutely fascinated. "He adopted you there? In the islands, you said? Islands in the Caribbean?"

"Adopted, purchased, scooped up—yes, he did. I'm not disclosing any secrets here, for you'd soon realize that the Beckets are a rather mixed assortment. I am the oldest, although Courtland likes to believe himself our keeper, and Cassandra is the youngest. The rest all fall somewhere in between, whether thinking of their ages at the time they became a part of the household or when they were born."

Julia, having grown up as the only child in her father's household, often envious of her friends and their many brothers and sisters, was eager to hear more. "How many of you are there?"

Chance wished he hadn't begun this conversation, but the woman should know what she was facing. "Eight, other than Ainsley. Quite the menagerie. Court, Cassandra, myself. My sisters, Morgan, Eleanor and Fanny. My brothers, Spencer and Rian. So you understand, Alice will not want for company."

Julia's head was spinning as she attempted to digest so much information given so quickly. All those names. Too many names. "I'm sure she will be delighted. But all those people. Becket Hall is probably enormous?"

Chance watched as a V of ducks slid across the current toward the shore. One in the lead, the rest following in that V, all neat and tidy and regimented. So unlike his family, his house, all of their lives.

He could never run far enough to get away.

"Becket Hall is large, yes. Large and rambling and fairly ugly." He stood up. "Shall we go?"

Julia got to her feet. "I believe I'll sup with Alice in our room this evening, sir. When shall we be ready to travel tomorrow morning?"

Chance ran a hand over his hair. "That's *my* decision? I hadn't planned on abdication, you understand, but I have begun to believe I've been overthrown. Shall we say eight?"

Julia smiled. "I think eight is a perfect time to continue our journey, sir." And then she gave in to curiosity yet again and pushed for more information. "Why, you may even have time to say your hellos to your family and still be back on the road to London early the next morning."

"A plan that would please me straight down to the ground, Miss Carruthers, much as that obviously disgusts you. But we both remember the amount of luggage I have brought with me. It turns out that I have matters to attend to up and down the coast, so I will be staying at Becket Hall—or at least returning to it every few days—until such time as I can escape to London."

"Really?" Julia said, trying to sift through the feelings his information had aroused, decide if they were feelings of joy or discomfort. "Alice will be very pleased, sir."

"Oh, yes," Chance said, then sighed, mentally picturing his brother Court's reaction to the news. "Everyone will be extremely pleased. Good day to you, Miss Carruthers. Don't remain outside without your cloak or you'll take a chill. I refuse to consider the prospect of being compelled to interview yet another nanny."

Julia watched him walk away, heading downstream along the bank, his hands clasped behind his back. Another woman might be intrigued by the man. The bereaved husband. The harassed, unknowledgeable but sincere father. The wretchedly handsome man with the brooding eyes and the full mouth of a soul who had been born for passion and adventure, even if he seemed woefully unaware of that fact. A man who'd seen an exotic place like Haiti, had even lived there. How? As a poor, orphaned boy at last discovered by Ainsley Becket and given a new but clearly unhappy life?

Yes, any woman would be intrigued, fascinated. Any woman would want to hold him, comfort him, help him.

Well, almost any woman.

Julia Carruthers longed to run after him and give him a good push in the back, sending him toppling headfirst into the river.

CHAPTER FOUR

CHANCE TOOK JACMEL for a run early the next morning, knowing the only way to keep the animal to a steady pace would be to first wipe away the memory of being locked in a strange stall all night. He then spent most of the day on Jacmel, either cantering ahead of the traveling coach or waiting by the roadside for it to catch up with him again, until he at last pushed into the coach to ride sitting beside his daughter.

It was dark now. Alice was soundly asleep. And Billy—had Julia Carruthers put the fear of God into the man?—had slowed to carefully pick their way through the moonlight over the last miles to Becket Hall.

A maddening day. A wasted day. And yet a lovely luncheon with Alice, who could chatter away nineteen to the dozen about everything and anything.

And all of that time, for every moment of the day, Chance had been unable to block Julia Carruthers from his mind. She was a servant, yes, but more than that, she was a woman. She might not be a society miss, but she probably knew more of her bloodline than he did of his; most anyone would. She was no worse than he, probably a good deal better, even if she had hired herself out as a child's nurse and he was living in a fine house in

Upper Brook Street, dressing in custom-tailored clothes and holding a fairly important post in the War Office.

He was the man he had made. A gentleman, in name if not by birth.

He rarely thought of the young Chance anymore, the ragged, barefoot boy who had angled for pennies on the wharf and slept wherever he could. He'd been known only as "Angelo's brat," until Ainsley.

He'd moved so far beyond that life, both in the islands and here in England.

But every turn of the coach wheels took him closer to Becket Hall, and the memories refused to go back where they belonged, into the far recesses of his brain. He blamed Julia Carruthers for that, although he knew such reasoning to be ridiculous.

Ainsley would like Julia Carruthers, damn him.

Yes, he publicly referred to Ainsley as his father and the others as his brothers and sisters, but in his mind all he saw was the end, that last day, that last memory. He would never forgive Ainsley that last memory.

Build a life, watch that life be destroyed. Love and refuse to love again. Protect yourself, adhere to the rules, refuse to be vulnerable or dependent again. Never, never trust.

Those were the lessons of that last memory. All of that. And Isabella's smile…

Julia cried out when Billy sawed on the reins. The horses all but plunged to a stop and she was tossed into Chance's arms from the other side of the coach.

"What on earth…?"

"Cow-handed fool!" Chance tried to disengage himself, but he had reflexively thrown out one arm to keep a sleeping Alice from tumbling to the floor of the coach, so that he could barely steady Julia with the other as she scrambled to right herself.

Julia had been dozing and was really only half-awake now as she pushed against him with her hands to right herself.

"*Ooof!* Miss Carruthers, please, for the love of all that's holy—"

"I'm sorry, sir. So sorry," she said, feeling her cheeks growing hot and blessing the darkness that hid that fact. "What happened? Why have we stopped?"

"Two very good questions, both of which Billy may be able to answer if my hands are not wrapped too tightly around his scrawny neck," Chance said, opening the door and jumping down onto the uneven ground. "You stay in the coach with—oh, never mind," he finished as Julia jumped down to stand beside him. "Billy? *Billy!*"

"Here, sir!"

"He's there," Julia said, pointing past the horses. "There, in the road. He's bending over something."

"Making it easier for me to boot him in the hindquarters. Is it too much for me to ask you to stay here while I investigate further, Miss Carruthers?"

"Probably," she said, knowing she should be agreeing with him, climbing back into the coach. "But Alice didn't waken and there's nothing out here anywhere save the road, the marsh and us. No trees, barely anything that could even be called a hill. What could be in the road? A sheep?"

"I suppose we could stand here and debate the matter, but I suggest I—we—do the obvious and go look," Chance said. He offered Julia his arm because otherwise she might trip over something in the darkness, and the woman was enough of a problem to him now without adding a sprained ankle to her list of detractions. "Oh, wait a moment more. Stand here while I get a pistol from the coach."

"You think the sheep is armed?" Julia ignored both the offer and the order as she lifted her skirts and made her way past the horses to where Billy was standing very still in the roadway.

"Billy?" she asked, then realized that the coachman was staring quite intently, not down at the roadway but over to one side, where the marsh grasses grew waist-high.

"I'm that sorry, miss. I didn't used to be such a looby," Billy said, then slowly raised his hands up over his head. "He said not to do this until you came looking, miss."

Julia's eyes had become more accustomed to the darkness, and now the moonlight helped illuminate the scene in front of her.

She could see that Billy had shot his hands into the air because a young man kneeling in the marsh grass was holding a large, ugly pistol directed at the coachman's chest.

The dark object in the road was really two dark objects, both of them human forms, neither of them moving. Julia went to her knees in front of the closest figure, who seemed little more than a boy.

"Lower your weapon, boy," Chance said from somewhere behind her. "Yes, I can see you, and by the way that pistol's shaking in your hand, I believe I'm the better shot. Billy, stop acting the looby. Lower your arms and relieve the halfling of his pistol before he hurts himself."

"Me, sir? Begging your pardon, sir, but a pistol is a pistol, even in the hands of a boy. And this one's cocked."

"Oh, for pity's sake," Julia said, looking first to Billy, then to the young man, who shook as he held the pistol, and lastly to Chance, who looked quite dangerous. And not at all afraid. She wished she could say the same, but she was actually terrified…which had the happy result of making her very, very angry. "We've got two boys bleeding to death in the road and no time to worry about who is the better shot, for clearly the best shots have already been taken. Billy, never mind the pistol. Fetch a lantern from the coach."

"Hoppin' right to it, miss!" Billy said, then turned and ran back toward the coach, directly disobeying Chance's order.

Chance continued to hold out his cocked pistol, even though he knew he was too far away to do more than aim, pray and shoot, probably hitting the infuriating Miss Carruthers, who had gotten to her feet in order to walk around one body to the other. "Miss Carruthers, if you would do me the courtesy of standing still—"

But she was down on her knees again, a hint of moonlight illuminating her blond hair but not her features that remained a shadowy profile as she looked up at the third man. Boy. Very nearly boys, all three of them, not men. And one of them would never grow to manhood. "I'm so sorry. I can't help this one, but I may be able to help the other, if you'll let me."

"Georgie? Georgie's dead?" the boy said, then called out, "Georgie! Georgie, you're not dead!"

Chance took the opportunity to advance toward the group and remove the aged pistol from the terrified boy's hand. "Did you shoot him?"

The boy dropped the pistol and turned wild eyes on Chance, speaking between sobs. "No, sir! They shot him. Two of 'em. They shot our George and our Richard. They shot at us when we wouldn't give 'em the tubs and Georgie told 'em to bugger off. We dropped the tubs and ran. We ran forever till we lost 'em. Then Georgie fell, right here. And Dickie, too. We never should have done it. We should have waited—what am I goin' to tell our mam?"

Julia listened to the boy even as she pushed aside the dark blue smock on the wounded Dickie to see the even darker ugly hole in his shoulder. "Help me turn him, Mr. Becket, please," she said, as the boy was unconscious, his breathing shallow.

"What?" Chance had lowered his pistol as he listened to the third youth's sorry tale, not paying much attention to Miss Carruthers except to note that she certainly did seem to enjoy the role of heroine. "What the devil are you doing?"

"Trying to save this boy's life, obviously. He's been running and all the while bleeding like a stuck pig," Julia said as Billy stood above her holding one of the large lanterns he'd taken down from the side of the coach. "I think the ball went straight through, but I want to be sure. Billy—hold the lantern closer while Mr. Becket and I turn Dickie and have a look. Mr. Becket? Your assistance, please?"

Was there any choice? Besides, the third youth was sitting on his haunches now, sobbing; he'd be no further trouble. Chance put down the pistol and dropped to his knees, carefully lifting the unconscious boy enough to roll him onto his side. "Well, Miss Carruthers?"

"In one side and out the other, Mr. Becket. I think he simply fainted, probably because he's lost so much blood."

And she was right, as Dickie roused quickly enough a few minutes later when Julia poured the contents of Chance's flask over the wound, the boy coming up wide-eyed and yelling for his mam.

By now the second coach had caught up with them, and as Billy and Chance stood guard in case the boys had been pursued, Julia rummaged in her portmanteau for an old slip and tore some of it into strips she tied around the cleaned wound.

"Are we far from Becket Hall, Mr. Becket?" she asked as she sat back on her heels, looked up at him in the moonlight. "We need to take Dickie with us. And poor George, as well. How is John?"

"John? You mean the one over there, retching into a ditch? Clearly past managing anything at all useful. You know these boys are smugglers, don't you?"

"Yes, I heard John mention tubs. Tea or brandy, do you suppose? Well, it's of no matter. They came afoul of someone, didn't they? What nonsense, to be just three of them out here on the Marsh."

Chance smiled a not-quite-amused half smile. "I suppose when *you* are out smuggling, you only travel in groups of ten or more."

"Ten? I should say not. More like dozens, Mr. Becket. Only a fool doesn't align himself with one of the gangs. And I have not run with the freebooters, sir, although I would lie if I said I didn't know many of them and haven't heard their stories. Poor Georgie," she said, looking at the body sprawled facedown in the road. "He couldn't have been more than seventeen, could he? His poor mam."

Chance glanced up at the moon. "And now you want me to transport all three of them to Becket Hall. Feed them, hide them, endanger my family with their presence. Has it by any chance occurred to you, Miss Carruthers, that I am a representative of the king and that the proper place for my two *prisoners* is Dover Castle? Dover Castle, then on to London where they will either be hanged and gibbeted or duly whipped and transported."

Julia put a hand on Dickie's shoulder, easing him back onto the ground. "He doesn't mean that," she said soothingly, then got to her feet to all but go belly to belly with Chance Becket. "If you're quite done putting the fear of king and courts into these poor boys?"

"Oh, bloody hell," Chance said. "Billy!" he called out, still looking at Julia. "Get the boy and have him help you load his brothers into the second coach. I want to be moving again in five minutes."

"Ah, now, sir, couldn't Nathan be takin' up the other end with me? Big, strappin' boy, Nathan."

Chance looked toward the groom, then toward the weeping boy. His jaws tightened as he remembered the time when, no more than fifteen himself, his wrong move had cost another man his life and how Ainsley had driven the lesson home. "No. He'll be less inclined to reckless acts after carrying his own dead brother. There are some weights a boy must live with if he's to learn to be a man."

Billy nodded. "Rodolfo. Right you are, sir. I'm just gettin' old and soft."

"And growing deaf, as well. I told you to get the boy and load the others." Then he gave Billy a pat on the shoulder as the man shuffled off.

"Thank you, sir," Julia said, totally confused by the exchange between Chance and Billy but knowing enough not to ask any of the many questions that had popped into her head. Such as, who was Rodolfo? And what so-sober memory did Billy and Chance share? So she merely watched, her heart aching for the boy, as Billy and a sobbing John picked up Georgie by his wrists and ankles and carried the body back along the road.

She'd seen dead bodies before, seen wounds before, but she was not nearly so calm as she pretended to be, because she'd always had her father by her side and in charge. Far easier to follow orders than to be responsible for giving them, responsible for the person needing her help.

"Dickie told me he and his brothers had gone to retrieve their small share of a larger run," she told Chance, feeling the need to fill the silence between them, speaking quickly, probably saying too much. "No one was supposed to do that until the entire gang could assemble tomorrow night, meet up with the land carriers. But Georgie wouldn't hear of that for some reason or other. These two men John spoke of must have spied them out and followed them. Now the entire haul may be lost, not just their portion of it, and the gang will be forced to find a new hiding place for freshly landed goods. A mess all around. Dickie and John had best be gone from the Marsh before anyone else knows what happened. His mam and any other family, as well."

Chance cocked one eyebrow at her, rather amazed by her knowledge and her deductions, not to mention her cool head in the midst of this crisis. "Obviously you've been giving all of this some considerable consideration. You expect retribution from the boys' compatriots?"

"Don't you? Freebooting is a desperate business and demands total secrecy. Through their eagerness, Georgie and his brothers may have lost the entire proceeds of a smuggling run. Possibly tons of goods, all paid for and brought to shore, hidden. Considerable work and cost are involved, sir. Someone will be very unhappy and want revenge. Dickie made mention of a black ghost but then quickly begged me to forget I'd heard what I'd heard."

"That would probably be wise. Excuse me," Chance said tightly and went after John, who was now wringing his hands and crying yet again. He took the boy roughly by the elbow and steered him into the tall grass beside the narrow roadway. "Stop wailing like a little girl. Stand up straight and look at me. Your brother told the lady about a black ghost. Now you're going to tell me."

John's eyes went wide. "Oh, no, sir. He did no such thing. None of us never would, sir. Dickie's just hurtin' bad, that's all. He never said that."

Chance ruthlessly squeezed the boy's upper arm. "Dover Castle, boy. Ever see a body hanging in gibbet chains? The blacksmith comes and fits you for your very own set. Grown men have been known to keel over dead just seeing the smithy come at them with the measuring stick. And it all starts at Dover Castle. I know the way—you and your brother could be there by morning. Of course, with that hole in him and with no one to doctor him, he'll be dead soon and you'll probably hang alone. Crying and pissing your pants as they drag you to the rope, your mam there to watch."

He gave the boy's arm a shake. "*Tell* me."

"We…we travel with him now, sir. The Black Ghost. Him and his men protect us from the others. From this side of Camber to Appledore and all the way to Dymchurch, sir. We're almost all together now, with the Black Ghost watchin' over us."

"Is that so?" Chance did his best to control his breathing, his temper. "The others, John. And who are the others? The ones who came after you?"

"I can't say, sir." When Chance squeezed again, John rushed into speech. "I don't know, sir, that's what I mean. Hundreds of them, all together. From Lunnontown, we think. We had to join together, too, or else lose everything. We're the Black Ghost Gang now, sir. We can't say it because nobody is to know but us. Never say

Black Ghost, sir. Dickie never should have said that. But Georgie, he said we didn't need to listen to nobody what won't even show his own face and…oh, sir, what do I tell our mam? Georgie was her favorite of all of us."

Remembering what Julia had said, Chance asked, "How many of you are there?"

Johnnie wiped his runny nose on the sleeve of his smock. "Twelve, sir. Da's gone, drowned on a run these two years past, but there's still twelve of us." He half choked on a sob. "E-eleven, sir. And now they seen us. They know who we are. Now they can find us. We're all going to be dead, like Georgie. Mam and Dickie and me, even the little ones. The Black Ghost can't help us now. Maybe the Black Ghost will even want us all dead, too. We was told to stay away until tomorrow night and we didn't listen. What should I do?"

"Christ," Chance muttered, then pulled the boy roughly into his arms. He let John weep against his shoulder while he told himself this boy was nothing like he had been years ago, when he knew that wasn't true. Desperate was desperate, no matter what the cause. Desperation was a taste, a smell, a fear you took to bed with you at night and woke with again in the morning.

"We really should be goin' on, sir," Billy said, grinning as he dug one booted foot into the stones. "I'll take young Johnnie off your hands, now that you're done teachin' him a lesson and all."

Chance disengaged himself from John's clinging arms. "Maybe I'm getting old and soft myself, Billy."

"Don't worry, boy, it'll all come back to you," Billy whispered with a wink, then took John by the shoulders, handed him his own filthy handkerchief, called him a good boy and led him back to the second coach.

Chance looked toward the lead coach to see that Julia had been watching him, had seen him with the boy. Had probably overheard him as he'd spoken both to Johnnie and Billy. Without a word she turned, hiked up her skirts and climbed back into the coach.

Leaving Chance to stand in the moonlight, silently cursing the Black Ghost. "*This* is how he hides?" he asked the night at last, then headed for the coach.

"Will your father—will Mr. Becket be upset that we've brought the boys to him?" Julia asked when Chance was seated across from her once more and the coach was moving yet again.

She could see his wry smile through the darkness. "Upset? Miss Carruthers, tonight will be probably the first time I will have pleased Ainsley Becket in thirteen long years."

Julia said nothing more but only sat in the darkness to consider the London gentleman whose knowledge seemed to reach far beyond concerns such as the cut of his coat or the latest society gossip, her mind full of questions, possibilities…and more than a little apprehension about what might await her at Becket Hall.

CHAPTER FIVE

LOW CLOUDS AND A SLICE of moon allowed Julia to see some of the facade of Becket Hall as she stood in the courtyard looking up at the huge stone building.

They'd driven up a wide, curving gravel path that was happily well-tended, to stop in front of the large central section of the house that seemed to be in the shape of a large U—although it could be an H, as she couldn't see if the wings also extended toward the Channel she knew to be behind the building.

"The house doesn't overlook the water," she said mostly to herself, but Chance heard her.

"There are terraces," Chance told her as he lifted the sleeping Alice from the coach. "But only a fool would face a house toward the Channel, Miss Carruthers. Then again, only a fool would order so many windows built into that side of the house."

They had long ago, somewhere between London and Maidstone and the incident on the Marsh, given up the notion that he was her superior, with she his docile servant (or at least she had), so Julia didn't think twice before asking bluntly as she reached back into the coach to retrieve Alice's small traveling bag, "Then I am to consider Mr. Becket a fool?"

"That would probably depend on where he decides to put you. If your bedchamber overlooks the water, you may think so once winter comes and storms begin to blow, rattling those same windows. But, no, you'll be in the nursery with Alice, which I believe to be even worse, as your chamber will be directly on a corner. Shall we? Billy, go pound on that door knocker, will you?"

Julia moved close beside Chance as they climbed up one of the wide stone staircases to a large stone porch, attempting to block Alice from the salty breeze that found them even in the shelter of the immense building.

"What about the boys, Mr. Becket?" she asked, holding the hood of her cloak over her head as the wind whipped at it. "Someone should be sent for the doctor, I believe."

"First let's get Alice into the house, Miss Carruthers. Billy well knows what to do."

"Really? Let us only hope he well knows better than he drives a coach."

Chance took a moment to smile at this, then disappeared as the large front door opened and light spilled onto the porch. Fifty servants scattered about Becket Hall and its outbuildings, at the least, and Jacko opened the door? Had Chance's luck gone from bad to even worse? "Jacko," he said, keeping his tone even if not cordial. "He's got you butlering now in your declining years?"

Julia squinted, trying to see the man as her eyes became accustomed to the brightness of the light that outlined a tall, wide shape that stood in the doorway. She watched as two thick arms came away from the man's sides before he jammed his hands onto his hips, the breadth of him now, elbows out, all but filling that doorway. Not loosely, sloppily fat, like Mr. Keen, the Hawkhurst baker, but just big and very, very solid. Stone-wall solid.

And with a voice that sent a chill down Julia's spine. "Here now, look what the sea dragged up. No, no, never the sea. Can't get your dainty city feet wet, can you? What's the matter, boy? Running from creditors, are you? Or did you wink at the wrong woman? Thinking to hide here? Not under my skirts, you won't."

Julia could feel Chance tensing beside her. "Skirts? But it's a man, isn't it?"

Chance sniffed, shook his head. "It's Jacko. And if he ever wanted to wear skirts, Miss Carruthers, I can assure you I'd be the last one trying for a peek beneath them. Come on or he'll just pose there spouting nonsense to amuse himself and have us standing out here all night."

"Oh, so that was in the way of friendly banter then?" Julia asked, knowing she'd heard nothing friendly in anything Jacko had said, no matter that he was dressed as a gentleman.

"Could it be anything else, Miss Carruthers?" Chance asked through clenched teeth, then shifted his blanket-wrapped daughter in his arms. "I've got Miss Alice here, Jacko, as Ainsley obviously didn't get my letter, so you can either leave off your crowing and let us in or take a bow, then shut the door on our faces and we'll be on our way."

The man stepped forward, the light from the dying flambeaux on either side of the door at last revealing his face, showing his age to be somewhere older than Chance Becket and younger than Moses when he'd come tripping back down the mountain with those clay tablets in his arms. More than that, she really couldn't tell.

Julia didn't know whether to smile or run screaming for the safety of the coach. For this was a round, happy face. Even a jolly face, with eyebrows raised up high on its forehead, a large nose with a bulb at the end, a carelessly trimmed mustache and small beard surrounded by apple cheeks. His smile was wide and exposed huge white teeth that were all odd-sized and oddly spaced.

The eyes? The eyes showed amusement, even playfully twinkled. The skin around the eyes crinkled when he smiled. Oh, so jolly. Jacko would probably look jolly even as he was carving your beating heart right out of your chest.

"You've got the babe with you?" Jacko asked, his head coming forward on his thick neck, as if this part of him, at least, wanted a closer look. "God's backside, you do! Well, get in here, boy. Don't leave the child out in the damp. God gave you brains, didn't he?"

Julia bit her lips between her teeth and waited for Chance to precede her into the large entrance hall, then followed after him, making sure she stood as far from Jacko as was possible without physically crawling beneath the long table pushed against a side wall.

Jacko kicked the door shut and turned to look at

Alice, who had awakened at last and was already look-ing at him. "Hello, princess," he said, his voice tender now, his delight obvious.

"Hello," Alice responded sleepily. "I'm not a prin-cess. You're funny."

It was true, Alice wasn't afraid of strangers. But Julia didn't trust that smile, that laugh. She knew a danger-ous man when she saw one. Jacko was like a dog you met on the village street, seeming pleasant enough but just as likely to bite as to wag its tail.

"She's very tired," Julia said, stepping in front of Chance, as her concern for Alice outstripped her reluc-tance to draw this man's attention to her. "We need to be shown a room where I can get her into bed. Thank you."

Jacko cocked one eyebrow and looked past Julia, to Chance. "Not the wife. I remember the wife. Didn't say two words to me, but I remember her. Who's this?"

Chance held his temper as Alice slipped her thin arms up and around his neck. "Miss Carruthers is Alice's nurse, Jacko. And my wife is dead these six months, as well you know. I've brought Alice to stay here, within the warm, loving bosom of my family. Now I'm taking Alice up to the nursery, as I know the way, and you can tell Ainsley I'm here. Or you can go to hell."

Julia let out a half cough, half choke, then lifted her skirts to follow after Chance when he headed up the staircase, as being left in the hallway with Jacko wasn't the most appealing thought she'd ever entertained.

She made it halfway across the hall before a large

hand grabbed her at the elbow and pulled her to a quick halt.

"You don't look like a nanny. Too pretty by half, and you look like one who really sees what's around her. Why's he here? Why's he *really* here, pretty girl?" Jacko asked quietly, smiling down at her.

"If you have questions for Mr. Becket, you should direct them to him," Julia said, wondering briefly if she might faint. "Please let go of my arm."

"Leave off, Jacko. She's good enough. Knows what she's about, this one does."

"Billy?" Julia asked, blinking, as the coachman rolled his wiry body into the hallway. What on earth? Servants didn't come into the front of the house, most certainly not a coachman wearing all of his travel dirt and with mud still caked on his boots. And most definitely not any servant carrying a half-eaten drumstick.

Billy's walk was suddenly more assured, the tone of his voice much more forceful, and Julia realized that this was the real Billy she was seeing now and not the awkward, scrambling little man who worked as Chance's fairly cow-handed coachie—probably playing that role for her benefit, now that she considered the thing.

"Billy boy, there you are, ugly as ever." Jacko let go of Julia's arm. "You can go up now, miss. Third floor, then turn to your right and then your left and follow your pretty nose to the end."

Julia didn't move other than to rub at her arm where Jacko's sausage-thick fingers had been. "You're seamen. Both of you. I should have realized…I should have—"

She shut her mouth, remembered Billy's description of her: *Knows what she's about, this one does.*

And she did, didn't she? She hadn't lived in Hawkhurst on the edge of Romney Marsh for all of her life without coming to "know what she's about." Knowing what Billy and Jacko were and even what those three unlucky young boys had been "about." Knowing that asking too many questions in Romney Marsh could mean she'd soon know too much for anyone to be comfortable.

But there was one question she had to ask. "Billy? Will you please tell me what you have done with the boys? Have you sent for the doctor? They're harmless, Billy, just boys."

"What's she running her mouth about? What *boys?*"

"The lads will be fine, missy," Billy said, ignoring Jacko's question as he looked at Julia. "Excepting the dead one, of course. He'll still be dead. Odette's with the other one. If she can't fix him, he's good as fish bait anyway. No harm will come to them, rest your mind on that. Mr. Chance, he gave orders. You go on upstairs now, missy."

Julia opened her mouth to ask something else—so many questions already half-formed in her mind!—but Jacko was looking at her again. "Thank you, Billy. Our…the baggage?"

"Already waiting on you, missy."

"Thank you again," Julia said as she clutched the small traveling bag to her and neatly sidestepped Jacko. She didn't break into a run until she reached the third floor, barely remembering anything of her surroundings on the way up, except to think that Mr. Ainsley Becket, whatever and whoever he was, must possess amazingly deep pockets.

She had, however, found time to think up at least a half dozen pointed questions for Mr. Chance Becket!

Julia pushed wide the already opened door that led to the nursery—again, an almost ridiculously well-appointed room, larger than the entire vicarage in Hawkhurst—then followed the sound of voices into an adjoining room to her left. There she found Chance Becket and little Alice, Chance doing his best to pull the blue gown up and over his child's head.

"Here, sir, I'll do that," Julia said, stripping off her pelisse and tossing it onto a nearby rocking chair that, goodness, had carved swans' heads for arms. She opened Alice's traveling bag and pulled out a night rail. "I imagine you'll be wanted downstairs."

"Do you really," Chance said, stepping back to let Julia take over the chore of undressing a child so sleepy her arms and legs seemed boneless. "You took your sweet time, Miss Carruthers. I already know you're a curious sort. Did you allow yourself a tour?"

Julia lowered the night rail over Alice's head, tucked her arms into the sleeves, then kissed the child's cheek as she worked to push back the coverlet and slip Alice's legs between the sheets. "Someone knew we were coming, Mr. Becket," she said as she stood up again. "Those are fresh sheets on Miss Alice's bed. There are fires in the grates. And there are newly lit candles. We were expected."

She watched as Chance ran a hand over his hair. He'd had a long two days, definitely a long evening tonight. He looked almost adorably rumpled, some of his hair having escaped the ribbon, and there was a hint of strain around his eyes. Obviously this was not a happy homecoming.

"True, Miss Carruthers. Jacko knew. He simply preferred to pretend he didn't. I was expected last night, however, and when I didn't arrive I may have disappointed someone. Jacko wanted me to be quite sure I understood that."

Julia shook her head. "Well, I don't understand. Why would you plan to leave your daughter here? You obviously detest the place and dislike your family, at the very least."

Chance's look was cool and level. "If we're done here, Miss Carruthers?"

He knew what was coming even before he saw her lift that maddeningly expressive chin. How in the name of Hades had he been so stupid as to hire this confounding woman?

Ah, desperation. It had been out of desperation, of course. Once he'd sent the letter off to Ainsley, once he'd made up his mind that he had no logical recourse but to go back to Becket Hall with Alice, he'd had no choice but to stay with his plans, even when Mrs. Jenkins proved unacceptable.

Those were his reasons, along with the way Julia Carruthers had appealed to him physically. A welcome surprise to sweeten the large bite of crow he would swallow once he stood in the same room with Ainsley Becket.

Even now, when he knew Julia was about to say something totally unacceptable and clearly out of line with her duties, all he wanted was to undo that ridiculous bun that was once more half sliding off her head, to learn if her honey-blond hair felt warm and silky under his hand.

"I would speak to you in the nursery, sir," Julia said, and he nodded, knowing the only way out of this bedchamber was via that nursery and that Julia Carruthers would probably physically tackle him if he attempted to leave without listening to her as she gave her opinion on whatever was sticking in her craw.

Mrs. Jenkins, nipping gin and all, would have made a safer choice. Any woman who had not been raised near the coast in Kent would have been a better choice. Someone oblivious, someone who would keep her nose in the nursery and her opinions to herself.

But he had picked Julia Carruthers. And this woman *knew*. But did she know enough to watch her tongue?

If he managed to stifle her now, it would be only a temporary victory—and perhaps a very costly one, as well. For Julia was certain to pick at him and pick at him until she'd said what she felt needed to be said—probably at the most inopportune time and in the most dangerous company.

Chance retrieved his greatcoat and hat and followed Julia as if he were a schoolboy summoned to the headmaster's office. Once they were in the nursery, he stood with his back to a piebald hobby horse he could remember as Cassandra's favorite and ruled his expression unreadable.

And, fool that he was, he'd hope that Julia had some budget of complaints about something other than what had been made so glaringly and disgustingly obvious to him. "Well?"

Julia's heart was pounding so loudly she was sure he could hear its every beat. She pointed in the general direction of the center of the house and said, "You know what's going on here? This Jacko person? And Billy? I never thought that Billy…although I should have… I've seen many a man like him walking the streets of Hawkhurst. They're seamen—at least, they were. And men who have been to sea very often feel a kinship for the smugglers. Georgie and his brothers did a very dangerous and stupid thing that could bring trouble raining down on everyone. What's really going to happen to Johnnie and Dickie? Are they in danger here?"

Chance clenched his hands into fists. She was going to ruin everything.

He had to shut her up. Now.

"I believe I can see where that vivid imagination of yours is taking you. Yes, Billy and Jacko were once sailors, years ago, and came here to Romney Marsh when we left the islands. But Billy's far too lazy and Jacko far too fat and happy here for either of them to care about anything but their own comfort. This is Becket Hall, not your childhood home in Hawkhurst. You're exhausted, Julia, darling, and our adventure on the Marsh and your very natural fatigue have made you fanciful," Chance said, still with his back to the door and as, with eye shiftings accompanied by jerks of his thumb, he directed her attention to that open door.

Darling? Julia took a step back. What on earth? Someone was out there? Someone was listening?

And then she shut her eyes, realizing the mistake she'd made, before opening them wide again, looking straight into Chance's face. "That is…oh, I don't know what's wrong with me. Those poor boys, come upon by robbers out there on the Marsh. A person who grows up in Hawkhurst hears stories of the old days, you understand, and I was so tired, tending to Alice all day—she's a sweet child, but her own fatigue made her a little fractious, didn't it? I'm so sorry…" She took a deep breath, let it out in a rush and pushed on, taking her cue from him. "Dearest Chance. I'm seeing bogeymen, aren't I? That will teach me to allow my imagination to wander."

"Yes, it will, won't it," Chance said, looking into Julia's frightened eyes and marking the rather alarming lack of color in her cheeks. She might be pluck to the backbone at times, but she could also topple in a faint at any moment. "But Alice is asleep now and we're alone. Just let me close this door so no one disturbs us. I haven't kissed you in hours."

Well, that brought the color back into her cheeks!

"But…but don't you think you should seek out your father…that is, Mr. Ainsley Becket? Jacko must have told him you've arrived."

"He can wait. They can all wait. I can't," Chance said in a near growl, walking over to the door to the hallway now that he'd given anyone who might have been listening time to hide out of sight. He stepped into the hallway himself, and it was empty, as he'd expected, then backed into the room and closed the door. Locked it.

"Was…was anyone out there?" Julia asked, whispering.

He could say no. But that wouldn't put the fear of God into her, would it? Besides, he knew Jacko. Jacko may have the size of a bear, but he moved like a cat. He knew the man had been there listening. "Yes, I saw Jacko, the back of him, sneaking into a room down the hall."

"Oh, good God in Heaven," Julia said as she clasped her hands in front of her to keep them from shaking. "Do you think he heard me?"

Chance stepped closer. "I'm sure he did, but you didn't say anything too dangerous. You're concerned for the idiots we brought with us, that's all. Ease your mind on that head at least, please. The boys and their family will be leaving the Marsh in the morning. I'm having them sent north, to my estate near Coventry, well clear of here. Now say whatever else it is you feel you must say and then we won't discuss any of this again."

Julia backed up two paces, because he was standing so close and she was suddenly very aware that he had earlier called her "darling." She mined her brain for the list of questions she had for him and came up with the first that she recalled. "Why is Billy your coachman? He's an atrocious coachman."

Chance smiled. "I knew you'd have questions, but I hadn't considered that one. But fair enough. Billy is my coachman because I choose that he be my coachman—and probably because he believes his life's work is to protect me, from only God knows what."

"He still walks as if he's on a rolling deck," Julia said, hoping to ease the tension that seemed to be increasing between them, a tension that had little to do with the questions in her head or the growing fear in her heart.

"He does that, doesn't he?" Chance said, smiling. "Jacko was also a sailor, as you already guessed. Ainsley was a sailor. Most anyone you encounter here at Becket Hall might have gone to sea at some time. After all, we lived on an island. But that's all it is, Julia. When we left the islands and came here, everyone gave up the sea. They gave up anything to do with the sea. Do you understand me?"

"You're telling me that no one at Becket Hall is associated with the smugglers or even knows or cares about them. I understand." She bit her bottom lip between her teeth as she looked at him, as everything seemed to fall into place for her, the pieces of the puzzle now all fitting together tightly, showing her a picture she'd rather not see. Did he think her a fool? "They know you are a part of the War Office."

"Yes, they do," Chance said, his expression going dark, unreadable. "And the war is on the continent, not here in Romney Marsh."

Why did she keep pushing at him? But she had to know. "True enough. But the Owlers are here, and they trade with the enemy. Did you really bring Alice to Becket Hall because you believe she should be here or are you using your own daughter as an excuse to spy on the smugglers for the king?"

"One does not necessarily make the other true. I had only planned to bring Alice home. And, my dear, as it stands, I don't have to justify my actions to you."

"No, you don't. But please don't dismiss me as some

foolish London society miss who has no notion of what can happen here. Do you know the history of the Hawkhurst Gang? You made mention of my birthplace, but I doubt you know all that I know. The worst of it happened a long time ago, but the stories still are told and retold in Hawkhurst."

"I only know that some five or six men were hanged in chains for murdering a king's officer, their bodies strung up along the roadway for all to see. But that was—what?—sixty years ago?"

Julia nodded her agreement. "They butchered one of their own at the same time, a man who was going to give the king's testimony against the gang. The gang had grown too large, too powerful. Smuggling isn't only a dangerous but necessary occupation for desperate people wishing to feed their families. Many people became very rich, both here and in London."

"The government destroyed the Hawkhurst Gang, and many more like them. There are better patrols now, Julia, more troops assigned to capture smugglers. The Crown has the situation under control—or will very soon. The war and the shortages war causes have simply stirred things up for a while, that's all."

Julia wasn't convinced and was far from satisfied with his reasoning. Hadn't she only a fortnight ago drunk the last of the contraband tea left at the church just days after her father's funeral? She had to make him understand.

"The Hawkhurst Gang thought nothing of murdering people who got in their way, people who saw too much, said too much. People like Dickie and Johnnie.

People like us, who have stumbled over what they'd done. And from what Dickie said, it would seem there are more large gangs out there now who could be very much like the Hawkhurst Gang. This Black Ghost, for one."

Chance felt a tic beginning in his left cheek. "You never heard that name, Julia. Never. Never so much as think it again. And I won't keep you here if you're going to worry yourself to death. I can send you back to London tomorrow morning, if that's what you want."

Julia shook her head, feeling suddenly stubborn. "Not unless Alice travels with me."

Chance cursed under his breath as he stabbed his fingers through his hair. "Do you honestly think I would let Alice come to any harm? This is my *family*, Julia. It may not seem so to you so far, but they would kill for me, and I would kill for them. Any one of them. And I would never harm them. Never. Jacko and Billy? I consider them family, as well. Everyone at Becket Hall is family. No matter how stupidly they—"

Julia watched as Chance brought himself back under control. She longed to ask the *real* question: did he think members of his own family had joined the smugglers? Because she'd certainly gotten that impression through his few terse comments to her in the coach after they'd found the boys.

And yet, was that so terrible? Her own father allowed contraband to be stored in his church before the smugglers could move it inland. Everyone in Romney Marsh and other coastal areas, in some way, large or small, was involved with the smugglers, knew some of the smugglers, benefited from the goods that were left as payment for the use of an outbuilding or the loan of a horse. Her best gown, the yellow silk, had been fashioned from a bolt of cloth left for her at the vicarage one night.

"The matters of business that will keep you here for a few weeks," Julia asked, "do they have anything to do with the smuggling trade? No, please don't answer. I shouldn't have asked. We shouldn't even be having this conversation. Not any of it."

Chance smiled at her. "At last. Yes, Julia, we shouldn't be having this conversation. But I will tell you, I am not here to run about, hoping to capture smugglers and bring them to Dover Castle to be tried and hanged. I'm only charged with speaking to the Waterguards and such up and down the coast, hopefully putting some of the fear of God into them so that they will do what needs to be done. Because they certainly haven't yet, have they, or Georgie would still be alive and thinking of no more than hoping to steal a kiss from some young girl."

Julia nodded, agreeing with him. The pity of the smuggling trade was not only that it was so necessary to survival but that generations of Marshmen knew no other way to feed their families.

"I…I suppose you should go downstairs. Your…your father may be waiting to see you."

"I'm sure he is, along with at least one of my brothers. As I remember it, your chamber is over there, on the other side of the nursery. Will you be all right? No bad dreams about bogeymen coming to truss you up and toss you in the Channel?"

"I believe they buried the king's man alive as he stood in a hole and tossed the other man down a dry well, then dropped rocks on him until he stopped moaning. But as you said, that was long ago." Julia hugged herself, rubbed at her arms as a chill overcame her. "No, I'll be all right. I believe you. That all happened very long ago. The world is much more civilized now. Besides, Billy has vouched for me," Julia said. "Good night, sir."

Chance let her get nearly to the door to her chamber before he stopped her, turned her around at the shoulders. "Jacko overheard us, remember? The man gossips like an old woman. By noon tomorrow, they'll all think we're lovers. That means you're mine, and no one associated with Becket Hall would even think to harm anyone or anything that's mine. I'm sorry I could come up with nothing better, but at that moment it was the only thing I could think of to…well, to shut you up. Do you want me to tell them otherwise?"

At last he had come close to admitting that, yes, there could be danger here at Becket Hall because of what they'd seen and heard on the Marsh. Julia felt her heart begin to race again and willed herself to be calm. "I knew what you were doing, once you did it. But I'm only the nanny. No one will care what our…association might be."

"So you don't mind being my mistress, Julia?" Chance asked her, drawing her closer.

"We both know I'm hardly that," she said, hoping she sounded firm, sure of herself and unafraid of him. She couldn't let him know how she felt as he stood so near,

near enough for her to see the golden flecks in his stormy green eyes.

"True. But you're a very brave woman, Julia. I saw that firsthand, out on the Marsh. And a very intelligent one, as well. No one here would be surprised that I'd found you…decidedly attractive."

Why was she still standing there? Why was she still talking to him and not running into her room, hoping there was a key in the door so she could lock herself away from him, from those eyes of his that kept drawing her in, closer? Closer. "And would they be surprised that you would have your…your lover pose as your own child's nanny, insinuate her into their household?"

Chance grinned, even as he lightly rubbed the pads of his thumbs across her remarkable collarbones. "Hardly, Julia. Hardly. In fact, I imagine they'll be delighted with my transparent effort to disguise our true relationship until such time as I'm ready to reveal the truth. Besides, as you said, Billy has already approved you, no mean feat in itself. We're a rather unique family."

Julia took a shaky breath in an effort to appear calm, collected. But this man knew his impact on her senses and he was letting her know that he knew. "Saying, however, does not make something so. If you think I'd feel safer? As long as you and I know the truth of our…our association…" Her voice trailed off as she felt herself becoming even more lost in the deep green depths of his eyes. "That is…you and I…I would not *ever*—what are you doing? Stop that."

Chance had lifted his hands to her hair and begun working at that infuriating, intriguing bun. "Did no one ever tell you, Julia, that a beautiful woman attempting to look prim and proper is more often than not a siren song to a man? I've been wanting to do this from the moment you walked into my presence and began taking over my household."

Julia felt the band on her hair coming free and the weight of her hair slipping down past her shoulders. He placed his hands on either side of her face below her ears, then slipped his fingers up and into her hair, sending shivers skittering throughout her body.

She should stop this. Stamp on his toe, slap his face. Something.

But, oh, it felt so good. His hands were warm against her skin, and his face was so close to hers, his full lips curved in such a wickedly intriguing smile. Her world filled with him, and only him, and all her defenses had deserted her.

She closed her eyes.

"Sleep well, Julia," he said—breathed—against her temple. "You're tired and Ainsley awaits. We'll continue this another time."

Chance watched as she opened her eyes to look at him in surprise. And perhaps disappointment? He hoped so, as he was more than disappointed himself. "You see, Julia? I'm a gentleman. But a gentleman on a very short leash and now returned to the bosom of his not-always-gentlemanly family. You might ask my sisters to hide you, but it would be safer, I'm sure, if you were to leave here, return to London."

"Return to London? So that's what this has all been about? You want to frighten me into leaving?"

"What I want and what I think best are two different things," Chance told her. "But you should leave."

"I don't want to return to London," Julia said before she could realize the implications of that admission. "I mean, I want to stay here, with Alice."

Chance trailed his fingers down her cheek, then looped two fingers into the top of her modest gown, traced the skin just at the uppermost swell of her breasts. "I don't know which of us is most dangerous to the other. But we'll find out, won't we. Again, *darling,* good night."

Chance turned and headed for the hallway, scooping up his greatcoat as he went, silently cursing himself for having nearly lost control of his hard-won civilized demeanor that had been more than a dozen long years in the making.

He shouldn't have come back. He'd cut the ties, loosed the bonds, made a new life for himself. And all it had taken were a few words from Jacko, a lungful of sea air and one beautiful, too-curious virgin to turn him back into the wharf rat he'd worked so hard to forget.

CHAPTER SIX

AINSLEY BECKET STOOD in the shadows and watched as Chance carelessly descended the wide marble staircase. The younger man kept his hands at his sides, his confident grace, as always, reminding Ainsley of how deftly the young Chance had sidled through a wharfside pub crowded with drunken sailors, smoothly lightening the load of coins in their pockets.

Ainsley had sat with his back to the wall and idly watched the tanned, barely clothed, underfed boy ply his trade. He was only amusing himself, especially when he saw the boy bump into Billy, murmur an apology and then walk away after Billy cuffed him on the ear. The boy had grinned widely then, even as he'd pretended to howl in pain, with Billy's pocket now empty and the seaman none the wiser.

"Fool's too drunk to know he's been dipped. Do we tell him, Cap'n?" Jacko had asked, using his mug of ale to point at Billy.

Ainsley hadn't answered. He was already on his feet, for one of Edmund's men had taken hold of the boy's arm and was leering down into the suddenly white, pinched face. Saying something, whispering to the boy.

"Damn him, I warned Edmund about that one," Ainsley had said as the seaman made a grab at the boy's crotch. "He'd poke a knothole." Then he'd looked down at Jacko, who was taking another drink from his mug. "You with me?"

"Better with you than against you, Cap'n, although I would remind you I said not to come in here. Back to the wall or nay, never drink in another man's pub," Jacko had said in that lazy, smiling way of his. He'd put down the mug and pushed his thickset body out of the chair. Both men had slipped out their knives, holding them low at their sides as they'd pushed their way toward certain trouble, Jacko whistling Billy to heel.

The rest of that evening remained a partial blur in Ainsley's memory, although the chipped tooth in the front of Jacko's mouth was one reminder. By dawn, the three of them had been nursing their wounds, some greasy bastard named Angelo who stood behind the small serving bar had been made the richer by ten gold pieces, Edmund was short three of his crew and Ainsley had acquired a brat. He'd thought it an amusing bit of justice that he'd put Billy in charge of the boy.

How old had Chance been when he'd come to the island? Eight? Ten? And a man nearly grown by the time—Ainsley closed his eyes, let the pain roll over him, not as crippling now, but still there to remind him, then finished the thought—by the time they'd all died and gone to England.

"It's good to see you, boy."

Chance paused with his right foot on the stone floor of the wide entrance hall, then moved again, turning to his right, following the sound of Ainsley's voice. "Sir," he said, then held out his hand to the man. Nearly five years had passed since they'd spoken, communicated in any way. "Thank you for not sending Jacko to the door with a brace of pistols."

"And why would I do that? This is your home, Chance. Alice is welcome here. Come along, I've got brandy warming by the fire in my study."

"Yes, sir," Chance said and followed Ainsley down the dimly lit hallway, secretly pleased to see that Ainsley continued to dress all in black, but that he still walked like a man who owned the world while gracious enough to share it with lesser mortals.

He'd been a god to Chance, his savior from a fate Chance hadn't really understood until Billy had taken him aside and explained in graphic detail what the sailor had wanted from him that night in Angelo's pub. His savior in all things.

How Chance had worshipped Ainsley, the tall, deceptively powerful man, his tanned face lean and strong, his sharp eyes missing nothing, his voice quietly commanding respect, his smiles rare but wonderful to behold.

He was still strong and straight, but there was some silver scattered now in his black hair, and the lines in his face had carved deeper, especially across his brow. Time does that to a man. As does pain.

Strange. Chance had never thought about Ainsley growing old, being anything but invulnerable. Even that day, that last day, he'd been the one who'd kept his head, who'd held them all together. Chance had hated him for that.

They entered the study, Chance following behind Ainsley.

Books. Ainsley's study was filled with books. Books on shelves that lined every wall and disappeared in the dark as they climbed toward the ceiling. Books piled on every surface, stacked on the floor. A newspaper not more than three days old was spread out on one of the tables, along with several maps.

Chance walked over to the table, taking hold of one of the maps at one corner and pulling it around so he could better see it. Several areas were circled with thick black ink, on both land and sea. "You're following the battles?"

"Other people's wars are often interesting, although nothing has been quite so intriguing since Trafalgar. England lost a good man in Nelson."

Chance dropped the corner of the map. "Yes. Maybe one day they'll raise a monument to him somewhere. In the meantime, they're allowing his beloved Emma to starve. I heard she's been imprisoned for debt, actually. Ainsley, it's been a long day and I'm really rather tired...."

"One drink, Chance. Just one. And some conversation."

The fire in the grate had been freshly fed, as if Ainsley had planned on a long night, a plan Chance didn't share. He waited for the man to take his seat in one of a pair of wing chairs in front of the fire, then sat in the other one, a low table between them holding a brandy decanter and two snifters.

Ainsley lifted his snifter, swirled the liquid a time or

two, then sipped. With the glass still in front of his face, he looked at Chance over the rim. "Once more, Chance, my condolences on the loss of your wife. Or perhaps you didn't receive my letter. The others would have come to you—"

"If I'd let you all know in time. Yes, I'm aware of that. Arrangements were necessarily rushed. Beatrice was interred in her family's mausoleum in Devonshire."

"I know her father died a few years ago, but didn't her mother offer to take Alice for you while you're so busy in London?"

Chance held his own snifter, pretended a great interest in the swirling brandy. "Priscilla wed again last year. Beatrice's brother holds the estate now, and Priscilla is off traipsing some moor in Scotland with her new husband." He looked at Ainsley. "But if you don't feel Alice can stay here, I—"

"Alice will be fine here. The girls can't wait to see her, spoil her. I only worry that she'll rarely see her papa. When were you last at Becket Hall, Chance? I believe that was when Alice was a mere infant in arms. She's—what—five now? Six?"

"Five," Chance said, still looking straight at Ainsley. "Beatrice didn't care for the country."

Ainsley smiled one of his rare slight smiles. "Don't blame a dead woman, Chance. That isn't gentlemanly. How long have we two been together?"

Chance turned his gaze toward the fire. "I was nine or ten when you bought me from Angelo, seventeen when...when we left the island."

"So now you're a grown man of thirty years, and I'm

nearing fifty. Thirteen years, Chance. I won't ask you to forget, but can't you find some forgiveness somewhere? I lost her, too."

Chance put down the snifter and got to his feet, turned his back to the man. "You make it sound as if I was in love with her."

"Weren't you? With all the ardor of a seventeen-year-old boy? That's nothing to be ashamed of. She was only two years your elder."

"And *your* wife," Chance said. "*You* let Edmund—"

"I did, yes," Ainsley said, also getting to his feet. "Look at me. Look at me, Chance. No more running, no more hiding from the truth. I accept all blame. None of it is yours. I had everything. At last, I had everything. But I wanted more, and that's what destroyed us. Not Edmund. Edmund was what he was. *I* am responsible. For her, for all of them."

"God. Oh my God." Chance collapsed into the chair, pushed his fingers through his hair, not even aware that the ribbon holding it in place had slipped off so that his darkly blond hair now was thick and loose to his shoulders.

The years fell away.

Ainsley felt a stab of regret, once again seeing Chance as he had been. Young, strong, unafraid. Before pain and loss had turned him inward, before civilization had smothered all his fire. The Chance he'd watched grow to young manhood could climb the rigging like a monkey, a knife between his teeth to slice away sail in a storm, then triumphantly yell into the wind, dare it to blow him into the sea. The Chance he'd known had loved life, every moment of it. Ainsley felt the loss of that boy, he felt it keenly.

But now the past was here with them, in the open at last. Now, maybe, they could finally make their peace.

Ainsley sat down again, folded his hands in front of him or else he knew he'd be unable to restrain from leaning forward, stroking the boy's hair. "What's wrong, Chance?"

Chance turned troubled eyes to Ainsley. "I didn't know you knew. Did she know?"

Ainsley didn't make the mistake of thinking Chance was referring to his last statement, his acceptance of his own guilt. "Yes, Isabella knew you loved her. She loved you, too. She loved you all. But she was my wife. That sort of love is different, the love of a woman for her husband, a husband for his wife. You know that, you've been married."

Then Ainsley watched for Chance's reaction. He saw a tic begin in Chance's left cheek, a sure sign that the boy—no, the man—was holding his emotions in check only with great difficulty.

"I failed Beatrice," Chance said at last, quietly. "We married for mutual convenience. Her family needed money—even the London residence they gave us was heavily mortgaged—and I wanted her family's name to get me into society, through the right doors. Even to the War Office."

He pushed his hair away from his face again, sighed. This was hard, so very hard to say, so he'd say it quickly. Not because he'd loved Beatrice, because he hadn't. But he had failed her. "My wife took a lover shortly after

Alice was born, and we never shared a bed again. She…she died a few days after some back-alley drab got rid of his baby for her."

Chance picked up his snifter. "There. Now you know. I wanted to leave it all behind. The island, you, everyone. I wanted to find a new life, a calm, ordered life. A *normal* life. I wanted to forget who I was, what I was. But it seems we have more in common than you think, Ainsley. We both let our wives die to feed our own ambition."

Ainsley remained quiet, and for some time the only sound in the room was the crack and sizzle of the fire.

"You have Alice. I have Cassandra and all of you. We live for them, Chance. We can only hope to live long enough to make up for our mistakes."

Chance's head shot up and he glared at Ainsley. The past was the past. They'd talked. They'd even discussed. Now it was time to move on. More than time. They were both grown men now and at last on an equal footing.

"How, Ainsley? How do you *make up* for past mistakes? By making the same mistakes again? What happened to all your fine plans to come here, keep the girls safe, at the very least? Bury the past, you said, let the past lie, let it die. Did you become bored stuck out here in your self-imposed exile? Did you feel the need for another adventure? Don't tell me you need money."

Ainsley put down his snifter. "I have no idea what you're talking about."

"Really? I'm supposed to believe that?" Chance drew his hands into tight fists, as if to rein in his temper. "Then explain to me, please, why one of the boys

I dragged here with me tonight talked about the Black Ghost Gang."

"What?"

Chance sat back, stunned. No one could fake that look of complete shock, not even Ainsley. "You…you don't know? Billy didn't tell you?"

Ainsley stood up slowly, suddenly feeling very old, very tired. "He told me what happened on the Marsh, about this Miss Carruthers of yours whom Billy seems to have cast in the role of heroine. But that's all."

Chance also got to his feet, his mind racing, racing toward one particular name. "Then you're not riding out as the Black Ghost, you're not running a gang of smugglers here on the Marsh? I know that's what you were about in Cornwall, before you had to run or be hanged. I assumed you—"

"Excuse me," Ainsley said coolly, already headed for the door.

Chance followed all the way to the second floor and down the hallway, until Ainsley stopped in front of the door to Courtland's bedchamber.

So they'd both had the same thought.

Ainsley tried the latch, but the door was locked. He pulled out his timepiece. Nearly midnight. "The young fool," he said, brushing past Chance and back down the hallway, down the staircase, not even breathing hard as he pushed open the double doors to the main drawing room. "Jacko? Damn you to hell. You knew, didn't you?"

Chance watched, reduced to no more than a spectator, as Jacko leaned over the low table in front of the couch, throwing dice one hand against the other one more time before pocketing the dice in his coat.

"Well, look who's come up for air. Maybe it's a good thing you came back, boy, shake things up a bit here in the backside of beyond. What's the matter with you, old friend, you couldn't find a way to bury yourself tonight? No taste for Milton's dreary poetry? No interest in Greek primers? No sackcloth and ashes to be found?"

"Point taken, Jacko, thank you," Ainsley said, folding his arms across his chest. "I'm a dull stick who has spent too many years grieving, sulking and turning my face from the world. I'll grant you that. But, by God, man, how could I be so blind? How long has this been going on? Courtland's out there, isn't he? Are the others with him? Spencer? Rian?"

Jacko nodded, his great head all but touching his chest. "Rian and Spence are gathering up some babes and their mama, to bring them here before they're sent out of the Marsh. But that's all, I swear it. Court? Nobody knows what Court does and nobody asks. He's his own man and has been for years. Or would you rather they were all kept in leading strings? Or run away, like that one there did, turn his back on every one of us."

"Feel better now, Jacko, with that off your chest?" Chance asked silkily.

Ainsley began to rock slightly on his heels as he tapped his hands against his folded arms. "I'm an idiot. A blind, selfish idiot."

"Don't be so hard on yourself, Cap'n," Jacko said, and Chance raised one eyebrow. Jacko never called Ainsley "Captain" anymore, not since they'd arrived in

Romney Marsh. That title had been reserved for Geoffrey Baskin and had been buried along with him. "But you might want to give a thought to this one here. Told the boys he found he was going to take them to Dover Castle. It's him you have to worry about, what he might take a mind to do to his own."

"I'll ignore that, Jacko," Chance said tightly as he stood beside Ainsley. "This time. But never again. Court isn't the only one who is his own man. Now let's hear you tell the captain what in bloody hell is going on around here."

CHAPTER SEVEN

JULIA AWOKE ALL AT ONCE, realizing that something—or someone—was on the bed with her. She opened her eyes, expecting to see Alice sitting at the bottom of the mattress. "Hello. Who are you?" she asked the child of twelve or thirteen who was still bouncing as she grinned at her.

"I'm Cassandra, except that everyone save Papa and Chance calls me Callie, which is a wickedly common name, but I like it. And you're Julia. Don't tell anyone I'm here. I'm supposed to be in bed with a horrid cold."

"Your nose is a little red," Julia said, pushing herself up against the back of the bed as she smiled at Callie. She reached for her father's pocket watch that she had put on the bedside table, opened it and saw that it was nearly eight o'clock. "I've slept entirely too long."

"You're worried about Alice? Don't be, please. Edyth has already fed her and washed her and dressed her, and now Alice is downstairs, where my sisters can fuss over her," Callie said. "Edyth's very competent, Papa says. She was my nurse when I needed a nurse. I don't now, of course, because I'm all grown-up. I haven't been in the nursery for *years.*"

Julia couldn't help but smile at this. What a pretty child, with a small heart-shaped face, her high cheekbones still nicely padded with baby fat. Huge brown eyes dominated the face also remarkable for its full, pouty lips. And Callie Becket had enough light brown hair for any two people, much of it in long, loose ringlets that bounced as she bounced.

"My nose is only red because it will insist upon *running* all the time," Callie informed her, then tilted her head to one side. "I wish I had hair like yours. It's so wonderfully straight, isn't it? I have more curls than Odette, but she's supposed to have them. At least, that's what she says."

Julia blinked at the name. Odette. Wasn't that the name of the servant who'd been put to taking care of Dickie? "Is Odette your housekeeper?"

"No, silly." Callie put her fists on the bedspread and leaned closer. "Odette's our *mambo*. She is very powerful, but not so much as her father was. *He* was a *houngan* and he could turn people into *animals* for days and *days*. She said she'd change me into a pigeon and roast me for dinner before I could change back if I got out of bed again. So you won't tell, will you?"

"I…I probably shouldn't, should I?" Julia said, wondering if it was possible she was still asleep and caught up in some strange fantastical nightmare. "Why is Odette a *mambo?*"

Callie rolled those huge, expressive eyes. "Because she's a very special voodoo priestess and very powerful. Everyone knows that." She sat back on her haunches and opened the top two buttons of her night rail, then pulled out a thin golden chain. "See this? This is a *real* alligator-tooth amulet Odette made for me."

"Is that so?" Julia said, looking at the rather brown, stained thing that, yes, was most definitely a tooth, thankfully too large to be human. "And why do you have that, Callie?"

"It's my *gad*, of course, my guard. We all have one." Callie's voice dropped to a whisper. "It's very, very special and keeps me from harm, keeps the bad *loas* away. I never take it off, never, except one time a year to soak it again in the *mavangou* bottle, of course. It needs to feed on the magic to keep the bad *loas* away. Odette is very put out with Chance, because he hasn't allowed her to soak his *gad* in a prodigiously long time."

"Really?" Julia was becoming more intrigued by the moment.

Callie rolled her eyes again. "Oh, yes. We're just lucky he's still alive. It's really very reckless of him. Odette becomes fatigued, always lighting candles and saying prayers for him."

"Prayers, is it?" Julia slid her feet out from under the covers, stood up and reached for her dressing gown. "I think I understand now," she said, slipping her arms into the gown, then tying it tightly at the waist. Her father's education had been centered mostly around things religious, and he had told her about the rituals of many other religions, most especially the "poor heathens" who worshipped strange gods, indulged in magic and other "fanciful nonsense," as her father had termed it. Wearing an alligator tooth seemed to fit this description. "Odette came here from Haiti, didn't she?"

"From Saint-Domingue," Callie said. "There were many problems there, many wars, but Odette doesn't like to talk about Saint-Domingue, or what is Haiti now—or anything that happened on the island. Very bloody times. I don't remember them at all, because I was just a puling infant when we left there and came here. That's what Jacko said. A puling infant. I don't think that's nice, do you?"

Julia remembered Jacko. "That was probably only friendly banter," she said, hiding a wince. While Callie jabbered away like a magpie, Julia gathered up the underclothing and the gown she had thankfully taken the time to lay out before at last crawling into bed last night. She stepped behind the screen in the corner and hastily dressed herself, trying to pretend she was unaware that nature was calling to her.

Callie shrugged as she climbed down off the bed. "Jacko loves me," she said, buttoning her night rail once more. "And Odette says people can't help what they look like, so even if Jacko looks like he eats little girls for breakfast, that doesn't mean he does. I have to go now, before someone comes to see how I feel today and I'm not there to tell them. You really should go downstairs, Julia. We've got coddled eggs today. Aren't you hungry?"

"I'm famished," Julia said, realizing that was true. "How do I get to the kitchens?"

"Why would you go there? I heard Edyth tell Birdie that she's supposed to move your things downstairs to the bedchamber next to mine so that Edyth can stay up here with baby Alice, like she did when I was a puling infant. Papa's orders."

Julia's heart managed a small hiccup in her chest. "I'm...I'm to be moved downstairs, with the family?"

Callie nodded. "Papa says you're Chance's very good friend and our guest and you're going to be a wonderful companion to us girls while you and Chance are here. I'm going now. Remember, you didn't meet me yet."

Julia gave the girl a small, weak wave, then sat down on the bed. Guest? Wonderful companion? *Very good friend?* Good God, it was happening. She was being introduced to this family as Chance Becket's *mistress.* What sort of ragtag family was this?

And she shouldn't tell anyone she'd seen Callie. Of course not. She hadn't seen those boys on the Marsh. She must pretend she doesn't know that there's something decidedly havey-cavey about Jacko and Billy. She shouldn't ask questions about anything, anyone.

No, she shouldn't. What she should do is finish her toilette as quickly as possible, pack up her belongings and demand to be taken to the nearest coaching inn. That's what she should do!

But she wouldn't.

"I've never been quite so fascinated in my life," Julia told her reflection in the mirror above the bureau as she dried her face after splashing it with—how wonderful!—the warm water she'd found in the pitcher.

Although even the presence of that warm water bothered her. How had the servant who'd brought it done so without waking her? Did the servants in this household wrap their footwear with strips of blanket to muffle the sound?

"Stop it, Julia," she told herself as she rummaged through her bag for her brush. "You're being fanciful.

You were exhausted and you slept like the dead. Some-one could have run through this room shouting that the Frenchies were coming and you wouldn't have budged."

She sighed, decided she'd convinced herself, and then brushed her hair, smiling at the thought that straight-as-sticks pale hair could possibly be better than Callie's marvelous tumble of warm golden-brown curls.

She pulled back her hair with both hands, preparing to twist it into a bun, then stopped. If she put up her hair, Chance—dear Lord, she was now very easily thinking of the man as Chance, not Mr. Becket!—might decide to tug it all loose again.

Was that a good thing or a bad thing? And would she go straight to hell for even asking herself that question?

Hastily tying her hair at her nape with a green gros-grain ribbon that matched those on her three-year-old gown, Julia made up her bed and packed up the re-mainder of her belongings, not much caring for the idea that anyone else would see her meager wardrobe with its discreet patches and darns.

Before heading downstairs, she then pulled back the heavy drapes on one of the large windows, her breath catching as she saw the sand-and-shingle beach not one hundred yards away and the Channel beyond, brilliant sunlight dancing on the water and not a hint of mist in sight.

How beautiful. How wonderfully, wildly beautiful.

She leaned closer to the glass. Yes, that was a ship out there, moving parallel to the shore. "I can almost make out the flag...."

"It's French. But not to worry, we're not about to be invaded. They just like to sail back and forth out there beyond the range of our guns and make a grand show once and again."

Julia spun around, one hand to her chest, to see Chance Becket standing not three feet from her. "Does everyone tiptoe here?"

Chance smiled. "Your eyes look even more green this morning. I imagine it's the gown. Pretty. Did you rest well?"

"I did, yes, but I will probably never sleep again, unless I find a key for the door," she told him, doing her best to ignore the fact that Chance had forgone his city attire in favor of fawn nankeen breeches above shiny black top boots, his full-sleeved white shirt open at the neck. He wore a dark brown leather vest he'd left unbuttoned. It looked as soft as newly churned butter.

She could see a thin strip of well-worn dark leather hanging around his neck and wondered if an alligator tooth hung at the end of it, then realized she'd been staring. Would like to continue staring. She folded her hands in front of her, then looked at those hands with some intensity.

Chance watched as Julia bowed her head, the sunlight streaming in through the window setting off small sunbeams in her hair. No bun today, which was a large improvement, but all her glorious hair still, alas, swept tightly away from her face. His fingers itched to release that confounding ribbon. Amazing how women could drive a man nearly wild by showing themselves to be so obviously chaste.

He'd been too long without a woman. Either that or Julia Carruthers was a witch.

"Yes," he said, turning his thoughts away from treacherous territory, "I know you had a visitor. I stopped to see Cassandra on my way up here. She told you Ainsley has stuck his thumb in my business?"

Julia busied herself in taking off and folding up her paisley shawl that she'd believed she might need downstairs. Silly. It was warm in Becket Hall. Excessively warm. At least in this suddenly very small room. "I'm to be moved to a bedchamber downstairs, where I, as your very good *friend,* will be treated as a guest while I amuse your sisters. Yes, I know. Will you provide me with a tambourine? Trained monkeys usually have those, I believe."

"Such a sharp tongue. I don't know what made either of us believe even for a moment that you had the makings of a nanny." Chance sat down on the edge of the bed, patted the smoothed coverlet. "Didn't you sleep in here last night?"

She rolled her eyes. "Some people take care of their own needs. I slept in that bed and I made up that bed this morning. I'm more than capable of caring for myself. And while we're on the subject of acceptable manners—you don't belong here."

"Here being this room, sitting on this bed? Or here being Becket Hall?" He stood up. "No, don't answer. I've come up here to tell you that Dickie and Johnnie, their mother and the remainder of her brood are already traveling north to my estate. They were escorted on their way after a fine but necessarily short moonlight service for the departed Georgie, who now resides in an unmarked grave on the Marsh. Harsh but unavoidable, for planting him in the local churchyard would raise too many questions. Better they all merely disappear."

After all, Chance thought fleetingly, that had worked well enough for the Becketts. Up until now, at least.

"That…that was both cruel and good of you, I suppose," Julia said, knowing how much her father would have disapproved. "Thank you for telling me."

Chance tugged at his earlobe. "I've more to tell you, although you've already guessed, with Cassandra's help. Thanks to Jacko's eavesdropping ways and, yes, my impromptu thought to divert him, Ainsley believes the two of us are…shall we say, *involved.* Because that misconception places you under my protection, I've decided to allow him to continue to think that way. You'll be safer here at Becket Hall than you were in your mother's arms."

"My mother handed me to my father when I was but three months old and ran off to France with her second cousin," Julia told him, the memory too old to cause her any pain. "Perhaps you have another comparison?"

She held up her hand. "No, please don't bother. And please don't tell me I'm being treated as a guest as a result of your very deliberate lie. I'm being kept where I can be watched, to make sure I don't go haring off to the local Waterguard to turn you all in for a king's reward. Feed me well, house me royally and gain my silence. I suppose nobody wanted to dig a second grave on the Marsh today?"

"My, what a fertile imagination for a vicar's daughter." Chance shook his head, wondering if he could have made a worse choice of nanny for his daughter if he'd hired a Bow Street Runner for the job.

Then again, how could he have known Courtland would turn into an idiot?

"And what would you tell the authorities, Julia? That you helped a dastardly family of smugglers to flee the Marsh? That your host employs old seamen on his estate? Ainsley's well-known here and well respected. Who, of the two of you, looks guilty?"

Julia bit her bottom lip for a moment, then said, "You. You look guilty."

Chance threw back his head and laughed. "My God, woman, you're right. Do you think it's too late to ride after Dickie and his brother, turn them over to the lieutenant at Dover Castle? That may be the only way I can save myself."

"We're talking in circles," Julia said, then sighed. "I've nowhere else to go at the moment and no way to leave here, and we both know that. And in any case, I don't want to leave Alice until I know she will be happy here once you've gone back to London. But then I'm leaving."

"To go where? Back to London? Back to Hawkhurst?"

"You really are an annoying man," Julia said, exasperated with the entire conversation. "And I'm hungry."

She got as far as the main room of the nursery before Chance stopped her by placing a hand on her forearm. He had to get through to her, make her understand, make her *believe*. "My family are not smugglers, Julia.

I give you my word on that. But that does not mean that any of us would turn over two frightened boys to be hanged or transported."

Julia took a steadying breath. "If I say I believe you, will you let go of my arm?"

Chance loosed his grip. "God, you're impossible."

"And you're insulting," Julia said, gathering all her courage and not even bothering to wave goodbye to her common sense. "I saw your reaction last night when I told you about this Black Ghost of Dickie's. You *know* him, whoever he is. Don't you? Is that why you're here, why you're really here? Are you simply using Alice as your excuse?"

Chance stood in front of the closed door to the hallway, blocking her escape, if that was going to be her next thought.

"All right," he said, "I'll tell you the truth. My only reason for coming back here—God, why did I even *think* about coming back here? My only reason was to bring Alice here, away from London, with people I could trust to take care of her. Unfortunately my superior at the War Office decided I should remain here for a while, poke about, possibly find out why, with all the troops we have stationed along the coast, smuggling is growing more prevalent, not less so."

"A fool would know that. Half the troops are in league with the smugglers, for one thing," Julia said. "And, for another, the local smugglers are giving way to large gangs financed by wealthy men in London. Go to London if you want to find the source and most of the profits."

Chance tugged on his earlobe again, realization

dawning on him. "How involved was your father with the local Owlers? Did he simply turn his back while his church was used to store smuggled goods before they could be moved inland? Or did he go out on the runs?"

Julia set her jaw. "My father was a man of God, a man who cared deeply for those in his care and did everything in his power to alleviate their suffering."

"Which doesn't answer my questions, does it? But it does tell me what I already knew. You know the reasons and the consequences and can be trusted as much as anyone can be trusted. But we'll keep up the facade, I believe. Jacko might not be as easily convinced or as impressed by those beautiful eyes of yours."

"Stop that," Julia said, angry. "Just stop that. Wasn't last night enough for you? Believe me, I'm suitably cowed. I'm more than aware of my current situation. I know I'm alone here and under your so-called protection. Please don't expect me to listen to your lies, like some impressionable girl. You have my promise that I'll never say anything about what I saw last night or what I believe or don't believe about what might be happening here at Becket Hall and even where your loyalties might lie. Is that enough? That has to be enough."

Chance stepped forward, ran the back of his index finger down her smooth, pale cheek. "For an intelligent woman, Julia Carruthers, you can be quite naive. Do you really believe I'm not…attracted to you?" He leaned forward, whispered his next words in her ear. "Or that you're not attracted to me?"

Julia kept her arms at her sides, her hands drawn up into fists. "You're no gentleman."

Chance pulled his head back slightly, cupped that determined chin of hers in his hand. "No, I'm not, am I? I'd had hopes, but I'm afraid it's true, no matter how long it takes, blood will out. Lucky, lucky me."

"Don't—" Julia said just before Chance brought his mouth down on hers. He smiled as he kissed her, she could feel that smile against her lips even as her knees threatened to buckle beneath her.

She wasn't resisting. Alas, she also wasn't responding. Chance stepped closer, so that their bodies touched, and cupped his hands on either side of her face, directing all his energy into coaxing her mouth to soften, to respond.

He needed her soft, compliant. Willing to stay where he could watch her, too occupied with him to poke that pretty nose of hers where it didn't belong.

What he hadn't counted on was his own reaction to their kiss. The sudden need he had to feel her warm and willing against him.

"Open your mouth for me, Julia," he whispered against her lips, feathering them with light kisses. "Let me in.…"

Julia heard herself whimper involuntarily as her senses swam, as she felt her body fill with a yearning words couldn't describe, urges her mind refused to understand. She only knew that fighting him—or simply her traitorous self—wasn't an option.

"Oh, yes, Julia, there's a dear," Chance breathed as he felt her melt against him. He deepened the kiss, lightly brushing the tip of his tongue across the roof of her mouth.

She didn't know what to do, how to respond. But, oh, what a lovely invasion! Julia needed an anchor or she'd float away. She raised her arms and grabbed on to the full sleeves of Chance's shirt, not touching him yet pulling him closer.

Her obvious inexperience intensified Chance's reaction to her. For all her bluster, all her show of bravado and independence, she was unschooled in the ways of a man and a woman. Unschooled but, bless her, not uninterested.

Not too quickly, he told himself, even as he slid his hands down her sides, to her waist, then slowly brought them up again, lightly cupping her breasts. She was slim and long-waisted, her breasts high and firm. Her body structure was so different from those smaller, rounder bodies now in fashion in London.

Artfully placed curls, dimpled cheeks; soft, giggling girls of little conversation and less wit. These were the young women the gentlemen of the *ton* favored now. They'd all bored him, even his own wife. Just as she had been bored by him.

Then again, Julia had just told him what he'd finally learned after fighting that truth for more than a dozen years: he was no gentleman.

She fit against his body, his hands, with the sleek strength and suppleness of a racehorse, the fine, clean lines of a greyhound. Made for speed, for grace, and with a great heart for the race.

Ridiculous! She was a woman. No different from any

other woman. Many would call her too thin for love-making.

But none had ever kissed her. Had ever held her.

Chance broke the kiss, knowing he was becoming fanciful. He had to concentrate on the matter at hand and Courtland's idiocy. "No one will question our association now, Julia, not even Jacko," he said, touching her softly pink and swollen bottom lip with the tip of his finger. "You look well and truly kissed."

Before Julia could think, she stepped back and slapped Chance hard across the face. "And what will your family think of *that*, sir?"

He put his hand to his cheek. Damn, it stung. He'd probably wear the mark of her hand on his skin for most of the day. "They'll think, Julia, that at last Chance has met his match with this woman of his and that it's damn well time."

"I don't understand. Why would your family allow your…your mistress under the same roof with your daughter, your sisters? Are you Beckets that uncivilized?"

"Do we give a tinker's damn what anyone else thinks of us? No, Julia, we don't. However, I am probably the exception, so please don't shriek and faint when I introduce you to my sisters as my affianced wife."

"So you'll lie to your sisters, your own daughter? I don't believe you. All of this deception because of what I saw and heard on the Marsh last night?"

"Among other concerns I or anyone in my family might harbor, yes. Not that we're announcing the banns, as I'm still in mourning. In other words, our betrothal is for here and for now, that's all. Give me a month, Julia. I won't press my attentions on you again. After a month, it won't matter who you talk to or what you think you know."

Julia protectively pressed her hands to the center of her chest, then realized she had waited much too long to worry now about her modesty. "It's…it's as if I were a prisoner here at Becket Hall."

"True enough." Chance smiled as he held out his arm to her. "Nevertheless, Miss Carruthers—welcome to the family. Shall we go down to breakfast?"

CHAPTER EIGHT

JULIA SAT IN THE MAIN salon at Becket Hall, her stomach comfortably full after a plentiful and well-prepared dinner, wondering how long she would have to wait before she'd be allowed to retire to her newly assigned bedchamber on the second floor.

She hadn't seen Chance Becket all day. He'd simply left her alone outside the morning room to muddle through coddled eggs on her own, and she really was more than a little angry with the man. Even if he had looked so very handsome tonight at the dinner table, arriving late, with no apologies and only a warning squeeze of her shoulder as he bent to kiss her cheek before taking up his own chair.

Callie had giggled, and Julia had known that her cheeks had gone red. But then everyone had started talking at once again and Julia had had to choose whether to sit and stew or join in. She'd joined in. And taken peeks across the table, drat that huge candlestick, to see if Chance might be looking at her.

He had been, several times. But was that because he wanted to see her or because he thought he should appear as if he wanted to see her?

If only she could forget that *assault* on her person

this morning. And, more especially, her reaction to Chance's kiss, the intimate way he had touched her, the words he had spoken to her. *Open your mouth...let me in....*

She felt caught up in a dream, one that could just as easily become a nightmare. Even now, Julia's head was still spinning from everything that had occurred from the moment the coach had stopped on the Marsh last night.

She'd come face-to-face with the most benevolently frightening man she'd ever seen. She'd met Cassandra and the rest of the Beckets. She'd been kissed by Chance Becket.

She'd kissed Chance Becket.

At least the family called "happily uncivilized" by Chance Becket had adopted the trappings of civilization. Becket Hall was wonderfully appointed, if located in a very isolated area of Romney Marsh.

And his sisters were delightful.

Morgan Becket amazed Julia, simply amazed her. The young woman was exotic, with darkest brown hair and deep gray eyes. She had the glow of the sun about her on her flawless skin and she seemed...ripe. Yes, that was the word. *Ripe.* Lush. Stunningly beautiful. But perhaps what was most beautiful about Morgan Becket was that the girl seemed to have no idea of that beauty— or, at the least, did not act as if she cared.

Morgan Becket walked and spoke as if she wore breeches, not her simple but well-made palest blue gown, more than once quietly cursing her skirts for tangling when she crossed her legs at the knee.

She'd told a story at the dinner table, a more than slightly bawdy joke, then waited until Ainsley Becket had smiled a small, indulgent half smile before she'd laughed.

Julia thought at the time that Morgan hadn't really understood the joke but had simply parroted something she'd heard and hoped for a reaction from her family.

For as lively and animated as Morgan was, another Becket "daughter" was quiet.

Julia looked across the large room, pretending not to watch as Eleanor Becket adjusted the skirt of her simple gray gown over her legs, then bent to rub at the calf of one of them. Eleanor was small and slight, ethereal-looking, with huge brown eyes in a gamine face that wore a much too serious expression for such a lovely young woman.

"Her leg pains her," Cassandra whispered as she sat down beside Julia. "We don't notice."

"I'm sorry," Julia said, quickly lowering her eyes. "I didn't mean to stare."

"Elly didn't see you looking," Cassandra assured her, then popped another sugarplum into her mouth. "Now please pretend you are enjoying my company very much or else someone will take it into their head to send me back upstairs to bed, and I'm heartily sick of being sick in bed."

Julia smiled at the girl. "I think we'd be smart to keep Alice away from you. You may be a disquieting influence on her."

Cassandra considered this. "No. That would be Fanny. Odette says she's got the devils in her. I'm simply spoiled straight down to the bone because Papa thinks I look like Mama, and he loved her very much."

"Is that her portrait above the mantel?" Julia asked, sure it was, for Cassandra looked very much like the smiling young woman in the portrait, captured in all her youth and beauty. The woman's hair was darker, but the smile was so like her daughter's it was almost uncanny. "She's wearing the most beautiful gown. All those colors!"

Cassandra looked at the portrait. "Odette says Mama called it her rainbow gown. Papa found the silk somewhere and brought it to her as a present. But it's gone now. It got lost."

"Callie, why are you still here? I went to your room to tuck you up and you weren't there."

Cassandra Becket sighed theatrically and Julia hid a smile behind her hand.

"You didn't want to tuck me up, Fanny," Cassandra said. "You wanted to ask me questions about Julia. What's she like, Callie? Will I like her, Callie? Why don't you just sit down and find out for yourself?"

"You're an odious child," Fanny said in an offhand tone that told Julia she'd offered those sentiments often in the past, and then she smiled at Julia. "Callie's such an infant. Come along, *infant,* you belong in bed. If Papa comes in here after his brandy and cigar and sees you, he'll look at you. You don't want him *looking* at you, do you?"

Apparently Cassandra did not. "I have to go upstairs now, Julia," she said, scrambling to her feet. "But don't worry, I'll see you in the morning."

Julia watched Cassandra and her sister Fanny leave the room holding hands, Cassandra already chattering to her sister, Fanny nodding her blond head as she smiled a delightfully wide smile down at Callie.

"Fanny makes it sound as if Papa would punish Callie if he found her still here," Eleanor said from her chair. "It's hardly that. Callie's been sick, and no one wants to worry Papa about anything."

"I see," Julia said, not seeing at all. Ainsley Becket certainly hadn't given her the impression that he needed to be shielded from anything. He'd generously included her in their dinner conversation and seemed to listen with both ears when she'd talked about her late father and their life in Hawkhurst.

Julia had gotten the feeling that there was nothing Ainsley Becket saw or heard that he didn't remember. And that some of what he'd seen and heard still hurt him very badly.

"You're feeling overwhelmed, aren't you?" Eleanor asked, sitting very still in her chair, her hands folded in her lap. "We Beckets can be a bit…daunting."

"Not to mention numerous," Julia said as she stood, walked over to seat herself in a chair closer to Eleanor. "I should like to write all of your names down on scraps of paper, then pin them to you until I can sort you out."

Eleanor's smile was glorious, lighting her entire solemn little face. "I felt the same at first. Perhaps I can help?"

Julia wondered what Chance's answer would be to that question, wondered how much he really wanted her to know about his "family." But then again, Chance was with Ainsley and his brothers, still in the dining room. "Yes, please. As you said, I am feeling a little overwhelmed."

"But certainly not because we all look like peas from the same pod," Eleanor said, then sighed. "I'm sure Chance told you at least that much? That we're Papa's children but not really his children, except for Callie?"

"Yes, he did tell me that." Julia looked toward the closed double doors to the dining room, hoping they'd stay closed until Eleanor had told her more about her siblings, most especially about Chance.

"Oh, don't worry," Eleanor said. "They've left the dining room by now and are shut up tight in Papa's study, all of them ringing a peal over Courtland's head for some reason or another, or so Morgan told me. They've been at it all day, and I doubt they'll be coming in here any more tonight."

"Courtland's rather a serious sort, isn't he?" Julia asked, remembering the man who had sat across from Eleanor at the dinner table. Courtland Becket was tall but shorter than Chance and built along sturdier lines. Only his longish, unruly light brown wavy hair softened his features and kept him from looking petulant rather than intense.

"Courtland enjoys being dour and sober," Eleanor said, then sighed. "Life is very serious to Courtland. I think Callie's the only thing that keeps him from becoming positively grim. It's as if the weight of the whole world is on his shoulders, and what isn't there, he'll pick up for the rest of us and carry it. He feels responsibility for everyone, you understand."

"But he's not the oldest," Julia said, remembering

what Chance had told her at the inn. "Chance is the oldest. I'm sure he told me that."

"Yes, all right, we'll do it that way," Eleanor said. "There are two ways, you understand. Our ages or when Papa found us. Chance was both the first and the oldest. Papa always kept him close, so that's why it's so difficult that…"

"That Chance doesn't visit Becket Hall very often?" Julia supplied helpfully, trying not to sound too eager.

"They had a falling-out when…some years ago. It's why we're all so glad he brought Alice here—and brought you here. To be fair, I think he tried to mend things before, by bringing Beatrice and Alice here, but his wife made it very plain that she wanted nothing to do with us or with Becket Hall. She called us a "barbarian menagerie" and much worse than that. Of course, Fanny did put a dozen frogs in her dressing room, with Callie's assistance, which didn't really help matters."

Julia laughed. "No, I suppose not. How old is Fanny?"

"Sixteen, so she's not the one I should tell you about next, although she is one of the last Papa adopted. Both Fanny and Rian the same day."

"Those are Irish names, aren't they? They're really brother and sister? By blood?"

Eleanor shook her head. "No. But they were orphaned at the same time. Rian is six years older than Fanny. They used to be very close, but now he and Spence call her a pest. And she is, I suppose. Not quite a child, not quite grown. She still thinks she should be running free and even refuses to put up her hair."

"Spencer," Julia said, remembering the dark-haired young man who'd sat at the table looking very much as if he longed to be somewhere else, anywhere else. "He and Morgan seem somewhat alike—in their coloring, that is."

"Some Spanish somewhere or even Portuguese," Eleanor said, nodding. "At least Papa thinks so. They're both very…passionate people. And when they argue? It's really almost funny, unless Morgan is throwing something."

Julia pressed her hands to the sides of her head. "I think I'm even more confused now. Eight of you! I know that isn't a large family, especially here on the Marsh, but I had no siblings at all. Now let me see if I have this correctly. Chance is the oldest, then Courtland, then—Rian or Spencer?"

"Spencer by a year. Then me, then Morgan, then Fanny and lastly Callie. Papa hadn't planned on us girls, not at all, but here we are."

"So you're the oldest girl," Julia said, believing that would mean she had known Chance the longest. "What was it like growing up on the islands?"

Eleanor looked at her hands again. "I have no idea. Papa…found me on his way here, to England. I'm his bit of flotsam, I suppose." Then she smiled. "Well, that's the lot of us. And if you don't mind, I think I'd like to go up to bed now. You'll be all right here by yourself? Morgan or Fanny might come back downstairs, but I can't be sure. You can ring for someone if you need any-thing."

Julia watched as Eleanor left the room, a graceful figure, only slightly favoring her left leg. Then she sat back and counted Beckets on her fingers and decided she liked Ainsley Becket very much, for he had chosen to provide for all these children, now mostly adults.

And they must have great affection for him, for none of them had left, save Chance.

Julia looked about the large, lavishly appointed room, enchanted once more by the portrait hanging over the fireplace, then realized that she was the lone female and could soon be surrounded by five Becket males. Did she really want that? Was she really ready for that?

It had been difficult enough sitting at dinner this evening, being welcomed to the family, and she'd felt a fraud as she'd coaxed Eleanor into telling what very well could be family secrets.

She probably should go to bed, as she'd really like to rise early, be ready to walk on the beach the moment the morning mist dissipated. She hadn't been out-of-doors all day, what with settling in both herself and Alice, and both she and the child could use a bit of fresh air.

But first, Julia decided as she climbed the stairs, she would check on Alice in the nursery.

CHAPTER NINE

CHANCE STOOD IN THE shadows, his arms folded across his chest, and watched as Odette approached Julia's bed.

She carefully turned down the bedspread, exposing the sheets, then moved to the top of the bed, to the pillows. In the light of the small bedside candle Chance could see that, unbelievable as it seemed, Odette had begun to show her age.

Not that anyone would dare ask how old she was, not even while on a ship just setting sail for the other side of the world, and the person shouted the question across the water while Odette was trussed to the dock with a stout rope.

There were threads of silver at last in the heavy rope of braids Odette wore tightly coiled around her head, and a pair of gold-rimmed spectacles was squeezed onto the bridge of her short, wide nose. She dressed all in black and had ever since that final day, all her vibrant colors gone. Her tall frame had at last begun to thicken, along with the swollen bare ankles he could see above the decrepit carpet slippers she always wore.

The pillow on the near side of the bed had been pushed aside now, and Chance watched as Odette reached into one of the many pockets she had sewn into all of her gowns and withdrew a small cloth bag.

He could hear the mumble of her voice but not quite decipher the words of her melodic chant. He waited as she touched the bag to the sheets. Here… here…there.

Only when she'd put the bag back into her pocket did Chance step forward, saying, "Was that in aid of keeping her here or sending her away? And don't try to hand me a bag of moonshine that you've begun to practice anything but white magic."

Odette didn't flinch. Nor did she turn to look at him. "She will stay where you stay, go where you go and never betray you."

"That's almost poetic. And this works? This bag of weeds and bones or whatever the hell you've got there? Did it work on Beatrice? I think not."

Now, at last, Odette turned around to face him. "I did not bother with that one. She did not have your heart and you did not have hers. Come to me tomorrow. It is more than time to renew your *gad* in the *mavangou*. There are bad *loa* here now, and there will be more."

Chance involuntarily put his hand to the middle of his chest, his fingers rubbing against the browned alligator tooth that lay there. He was a grown man and didn't believe in Odette's voodoo ways. But old habits die hard. "I don't believe in bad *loa*. Just bad luck. Bad luck and stupid decisions. I only wear this to keep a fanciful old woman happy."

"And you are only in this room because you want to make yourself happy, no matter what the master says.

I've turned down the bed and spread the welcome. The rest is up to you."

"I don't know if I should wonder if you've been listening at keyholes or believe in your powers and thank you for your help—or curse you for thinking I'd need it."

Ah, finally. He'd roused a smile from the woman, as well as one of her deep, rumbling laughs. "Cassandra helped me prepare this year's *mavangou,* and it is very potent. Both gunpowder and Shrove Tuesday ashes. But do not come to me until nine tomorrow morning," she said, moving slowly toward the door. "These bones grow old in the cold and damp of this inhospitable island, and I don't move as I did in the warmth of the sun."

He watched Odette go as the affection he felt for her took him back to the days when she had fed him, watched over him and more than occasionally let him feel the back of her large-knuckled hand across the back of his head. She'd cared for all of them, taken them all under her wing, into her heart.

But never the way she had with Isabella or with Cassandra. It was Odette's curse on herself that she hadn't seen what would happen that last day, that her religion, her beliefs, all her charms and chants, hadn't revealed the evil.

Yes, Odette had aged far beyond her years. They all had.

Chance mentally shook himself, pushing away the memories, and looked at the bed. Julia's bed.

He needed to do what had to be done. Odette's powers to one side, the best way to ensure Julia's silence was either to kill her or make love to her, and killing her wasn't an option. But women became more malleable once they were bedded, if the man bedding her knew what he was about.

Beatrice had been the exception. Only after Alice's birth had he discovered that she'd been in love with another man even before their marriage. If he'd known then what he knew now, he would have given them a fat purse and his best wishes, then pointed out the way to Gretna Green.

But then, Chance knew as he straightened the pillow on the bed so that it lined up with the others, he wouldn't have Alice.

The clock on the mantel chimed the hour. Ten o'clock. Where the devil was the woman? He needed to be back downstairs by midnight to help Courtland go clean up his mess.

But they'd all agreed. Julia Carruthers was here, she knew too much and they couldn't really let her go right now. Ainsley had told him, "Control her. I believe she understands she is to keep silent. But never put all your coins on only one number, Chance. Better to cover your bets."

"That means cover *her,* if you're not understanding this, my grand stallion." Jacko had laughed then, and Chance had taken a swing at him, only failing to connect with the man's grinning face because Ainsley had caught his arm in midpunch.

"London life making you slow, pup? I remember when you moved better than that," Jacko had said, still holding a mug of his favored rum. The man hadn't so much as flinched or taken up a defensive posture. Then he'd smiled and stroked at his beard. "If you don't want her…"

"Jacko," Ainsley had said quietly, lightly placing his hand on Chance's chest. "Why don't you go see what the others are up to in the morning room? I'll join you shortly." Once the man was gone, he'd turned to Chance. "Let it go, son. Jacko's old now. He lives in his past and fights with his mouth."

Chance had done his best to shake off his anger and only said to Ainsley, "Yes, thank you. I'll join you later." Then he'd grinned and said the words that still echoed in his mind, shaming him, as they'd been said to bolster his feelings at Julia's expense: "Ah, the sacrifices I must make for my brothers."

He turned now as he heard the sound of the door latch being depressed and waited for Julia to see him as she entered the room carrying a candle in a glass-topped holder.

Julia turned to shut the door and turn the key in the lock. She'd had enough of people traipsing in and out of her bedchamber as if it lay en route to the dining hall or some such thing. She pocketed the key, then sighed wearily, because Alice had wakened when she'd gone in to her and she'd had to read her two stories before the child had fallen asleep once more.

What a long day, what a long few days. A month of days all tightly packed into three interminable, eventful days. She was already reaching behind her with one hand to begin unbuttoning her gown as she turned toward the bed. And at last sensed that she was not alone.

"*You.*"

Chance, who had been leaning against one of the tall bedposts, stepped forward, smiling. "Yes, *me*. And now that we know where I am, where have you been?"

Julia walked over to a table and put down the candle holder before he could see it trembling in her hand. "I have been with your daughter, saying good night to her for the second time, which is one more time than you said good night to her. Sir."

Chance winced. "Christ. How could I have forgotten…?"

"I imagine if something is not done regularly, that something is easy to forget," Julia said, deliberately refusing to acknowledge the quick flash of guilt in the man's eyes. "And now, if you don't mind, I'll ask you to leave. I'm tired and I wish to go to sleep. *Darling*."

Chance stayed where he was. "We'll assign a maid to you tomorrow, to take care of your personal needs. In the meantime, perhaps you'd like some help with those buttons. *Sweetheart*."

Julia felt her chin go up and her hands ball into fists at her sides, both automatic, stubborn responses to what her body, at least, felt to be the threat of imminent attack. "You weren't amusing the first time and you promised there would not be a second time."

"Amusing?" Chance smiled as he began walking toward her and she, wonderfully brave or helpfully inquisitive, stood very still and watched him. "Is that what you call what happened between us this morning, Julia? Amusing? I think I'm insulted."

"Really?" she said, her heart pounding. "I'd say you were insulting." Then she walked away from him, all the way across the room, to stand with her back to the closed draperies, her arms crossed below her breasts. "Now go away."

"I can't," Chance said, spreading his arms. "You've locked the door."

Julia pushed her hands into the pockets of her gown, her fingers closing over the cool metal of the large key. "Oh, blast," she said angrily, then took a deep breath, let it out slowly. "All right. Say what it is you came to say and then go."

She believed he'd come here to *talk?* Lord love the woman. But very well, they'd talk. "I wanted to thank you for today, Julia. Ainsley was quite impressed. My sisters believe you to be extremely pleasant, my brothers are envious of me and my daughter, it would appear, would be a sad child indeed if you weren't here. And you didn't stab me with your fork when I kissed your cheek in front of my family tonight at dinner. So for all of that—" he spread his arms again, palms up, as if to show that they, and he, were empty of anything in the least nefarious "—thank you."

"You're welcome," Julia said, then lowered her head, looked at him through her lashes, totally unaware of what she was doing. But she did feel flattered and quite pleased. What a pathetic fool she was, she should be ashamed of herself. "Your sisters like me? I think they're very nice. Very different but very nice. Callie is a rare handful, isn't she?"

"They all are, in their way. Except for Eleanor. Although I will warn you, that little bit of nothing has a will of iron. I, for one, would think twice before I crossed her."

Julia couldn't help herself. "I noticed that she walks with a slight limp. Callie says her leg gives her pain."

"And you, uncurious as ever, want to know what happened to her, yes? Was she born that way? Was there an accident?" Chance said, moving closer, shortening the distance between them.

"No," Julia said quickly. "No, I don't. If Eleanor wants me to know someday, she'll tell me. I won't ask about Eleanor or any of your sisters or brothers. I won't ask about Ainsley and I most especially will not ask about Jacko or Billy or any of the others I've encountered thus far. Mr. Becket's servants, that is."

"And a motley collection they are, yes. All colors, all shapes, all sizes and more than a few languages among them. At least two missing a hand each, one of those a woman. And one with a wooden leg—that would be Bumble, our cook. I don't think there are more than three or four who have all their own teeth, either. We had one who'd lost an eye, wore a fine black patch, but I've heard Ricardo put his good eye to finding himself a fine countrywoman in Dymchurch who doesn't mind his feet stuck under her kitchen table."

Julia put a hand to her mouth to cover her smile. "Certainly none of them remind me of your fine London butler or your footmen in their fancy livery. Everyone here…everyone just seems to be here because they want to be here, and as long as they're here, they'll help out."

"What a lovely and very apt way of putting it," Chance said, shortening the distance between them yet again. Slowly. Slowly. All good things come slowly.

Julia shrugged. "The house is so formal, but the people are not. I…I do think it *is* all very lovely, frankly, although I believe I can understand why your late wife wasn't quite so delighted. Becket Hall is most certainly not Upper Brook Street."

"Becket Hall is our land ship," Chance said, realizing his words were very close to the truth. "Stone and mortar rather than wood and sail. An aging crew, retired from the sea. Someone should write an epic poem."

"Perhaps someone has, in a way," Julia said, nervously twisting her hands together. "'The helmsman steered, the ship moved on; Yet never a breeze up-blew. The mariners all again work the ropes, Where they were wont to do. They raised their limbs like lifeless tools— We were a ghastly crew.'"

Chance stepped back as if she'd slapped him. "Samuel Taylor Coleridge."

"'The Rime of the Ancient Mariner,' yes." Julia shrugged her shoulders. "I'm sorry. I don't know why that came into my mind."

"No, no, that's all right. It's a fanciful story. The mariner saved by an albatross, only to slay the bird and have it hung around his neck as penance. Ainsley puts more stock into that fantasy than most."

Unbidden, another bit of the poem sprang into Julia's head. "'The other was a softer voice, As soft as honeydew: Quoth he, 'The man hath penance done, And penance more will do.''" Now she was becoming fanciful as well as scaring herself. "It's growing late.…"

"Yes. Yes, it is," Chance said, snapping himself back to attention and to the matter at hand. "You're an interesting woman, Julia. The vicar's daughter, who knows too much about what goes on in the Marsh, who has no qualms about tending to bloody wounds...who spouts poetry."

He pushed his fingers through his hair. "I don't know if you're the luckiest find a man could stumble over or his just punishment."

Julia swallowed down hard, amazed at how vulnerable Chance Becket looked to her at that moment and how in charity she was with this maddening man who harbored so many secrets. So many, she felt sure, sad secrets. "This hasn't been an easy homecoming for you, has it?"

Chance looked at her and laughed softly. "You noticed? And here I thought I was putting such a fine face on things."

The room was becoming smaller, more intimate. And he was becoming very aware of how alone he had been for so very long and how sweet it would be to have someone to hold, someone to care for him. Someone who someday he might even be able to talk to....

Julia felt so sorry for the man, both for the man and the boy he'd been. If he were Alice's age, she would take him in her arms and try to comfort him. "Yes, I did notice. And my presence here isn't making any of what's going on here easier for you."

He shook his head, shocked to realize what he would say next was true. "No, Julia, there's where you're wrong. Frankly I can't imagine being here without you. God knows what I would have done if you hadn't been there on the Marsh with me last night. I might have…might have been stupid enough to destroy everything."

Should she pretend not to understand what he meant? But what was the point in that? "If Dickie had not said *Black Ghost* to me, and me to you, you may have done your duty. Then Dickie may have said the words to someone at Dover Castle." She closed her eyes for a second, then said the rest. "And brought the world down around your family's head."

"Billy would have stopped me," Chance said before he could measure his words. Too close, too close; this woman was much too close.

Julia put her hand on Chance's arm. "Do they really spy on you in London? Don't they trust you?"

Now Chance laughed in genuine amusement. "Billy *protects* me. Or at least he'd like to think so. Don't become too fanciful, Julia, not everything is a mystery to be solved."

You are. Julia closed her eyes and turned her head away from him as she prayed she hadn't said the words out loud. "I'm tired. Please."

Chance reached out to lightly touch the side of her throat. "There's still those buttons to contend with," he said quietly.

"I can manage them, thank you." She didn't look at him but kept her head turned, refusing to believe that she wanted him to keep touching her, even as his fingers drifted to her cheek and then lightly to her chin.

"Look at me, Julia," he said, the slight pressure of his fingers beneath her chin. "Look at me. What do you see in my eyes?"

"I…I don't know," she said, her own eyes searching his face, drinking in the beauty of him, the restrained but probably never to be conquered strength of him. "I think you frighten me."

"Oh, no, not that," Chance said, dipping his head to nuzzle at the silky skin below her ear. She tasted as good as he remembered. He whispered into her ear, "Don't be frightened."

Julia took an involuntary breath as tiny shivers of awareness spread like silken cobwebs, tracing over her shoulders, down her arms. She could feel her nipples pressing against her undershift.

He slid his arms around her, pulling her closer, and she wondered if he'd felt as alone as she had and if he, too, felt less alone now.

She was weakening. Chance knew it. Knew it and cursed himself. Cursed Ainsley and Jacko and Courtland. All of them.

Then he cursed himself again, because he wasn't here with this woman on orders from anyone. He was here because here was where he wanted to be. Holding her. Tasting her. Introducing her to what it felt like to be a man and a woman together.

"Never be frightened of me," he said as he raised his head slightly, then brought his mouth down on hers. Slanted his lips against hers until she opened to him, then plunged inside.

Her arms came up of their own volition, it seemed, for Julia was now holding him, clinging to him, the small fires he had lit this morning now bursting into flame with a vengeance.

She didn't know what she felt or even why she felt it. But she wanted to learn, to feel more, because she was sure there would be more. "Please," she murmured against his mouth, then gasped as she felt his hand cup her breast.

Holding the kiss, with his right hand Chance released the row of buttons that ended just below her waist, then pushed the material from her shoulders, along with the straps of her simple cotton shift.

Julia felt the night air on her bare skin, cool and surprising, before Chance covered her breasts with his hands, lightly rubbing the pads of his thumbs over her.

She should stop him. This was madness. She didn't even know this man. She'd never known a man, not in her nearly one and twenty years, had resigned herself to spinsterhood. *Which is no excuse.*

"Go away," she breathed without realizing she'd spoken aloud as Chance kissed her cheek, her chin, began nibbling maddeningly at the tingling skin of her throat.

His hands stilled on her breasts. He would never force a woman. He'd seen enough to have given him a horror of that sort of display of physical dominance. "You want me to leave?" he asked, then gave in to the desire to lick at her magnificently straight collarbone with the tip of his tongue.

Julia tipped back her head, breathing hard as she looked up at the dark ceiling, mentally waving goodbye to her common sense and a lifetime spent believing she had a clear understanding of right and wrong. "No," she then said honestly. "I…I was talking to my conscience."

"God, you're a fascinating woman, Julia Carruthers," Chance told her, then scooped her up, carried her over to the bed, gently laid her against the cool, fragrant sheets.

He joined her on the bed, taking up where he'd left off, kissing her mouth, touching her breasts.

She knew she was naked to the waist, exposed to his eyes, but she didn't care. Still, what was fine for the goose…

He was dressed casually again, just evening shoes, hose and skintight fawn breeches, not even the vest of this morning covering his snow-white, generously sleeved shirt with the collar opened, exposing a small part of his tanned chest and a few golden curls. She ached to touch him.

Julia tugged at the buttons, amazed to find herself feeling frantic now, as if his touch on her breast was somehow urging her on to her own explorations. If only she could remember how to open a button.…

"This is much better done without clothes, sweetings," Chance told her, covering her hand with his own. When she didn't disagree, he pushed away from her and stripped off his shirt and the *gad* around his neck before blowing out the bedside candle. He hardly needed protection from Julia. Only then did he rid himself of the remainder of his clothes.

She was an eager virgin, yes, but that didn't mean the sight of a naked male body could be counted on to increase that eagerness. He joined her on the bed once more, his hand going to her waist even as he leaned over her, kissed her again.

And again. And again, trying so hard to remember that it was him seducing her, as she not only allowed his kiss but set her own tongue to dueling with his…all the while he deftly relieved her of her clothes before covering them both to the waist with the soft bedsheet.

He held her close as he lightly stroked her bare back, reveling in the way that back curved, the enticing indentation that marked her spine. And she did the same.

He had lightly nipped at the lobe of her ear. Now she did the same to him. The eager student, learning, practicing what she'd learned.

Chance felt sure he was about to go out of his mind…even as he reveled in the role of teacher.

He taught her that her body was a garden of delights for both of them.

He suckled at her breasts, his blood singing when she began to moan, pull his head closer, hold him very still as he laved her nipple with the roughness of his tongue, held her breath as if to move either of them would utterly destroy her.

Julia felt herself floating on a cloud of sensations she hadn't even dreamed possible. His hands on her. His mouth. On her.

She could stay like this forever or so she thought until Chance began moving his hand lower. To her waist. To trace delicate circles on her belly. To move lower still, to slip between her thighs and touch her so very intimately, even as she clenched her teeth, suddenly aware that what she'd been feeling had been only a prelude to the aching wonder she felt now.

The anticipation of something wild, something wonderful. A willing step off that cloud and into the unknown.

Julia could feel his hard body against hers, his manhood that she could only imagine sunk deep inside her...and for the first time she felt fear.

"It's all right, Julia," Chance breathed against her ear as he felt her body tense. "This is the way it's supposed to be. This is why we were made the way we were made."

And all the time he was touching her. Stroking her. Learning her. And when she relaxed her thighs, when she sighed, he felt a surge of power run through him that he had to shut down immediately or else disgrace himself.

He was losing control. He never lost control. She was unschooled, her lovemaking tentative, almost clumsy. But still so eager. And now so trusting.

And he was a bastard of the first water.

"Nature makes certain that you're ready for me, sweetings, and you are. You're glorious," he told her, gentling her as he would a timid young colt. "There will be some pain, I won't lie to you, but only this once, and I'll make you forget it. I swear I will."

"Hold me, please," Julia said, her eyes closed as she reached for him. "Don't talk. Just...just do it."

There never was a bastard like him.

Chance kissed her yet again, then levered himself over her, settled himself between her thighs and let nature do the rest.

Julia felt the pain, digging her nails into the hard flesh of Chance's back, knowing she'd just crossed over from maidenhood to womanhood and knowing there was no way back.

And then he began to move. She could feel him take possession of her, moving inside her, and she was the eager pupil once more. She moved with him, tentatively at first, and then, as the heat grew, as the *need* grew, so did her courage. Holding on to him as his breathing became even more rapid and shallow than hers, as she felt the sweat break out on his skin, as she felt something inside her grow and bud…and burst into bloom.

Chance felt her give over, give in, let her body take her where it wanted to go.

He didn't have that luxury.

Muttering a curse under his breath, he withdrew to all but collapse on Julia as he spilled his seed on her belly, then lay there, his strength gone, his passion released but not wholly satisfied.

"Stay here, sweetings, don't move," he told her quietly, then retrieved a towel from the washstand in the corner. He sat on the bed and slightly pressed the towel between Julia's legs, then wiped her belly. "Are you all right?"

All right? She was mortified! She was lying there naked. She'd just given herself to this man, and now somehow something very beautiful had become something very tawdry as he wiped away the seed he hadn't cared to spill inside her.

"I'm fine," she said, glad for the dark that was broken only by the small candle she'd brought to the room with her. "Could…um…could you please leave now?"

Chance tried for some humor, something to lighten what was rapidly becoming the most awkward moment of his life. "Are you speaking to your conscience again?"

Julia pulled the covers up to her chin. "No, I'm not. Please…just go. I don't know if you feel some small need to talk now, to *discuss* what just happened, but I must tell you that I most assuredly do not."

Chance nodded, then reached for his clothing, quickly pulling on his breeches and stabbing his arms into the sleeves of his shirt, not bothering with the buttons, then lowered the *gad* over his head. His hair was hanging loose, and when Julia dared to peek at him in the semi-darkness, she caught her breath. He looked so beautiful and yet so dangerous. Untamed yet vulnerable.

And he had just made love to her, to the spinster daughter of a Hawkhurst vicar. The world had turned upside down, and Julia still wasn't quite sure how that had happened.

Would he please just *leave!*

"We'll talk tomorrow."

Julia nodded, not trusting herself to speak.

"I'm serious, Julia. We will talk."

Then Chance snatched up his hose and shoes and headed for the door. Stopped.

"So much for a gracious exit. Julia, I'm still locked in."

The most ridiculous thing happened. Julia smiled. Then she giggled. She laughed until tears came to her eyes and then she began to cry.

She was still crying when Chance, having retrieved the key from the pocket of her gown, and without another word, left her, closing the door quietly behind him.

CHAPTER TEN

CHANCE WASHED HIMSELF hastily in cold water, then pulled on the clothing Billy had laid out for him. Black. Black from throat to ankle, including a pair of black boots he'd left at Becket Hall when he'd gone to London, boots that went to the knee in the back, up and over the knee in front. Boots last worn on the deck of the Black Ghost.

He tied a length of black silk around his waist, another around his throat, then slid his favorite knife between the sash and his waistband.

A black knit toque would completely cover the hair he pushed up inside it as he opened the door and stepped into the hallway.

"My, my, my. You are having a busy night, aren't you, Chance?"

Morgan. Chance turned to look at his sister, who stood with her back to the wall, her hands tucked behind her and rhythmically pushing against that wall, so that she seemed to gracefully move while standing in place. "What in bloody blazes are you doing here? And what in God's name are you wearing?"

The girl stepped away from the wall and spread her arms wide before turning in a full circle. She, too, was in black from head to toe. "You don't recognize your own clothes, brother mine? Anyone else would have noticed if I'd raided their wardrobes, but you weren't here to notice, were you? Yet here we are. I thought you'd never leave her room. Honestly how anyone would rather rut like a boar than ride the Marsh, I'll never know, but to each his own, I suppose. Come on, they'll be waiting for us out at the stables."

Chance scrubbed at his face with his hands, then chuckled darkly. "You're seventeen, Morgan, if I'm remembering correctly. Too young to be so jaded but not too old to be spanked and sent back to the nursery."

She pulled herself up straight, unaware that the action only served to accentuate the lush swell of her breasts beneath the black silk. When had she grown up? How had it happened without him ever noticing?

Her dark brown hair was tucked up inside a drooping knit toque, but one thick lock of hair was visible, hanging from her forehead and sweeping down the curve of her cheek, ending beneath her chin. Her stormy gray eyes seemed to dance in mischief. Beautiful. Wild. The girl was becoming a woman, even if she didn't know it.

"I've ridden out before, Chance. I *have*. What's one more, when there are already so many? I didn't have to come here. I just thought…I just thought you would…"

"You thought I'd be pleased? That I'd enjoy being in on the *joke*? Ainsley definitely has had his nose too long in his books, hasn't he? You've gone wild out here on the Marsh."

"I've grown *up* out here on the Marsh. And I *help*. What do *you* do, big brother?"

"What do I do? I count to five, little sister, and if I don't hear the door to your bedchamber slamming shut by then, I'll find a rope and tie you to your bedpost. Wait. First, I'll relieve you of this, thank you," he said, snatching the wicked-looking knife from the black sash she'd tied around her waist. "What a piece of work you are. And now, Morgan…one…two…three…"

Morgan stood and glared at him a moment longer, her full lower lip pushed forward in a defiant pout, then turned on her heels and ran down the hallway.

Chance shook his head and watched her go. "God save the man who tries to tame that one," he muttered, placing the knife on a nearby table, then headed for the servant stairs and the door closest to the stables.

Morgan had been right. He was late, and they were waiting for him, already saddled, mounted, prepared to move. A good three dozen of them, at his quick count. All men from Becket Hall.

Jacmel also waited, tied to the fence rail, and Chance made short work of vaulting into the saddle. "My apologies for my tardiness," he said as Billy handed up a pistol Chance pushed into his waistband. "You're not dressed for the occasion," he said then, grinning down at the sailor-cum-coachie.

"The day I set sail on a horse is one you'll never see," Billy said, shaking his head. "Bad enough to sit up behind them. They fart, you know. And stink worse'n a shark three days dead on the deck in the hot sun." He hesitated, then added, "You be careful, you hear? Stay near Court, get each other's backs if it comes to a fight."

Chance grinned. "Such concern. Will you give me a kiss goodbye, too?"

Billy's lined face went flat, his eyes cold as he laid a hand on Chance's thigh. "You've been living soft, boy. Living high. I'm just askin' you to follow, not lead on this one. You understand? Court. Follow Court."

"Oh, yes, I can see the wisdom in that. He's led everyone so well while I've been gone, hasn't he? Led every man here within an inch of the hangman."

Chance felt a leg against his as Courtland brought his own mount up close beside Jacmel. "Nobody asked you along. We've been muddling through without you for a lot of years, we can muddle through now."

Chance looked at his younger "brother," so much the man now, with his shaggy sandy hair, his too-solemn face, that close-cut beard he'd adopted.

Chance had been the only one, until Ainsley had dragged Courtland to the island and handed him over to Odette. Small, bloodied, whip marks on his bony back. Ainsley had named him because Courtland hadn't said a word, told anyone his name. He hadn't said a word for about four years after coming to the island, not until Ainsley had brought Isabella there, introducing her as his wife. His first words had been spoken to her: "Your laugh is so pretty."

Courtland had become her pet, her adoring pet, and when Cassandra was born, it was Court who had assigned himself the role of her protector. He had been how old when Cassandra was born? Probably thirteen, as old as she was now.

Courtland had been holding Cassandra that day

when the Black Ghost limped home to the island. Standing on the beach, up to his knees in the clear blue water. Not a tear in his eyes or a word passing his lips. Holding the infant...

Chance shook off the memory. Too many memories. He shouldn't have come back. "For a boy of few words, you make a nattering man. Are we going to talk or are we going to ride?" he asked, daring Courtland to take the next step.

"Listen up," Court said, turning his mount, a coal-black stallion with only a small white blaze on its face. He stood in the stirrups as he addressed the company, and Chance noticed that his brother was wearing a black silken cape tied at the neck. A flair for the dramatic, his brother. "They may have shifted most of the haul by now, but we don't know that. What they haven't carried inland, they'll be guarding. Our land party awaits word at the usual place but won't move until we've had ourselves a look. And maybe a fight. Are you ready for a fight, boys? Are you ready to take back what's ours and maybe send a few thieving bastards to hell?"

Dozens of fists and as many shouts shot into the air and Chance cursed under his breath, his heart sinking. *Boys,* Court had called them. He knew these men. He'd sailed with these men. But that was thirteen long years ago, and some of them hadn't been young then. *A ghastly crew.*

He wished Ainsley would be riding with them but hadn't expected him to. Did Ainsley know that Spence was riding with them? That Rian was riding with them? That all of his "sons" were riding out while he sat in his study, so turned away from life even the thought of a fine fight couldn't rouse him?

They had all lost so much when Isabella died.

Chance used his heels to turn Jacmel and ride out of the stable yard with the others, bringing his mount beside Court's as they rode along shoulder to shoulder in the moonlight and ground mist.

"The silk cape is possibly overdone, if you want my opinion," he said.

"Everyone needs to know who leads, Chance. And the cape adds to the mystery. Dramatic, yes, I agree. But it serves its purpose. If something were to happen to me, Spence could take over, with no one outside of Becket Hall the wiser."

Chance moved on to another subject. "How long have you been putting Spence and Rian in danger, Court? I asked last night, but you didn't answer."

Court kept his eyes looking straight ahead. "They're grown now. They make their own choices."

"Really. And Morgan? What about her? She told me she's ridden with you. Not, she says, that you noticed."

"That's a lie. Morgan has never—hell's teeth, Chance, she hasn't! Damn her!"

"Damn somebody. Ainsley had better think about marrying her off before she does something even more reckless," Chance said tightly as they came to a worn track and turned to follow it, two abreast. More horsemen were joining them, appearing one by one out of the mist from the direction of the village, falling into line. There had to be sixty of them now. It would have been easy for Morgan to slip unnoticed into such a group.

"We were too busy figuring logistics last night to go into it, but tell me, how did this all start? Better yet—why?"

They rode on in silence for a while, until Courtland said, "You remember Pike, don't you?"

"Pike? Of course I do. Ship's carpenter. He worked for months making Cassandra's cradle. What of him?"

"He's dead, that's what of him. Not quite a year ago. It turned out his wife's brothers were part of a small gang of smugglers from Lydd, and Pike went on a run with them, thinking it would be a lark, I suppose."

"That sounds like Pike. Go on."

"There's not much to say that you haven't already guessed. They crossed the Channel—rowed the whole way—but when they landed with their haul someone was waiting for them. Four of the crew and one of the brothers were sent back to Lydd with two messages."

"What were the messages?"

"The first was that no goods would be moved unless both the men and the goods were under the protection of the Red Men—they move about the villages quite openly, too, with their red sashes for all to see. Bloody arrogant, but not so arrogant that they travel in groups of less than a score or so."

Chance patted Jacmel's sleek neck, as the horse clearly wanted to run. "Not yet, Jacmel. Not yet." He turned to Court. "And the second message?"

"Heads. Heads in a box. Two of the brothers. And Pike's. You take any message from that you want to take."

Chance said nothing. There was nothing to say. Courtland and the rest of them had dug up the Black

Ghost and set him riding, uniting together to protect the many small independent groups of smugglers in the area. And all the time hoping to hell for a fight—and some revenge.

At last, as the horses moved carefully through chill standing water, he said, "Why the Black Ghost?"

And at last Courtland smiled, ruefully, obviously at his own expense. "Idiocy. A touch of madness. It was stupid of me, Chance, I know that. But there's nobody to make the connection, trace it back to Ainsley. We've been safe here for thirteen long years. Safe and bored."

Chance looked toward the horizon, which was a good distance away on this flat, treeless land. "We'll soon remedy that, brother," he said, pointing toward the long, winding trail of lit torches moving inland. He pulled the thin black scarf Billy had left on the bed for him up and over his nose, just as Court did, just as they all did.

"Yes. Everyone's seen them and knows what to do. The majority are land movers and will drop their loads and run when they see us, but their guards will fight. We'll get some revenge on the Red Men Gang tonight," Courtland told him. "And with any luck, we'll get back most of the haul, too."

Chance turned in his saddle to see that the riders were fanning out now, making the party into one long line of darker shadows in the mist. Saddle horses, dray horses, horses more used to pulling a plow. Old men, young men. Boys. All fighting for their own. He felt his own heartbeat increase as the itch to be moving, riding headfirst into the danger, came up to greet him like an old friend, long forgotten but definitely welcome.

There was always the planning, the hunt. But land or sea, nothing surpassed a good fight.

Romney Marsh might physically be a part of England, but those who lived there believed mostly in Romney Marsh, just as the family and crews had believed in the island. Their land, their lives, their fight, and the devil with anyone who got in their way.

Tales of this night's work would reach London and not be well received. England was already at war with France and soon to be at war with America, if the rumors could be believed. No one wanted a third war on their own English shores, between their own English citizens.

Chance pulled down his mask to grin at Courtland. God, but he felt alive. Alive in a way he hadn't felt in a long, long time. "Well, shall we, brother? It's been a while since I've broken the king's law."

CHAPTER ELEVEN

JULIA STOOD IN FRONT of the long mirror in her bed-chamber, surprised to find that she looked the same this morning as she had last night. She should have been able to see some difference, for she most certainly felt different.

She raised her hands to her breasts, covered once more in her simple cotton shift, and for the first time in her life thought of her body as anything more than that—her body.

That Chance could show such delight in that body, that he could bring such delight to that body?

"We're all God's creatures, Julia," her father had told her the day she'd come running to him, sobbing, telling him that she was bleeding, she was going to die. "Today, my sweet girl, you have taken one more step in His plan for His creations. Today, Julia, you are a woman."

Julia smiled, that smile a mixture of sadness and wry amusement. "No, Papa, not then," she said quietly, acutely missing the man who had been both father and teacher. "Last night I became a woman. But if God has a plan, Papa, it's still His secret."

She crossed over to the bed and picked up the length

of black grosgrain ribbon that had last been tied around Chance's hair. She'd held it tight in her hand all night, like some silly, simpering fool.

She should give it back to him. She really should.

Instead she walked back to the mirror and watched her reflection as she tied the ribbon around the left strap of her shift, then tucked it inside, next to the skin of her breast, over her heart.

"There," she told herself, lifting her chin. "You are now most definitely a pitiful, pathetic penny press heroine with more hair than wit."

Julia quickly finished dressing, having declined the assistance of the maid who had come scratching at her door earlier with hot chocolate and toasted bread and butter. She'd needed to be alone.

But now she needed to be with people so that she had something else to occupy her mind other than what she would say when she next saw Chance Becket.

She found Alice in the nursery, Callie with her, the two of them happily investigating cupboards for toys that had been tucked away when the older girl had left the nursery, while Edyth watched them, a smile on her homely face.

The drapes had all been pulled back from the windows, and the morning sun streamed into the large room, making blocks of sunlight on the large Aubusson carpet that could have graced the finest London drawing room if it weren't here, in the back of beyond.

The sunlight reminded Julia that she had wanted to walk out this morning, see the house and sea, smell the air.

"Good morning, ladies," she said, and the two girls turned to grin at her. "Who would like to accompany me on a walk down to the water?"

Ten minutes later, after being assured that both children had eaten and with all three of them wearing pattens Edyth had told them they could find in the hallway behind the kitchens, they were off.

Holding tight to Alice's hand, Julia followed Callie, who ran ahead, waving her arms as she danced her way toward the water. "Oh, go with her," she told Alice, who was tugging on her hand now. "Just be careful."

Julia watched the children as they ran up and down the waterline, pretending they were gulls, swooping with their arms, daring the water to lap at their feet.

That's when she looked to her left and noticed in the distance, around a curve in the waterline, the marvelous sloop anchored not fifty yards from the shore, its sails secured as it rode high in the water. She was much too far away to see it clearly, but it looked to be perhaps sixty feet in length and well kept. There were also a few smaller boats pulled up on the shore and turned upside down, cork-strung fishing nets spread over their hulls to dry in the sun.

The presence of the boats didn't surprise her. Becket Hall was, after all, sitting right next door to the Channel.

The French ship was still out there, too, small in the distance, still sailing parallel to the shore. She watched it for a while, then turned about to look back at Becket Hall.

She couldn't decide if the house looked as if it had been dropped there from the sky or if it had grown up from the land. There was something of the fortress about it, even with the sun winking off the multitude of windows and with its large terrace and gracefully curving staircases at either end of the terrace winding up from the ground.

From her vantage point and in the same direction as where the sloop was anchored, she could see what had to be the large stables, as well as a multitude of outbuildings of all shapes and sizes, all of them at a good distance from the Hall.

Keeping one eye on Alice and Cassandra, Julia walked along the shoreline, seeing where the shoreline, in the distance, rather than being flat, rose into low chalk cliffs, with the waves crashing up against them. She wondered if there were caves there and if the smugglers used them to hide their hauls before moving them inland.

Then she decided she shouldn't think about such things.

"Look, Julia, look!" Alice called out as she held out her arms and ran. "I'm a gull, I'm a gull!"

Julia laughed and waved, then, feeling secure in Cassandra's presence, turned inland herself, heading for the large stable yard and the buildings that had been fashioned to blend in with the architecture of the stone house. She skirted the three-railed fence, carefully picking her way, then looked up and gasped. A village?

No. Not a village. A street, only one, but with houses on both sides and a few small shops. And all of it not a quarter mile from Becket Hall.

She hadn't seen any of this the night they'd arrived; it had been much too dark. She'd had no idea....

"We're fairly self-sufficient here on the estate, Miss Carruthers."

Julia gasped, then turned to see Ainsley Becket standing not ten feet from her. "Mr. Becket, good morning," she said, dropping into a quick curtsy. "I...I, um—"

"I saw the girls, yes. They're amusing themselves. I'm so pleased Cassandra has company now. As well as Alice. Would you care to walk with me?"

"I'd like that, yes," Julia said, and when he inclined his head toward the low rise leading up to the small houses, she fell into step beside him.

Ainsley Becket was tall and lean and very fit for a man she believed to be on the sunny side of fifty. He had silver threaded through his black hair that he wore shorter than his adopted sons, with only a stray lock or two blowing across his forehead in the breeze coming from the Channel.

"Chance would have told you that we came here some years ago," he said as they walked along. "My family, myself and most of the crew from the two ships that brought us here. Their wives and families, as well. You'll see bits of those ships everywhere, in the walls of the houses. We left the sea, you understand, and made certain we wouldn't be tempted to go back again."

"But you have the sloop?"

"Yes. It amuses Jacko. He occasionally runs it toward any French vessel that sails too close, only to watch the Frogs hop away."

Julia laughed, for the first time finding something that, if not serving to make Jacko endearing, at least made him seem human. "Chance was a sailor, as well?"

"I owned two ships, Miss Carruthers. There is a vast difference between owning ships and being a sailor. I made my fortune carrying other people's goods from place to place. Mostly I would say I was a bookkeeper."

"A trader," Julia said, keeping her gaze on the uneven ground as they walked and not believing a word the man said. Ainsley Becket had the look of a man who'd spent a lot of years standing on a deck, squinting into the sun.

When she looked up again, it was to see a huge wooden carving that stood at least twenty feet high. "Oh, my goodness!"

Ainsley laced his fingers together behind his back, this strikingly handsome man, dressed all in black and with bluest-blue eyes older than time. "The bowsprit and figurehead of my best ship, Miss Carruthers," he said, gesturing toward the marvelous carving. "The boys refused to part with her."

"She's a mermaid, isn't she?" Julia asked, still amazed. It was as if someone had sliced off a portion of the very front of a ship, then planted it in the ground, braced it with thick beams. The large painted figure had a lower body of silvery-blue scales and a graceful, sweeping fish tail, and her bare breasts were partially covered by her long golden-yellow hair. She seemed to be looking off into the distance, always the first to see something new as the ship cut through the water.

"Pike carved her. One of my men," Ainsley said, placing a hand on the polished wood the mermaid was attached to, stroking that wood almost gently. "Now she looks from the land to the sea. I wonder if she's ever lonely for it."

"Are you, Mr. Becket?" Julia asked before she could guard her tongue. "Oh, I'm sorry. I shouldn't have asked that."

He offered his arm and then turned away from the figurehead, from the double row of small cottages behind it. "I made my fortune in the islands, Miss Carruthers. But it was time to come back to England. The girls, you understand. The boys were one thing, but not the girls."

Julia nodded. "Yes, I understand. You've built a world for them here, haven't you?"

"Yes…excuse me," Ainsley said, removing the support of his arm as he turned and walked, his strides long and purposeful, toward the large fenced-in area where several horses grazed.

Julia looked toward the shoreline to see Cassandra and Alice were busy picking up mussel shells and arranging them on the wet sand, and then lifted her skirts and quickly followed after him.

By the time she caught up, he was standing at the fence, stroking the neck of a large bay horse that had stuck its head over the railing.

"Oh, he's hurt," she said, seeing the dried blood on the animal's flank.

"Spence's horse," Ainsley said as if speaking to himself. "Damn."

Julia had been forgotten, she knew, as she watched Ainsley take off again, this time his long strides leading him toward Becket Hall.

Suddenly she wanted the girls with her and all three of them back inside the safety of Becket Hall's strong walls. She wanted to see Chance, be assured that he was all right.

"Girls!" she called out as she ran, knowing she was still too far away for them to hear her as the increasingly stiff breeze carried her words away. "Girls! Time to go back!"

Cassandra finally looked up, waved to her. "Julia! Come see what we've found!"

Julia stopped running, willing her heart rate to slow, and pinned a smile on her face as she neared the girls. Obviously they had been digging in the sand. "Sunken treasure, no doubt?"

Cassandra shook her head, shaking her hands in front of her, trying to rid herself of clumps of wet sand. "Everybody knows there's no sunken treasure here. It's only an old boot." Cassandra's eyes sparkled with mischief. "We think there's still a foot in it, don't we, Alice?"

"Julia?" Alice asked, hugging herself as she gave a delightful shiver. "Will you look for us?"

"I most certainly will do no such thing," Julia told them, pulling a handkerchief from the pocket of her pelisse and using it to wipe at Alice's hands. "Callie is only teasing you, aren't you, Callie?"

The girl shrugged. "Who knows? Who knows what goes on here in Romney Marsh?" she said, wiggling her sandy fingers at Alice, who gave a small squeak, then buried her head against Julia's side.

"All of you Beckets are a handful, aren't you?" Julia said, then felt her heart do a small flip in her chest as she looked toward the terrace to see Chance standing there, watching her.

Suddenly she couldn't breathe.

He stood with his legs apart, wearing long, heeled boots that covered his knees, his shirtsleeves billowing in the breeze and his hair blowing long and wild about his head. He'd worn London clothes comfortably, but dressed as he was now, the man looked…he looked *free*. More at his ease than she'd seen him before. Or was that proud stance that of any man who'd recently bedded himself a virgin?

And where had *that* salacious thought come from?

No, he had the look of a man who felt very much in charge of his own world. A man who had very possibly played at riding about the Marsh at midnight on some reckless adventure.

In any event and for whatever reason, the sophisticated, well-dressed gentleman she'd met in London was well and truly gone now, as if he'd never existed. Even at this distance she believed she could feel Chance's strength, some new passion that had stirred his blood, raised his spirit.

Or perhaps this was an old passion come back to him.…

Julia involuntarily lifted a hand to her left breast to press her fingers against the grosgrain ribbon hidden beneath her gown, then quickly turned the gesture into a nervous wave.

He raised a hand and waved to them, as well, and Alice waved back before breaking into a run, Cassandra following.

Julia began walking toward the house, ashamed to realize that she had every intention of using two young, innocent girls as the shields she would hide behind as she came face-to-face with—dear Lord—with her *lover.*

CHAPTER TWELVE

"LOOK AT YOU LITTLE beggars. No bonnets, your cloaks full of grit. What were you two doing down there—rolling on the beach?" Chance teased as the girls skipped toward him across the terrace.

Alice giggled, and Chance took a moment to rub the top of his daughter's head. Children were so forgiving, thank God.

"We found an old boot, Papa, and Callie thinks there's still a *foot* in it," Alice said, her eyes wide as she looked up at him. "But Julia wouldn't peek for us."

"Really?" Chance looked over the girls' heads to wink at Julia as she walked toward him and he felt something punch him hard in the stomach. How her hair shone with the sun dancing in it. And the lady didn't seem to worry about freckles on her fair skin or she actually liked the feel of a sea breeze ruffling her hair. Did she know how soft, how approachable she looked today? No, she couldn't, or else that horrible bun would be back in full force.

"Julia was off talking with Papa," Cassandra explained. "And then when she came back she said it was time to come inside. We've been outside barely at all, and I don't think that's fair. She should have looked in the boot. But I *am* hungry, so I suppose I'll forgive her."

Speaking with Ainsley? How interesting. "I would have supposed she would have hopped straight to investigating," he said, still looking at Julia, who returned his look without blinking. "She's usually a very curious lady is our Miss Carruthers."

And probably is now, he believed—just not about old boots. "Go on now, you two. Cassandra, take Alice and run upstairs to Edyth. And take off those pattens before you go into the house, hear me," he called after them, "or someone will be handing you both brooms and a strong sermon. We don't make unnecessary work for others here at Becket Hall, remember?"

Julia had heard everything through the sound of her own blood pounding in her ears, and from somewhere in her brain came the words: *We run a tight ship here.*

But certainly not a very formal one. Ainsley Becket was in charge, along with Jacko. That much was clear to her. The Becket "children" could be the ship's officers. And everyone else seemed to simply be part of the *crew*, all putting their hands to whatever needed doing.

There was such affection here and yet so much respect. A *bond* between everyone that she greatly admired yet didn't completely understand, as if they were all parts of the same whole. Or shared in the same secret.

She watched the girls go, the two of them giggling and holding hands. She was going to smile to Chance Becket now and say good morning and pretend nothing had happened between them last night and that she wasn't aware that what happened between them last night wasn't *all* that had happened last night.

Then she opened her mouth and said precisely what she hadn't planned to say. "You all went out last night to see if the haul was gone, didn't you? Because the people who shot those boys also discovered where the goods were being stored, and you wanted to save what you could before they could round up a land party to take it all away."

Chance looked at her, one eyebrow raised. He may as well have left the woman a detailed note telling her where he'd be off to and why after leaving her bed. "Was all of that a question or a statement?"

"Spencer's horse is injured. I can't be sure, but I think he was grazed by a bullet."

"Spence's horse? And how do you know it's Spence's horse?"

"I was walking with your—with Mr. Becket, and he mentioned it. He…he was upset."

"Is that so? So you and Ainsley were out walking. Was it an interesting walk?"

"He took me to the village. I had no idea it was there. You're all your own community."

How much did she know? How much had she guessed? He carefully measured his next words. "There have been additions and deletions over the years, yes, but we remain fairly self-sufficient. At the moment we're missing a carpenter."

"Pike," Julia said in all innocence, remembering the name Ainsley had told her, then quickly bit her lips together for a moment, as Chance was now looking at her curiously. What on earth had she said wrong this time? "Mr. Becket told me Pike was the ship's carpenter who carved the mermaid that was once the figurehead on one of his ships. And I'm not telling you anything you don't already know, am I? Does your cheek hurt?"

He raised a hand to his cheek. Cold compresses had gotten rid of the worst of the swelling, but it was still tender to the touch. This woman missed nothing. "A lucky punch. The man didn't get in another," he said, then smiled. "And, since I know you'll ask sooner or later, Spence is fine. Odette's with him."

"Then he was injured, as it was Odette who was put in charge of tending Dickie's wound."

"Right on both counts, congratulations. Spence's wound is little more than a scratch. The boy believes he's invulnerable. The scratch will only do him good."

Julia hadn't really spoken with Spencer Becket yet, but he had made an impression on her. He wasn't as tall as Chance or Courtland, but he was...intense. Yes, that was the word. His eyes were dark, nearly black, below low, sweeping, dramatic brows. His black wavy hair had been cut to just below his nape and was wild, unruly, constantly falling onto his face, only to have him give his head a quick shake in order to be rid of it. Possibly an arrogant shake? Handsome, as were all the Beckets each in their own way, but with the look of dangerous passions only held in check by a strong will.

Julia looked at Chance, made a comment based on what Eleanor had told her. "Your brother is Spanish."

Chance shrugged. "Probably, along with who knows what else mixed in. We're mongrels, Julia, all of us, and rather proud of that fact. The problem with Spence is that, however he came by his blood, that blood often runs hot and his brain doesn't always tag along on the journey. I was probably twelve or thirteen to his five when Ainsley brought him home, so I never paid him much attention, to be truthful. But he was wild when he came and he's stayed wild."

Julia could ask more questions, she supposed, but as she was so nervous she was barely listening to the answers, that didn't seem fair. Had the raid been successful? Had they recovered their goods? Where was the haul now?

But those were silly questions and really should be none of her concern. She knew only that there had been a fight and both Chance and Spencer had been injured. The thought of Chance hurt, possibly dying? Why did that upset her so? Why did half of her want to pummel him for being so reckless, while the other half of her wanted only to hold him?

"I should go in now," she said, backing up a step, but Chance put a hand on her arm.

"Not yet. I want to speak with you about what happened between us last night, Julia," he said, his voice low, his deeply green eyes gone dark. "Please."

"Why? What is there to say? You bedded a woman, then went riding out on the Marsh to do God knows what. And I...I must be *insane.*"

He'd hurt her. God, he'd hurt her. Damn him for the bastard he was. "I'm sorry, Julia."

His apology brought her up short, and made her instantly furious with him. She'd been nervous? Why on earth had she been nervous? "*Sorry? You're sorry?* Is that so, Mr. Chance Becket? Well, I'm *not* sorry. Now what do you have to say to *that,* Mr. Chance Becket?"

Chance was suddenly so off balance he was surprised he still stood upright. "You cried."

"I also laughed. I also *allowed* what happened. Please don't tell me you thought you'd…you'd—"

"Taken unfair advantage of you," Chance said quickly, not really wanting to hear the word *ravished*— or worse—coming from Julia's mouth.

She lifted her chin. "Because you did no such thing. I am perfectly well aware of what I did."

But not why she did it. Chance mentally flinched as his conscience pushed out from under the rock he'd placed over it and shouted accusingly in his brain. Not that it had ended that way for him. But it had begun that way, and he should burn in Hades for that.

"So," he said, measuring his words, "you and I both knew what we were doing last night and neither of us is sorry, although I could argue that I knew much more than you."

Julia turned her back on him. "There's no need to be crass."

"No, there's not. But there is another need, Julia. Marry me."

Julia's eyes went so wide she momentarily feared they'd pop out of her head and drop to the stone terrace, and wouldn't *that* be embarrassing! Then she swallowed painfully and turned to face him once more. "I'd really rather not do that, thank you for asking."

Chance stabbed his fingers through his hair. "Damn it, Julia, it's not as if we have a choice."

"How very…flattering," Julia said, looking up at him, her palms itching either to slap him or to run her fingers through his windswept hair. And slapping him was beginning to win out. "I still must decline the offer."

"Julia, think, please. I brought you here. I've gotten you involved in something very dangerous. I've allowed my family to believe that we're betrothed. All of this is damning enough, but now I've completely compromised you and I'm not even sure I understand why I did what I did."

"My, what flattery. But I believe I understand the why of what you did—what we did," Julia said, twisting her fingers together in front of her. "Keep the silly spinster busy spinning daydreams and she won't be any trouble, won't keep poking her nose into matters that don't concern her. I must say, reflecting back on the thing, the idea had some merit."

Chance couldn't hold back a short closed-mouth cough, as Julia had hit so close to the mark, then decided to go on the offensive. "That's insulting to both of us, Julia. You're an attractive woman, a highly attractive woman. I may be ashamed of myself, of my behavior, but I am not sorry I came to your chamber last night. I think we could have a good life together. You seem fond of Alice, for one thing, and you even appear to enjoy my family. I've thought about this, Julia. I've been thinking about you all morning."

"Yes, after leaving me last night, already knowing you could be riding off willy-nilly to get yourself captured or killed."

"So much for your opinion of my abilities, thank you. And as I recall the thing, you asked me not to speak. You asked me to leave."

"Do you always listen to silly women?"

"Julia, we're going round and round again."

"And backward. Please don't forget backward. I'd better enjoy arguing with you, Chance, if we could also sometimes move forward."

"We are moving forward, damn it. Marriage is the only answer."

Julia stood very still. She was a romantic fool, that was obvious to her now. And she was destined to end her days caring for someone else's children or possibly raising cats. "Why did you marry Alice's mother? Was it for love?"

It was time to be honest, Chance knew, more than time. "No, Julia. Ours was a marriage of mutual convenience. I'm ashamed now to say that, no, I did not love Beatrice, and she did not love me."

"Mutual convenience, was it? Much like the marriage you speak of for the two of us, I would suppose. And with the unspoken knowledge that affection for each other has nothing to do with that union. No, don't talk to me of marriage, Chance, for I am foolish enough to want more or nothing," Julia said, believing she'd lingered long enough, revealed more than enough. Besides, she may have won this time…or lost, very badly. She turned and headed for one of the many sets of French doors that led into the mansion, willing herself not to break into a run.

This time Chance was wise enough not to try to keep her at his side. Better he should walk down to the shoreline, then keep walking into the water until it was over his head. When had he last been this stupid, behaved so badly? What was it about Julia Carruthers that tied his tongue in knots and had his brains scurry off on holiday—leaving him bereft of allies in this battle of wits and wills…and desires. God yes, desires. He believed he could still feel the smooth texture of Julia's skin against his hands.

Did he really want to marry her?

He could think of worse fates.…

At the sound of one pair of hands slowly clapping in a sort of mocking applause, he turned to see Courtland ascend the last few steps of the west staircase and begin walking across the terrace toward him.

"Bravo! Bravo, Chance. Oh, yes, I heard. I stayed out of sight on the steps, but then I listened to every word, just like Jacko would do, our friend who has never lost his love for putting his ear against keyholes. I can see you have our Miss Carruthers tightly wrapped around your little finger, brother, just as you said you would. You know, I should head up to London, get me a bit of that fine town bronze you wear so elegantly."

"Shut up, Court," Chance said, walking over to lean his forearms on the stone balustrade and look out to sea. "I'm already painfully aware I've bollixed things. Curse the woman. I don't know if I should send her packing or take her back to bed. Someday perhaps someone will be able to explain women to us clumsy males."

Courtland joined his brother, also leaning his forearms on the balustrade, the tension between them for the first time in a long time not in evidence. "If someone does, they can begin those explanations with Morgan, then go on to Fanny and Cassandra."

"Not Eleanor?"

"Elly is a lady, thank God. She sings, she paints, she plays both the harp and the piano Ainsley provided for her. She doesn't sneak out to ride with the Ghost, like Morgan—you were right about that, by the way. And damn me if she isn't proud of the fact."

"Did you lock her in her rooms and threaten to limit her diet to stale bread and ditch water?"

"You don't threaten Morgan, Chance. She's too headstrong for that and would only do the opposite of what I've told her, even if she didn't want to, just to prove she is in charge of herself. Odette's asked for an increase of her budget for candles, she lights so many candles to chase Morgan's mischievous *loas* away."

Chance grinned. "You have your hands full here, don't you? So that's Morgan. What about Fanny and Cassandra?"

Courtland shook his head. "Must we? Oh, very well. Fanny insists she can do anything Rian can do, better, and sometimes she's right. She's nearly as bad as Morgan, as a matter of fact, and Rian encourages her. And Cassandra? That child can plague a man straight out of his head, dancing around after him like some curious, adoring puppy. Thank God Alice is here now to occupy her."

Chance smiled at his brother. "Maybe you should think about escaping to London. But you enjoy it, don't you? Riding herd on everyone else, that is, playing at mother hen. Yet perhaps not enough to keep you completely happy or else you wouldn't be gallivanting about the country in that ridiculous cape long after you'd avenged Pike's murder."

Courtland chuckled ruefully and then both men were silent, watching the French ship finally pass out of sight, heading toward Dover Castle but still safely out of the range of English guns.

"Now that we're talking without shouting at each other, I hesitate to say this. But Ainsley's definitely coming awake," Courtland said at last. "I was in Spence's bedchamber a little while ago, when Ainsley came bursting in to ring a peal over the boy's head. A beautiful thing to hear. No one could ever chew up one side of you and down the other like Ainsley, all without raising his voice. And for once Spence was smart enough to keep his own mouth shut."

Chance felt his spine stiffen. "Thirteen years, Court. It's been thirteen years. About damn time he woke up."

"True. You, too."

Chance pushed back from the railing. "And what does that mean, brother mine?"

Courtland remained where he was, still looking out to sea. "So much for the flag of truce between us. You know damn well what that means. How can he ever forgive himself when his oldest son won't forgive him? You were closer to him than anyone, Chance, and the first to abandon him."

The words hurt, cut deep, and Chance was stung into defending himself. "Do you know how many bodies we slipped into the sea when we reached deep water? Picking up those bodies, laying them in tarps, sometimes a piece at a time? He sent you on board with the younger ones. You didn't have to be there with the men when they found their women raped and—"

"I was there when it happened, Chance. I saw more than enough before escaping to the interior and saw what was left when we came back," Courtland said flatly, at last pushing himself away from the balustrade to face his brother. "You seem to forget that. You seem to forget everything except your own anger and pain."

"You're right, Court, and I apologize. That was stupid of me. But Ainsley never shed a tear for Isabella," Chance said, a tic beginning to work in his cheek as, at last, he'd said what he thought, what had haunted him for so long. "Yes, he was the captain, and yes, he had to take control, which wasn't easy. But not one tear, Court. Not one. No revenge, either. Just his mighty plan to have us all disappear, start over, hide himself here like a coward. Turn us all into cowards along with him."

"Ainsley had no choice but to bring us here, Chance, and everyone agreed to the plan except you. As for Isabella? Oh, hell, do us all a favor, Chance. Go talk to Jacko."

"Why would I do that?" Chance's heart was pounding now, and he didn't know why.

Courtland sighed. "Because he and I are the only ones that know—and no one is aware that I know—that I followed them that first night. Ainsley and Jacko."

"Followed them? Followed them where?"

Courtland put up his hands as if to say *no more*. "Go on. Talk to Jacko. It's not my story to tell."

"Where is he?"

"I would imagine he's where he is every day. Over in the village, drinking his way through the *Last Voyage*."

"I've never cared for that name," Chance said, looking toward the stables and the village beyond. The village, the encampment, the refuge…the hidey-hole. "Better to call it *The Retreat*."

"I know. We all know what your feelings are. But we were decimated, Chance, and we had to think of the women, the girls. Do you think he's dead?"

Chance didn't bother pretending he didn't understand his brother's question. "Edmund? If we believe the rumors, yes. Murdered by his own drunken men not a week later. I don't know if I want him dead or alive so I can kill him."

"I've always wondered, Chance—why didn't you listen to the men who wanted to take the Gray Ghost that same day, hunt him down? You, Billy and the rest. I know you were only seventeen, but they would have followed you. Christ, man. You'd been all but raised on the Black Ghost, Ainsley teaching you everything he knew, every trick, every ploy. He even stepped back and let you take down the *Marguerite* on your own. Jacko brought you one of the town whores to celebrate, remember? Isabella was furious with him."

"I'd rather forget all of that, especially the woman. But you already said it, Court. We had to protect the women. And half the men had lost their hearts and wanted nothing more than to die themselves. That's no way to go into battle with an enemy that outnumbers you in both ships and men. I knew we had to wait at least a few days until the ships were repaired and we could take after Edmund, but by then we were on our way to England. No, when I left the sea, I left that life behind me."

"And set out to educate yourself, make yourself a gentleman, a loyal subject of the Crown," Court said, nodding. "You know what, Chance? I don't think it worked. Not even after Billy took those so very damning letters from your luggage and brought them to Ainsley. The papers are tucked back into your luggage, safe and sound, and so very official-looking."

"Christ," Chance said, slamming his fist into the palm of his hand. "I should have known. Billy's first loyalty will always be to Ainsley." He looked at Court. "So? Is everyone now questioning *my* loyalty?"

"Jacko took some convincing, but no, we're none of us too concerned. Not now that you know you'd be turning in your own family. That must have been a shock to you."

Chance smiled ruefully at this obvious understatement. "I think you can safely say that. But you do know I'll have to make an appearance at every Revenue Office and such from here to Dover Castle, at the very least. I don't know how the boys are going to like that."

"Taken care of," Courtland told him. "By Ainsley, through Jacko. I'll have you know that you're using your position in the War Office to make discreet inquiries into any information the Preventative Waterguard might have about the Red Men Gang."

"So that the Black Ghost can find and destroy them." Chance smiled, shook his head. "You're right. Ainsley is waking up. Since nobody but those here at Becket Hall even know me, I should be safe enough. And I'll take Billy along, as well. While I act in my official capacity, he can visit the pubs with both ears open. Nobody ever notices Billy. Which also means we'll travel by boat, since Billy doesn't ride and he's never really mastered the coach."

"That sounds reasonable. Tell me something, Chance. If we hadn't been involved or if you hadn't found out—would you have complied with your orders?"

"I'm only to put the fear of God and king into the local officers, Court, not become a part of the troops, either on land or in one of the Revenue cutters. And believe me, none of it was my idea. I'd asked for leave only to bring Alice to Becket Hall."

"That must have been a difficult decision. Coming back, I mean."

"Not once I got here," Chance said, turning to look out over the Channel, then slowly turn back toward the mansion. "It's time I put my demons to rest, Court. Tell me about Ainsley, about what you saw. Jacko might feel honor-bound to tell Ainsley I asked. I don't want to be the cause of opening wounds that have finally begun to heal."

Court also looked up at Becket Hall. "Let's walk," he said, and the two men headed down the stone staircase, taking a path that would lead them around to the front of the building, then said abruptly, "Isabella wasn't buried with the rest."

Chance stopped on the bottom step, looked at his brother. "But…but I saw the tarp go into the water. Ainsley said a prayer over it. I don't understand."

"I know. Let's keep walking. I was in the house late that first night, gathering up what I could find of Cassandra's clothing, when I heard Ainsley and Jacko climbing the stairs. I don't know why I did it, but I hid from them and only could see Ainsley carry Isabella's body into their bedchamber, then Jacko standing in front of the closed door and looking about as fierce as I've ever seen him. I knew that it was too late to show myself. I honestly thought Jacko could have wrung my neck if he'd seen me."

"What was Ainsley doing behind that door?"

Court bent down and picked up a stone, then threw it into the distance. "Preparing her for burial. Dressing her in that gown she's wearing in the portrait in the main salon. When he carried her out, I could have sworn she was alive again. He'd washed her, dressed her hair. She was even wearing her dancing shoes. I had to clap my hands over my mouth to keep from calling out to her. If it hadn't been for the way her head was so…so loose on her neck…"

Chance put a hand to his own mouth, mumbled, "My God. Where did he take her?"

"I watched from the veranda as he and Jacko disappeared into the trees, then followed them. I had to, because now Jacko was carrying a shovel and a bundle of sailcloth."

"He buried her on the island," Chance said, "then pretended to bury her at sea with the others. Why?"

Courtland shrugged. "He needed to mourn her, I think now. Back then all I knew was that I was eavesdropping on something very private, something I shouldn't have witnessed. He sat beside her after he laid her in the middle of the sail, stroking her hair, laying his head on her chest, holding her hand. I've never heard such weeping as that, before or since. He kept saying that he was sorry, so sorry. He begged God to give her back to him. He cursed God. He howled, Chance, until I thought he'd never stop."

He took a breath, let it out slowly. "And then they buried her, and he went back to take charge again. Pull us all together, oversee repairs to the ships, get us out of there because we were all too vulnerable to another attack."

Chance bent his head, rubbed at the back of his neck, willed the tears not to fall. "I…I thought he'd turned coward. Worried only about getting away, hiding. First listening to Edmund and then leaving the sea, bottling himself up here. And I judged him, deserted him. What a miserable piece of work I am."

Court clapped him on the shoulder. "You're a proud man, Chance. If you went running, it wasn't just from Ainsley and our lives on the island. I don't want to get all maudlin on you, but I think you were running from *you,* as well. Running from the wharf rat. You wanted to be more than you believed you were. We all want more than we are. Can't fault a man for that."

"Why did I always think you were such a nuisance?" Chance asked, finally smiling at his brother. "You may be the bravest and smartest of us all. Although I'm not quite sure I like that beard."

"Cassandra hates it," Courtland said, rubbing at his chin. "I may keep it forever."

The terrible tension broken, the brothers laughed as they stood on the drive in front of Becket Hall, very much in charity with each other, which was a novelty in itself, and turned as one when they heard riders approaching.

"My, we are having a busy morning, aren't we?" Courtland said, crossing his arms in front of him. "That would be Lieutenant Diamond and a half dozen of his dragoons coming to visit. We think he's sweet on Morgan, God help him."

"And Morgan?"

"Who knows about Morgan and anything. To be truthful, I think she's practicing on him. Her feminine wiles, that is."

"Poor fellow," Chance said, watching as the lieutenant dismounted. "Are you sure Morgan is all he's interested in at Becket Hall?"

"We don't know. But now that you're here, with those impressive letters with all their official seals, I should imagine any doubts he may harbor about us will be settled. You're really coming in handy, brother, so very glad you could come."

Chance grinned. "Anything I can do to help the family. We sail together or sink alone. Shall I be pompous and important, do you think? Have the man wetting his pants?"

"I might enjoy watching that, yes, as long as he does it outside." Court swept an arm in front of his brother as if inviting him to pass ahead of him. "Shall we?"

CHAPTER THIRTEEN

JULIA HAD MADE THE mistake of entering Becket Hall via one of the pairs of French doors leading directly into the main salon. Now instead of hiding in her bedchamber, she sat beside Eleanor Becket and did her best to smile and nod at the right places while Eleanor told her about Becket Hall.

The house had been purchased, not built, which surprised Julia, Ainsley Becket having seen the immense mansion from his ship as they'd sailed toward their planned destination of Dover.

"Papa and Jacko immediately rowed in to shore, and very shortly after that we were all here. It seemed that the family who owned the house had only recently inherited it and much preferred town life but despaired of ever selling the estate. I don't know why. I love it here. So peaceful, so quiet. Not at first, of course, as everyone had to be housed here for some time."

What a preposterous humbug! Julia looked at Eleanor, wondering if the woman was truly naive or even more clever than anyone supposed. Eleanor was so very delicate, so reserved…so much not like the rest of the Beckets.

"Have you ever been to London?" Julia asked her.

Eleanor's smile was a marvel, making her even more beautiful. "No, I don't care to travel. Papa and I are very content."

"But not the others?"

"Courtland. And Cassandra is still very young. I think Morgan would like to see London, although she has absolutely no interest in becoming a part of society. Spencer is mad to have Papa buy him a commission in the Army, and I worry that Rian feels the same. It's a subject we don't dwell on in order not to upset Papa."

No, Julia thought, no one ever seems to want to upset Papa. "Leaving Chance and Fanny, I believe?"

"Yes, of course. Chance made his feelings plain years ago, but I really can't say what Fanny thinks. She is only sixteen, which is old enough to put up her hair, which she flatly refuses to do, as I believe I've already told you." Eleanor smiled. "What I didn't tell you is that I'm surprised she hasn't simply cut it all off. Court says she's an Irish demon, but he only says that in jest. I think."

Eleanor smiled toward the doorway. "There you are, Morgan. Julia and I were just chatting. Tell us, do you want to go to London or simply molder away here, as Spencer says?"

Morgan crossed over to a nearby couch, her strides carelessly long, her legs seeming to swing straight from the hips. Did the girl know the shape of her legs was outlined by the constraints of her skirt with each step she took? And it wasn't that her sprigged muslin gown was cut daringly low, it was that Morgan was simply one of those women who had been generously...endowed.

"London?" Morgan said, crossing her legs, and her slim ankles were exposed. "Is Chance leaving already? Are you planning to go back with him, Elly? I still say if Papa wants you to have a season on the marriage market, you should take the plunge."

"Morgan, please," Eleanor said, lowering her head once more.

Such a long, delicate neck, Julia thought. Eleanor Becket would cause quite a stir in London...if not for that limp. Julia didn't know very much about London society, but she was fairly certain its members could be cruel. *Papa* might harbor the same concerns.

"I'm sorry, Elly," Morgan said, reaching over to lightly touch her sister's neatly clasped hands. "I'm always saying something stupid, aren't I? I didn't mean to—oh ho, look who's here. Lieutenant Diamond. Do you want to watch while I make him stammer?"

Eleanor kept her voice down as Chance, Courtland and a tall, fair man dressed in the uniform of the dragoons entered the large room, still speaking to each other. "Morgan, you tease that poor man half out of his mind. Now uncross your legs and sit up straight, please. Lieutenant Diamond's truly smitten."

"And that's somehow my fault?" Morgan asked, grinning at Julia. "Besides, a little wool over the man's eyes is good for all of us. Don't you think so, Julia?"

"I suppose, Morgan, although I don't quite understand what you mean," Julia said, feigning innocence even as she feared her ploy wasn't working. "As long as you remember that a discarded suitor can turn quite mean."

Morgan frowned, looked at Lieutenant Diamond's back, looked at Julia again. "I hadn't thought of that."

"You rarely think through anything you say, Morgan," Eleanor said, sighing. "But you began this flirtation and now you're simply going to have to continue being flattered by Lieutenant Diamond's attention until either he or you leaves the area. That's only fair to the gentleman."

Julia watched as the lieutenant broke himself away from Courtland even as Chance left the room—heading for the stairs, she supposed—and walked over to bow to the ladies. She'd been right. Eleanor Becket knew quite a lot and only pretended she knew nothing. And obviously although Chance and Morgan seemed to trust Julia, Eleanor was still reserving judgment to some point. A complex young woman, this fragile flower.

Morgan held up her hand and the lieutenant bent over it, holding on to the hilt of the sword strapped to his waist. "Lieutenant, how good to see you again. Gracious, it's been an *age*."

"Only a week, Miss Morgan. Although it seems a month. I've been occupied with my duties, I fear," the lieutenant answered, then turned to Eleanor. "Miss Becket," he said and bowed to her as Eleanor regally dipped her head.

"Lieutenant. Please allow me to present to you Miss Julia Carruthers, my brother Chance's fiancée, although he's yet to make a formal announcement."

The lieutenant all but snapped to attention, his expression respectful, then bowed to Julia. "Miss Carruthers, my honor. And my felicitations."

Julia knew there was no way to correct Eleanor without making a total spectacle of herself. "Thank you, Lieutenant. But I do believe you're wanted across the room."

With one last look at Morgan, who smiled up at him from beneath her long black lashes, he was off and within moments was reading some papers Chance had handed him.

His orders. They had to be Chance's orders. And the lieutenant seemed suitably impressed, reading them quickly, then handing them back to Chance, bowing to him.

What a charade. And what brilliance. The lieutenant would be so happy to tell Chance anything he wanted to know…and Chance would share all of that information with the rest of the Beckets. With the Black Ghost.

Julia had to stifle a giggle, which meant she was a terrible person, indeed, and quite thoroughly corrupted. Chance certainly had played his cards successfully, as one trip to her bed and she had become a willing participant in the entire smuggling scheme. Shame on her.

She coughed into her fist to hide yet another giggle when Chance smiled at her, his eyes all but dancing, as if they shared a great secret.

"Oh, look at Chance, Elly," Morgan said, having turned sideways on the couch to watch the men. "He's positively delirious with love, isn't he?"

"Morgan, you're not supposed to notice such things," Eleanor told her quietly.

"Oh, pooh," Morgan said, turning around to look at

Julia. "Anyone with two eyes can see he's top over heels in love with her. Isn't he, Julia?"

Julia felt heat rising into her cheeks and wildly searched her brain for some other subject to talk about, one not so embarrassingly personal. "I…um…"

"Ladies?" Chance said, having walked across the room without Julia noticing. "We beg your pardon for deserting you, but we have much to discuss with Lieutenant Diamond and don't wish to bore you ladies with such matters. Darling," he ended, bending to kiss Julia's cheek. "I'll come to you as soon as I'm free, and we can further discuss the nuptials. I'll be counting the moments."

Julia wasn't in danger of giggling anymore, and her cheeks were certainly not flushed but had probably gone chalk-white. How dare he kiss her, say such things in front of his sisters, as if he was making an appointment to come to her bed? Why, weren't things already complicated enough without—

"Nuptials, is it? This soon?" Morgan said, sitting back and folding her arms beneath her breasts. "And him still in half mourning. Well, that's settled then, isn't it? You and Chance will be staying at Becket Hall for six more months before heading back to London. After all, Chance wouldn't want to cause a scandal."

"I don't think Chance cares a great deal about what society might think," Eleanor said consideringly, placing a hand on Julia's arm. "Julia? Is this what you want?"

Julia stood up, grateful her legs seemed able to hold her erect. "I…I suppose—"

"Wonderful!" Morgan said, cutting her off as she jumped up and wrapped her arms around her. She kissed Julia's cheek, then whispered in her ear, "Chance is brilliant, isn't he? *Now* Jacko will have to be satisfied."

Julia stood stiffly when Morgan stepped back, then somehow dredged up a smile. "If you'll both excuse me? I...I didn't sleep well last night and really believe I'd like to lie down for a while."

Morgan snorted—yes, *snorted*—and Julia suddenly wondered how many people knew that she and Chance...that she and Chance had...oh, blast!

"Excuse me," she said again and quickly left the room. She needed time alone to think up at least a half dozen horribly painful ways to torture Chance Becket.

Her mind filled with the glories of hot pitch and feathers, Julia was halfway into her bedchamber before she realized she was not alone.

"I beg your pardon. But who are you and why are you in my chamber?" she asked, already fairly certain of the answer to the first part of the question.

The tall ebony-skinned woman put down Julia's hairbrush and smiled in a broad white-toothed grin. "I'm Odette, of course, and I go where I wish to go. Today I wish to see you, so I am here." She shrugged. "Simple, yes?"

"Actually, I suppose so," Julia said, taking a seat beside the fireplace and motioning for the woman to sit down in the matching green chair. If she just thought of the accepted rules of every possible polite convention, then turned them on their heads, she would have gone a long way toward understanding Becket Hall and its inhabitants. "Callie mentioned you. She's very much in awe. You're some sort of priestess, I believe? From Haiti?"

Odette sat down, smoothing the skirts of her black gown over her knees, and her pride was evident in her ramrod-straight posture. "I come from Dahomey, my family stolen from our home to be carried across the sea and sold like cattle in the marketplace. Saint-Domingue, Haiti, the name makes no never mind. For me, I have learned my home is where I am."

Julia was amazed. And saddened. To read about such happenings was one thing, to see this woman, this proud woman, was quite another. "I'm so sorry."

Odette cackled, her dark eyes twinkling. "For what, girl? You had nothing to do with my life. I am happy here. Are you happy here?"

The abruptness of the question startled Julia. "Why, yes. Yes, I am. The Beckets are lovely people and I—"

"You belong to Chance now, and he to you." She stood up, reached into the pocket of her gown and extracted what Julia now knew to be a *gad,* the tooth thankfully small but still more than a little ugly. Odette lowered the thin circle of leather over Julia's head, the tooth falling at the end of the strip to hang down between her breasts.

Julia felt a shiver run up her spine, but she was certain that was her own superstition, not any power in the *gad.* "Why, thank you. It's…it's lovely, really. I'm truly honored. Has Chance renewed the magic in his?"

"It is done. The boy would not disobey me. We settled that a long time ago, when he first came to the island

and he put up a fuss about going into the bath I'd got ready for him." Odette grinned again and actually winked at her. "There's nothing I don't know about that boy."

Julia could feel color rushing into her cheeks even as she grinned. "You dumped him into the tub? How old was he?"

"Nine, or so we all decided. Too old for a young black woman to be sitting on him, stripping off his filthy britches and giving his bare backside a good whacking. Not that I could do that now, with him thinking himself a man grown. All you need with Chance is to let that boy know you won't swallow any foolishness from him, that's all."

Was that what this visit was all about? Odette was giving her instructions on how to handle Chance Becket? Did the woman think she needed lessons? Of course she did. Julia thought so, too. But she did take issue with the notion Chance was just a boy being foolish. "Is that what you call his stubborn pursuit of what he thinks is best no matter what anyone else might think? *Foolishness?*"

"Anything a man does that a woman does not like is foolishness in one way or another," Odette said, patting Julia's shoulder. "You stand up to him and only bend when you want to bend. Marry strength with strength, and together you will be invincible. All the shadows of his past will disappear and you will both walk in the sun."

Julia turned in her chair, put a hand on the woman's arm. "Wait, please. I'd really like to know more about Chance, about his childhood. About the island."

Odette smiled down at her. "Then ask him. The day he tells you, his heart is yours for the keeping. Do you want his heart?" The woman shook her head yet again. "No, say nothing. It is not yet time, I don't think."

"But you came here," Julia said as she lifted the *gad*. "You gave me this. Have…have you cast a *spell* on me? I mean, not that I believe such things, turning people into animals and such, but…have you?"

"I use my magic for good," Odette said, gathering herself up to her full height, which was impressive. "Callie is a child and likes stories, so I amuse her. Black magic is for those whose souls live in the dark, those who embrace the bad *loa*."

Julia nodded as if she understood, which she didn't. "Forgive me for questioning you, Odette."

Odette grinned again, not a shadow in her eyes. "Questions make no never mind. Only be sure you wish to know the answers. I must be off."

And, with no explanation as to why she must leave, Odette walked out, leaving Julia to sit alone in her chamber, to await Chance's arrival to, so he'd said, *discuss* the nuptials.

Well, the devil she would! If he wanted to speak with her, he could very well come find her, not expect her to be sitting there waiting for him. Besides, it was probably best to let him find her somewhere there was no bed in the room with her.

She went to the wardrobe to gather up her pelisse, then remembered she'd left it in the main salon. "Blast!" She pulled open drawers until she found the knitted shawl Mrs. Kester had made for her—to thank her for staying with her, holding her hand until the midwife had come and all through the birth of her son Henry—then headed for the back stairs.

This area of Becket Hall was new to her. She was fairly sure it would take three solid days to see it all, admire all the fine furnishings, but she did stop a few times to touch an exceedingly beautiful vase, to bend down to slide her hands over one of the silk carpets.

Eventually she made her way to a set of French doors in the music room and from there she was soon outside on the terrace and then making her way down to the shoreline.

The sun shone brightly, so that Julia wished she'd thought to bring her bonnet with her, and the breeze had stiffened, coming in from the Channel to ruffle her skirts and tease her hair around her head.

The wind coming in from the Channel on a fine day had always been considered invasion weather, and she wondered if Lieutenant Diamond and his men still believed a French invasion possible. What would it be like to look through one of the windows of Becket Hall and see a thousand small boats heading in toward the shore, the sunlight twinkling on ten thousand rifles, ten thousand bayonets?

Julia wrapped her arms around her as gulls circled overhead, and turned in the opposite direction of the stables and small village, minding her steps as the sand and shingle eventually turned mostly to sand. She then turned inland, as she'd heard the stories about the shifting sands of Romney Marsh and the dangers they presented the unwary.

Luckily there was a narrow path visible through the marsh grasses and the few hardy bushes that seemed to grow sideways, pointing her way inland. As she reached a small rise, it was as if all of the Marsh was displayed for her in its stark, mysterious beauty. Mostly flat land but with a myriad of towering church spires in the distance, visible to the horizon.

She smiled. Her father had told her he would like to think the abundance of churches reflected the deep faith of the inhabitants but knew, alas, that the church spires, rising up above the flat land, were often little more than navigational tools for the freetraders.

She looked back at Becket Hall rising majestically above a mostly flat land. No need of a church spire here, but only the lighted windows facing the sea, like so many beacons. So innocent, unless someone knew what she knew. Or what she thought she knew.

Julia saw the rider before she heard the hoofbeats and pressed the side of her hand against her brow to keep the sun out of her eyes as the huge red horse leisurely cantered toward her.

"Chance," she said to herself. "I'd be no easier to find if they tied a bell around my neck."

CHAPTER FOURTEEN

CHANCE REINED IN JACMEL a good ten feet away from
Julia and dismounted, tied the reins to the wrist-thick
branch of a small, scrubby tree. "Thank God you turned
inland, woman," he said, taking hold of her upper arms.
"Court and I were riding back after escorting the lieutenant and his men halfway to Dymchurch when I saw
you. Nobody walks along the beach in this direction unless they know the way."

Julia was shaking now, realizing she may have had
a lucky escape. "So there are quicksands?"

Chance let go of her arms and stabbed his fingers
through his hair. This woman was going to drive him
straight out of his mind. "Why did I even bother thinking I might have to rescue you? How do I keep forgetting that you grew up learning about Romney Marsh?"

Julia considered the notion he'd been concerned for
her, possibly even frightened. Either that or having her
disappear would cause more trouble than anyone
wanted, especially now that Lieutenant Diamond had
seen her. She much preferred her first thought but
couldn't dismiss the second.

So she pushed—just a little.

"For a dangerous area as this is, it's surprising that

there would be such a well-worn path, isn't it? But as you say, for those who know the sands, it isn't treacherous at all. Only for those who don't. I'm sure someone has warned Lieutenant Diamond away, told him of the danger to his men if they were to patrol here."

Lord save him from intelligent, prying women! Chance grabbed her by the elbow and drew her along with him toward the horse. "We'll walk back," he said tightly. "Just let me untie Jacmel. Did you enjoy your walk?"

"Most of it, yes. Jacmel," Julia said, also suddenly eager to change the subject. She realized that she was always eager to change the subject, mostly because she had said something she should not have said. "What does the name mean?"

"Jacmel is the name of a town I knew in the islands," Chance said dismissively, for although he would much rather not listen to more of Julia's stabbing remarks about the smugglers, he was likewise reluctant to discuss the islands. "Here," he said, digging into his pocket, one hand holding Jacmel's reins. "The moment didn't seem right earlier, on the terrace. But you should have this."

Julia automatically put out her hand, then goggled at the ring he'd laid in her palm. It was heavily engraved gold, with a huge green stone surrounded by tiny pearls. The sun winked off the stone, dazzling her, and she stumbled into speech. "I…I can't take this. I don't want to take this. Where did you get this?"

He'd known she'd ask that last question. Most women wouldn't have, of course, but Julia Carruthers had her own definition of how she should behave. "It isn't polite to ask such questions, Julia," he said, because, oddly, he wanted to hear her reaction to his small reprimand.

"Probably not," Julia said in what he was learning was her matter-of-fact bluntness, still staring at the ring. "Here, take it back."

Very nearly the straightforward answer he'd expected, almost to the word, as he had been thinking she'd say *absolutely not*. Still, her meaning was clear. And he *was* beginning to understand her. Anything he wanted, she automatically rejected out of hand.

So being a little contrary himself, he asked, "Would you like another stone? I thought the emerald would complement your eyes. But if you want sapphires? Or diamonds?"

"I simply want you to take this back," Julia said, all but shoving the thing in his face. "Or do you think I haven't figured out what you and Ainsley and Jacko and the others *did* in the islands? Why you're all so remarkably wealthy?"

"We were legitimate traders," Chance said, unaware that a tic had begun in his left cheek. "Or are you looking at that ring and seeing me with a cutlass between my teeth as I board and plunder ships? Is that what you've conjured up now in that maddening mind of yours, Julia? That we're nothing more than a crew of bloodthirsty pirates? And here I thought we were smugglers. Make up your mind, Julia."

She didn't know what to say and she definitely didn't know how to say it. Did she really believe she was residing with a retired crew of pirates?

No, of course not; that was unthinkable, unimaginable. But privateers? That possibility made perfect sense to her, as far as things went. And wasn't it odd that Chance had immediately said *pirates*, not *privateers?* Privateers were allowed, even sanctioned. But privateers commissioned by what country? England? America? Spain? Or even Napoleon's France? The possibilities remained frightening.

"I...I'm sorry," she said at last, sighing. "I shouldn't speculate, should I? When...when you wish to tell me, if you ever wish to tell me about the islands or...or anything, it will be your decision."

Chance smiled, feeling the moment over or at the very least postponed. "I don't wish to tell you."

"Oh," Julia said quietly, remembering Odette's words. He'd certainly put her in her place, hadn't he? "I...I see. But I still can't accept this ring. It's all about deception, and I could never look at it or your family without remembering why I was wearing it."

Chance's smile faded. "You are the most headstrong, obstinate, difficult, disobedient—aren't you going to interrupt me, tell me I'm wrong?"

"No," Julia said calmly, hoping he didn't know how exciting she found this moment and the man who was looking at her in such obvious frustration. "I was waiting for you to say something to which I might be moved to take exception. And you forgot *contrary.* My father always included *contrary.* Now take this blasted ring and get rid of it!"

Chance looked at her for a long time before he felt the corners of his mouth turn up and he gave in to laugh-

ter. "Well, if one of us is to be obedient, it might as well
be me," he said, taking the ring from her and tossing it
over his shoulder. "There. That's settled."

And she had just been thinking how dangerously
adorable he looked as he smiled at her? Julia's mouth
dropped open, and she pushed him aside on the path,
looking into the knee-high marsh grass. "You—you
idiot! Where did it go? Did you see it land? No, of
course you didn't. You were much too busy grinning
like an ape, weren't you. Of all the imbecilic, ridiculous
gestures—you really do carry off the palm, don't you?"

Chance watched in amusement, his arms crossed
over his chest, as Julia plunged into the high marsh
grass. "I thought you didn't care for the thing? Really,
Julia, it's difficult to please you when you keep changing your mind. Do you want to ask for my assistance?"

She turned to glare at him, and he was fairly certain
stronger men than he would have flinched. "I imagine
you do," he said, walking into the grass, still holding on
to Jacmel's reins.

"Be careful, you'll trample everything and we'll
never find the dratted thing."

"Don't concern yourself, Julia. I hereby vow to remain here until the *dratted thing* is found. Hours, days,
weeks. But only if you promise you'll wear the ring
once it is found. Otherwise? It *is* only a ring. Next time
I'll toss it into the Channel. Goodness, that sounds almost romantic, doesn't it? The spurned lover and all of
that."

Julia, bent over as she spread the grass and looked
down, mumbled something she hoped he wouldn't hear

and kept searching, feeling the damp penetrating her fabric half boots.

"Shame on you, if I heard what I thought I heard. And I really would rather not visit Hades, let alone live there. I, for one, consider this to be a grand adventure of sorts," Chance said, pushing deeper into the grass, as he had a fairly good idea of how far he'd thrown the ring. As he stepped forward, he thought he saw something glinting in the sunlight.

And he had. He bent down and picked up a brass button much like that worn by Lieutenant Diamond when he'd visited Becket Hall. Now what could he suppose the dragoons were doing there, on Becket land? Court had told him that the beaches there weren't used by the smugglers he and the crew protected.

Still, the track, as Julia had said, was obviously in use. "Damn it, Court, don't you know well enough never to soil your own nest," he muttered angrily.

"What did you say? Did you find it?"

Chance closed his hand around the button. "No, I'm afraid not, Julia. Wouldn't it be interesting if one of those gulls spied it from the sky, then swooped down and carried it off?"

Julia pulled a face at him and went back to poking through the grasses. *Foolishness.* That's what Odette had called it when she'd spoken about Chance's ridiculous behavior. "I'll have to tell Odette I was wrong to question her choice of words," she grumbled, using a thin dead branch she'd found to poke her way.

This was useless, impossible. On a par with finding a needle in a haystack. And the ring was gorgeous. How she'd itched to slip it on, see how it looked on her hand. She'd done the right thing to refuse it, she knew that. But she could at least have tried it on....

"Got it!"

Julia stood up straight, a hand going to the small of her back, as she'd been bending down for longer than she thought, and looked toward Chance, who was holding up the ring so that it glinted in the sun...and looking odiously pleased with himself. "And I presume you're now feeling quite proud of yourself?"

"You know, as a matter of fact, I am. But did you know you're speaking to me without really opening your clenched teeth? It seems to me that only females can do that."

Julia did her best not to throw the stick at him, then shot back, "Possibly, just as it's only males who can make perfect asses of themselves without growing a tail."

"Touché." Chance made his way toward her, Jacmel following, then escorted her back onto the path. "Your hem is damp, and I'm fairly certain your feet are wet. But if you don't mind, I'd like to linger here a little longer."

"Until I take either a chill or the ring," Julia said, then sighed. "Oh, very well. As long as we both agree that I'm only taking it to placate your family and that once this is over—whatever is going on here—that I will not hold you to the betrothal and once we leave here, the ring goes back to you. Oh, and that *you* explain everything to Alice."

Chance frowned. "Alice? Oh, Christ. My list of sins

with that child just grows and grows. Well that settles it. Now we'll simply have to marry."

Julia went so far as to give him a push in the chest. "You're impossible! We'll…we'll figure out some hum to tell her once this charade is over. That I must go care for an ailing aunt or something. Once I'm gone and she's happy here, you can come to visit and tell her we just didn't suit or something. Tell her…tell her I've run off with my aunt's butcher for all I care. For now just…just give me that dratted ring and let's be done with this nonsense."

"The butcher, is it? How lowering for me. Would you consider the local squire? I mean, I do have my reputation to think of here."

When Julia sort of *growled,* he hurried on, "Very well, very well. Agreed." He then handed over the ring, inwardly believing himself to be quite brilliant, for it would appear that he'd truly unsettled Julia. Which only seemed fair, as she certainly unsettled *him* with that talk about his daughter. "Although you may want to wash the thing before slipping it on your finger. It's rather sandy at the moment."

He wasn't even going to put it on her finger? Julia felt her heart plummet to her feet as she slipped the ring into the pocket of her gown, a reaction she didn't prefer to study. "And you agree to my terms. Just like that?"

"That is what you want, isn't it, Julia?"

"Well…yes, but—but what about that nonsense you were spouting about compromising me?"

Chance was enjoying himself again, probably too

much. Seeing Miss Julia Carruthers flustered was a sight to remember, hug close to his heart. "Yes, I remember, but you already said you wouldn't hold me to it. I believe you mentioned love and not wishing to marry without it. Or did I misunderstand you?"

"No," Julia said quietly. "You didn't misunderstand me."

"So it's settled. Because you see too much, you know too much and have unfortunately *said* too much and because you couldn't safely leave here unless you were under my protection and I'm, alas, not going anywhere for a while, we are now betrothed."

"But you won't…you won't come to my bedchamber again, will you?" Had she sounded at all sad about that? She sincerely hoped she hadn't sounded in the least disappointed. Certainly he hadn't sounded in the least romantic. Which was what she wanted. Really. Maybe…

"I'm not a monster, Julia. I won't be invading your bedchamber unless I'm invited."

"Well…well that's good, thank you," Julia said as they began walking once more. "Would you really have thrown the ring into the sea?"

Chance smiled down at her, and she thought she could see the devil peeking out of his eyes. "Only a woman would believe that, my dear. That stone is worth a small fortune. Even so, our agreement stands."

Julia refused to answer him other than to pull her arm free of his and walk faster.

He caught up easily. "Julia? Our agreement stands?"

"Yes, yes, it stands. And you…you're the most *foolish* man I've ever met."

"Foolish, is it?" Behind her, Chance grinned, his mood improving by leaps and bounds as he admired Julia's straight, slim form as she walked ahead of him. He still wasn't certain exactly where he wanted to go with Julia Carruthers, but that was no reason not to enjoy the journey. "That can't be the word you were searching for."

"Really? Only a man would believe that, *my dear.*" And then Julia mentally patted herself on the back all the way to Becket Hall, for, just this once at least, she had finally gotten in the last word with Chance Becket.

In fact, it wasn't until she was safely alone in her bedchamber that her smile faded and she realized she wasn't really happy at all....

CHAPTER FIFTEEN

AFTER JULIA HAD GONE upstairs to change, Chance ran
Courtland to ground in Ainsley's study, the pair of them
sitting silently, looking through the windows toward
the calm waters of the Channel.

"You're a cheery twosome," Chance said, going to
the drinks table to pour himself a glass of wine. "Don't
tell me Spence cocked up his toes. It was only a nick."

"Spence is fine, threatening Odette with mayhem if
she insists on keeping him in bed. We were just considering what to do next, if you must know," Courtland
said, picking up his own glass from the table beside his
chair. "Lieutenant Diamond didn't exactly arrive here
the bearer of good news."

"No, he didn't," Chance said, nodding to Ainsley,
who sat behind his desk, before taking up a seat of his
own. He rather sprawled on the maroon leather couch,
then pushed his hair out of his eyes. He had a black
grosgrain ribbon in his pocket and could tie his hair
back, out of his way, but was rather enjoying the casual
dress of Becket Hall, and the devil with starched collars and choking neck cloths and the rest. He had even
begun to look back fondly on the days when, as a boy,
he'd run barefoot through the warm sand. Memories

he'd for so long tried to squelch. Perhaps Julia was right, and he was *foolish*. And not quite paying attention, which was never good.

"I wonder," Ainsley said. "Is Red Men Gang the name they've given themselves or simply what the locals call them because of these sashes they wear?"

"Does it matter?"

Chance sighed, stretched his legs out in front of him to frown at his sandy boots. "Yes, Court, it does. Are we dealing with a ragtag crew of fairly disjointed individuals or are there brains somewhere and not merely brawn? The better we know the enemy, the easier it will be to plan how to deal with them."

Courtland bowed his head to his brother, grudgingly conceding the point. "Whatever the case, according to the lieutenant, this gang seems to be popping up everywhere up and down the coast all at the same time, more than twenty miles each direction, which is barely credible."

"I don't claim to be too familiar with the residents of this area," Chance said, "but I think we can be fairly sure that the leaders of the various small gangs would have several reasons not to share their power or mingle their hauls."

"Very true, Chance. There can be only one real leader to make the decisions. They'd be fighting among themselves before long, unable to agree who should be in charge," Ainsley said, leaning forward in his chair to rest his elbows on the desktop.

"Tearing each other apart like dogs the moment a single discrepancy showed up in the size of the loads,"

Courtland agreed, nodding his head. "Good men, for the most part, but definitely leery of strangers, and we all know that around here a stranger is anyone not from your own village."

"Then we're agreed that we're dealing with a large, well-controlled, strongly led and generously financed organization. Someone in London has to be in charge overall, possibly a cartel formed of both businessmen and the men who do the real work. Yes, even members of the *ton,* who wouldn't get their own hands dirty but who forward the money to bring goods across the Channel, then reap the lion's share of the rewards back in London when those goods sell for five or ten times their worth. Well-financed, well-organized, well-armed. Ruthless enough to set a few examples, like Pike, so that all the local gangs knuckle under and join them."

"You've really put considerable thought into this, haven't you?" Chance asked. "I agree they're ruthless. Killing Pike and the men with him—and now that boy I found on the Marsh—all to send the message that they're in charge. Have there been any other deaths?"

Ainsley nodded. "A few, Court tells me, but even a few is too many. There hasn't been so much bloodletting between gangs since the days of the Deal Boatmen. And the Hawkhurst Gang, of course. The legends might live on, but the worst gangs have been gone for more than fifty years, with the gangs working each in their own territory. There are rules—unwritten yes, but rules. The centuries have taught that everyone can coexist along the English coasts unless any one gang attempts to become too powerful."

"Which has become more and more the case over the past few months, according to Diamond," Courtland said as he got to his feet, began to pace.

Ainsley rhythmically rapped his fingers against the desktop, a sure sign that his mind was fully engaged. "Starting with Pike's senseless murder and this attempt to take over the local smugglers, frighten them to either disband and starve or work for the Red Men Gang for a pittance. It's all so familiar, boys, isn't it? Places change, the times change, but not much else. Certainly not people."

"And now we've stirred the pot by inflicting a few casualties on the other side," Chance pointed out, "thanks to the Black Ghost taking his revenge. We disposed of the bodies, but the good lieutenant is bound to hear about last night's adventure before long. Pity I don't think he's the sort who'd take a bribe to look the other way."

Courtland whirled on his brother. "What would you have had me do? It was only through Pike's widow that I could even find out how to contact the smugglers, let alone convince them I only wanted to guard them, not take a slice of their pie. And I needed a disguise, so not to bring holy hell down on us here at Becket Hall—"

"Ah, yes. The cape. Very impressive."

"Yes, damn it, Chance, it is, and I needed to make an impression. I wanted my revenge for Pike. We all did. We've lived here without incident for a long time, and a man like Pike should have died in his bed, not be brutally murdered. These are our people, they've accepted us without questions, and we have a duty to keep them safe. I just didn't think we'd end up riding out again and again."

Chance hazarded a look at Ainsley, who was now sitting back once more, his hands steepled just beneath his chin. Chance wasn't sure if the man was amused, contemplating mayhem or simply content to listen. "But you didn't tell Ainsley. If you were so sure what you were doing was right, Court, why didn't you tell him?"

"We've already been over that ground, Court and I," Ainsley said calmly. "The matter is settled between us."

Chance got to his feet. "So I'm no longer included in the family? Is that it? I was good enough to ride out with him last night."

Courtland turned on his brother. "You can't stand it that I'm in charge now, can you?"

"On the contrary, brother mine," Chance said, looking straight into Courtland's eyes. "I can't stand that you made such a bloody mess of things."

Courtland took a step in his brother's direction. "At least I didn't cut and run, turn my back like some judgmental bastard. *You* probably would have let Pike go unavenged. All we've seen is the back of you for most of the past thirteen years. What makes you think you can simply *stroll* back here and take over?"

Chance felt his hands tighten into fists and purposefully relaxed his fingers. "Nothing," he said, mastering his anger, refusing to contemplate whether Courtland was calling him disinterested, a coward or both. "Nothing makes me think I can come back here and take over. You're a man grown now, Court, and you stayed. I may not agree wholeheartedly with what you've done with this Black Ghost thing, but I'm here now and I want to help."

Courtland looked at the hand Chance extended to him. "Help, not lead."

"Don't push, Court," Chance said with a smile, but the warning was in his tone. "I give my word."

"Then we'll shake on it," the younger man said, grabbing Chance's hand. "I don't usually nearly come to blows twice in one day and with the same person. I apologize."

"As does Chance," Ainsley said from his seat behind the desk. "And now, before this old man begins blubbering at all this affecting sentiment being bandied about, Court, I believe Jacko has some ideas about how to better organize the men. He's at the *Last Voyage,* as usual. Go humor him, please."

Chance could see that Courtland wanted to decline but that his brother also understood that Ainsley's mild tone contained an order not to be disobeyed.

Once Courtland had bowed and left the study, Chance turned to Ainsley. "Even with that ridiculous beard, I keep forgetting he's no longer a boy. He's grown a temper as well as found his tongue, hasn't he?"

"I'd say his fuse is about the same length as yours. And we all make mistakes. That's how we learn. Sit down, Chance."

"You want to ask about my fiancée, I imagine. I just gave her a ring to seal our engagement." Chance returned to the couch, feeling not a single qualm about lying to Ainsley concerning his supposed plans to marry Julia.

"No, I don't wish to meddle in your private affairs, Chance. Except, of course, for how they might affect the rest of us."

"Everything is fine on that head. Besides, along with Alice still in Julia's charge, Elly has agreed to also keep her occupied with plans for the nuptials. Embroidering pillowcases and whatever other nonsense women believe necessary. And once things are settled here, I'll take Julia back to London. I see no more trouble, nothing for Jacko or anyone else to fret about anymore."

Ainsley lifted one well-defined black eyebrow. "Really? I have met the woman, you know, spoken with her. You and I haven't been together for any length in some time, Chance. Do you regularly delude yourself now?"

Chance threw back his head and laughed, then quickly sobered. "All right, I'll be honest with you. I'm thinking I may have to tie her to the bedpost to keep her nose out of our business, actually. It seems she grew up on stories of the Hawkhurst Gang and smuggling in general. Her vicar father either rode with the local smugglers before his death or, at the least, allowed them to use his church as a hidey-hole. No matter what, Julia is very much in sympathy with the smugglers."

Ainsley looked at him, just looked at him. And waited.

"You want me to say it all, don't you? Very well," Chance said, knowing no one had ever won a staring match with Geoffrey Baskin; a change of name and the passage of more than a dozen years hadn't seemed to change that.

"I want to know if you understand, that's all."

"Oh, I understand. She sees too much and she asks too many questions. Billy knows that because he was there with us on the Marsh when we stumbled over the boys, and what Billy knows, Jacko knows, along with God only knows how many others at the *Last Voyage*. And we both know how superstitious those two are about women, no matter that we aren't aboard ship anymore."

"Billy still walks as if he is, and Jacko has a sad past when it comes to women, so we'll excuse him."

"A sad past, is it? I heard it was a case of the pox with one and a bash over the head and a stolen purse with another."

"There's also the one in Santiago he found in bed with another woman—and if you ever repeat that, we're both as good as dead men," Ainsley said, getting to his feet, still straight and slim, handsome as well as impressive in his unremitting black. "I've spoken with Odette."

Chance smiled wryly, happy to be back on such close footing with the captain. "Yes, so have I. According to Odette, Julia will follow wherever I go and never betray me, so I suppose I should relax."

"She also said that Isabella and I would live to see our many children and grandchildren," Ainsley said as he rubbed at the back of his neck.

There was shared pain in the small silence that followed Ainsley's words.

"You're worried I might go all soft on her. Let my heart rule my head. Don't be. I'll watch her," Chance promised quietly at last, keeping his tone neutral.

"No, you'll take Billy and get on with your business, and we'll watch her. The moon's still right for another run tonight and Court will handle that, our crew guarding the men as they land and until the goods are safely concealed before they can be moved inland."

"They can't use the crude hidey-hole I saw last night. The Red Men Gang will certainly be watching for them there."

"Agreed, and we don't want another fight—yet. It's unfortunate, but we see no other avenue at this late date but to hide the goods in the village."

Chance put a hand to his head and began rubbing at his forehead, wishing he didn't have to ask the question. "Landing where?"

"On the sands, as they've done before. Nearly under my nose, which shows how senile I've grown. There have been mistakes made, Chance, and they will be remedied. But for tonight we've got no choice. Only two dozen small boats land at midnight, carrying silk, coffee, gin and brandy, rowing across the Channel, if that tells you how desperate these men are and why the goods won't be moved again until tomorrow night. They'll arrive exhausted."

"The sands aren't a good idea."

"Why? Because Court picked the area, not you? Everyone knows the sands are treacherous to anyone unfamiliar with them, so I don't expect any problems from the dragoons."

"Is that so?" Chance reached into his pocket and pulled out the brass button, tossed it to Ainsley. "I found this an hour ago in the tall reeds and grass not six feet from the path leading from the sands. From the shine still on it, it hadn't been there long."

"Sweet Christ and all the little fishes, as Jacko would say." Ainsley pocketed the button. "This is my fault,

Chance. I haven't been paying attention. I've let them all grow up wild and headstrong."

"You taught me. You, Jacko, Billy," Chance reminded him. "It's not too late for the others."

"No, it's not. But it could have been. Court is learning and doing well on his own, if not brilliantly, but there's still Spence and Rian to consider." Ainsley smiled ruefully as he stood up, came out from behind the desk. "You know, I think I rather fancy the idea of a cape and mask. That touch of drama and mystery."

"Oh, no. You're considering riding out as the Black Ghost? Don't you think you're past such adventures, old man?"

"I'll ignore that insult," Ainsley said. "I can plan here," he said, leaning over the table of maps and charts. "A leader leads, Chance, and teaches by example. You said that. We both know that."

Chance gave in to the excitement of the moment, his memories of following wherever Captain Geoffrey Baskin went, drinking in all he could learn, dancing in his brain. "Exactly so. And why should you have all the fun? Don't bother to deny it, you've got your blood up, Cap'n, and you're enjoying yourself. I remember that look. I sailed at your side for over eight years and I'm riding with you tonight."

"From boy to young man, and I've missed you. But, no, you're not riding tonight. I need you to find out more about these Red Men so that we can deal with them where they are before we bring the attentions of the Preventative Waterguard and the dragoons too close to Becket Hall."

Chance smiled. "Yes, I thought the same thing earlier. A wise bird never soils its own nest."

"Exactly as I explained to Court an hour ago. We never struck anywhere near the island. But enough of that. I've already told Billy to have the *Respite* ready for you in an hour, and that was thirty minutes ago. Go say your farewells to the inquisitive Miss Carruthers and be back here by the end of the week. Oh, and for God's sake, don't warn her to stay away from the windows tonight, because—"

"Because that would only ensure that she'd find a spyglass somewhere and keep watch until dawn. Yes, I know. I'll see you Friday. Try not to get shot or captured, if you don't mind. I do have my position at the War Office to consider—along with the length of my neck, which I like as it is, thank you. Are you sure you'll be all right? It's been a long time since you've been out on a run."

"Cornwall, when I was younger than Cassandra is now. I do recall my own incautious youth, as well as remembering why my brother and I found it necessary to leave there and travel to the islands. And I won't be out on a run, Chance, but merely waiting here on dry land. When I left the sea, I vowed never to go back, remember? That includes jaunts across the Channel. I told you, Court has held the Black Ghost's involvement to the shore and inland, thank God."

"Speaking of Court, does my little brother know you're taking command?"

Ainsley's eyes shone in real amusement. "Why do you think he was so ready to punch something?"

CHAPTER SIXTEEN

CHANCE LEFT THE STUDY, smiling, losing that smile when he remembered that he had to say goodbye to Julia before getting on with his business. Business that might be dangerous on some level but that had his blood running—although a smart man wouldn't let Miss Julia Carruthers so much as think she'd glimpsed a hint of that excitement.

He passed Morgan on the stairs, and she stopped him to ask, "What's going on? Court looks like a thundercloud, and when I asked if he's going out tonight he all but stripped off my hide and fed it to me."

"Good, that will save me the bother," Chance said, chucking her beneath her chin, believing he'd found the perfect fib to keep the girl out of trouble. "But I will give you a word of warning, dear sister. Ainsley knows."

Morgan's face went deathly pale. "Papa…he *knows?* He knows I sneaked out and rode with Court a time or two? Who told him? You tell me, Chance—which one of you tattled? It was you, wasn't it?"

"Who tells Ainsley anything? We all know he has ears everywhere," Chance said, winking. "I also know, were I you, I'd be on my best behavior for the next few weeks."

Morgan seemed to regain some of her bravado. "He won't do anything. Besides, Papa doesn't pay attention."

Chance patted her cheek. "Things change, Morgan. He's paying attention now."

She made a face at him before saying, "I don't really remember the island much at all, you know? Court said I don't need to either, that I should just remember being Morgan Becket of Romney Marsh. Was Papa really—"

"Oh, yes, he was, and the very best of them, too. You might want to think twice before getting on his bad side."

"Now you're just trying to frighten me."

"I know. Is it working?" Chance asked, grinning.

"I think so, yes. Does he really know what I've done? I mean, *really*? You told him? It had to be you."

"Don't worry, I'm sure he won't call you on the carpet. Just spend some time letting Elly teach you how to embroider or something."

"I'd rather die the death of a thousand cuts," Morgan said sincerely. "I read about that, you know. There's this method of torture, you see, and they—"

Chance raised his hand to silence her before he was gifted with all the gory details. "Thank God you aren't the oldest or you'd have trained the rest of the girls up to be hellions just like you. When I go back to London, I want to arrange for you to come up for the season next spring. We've got to marry you off, definitely. Let you become someone else's headache."

"Wretch. But I'll be eighteen by then, won't I? Maybe a year *will* help, and I'll be civilized by then.

Elly says she doesn't think London is ready for me yet," Morgan said not at all unhappily.

"And I agree with her. But I've some penance owing here, so I might as well start with getting you out of the way."

Morgan kissed him on the cheek. "I know you love me, so I'll let your insults pass. And I think I might enjoy London, riding in the park and all of that, as long as I can come back here once the season is over."

"You might find Becket Hall dull after London. Now do I have your promise you'll keep your nose out of the Black Ghost's business? Morgan? A season in Mayfair hobnobbing with all the handsome young lords hangs in the balance. Answer me."

"Oh, all right, I promise. But they're landing on the sands and will come along the beach to the village, so I'll see everything anyway. I'll just stay on the terrace, all hidden behind the balustrades, and watch."

Chance looked at her closely. "And how would you know that? Have you taken to listening at keyholes now?"

"No, I'd never do that," she said happily. "I just happened to see Court talking to Jacob as he was cleaning the grate in Elly's bedchamber and I traded a kiss for what he knew."

"Of all things wonderful. My sister has grown into a manipulating minx. You could get yourself in trouble, you know, toying with a man's affections."

"Pooh! Jacob's no more than a boy."

"As I remember it, Jacob is Spencer's age, a good several years your senior. Hardly a boy."

"He is to me. Besides, I wouldn't have done it if you

or Court ever told me what's happening, so if you're placing blame, place it on yourself," she said, seeming not the least insulted. "I only do what I have to do because you men think women are too *delicate* to know anything. But don't worry. I won't tell anyone I saw you leaving Julia's bedchamber late last night, and you won't tell anybody that I know what I know. And I *will* stay on the terrace."

Believing that was as close as he was going to come to having Morgan obey him and already wishing he didn't know so much about his enterprising sister—or she about him—Chance headed once more for Julia's bedchamber.

He was going to keep Billy waiting and would probably have to simply hope that Billy had folded his clothing and not merely stuffed them in a traveling case.

There also was no time to personally check and make sure Billy had remembered to pack such superfluous things as hose and several sets of fresh underclothes—Billy never having quite grasped the idea of changing his own underclothes with any regularity. Still, thank God he'd decided to leave Oswald behind in Upper Brook Street rather than have the valet poking his long nose around Becket Hall.

Chance stopped in front of the door to Julia's bedchamber, took a few slow breaths and then knocked.

Moments later Julia answered that knock, opening the door only slightly to peer out at him with one eye. One hour, she thought. Less than one hour after making their pact and already he was breaking the rules. That was rather nice—not that she'd let him know she felt that way. "I believe we'd agreed that you would not—"

"I'm here to say goodbye," Chance said, then smiled as Julia stepped back, opened the door for him.

She instantly understood and was immediately worried for him, drat the man. "You're going to Dover Castle?"

"And several places in between, yes. To perform the duties to which I have been assigned."

Julia rolled her eyes, then walked over to the window, feeling the need for some space between them. "Oh, please, don't ask me to swallow that crammer. You're off to see what the Preventative Waterguard knows about the Black Ghost. And don't pull a face at me, because it's you who is insulting me, not the other way round. What if someone finds you out, what then? Lieutenant Diamond didn't appear particularly stupid, except perhaps when he looked at Morgan."

Chance rubbed at his forehead. "I don't know why men plan wars. You females seem to have more talent for the finer points of the thing."

Julia would have laughed except for the fact that she was not amused. Rubbing her hands together so that she wouldn't be tempted to walk over to him, touch a hand to his cheek, she asked, "How long will you be away?"

"Ah," Chance said, closing the distance between them, "the lady will be lonely without me."

"Devastatingly so, yes. Just as I would miss any headache. Please answer the question. Did you know about this when you forced that ring on me? Am I supposed to wear it to protect myself from your family, keep them reminded that I'm…that I'm your property?"

"I didn't know I was leaving so soon but, yes, that was the general idea, and you knew it. But not the family. Jacko. Nobody likes to worry an old man, especially one who doesn't much trust women and who is built like a bull, with the temper to match. Now kiss me goodbye like a good fiancée, because the *Respite* is nearly ready to sail."

"You're going up the coast by boat?" Julia asked, if only to delay the inevitable: Chance kissing her, she unable to help kissing him back, the rotter. She'd barely been able to think of anything else but Chance, the way he'd made her body respond to his touch, and it had been impossible to convince herself that she could fool him into thinking she didn't hope for his attentions again. And again. For as long as he wanted her...even if he didn't really want her.

Chance frowned, as Julia had seemed to ask the question while not interested in the answer but was much more interested in simply looking at him. And a flush was making its way into her cheeks. His reaction to her, he realized, was lower than that and would soon become obvious. He had to leave—now.

"I haven't been on the water for a long time. Besides, I'll travel faster this way." He put his hands on her waist, drew her closer. "I won't be away from you a moment longer than necessary, I promise. I want to see you wearing my ring."

She lowered her head. "There's nobody here to listen, so you can stop that now."

"I must flatter you more often, as you respond so winningly." Chance laughed and tipped up her chin so she had no choice but to look at him again, because he very much liked the way she looked at him. But she immediately closed her eyes. Stubborn woman! "Julia, look at me. Where's the ring? Why aren't you wearing it?"

Julia stepped away from him and reached into her pocket to pull out the ring, show it to him. "It's too large, so I wrapped a ribbon around it until it fit, but now it's uncomfortable."

Chance took the thing and looked at it, then handed it back to her. "That's quite a bit of ribbon, isn't it? While I'm gone, have Morgan take you to see Waylon. He'll trim the thing down to fit you."

"Waylon? You have a jeweler here at Becket Hall?"

"No, but we do have a smithy in the village. Every crew needs a blacksmith."

Julia tipped her head as she looked at him. "You want me to take this obviously expensive ring to a *smithy?* That's preposterous."

"Not really. Waylon has worked with jewelry many times," Chance said, thinking back to the island and sitting on an overturned barrel to watch as Waylon dismantled some of the more distinctive jewelry to remove the stones, then melt the gold. Not that he was about to tell Julia about those particular memories.

"Very well then, I'll ask Morgan to go with me tomorrow. Didn't you say you should be leaving? Don't let me keep you." She so wanted him to go before she had to think too much about the fact that he would be gone.

"You're right, I should go," Chance said, suddenly uncomfortably aware that he might just miss this woman while he was playing at government agent and smuggler's spy. And for some unknown reason, he seemed to want to punish himself before he was on his way. "I'm still waiting for my kiss from my betrothed, remember? A kiss, an affecting few words such as *Godspeed and hurry back to me, darling.* Do you think you can manage that?"

"I don't think so, no. But do try not to be discovered doing something you shouldn't be doing. Alice would miss you, I'm sure. Have you said goodbye to her?"

Chance winced. "Damn. Alice. Is she in the nursery?"

"I would suppose so, but she might be napping. Do you want me to tell her?"

"I shouldn't, but yes, thank you. I'm…I'm not accustomed to informing Alice of my comings and goings, I'm afraid. Tell her…tell her that when I return we'll all three of us go on a picnic on the beach or some such thing."

Julia smiled softly, because he seemed truly upset that he had forgotten his daughter yet again. She didn't know what all was going on at Becket Hall, but the man certainly had something weighing heavily on his mind. "Alice will like that."

Chance smiled at her. "Thank you. And Alice and I will laze on a blanket and watch as you dig up that boot again, to take a look inside."

"Oh, really? I don't think so. If I'm lucky, the tide will have taken it." Then she walked over to him, stood up on tiptoe and kissed him on the cheek, because she now had truly run out of things to say to him. "There. And I'll pine for you endlessly. Now *go.*"

Chance had his arms around her before she could move away from him. "I think I need more than that miserly kiss, madam," he said, then brought his mouth down hard on hers.

It is amazing what a body remembers all on its own, Julia thought as she melted against him, her arms snaking up and about his neck in the off chance he thought to break the kiss before she was ready.

And she wasn't ready. Not when he was now cupping her breasts, rubbing his thumbs across the thin fabric of her gown, concentrating on her now-straining nipples. Not when he had somehow insinuated his thigh between her legs, pressing against her sex as their tongues dueled, as she dug her fingernails into his shoulders.

She was no young miss. She was a woman grown and now an awakened woman. And she was *not* going back to the way she had been, innocent, ignorant of just what being a woman meant.

Since coming back to her bedchamber from the beach to discover that she may have just snipped off her nose to spite her own face, she'd decided to take what he had to give her for as long as he felt inclined to do so. But she'd likewise decided to give back as good as she got.

Chance reluctantly slid his hands back down to Julia's waist, not because he didn't want her but because he was beginning to think she was experimenting with him, this woman he'd shown the pleasure men and women could share.

He might worry that another woman would believe

herself in love with him merely because he'd come to her bed, given and taken pleasure there. But Julia Carruthers wasn't other women and far from gullible. She knew why he'd come to her—she'd told him as much—and no one could believe herself in love with a man who would do anything so low, so base.

No, she didn't really want *him*. She wanted *it*. Miss Prim and Proper had turned overnight into a wanton, and that transformation was *his* fault.

So why shouldn't he reap the benefits?

Because he was a gentleman, damn it, and if not that, he was a man with at least some semblance of a conscience.

Chance pushed her slightly away from him, pressed several more kisses against her face, then stepped back. "I really have to go now."

"Yes…you really should. They'll be waiting."

"Don't worry. Billy hasn't boxed my ears in some time now."

He got as far as the door before turning around to take one last look at this woman who had so quickly gotten beneath his skin, annoying him, rousing him, maddening him.

Julia still stood near the window, looking at him as the early afternoon light haloed around her. She lifted a hand and pressed her fingertips to her swollen mouth, hardly able to believe she'd behaved so recklessly…and that she still wanted him so much.

"Oh, bloody hell," Chance said, turning the key in the lock and already unbuttoning his shirt as he stormed back across the room. "Let them wait."

Julia was in his arms again almost before she could register what was happening, and moments later, their mouths fused together, she was lying on her back on the bedspread.

The flare of passion was instantaneous and fierce. They kissed again and again, nipped at each other, tasted each other, and all while working to remove each other's clothes.

Julia's gown was at her waist before she could push Chance's shirt from his shoulders, so he finished the job for her, then began unbuttoning his pantaloons as he knelt over her, looking at her upper body with an intensity that she felt tauten her nipples in response.

"Hurry."

Julia had said the word. She heard herself say the word, her voice all but pleading with him. And she didn't care. She just wanted him to *hurry*.

She felt his hands on her thighs as he pushed up her gown, then slipped her underclothes down past her knees before settling himself against her. Just the thought of their shared state of partial dress, the urgency they both felt, ignited her passion to the point where such sudden, unseemly haste seemed perfectly reasonable.

Chance bowed his head toward Julia's breasts, licking the valley between them as he looked up at her, heard her sharp intake of breath. And when he covered her nipple with his mouth, the low, purring sound she made in her throat made him realize that not only was she ready for him, he was in danger of disgracing himself if he didn't take her, take her now.

He raised himself slightly to position himself better between her legs, then slipped inside her in one long glide, deep into the moist heat that awaited him. Captured him. Held him.

Julia wanted to lift her legs up and around him, as he had taught her last night, but her underclothes were tangled around her ankles. She whimpered in frustration and pulled him close against her so that she could hold him.

Chance felt his already nearly frantic passion building as his heart pounded, as he found it difficult to breathe. He plunged faster, deeper, while Julia matched him thrust for thrust.

There was nothing gentle here, nothing. This was two people in need, each of them demanding something from the other. A mindless coupling that moved them forward, took them deeper and higher and finally exploded all around them before they came crashing back to earth together.

And all Julia wanted to do now was hold him and kiss him and kiss him again.

And all Chance could think now was that he'd lost all control of himself and spilled his seed in Julia. And he didn't care.

Julia did her best to slow her breathing, and then Chance kissed her one last time, smoothed back her hair and left the bed to snatch up a towel from the washstand, keeping his back to her as he buttoned his pantaloons.

He turned to her then, reaching for his shirt, and Julia finally came back to her senses. She tried to push down the skirt of her gown even as she pulled the bodice up and over her breasts.

"No, don't do that, please. A man about to go off on a journey should carry with him the memory of why he can't wait to return," Chance told her quietly, pushing down her bodice once more, then kissed her breasts before stepping away again, smiling down at her. "Here, what's this?"

Julia immediately knew what he was referring to— the black grosgrain ribbon she'd tied around the strap of her shift. She put her hand over it, thanking her lucky stars that her *gad,* at least, was safely hidden in her dressing table. "It's…it's nothing."

"No," Chance said. He pushed her hand away and looked at the bow visible on her shift. "It's a tie for my hair. I left it here last night, didn't I?"

"You may have," Julia said, looking past him. Which was silly. She'd just made love with the man, certainly she could talk to him. But she couldn't. Now who was foolish?

Chance pushed a little harder, caught between amusement and bafflement, with just a bit of pride mixed in, not that he'd think about that right now. "And you're wearing it. Over your heart, too."

"I tied it there so I'd remember to give it back to you," Julia said, keeping her eyes averted. "Isn't Billy waiting for you?"

Chance would have pushed some more, but even a stupid man, he believed, could recognize when it was time to withdraw from the field. "Julia Carruthers, you are an endless source of wonder to me. Just when I think I'm beginning to understand you I… You're right, I've got to go now."

Which is how Julia came to be lying on her side, totally bemused, her skirts barely covering her hips, her breasts bared, like some creature in a Renaissance painting, watching Chance Becket walk away from her.

"Please be careful," she whispered as the door closed behind him and she sank back against the mattress, her eyes stinging with unshed tears. "Don't do anything brave."

CHAPTER SEVENTEEN

JULIA DIDN'T GO downstairs until the second dinner gong had rung, hoping to avoid conversation with the family in the main salon and holding on to Alice's hand because…because she was a selfish, craven coward, that's what she was.

"I like it here," Alice told her as, still holding Julia's hand, she jumped off the last stair, landing gracefully in her satin soft-soled slippers, her curls bouncing around her smiling face. "Everyone is so very nice, and I'm not stuck away in the nursery eating porridge. Although Buttercup will miss me horribly. Could I please go back upstairs and—"

"I don't think there's a place laid for Buttercup, sweetheart," Julia said, smiling, then swiftly said something to divert the child. "But I have heard that you will sit beside Callie at every meal now that you behaved so well at luncheon this afternoon, and she's almost as fine a companion as Buttercup, isn't she?"

Alice became very solemn. "She's better, but we can't tell Buttercup because she'll be sad."

Walking slowly, in no hurry to enter the dining room, Julia said, "I thought Buttercup was a boy rabbit."

"He *was,* but Callie and I decided that no boys should

be allowed in the nursery, so now he's a girl. We don't like boys. They're very fickle, you understand. We took a pact and everything."

Now Julia grinned. "Is that so? Well, my darling, I think that's very wise of you and Callie."

"She says so. That we're even brilliant, because boys are lower than snails, and that's quite low. Julia? What's a fickle?"

"Um…well…I suppose Callie meant that a fickle person plays with you very nicely one day and then ignores you the next—and for no good reason, too," Julia said, trying not to think of Chance as she explained.

"Oh. Like Court being nice to Callie, tossing a ball with her one day and then when she wants to play again today, calling her a pernikious brat and telling her to go away?"

"Pernicious, sweetheart. And yes, that's it exactly," Julia said as they entered the dining room to see half the chairs still empty. Spencer was there, his left arm in a sling, his expression bordering on petulant, as if he dared anyone to say he was still too sick to have left his bed, but he was the only male Becket present.

Julia knew where Chance had gone, but to see that Rian, Court and Ainsley were also absent? Clearly something was afoot. And just as clearly she shouldn't comment on that fact.

"Come sit next to me, Alice," Cassandra called out cheerfully. "We're all just sitting where we want to tonight, except for Spence, of course. He'd rather be in Hades than here with all us *girls*."

"Stubble it, brat," Spence growled halfheartedly, reaching for his wineglass as Julia sat down beside him.

Morgan, who was already seated across the table from her brother, made an elaborate business out of unfolding her serviette and placing it in her lap. "My, aren't you the cheery one, Spencer Becket. What's the matter? Wouldn't the other boys invite you along to play?"

"That means they're all fickles, and shame on them," Alice solemnly informed Julia as she tucked a linen serviette into the neck of the child's pretty pink gown, just as her father had done for her when she was a little girl.

"Yes, dear," Julia said, biting back a nervous giggle. "But we're polite ladies and we don't make such comments in company."

"Oh. But they *are* fickles, aren't they?"

While Morgan and Spencer continued their argument, Julia tapped a finger against her own lips before intoning seriously, "Porridge. Nursery."

"I'm sorry." Alice pulled a comical face and quickly turned to speak with Cassandra.

"Morgan," Elly said quietly from the head of the table, her chin lowered as she appeared to be inspecting her water glass, "that will be enough, thank you," and both Morgan and Spencer went silent, holding their argument to glares across the table.

Then Eleanor looked up, smiled at Julia, who was suitably impressed with the seemingly fragile young woman's quiet air of command. "Papa and everyone went to the *Last Voyage* to visit with our friends, something they do once a week, leaving us ladies on our own. Poor Spence couldn't go with them, not with his injured arm."

"Yes, your arm," Julia said, something contrary in her not about to willingly swallow Elly's fib. Either these people trusted her, let her in, or she would be as contrary as she wished to be. Even if her papa was sitting on some lovely cloud, tsk-tsking and racing to convince the other angels that he'd "raised the child up much better than this."

So looking, she hoped, merely idly curious, she asked, "How did you come to injure your arm, Spence? A sprain, I suppose? I did notice that your mount had suffered some sort of…misadventure. Did you fall off?"

"I most certainly did not," Spencer shot back angrily. "And where's Fanny? Why is she always late?"

Morgan dipped her spoon into the soup that had already been set before everyone. "To annoy you would be my guess, brother dear. Oh, here she comes now." Then in a low whisper Morgan added, "Bloody hell."

Julia, whose back was to the door, turned in her chair to see Fanny entering the dining room on the arm of Lieutenant Diamond. There was color in the girl's cheeks, but all the flawless Irish complexion around those two spots of color had gone deathly pale.

"Look who I found as I was returning from my walk," she said, her cheerful tone not accompanied by a smile. "Lieutenant Diamond has come to see Chance and Papa. I've told him Chance is gone about the king's business, didn't I, Lieutenant?"

"That you did, Miss Fanny. Good evening Miss Becket, Miss Carruthers, ladies—and, of course, Mr. Becket," Diamond said as he bowed, his eyes on Morgan, who was blinking rapidly in his direction, her flirtation just a tad overdone. "A fine man, your brother. But I did still hope to see Mr. Ainsley Becket on a matter that I'm sure is of no interest to you ladies."

Spencer belatedly got to his feet, also to bow, although his greeting was more in the way of a short, sharp nod of his head. "As Fanny also probably already told you, our father isn't here."

Morgan rested her chin in her palm as she leaned one elbow on the table. "Oh, hush, Spence. And on the contrary, Lieutenant. I find your brave work with the dragoons highly interesting…and *very* exciting."

"Morgan, sit back," Elly said, "Juanita needs to put down those bowls."

Julia was distracted for the moments it took Juanita to place a large bowl in the center of the table, then deftly follow up by transferring two heavy platters balanced on her beefy right arm to the table before turning on her heels and heading back toward the doorway that led to a set of stairs and the kitchens below.

Two things amazed Julia, had amazed her from the beginning, about the dining room at Becket Hall. One was that other than for the soup course (for everyone but Alice), the food was delivered in large bowls and platters, and everyone helped themselves, then passed the food to the next person. Highly informal, the Beckets dining as she and her papa had at the vicarage, with no attentive servants, no separate courses. Not at all, she knew from novels she had read, the way things were done in London society.

The other thing that amazed her, even more than Juanita's bulk or the soft white blouse and many-colored striped skirt she wore, was the fact that the woman had no right hand.

Chance had told her there were two servants—she must really think of another way to think of these people than the ill-fitting title of *servant*—one man, one woman, each missing a hand. But she had thought he'd been teasing her. Was the penalty for thievery still the cutting off of a hand? Not here in England but on those islands she was so curious to learn about in more detail?

What did not amaze her was that Juanita was a part of this very unique household.

Julia was brought back to attention as Alice tugged on her sleeve. "Is Morgan a flirt, Julia?" the child asked, thankfully quietly. "Callie just said she's an abomipal flirt."

Julia swallowed a laugh, at the same time wishing the inquisitive Alice had held her question until after dinner, when she took the child upstairs to the nursery. "Abominable, dear, and no, she isn't. She's merely young."

"No she's not. *I'm* young."

Julia patted Alice's hand as she reconsidered the wisdom of allowing Alice at table, then whispered, "Later, sweetheart. Look, Callie's spooning some peas onto your plate for you. Isn't that nice? You told me you like peas."

"I *love* peas. I just don't like soup. It's too dribbly," Alice corrected and turned back to her plate.

This finally let Julia free to listen to the conversation taking place as Eleanor, their hostess, allowed Lieutenant Diamond to remain standing—a clear sign that he wasn't going to be invited to break bread with the family.

"…unfortunately, we also discovered three fresh graves. Forgive me, I shouldn't speak of such things in front of you ladies."

"Only three?" Spencer whispered out of the corner of his mouth as he picked up his soup spoon, showing himself to be both daring and very young. "Perhaps the other two dug themselves out and ran away."

Julia's stomach did a small flip. Spencer had sounded quite happy. Had she really convinced herself that there was some sort of romance, some dash, in Chance riding out with the smugglers? There was no "romance" in dead bodies. Men most certainly were put together with more of a liking for bloodletting than were women, if she was to be any judge.

But even more than that, Lieutenant Diamond must be silenced, a thought that hit her only a heartbeat before Eleanor Becket said coolly, "There are children present, Lieutenant, the fact of which it should not be necessary to point out to a gentleman."

"And there's your problem," Spencer said in between mouthfuls of soup, his unruly black curls half covering his face, and Julia believed she could actually feel the heat radiating from him. "You can put a pig in a scarlet coat. Doesn't make him a gentleman. Does it, *Lieutenant?*"

Julia closed her eyes for a moment, then looked up at Lieutenant Diamond. There were inappropriate times, there were inappropriate questions. Alice had certainly proved both with her innocent questions. But then there was just opening one's mouth and flat-out sticking one's head on the block.

The soldier bowed twice, in both Spencer's and Eleanor's directions. "I accept that insult, sir, and offer a thousand apologies, Miss Becket. I only wished to inform your brother and Mr. Becket that these are dangerous times on the Marsh and becoming more so daily. It would appear we have our own war going on here, beyond that of our struggle against Napoleon."

Then the lieutenant turned smartly once more, to look at Spencer. "I see you've been injured, Mr. Becket. Perhaps you could indulge an officer of the Crown and tell me how you came about that injury? Is it…recent?"

"I'll bloody throw you out on your ear, that's what I'll do," Spencer said, lifting his left arm and ruthlessly ripping off his sling. He tossed the black silk on the table, clearly ready to leave his chair so he could put his words into action.

Julia couldn't help herself—she gave him a sharp, sideways kick under the table, the side of her shoe landing squarely against his anklebone. Spencer, who was already half out of his chair, abruptly sat down and turned to glare at her.

The tall, blond-haired soldier lifted his chin, looking down on Spencer. "My, Mr. Becket, guest as I am in this house, I must say your reluctance to cooperate with the king's representative in this area is most disconcerting. Almost, Mr. Becket, as if you have something to hide."

It was now or never, Julia decided. Either she was a part of this family or she wasn't.

"Oh, Spence, calm yourself, please," Julia said, laying a hand on his forearm. "There's no need to be so gallant in my defense."

Spencer frowned in obvious confusion. "I…but I want to—"

"Yes, dear, I know," Julia continued quickly. "I had only begged your promise not to tell Chance, that's all. I never meant to have you come under improper suspicion just to save my embarrassment."

"But I—"

"Spence, let Julia speak," Eleanor said from the end of the table. "It is, after all, her story to tell. Go on, please, Julia."

Julia's mind had been working nineteen to the dozen inventing a story that would completely protect Spencer, and now she took a steadying breath and looked at the lieutenant, whose fine English coloring was already, she noticed, going a little green.

"Miss Carruthers," Lieutenant Diamond said hastily, "I assure you, I would not wish to embarrass you in any way or ask Mr. Spencer Becket to break a confidence. Mr. Chance Becket would be—"

"My fiancée would be extremely put out with me if I did not answer questions put by you, sir," Julia told him, cutting him off, because this had to be said. "I was out walking by myself today—such a fine day, you'll agree—and foolishly believed the handsome bay horse inside the stable yard fence wouldn't mind if I stepped inside the fence to pet it. Well, it appears, sir, the horse did very much mind, and if it weren't for Spencer's timely arrival, I might well have been trampled. I have so little experience with horses, you see. I was very naive. They aren't like puppies, are they?"

"Oh, Julia, that's awful!" Alice exclaimed, and Cassandra quickly put her arm around the child and pulled her tight against her chest, effectively quieting her.

These Beckets worked well together, Julia thought quickly before continuing her enormous fib. "Well, sir, I came away with nary a scratch, but Spencer bruised his arm badly, and that poor horse suffered a nasty scratch against the fence."

She patted Spencer's arm, then folded her hands on the edge of the table as she smiled at the lieutenant. "I should have known I couldn't hide my reckless action from Chance and I will confess all to him when he returns. But if you could please, Lieutenant, be discreet if you should happen to see him as he is out and about on the king's business, I would greatly appreciate that kindness. Chance worries so over me, you understand."

Their food grew cool as Lieutenant Diamond apologized for a good five minutes and then finally took his leave.

In the silence that followed, Julia nervously counted to fifteen inside her head before anyone spoke. And then everyone spoke at once.

"Callie pinched me when I tried to talk. That wasn't nice," Alice complained, and Cassandra quickly apologized.

"That was brilliant, Julia. Diamond all but *ran* out of here, fearing for his commission and seeing himself in the mud on the Peninsula, going toe-to-toe with the

French like a *real* soldier," Fanny exclaimed as she used a large fork to skewer a thick lamb chop.

Morgan grinned. "You tell a fine tale, Julia. Horses aren't much like puppies? I could hardly keep from laughing and ruining everything. And Spence as the hero? Do you think the good lieutenant saw my eyes cross at that bit of nonsense?"

"Shut up, Morgan," Spencer ordered in the way brothers speak to annoying sisters as he retrieved his sling and tossed it to the floor. Then he turned to place a kiss on Julia's cheek. "Morgan's right, though. That was brilliant, and I was an idiot. I should have known Chance wouldn't let his heart cloud his judgment."

Now it was Julia's turn to go pale, a moment before she felt color running into her cheeks. "Yes...thank you, Spence."

Alice tugged on her sleeve. "Are you sure you aren't hurt, Julia?"

"Positive, darling," she said, hugging the girl close as she looked at Eleanor, who had yet to say anything.

Eleanor just looked at her, as Julia held her breath, then nodded in that ladylike, regal way of hers and went back to her soup.

Julia exhaled and picked up her own spoon.

"Spence?"

"No more, Morgan," he growled.

"Very well then, suit yourself. See if I care a snap if you bleed to death."

Spencer looked at his left sleeve and uttered a soft curse. Clearly his violent show of no longer needing his sling had reopened his wound.

"If you'll allow me to be excused, Elly?" he said, getting to his feet to bow to Eleanor. Julia could now see both the dark wet patch on his sleeve and the trickle of fresh red blood running down over the back of his hand.

Spencer made it halfway out of the dining room before slowly crumpling to the carpet in a faint.

And that fairly well put paid to the Becket's evening meal.

THE NEXT MORNING Julia and Morgan donned heavier capes, as the weather had turned damp and misty, and made their way along the shoreline to the village, Chance's ring tucked up in Julia's pocket.

"Do you know how Spencer is this morning?"

"Spence is fine. Odette took care of him, but she was angry. Couldn't even remember her English, but just kept railing at him in that mix of French and whatever it is she speaks when she's upset."

Julia shivered. "I don't think I'd like to be on the receiving end of Odette's anger. But Spencer really worried me last night."

"Spence is much too headstrong," Morgan said dismissingly, neatly hopping from the shale and sand up onto the wooden flagway that was wide enough for she and Julia to walk side by side. "Hot-blooded. Always wanting to play the hero. Papa should simply buy him a commission and let him trot off to war. It's all Spence wants. All Rian wants, too. They're both terrified the war will be over before they can get there."

"And this worries you?" Julia asked, carefully picking her way on the wet, slippery flagway.

"No. Not a bit. A person should do what a person wants to do. And it's even worse for us women." She stopped, turned to smile at Julia, her eyes sparkling with mischief. "Don't you ever wish to just *do* something? Forget about your skirts and your *fragile* nature and just do something? *Be* somebody?"

Julia frowned, truly not understanding whatever it was Morgan was trying to say. "I am somebody, Morgan, and so are you. And Mr. Becket is wonderfully lenient. You won't find such freedom of behavior in London."

"Then that's decided. I won't go. You tell Chance for me, would you? Tell him I most humbly decline his kind invitation—or something of that sort."

"Chance invited you to come to London for a season?"

"Uh-huh, but I won't go now, not if there are going to be a multitude of rules Chance would expect me to obey, because we'd both end up being very disappointed," Morgan said, turning to peer into the small, dusty shop window. "Oh, Ollie's waving me in. I suppose the leather has arrived for my new riding boots. Italian leather, you know. The very finest."

"But aren't we—never mind," Julia said, smiling at her own naiveté. From Florence to Spain to the French coast to Romney Marsh. "Shall we go inside?"

"No, no, I'll take forever. Ollie insists on new measurements each time." Morgan leaned closer. "I think he likes holding my feet and looking at my legs, but he's an old man now, and I don't see the harm, do you? I giggle and tell him my feet are ticklish, and he smiles and blushes."

"You're incorrigible, you know," Julia told her. "And I think I like you very much. Where is the blacksmith located?"

"At the end of the village and then another few steps along, in case the forge catches fire. I'll join you when I'm done or you can just walk back here, if you don't mind? Waylon's probably waiting for you."

"Will I have to giggle as I let him hold my hand to measure my finger?"

"Only if you want his wife to take a pitchfork to you," Morgan said, winking, and Julia headed toward the blacksmith shop, now able to see the smoke rising from the forge.

She couldn't help but notice people stopping, staring at her, so she lifted her chin and smiled, nodded to the ladies and kept moving, her pace increasing as she passed by the larger building displaying a burned-wood overhead sign, *Last Voyage*.

By the time she reached the smithy, Julia wondered if she had grown a second head, for all the curious looks she was getting, which possibly explained why she hadn't noticed she was being followed.

She'd pulled open one of the remarkably heavy doors and taken no more than two steps into the dark, over-heated shop smelling of hot iron, where a leather-aproned man the size of a door himself yelled at the young boy working the bellows on a nearly white-hot fire, when a voice behind her said, "Guard the door, Gautier."

Julia instantly froze in place, then turned about to see Jacko. Looming over her, smiling that delighted, deadly smile. Just the sort of smile Julia imagined the devil wearing as he welcomed newcomers to hell.

"Good morrow, Miss Carruthers," he said, gifting her with a rather insolent salute. "Gautier? I said, guard the door."

"*Oui*, Jacko."

Julia stepped back several paces, then peered around Jacko's heavy-shouldered bulk to see a small man in a tight-fitting red-and-white-striped seaman's jersey and rather ragged, definitely baggy drawers. Gautier smiled at her.

"From the *outside*, Gautier," Jacko said, still smiling at Julia, and the little Frenchman hit the palm of his hand against the side of his head, said, "*Mon Dieu, naturellement. Pardon*," and scrambled through the doorway, closing the door behind him.

Silly as all this melodrama seemed to her, Julia was becoming rather uneasy. "Precisely what do you think you're doing, Jacko?"

"I think that's obvious, don't you?" He turned and lowered the bar onto the hooks attached to the door, then called out, "Waylon! Take the boy and leave. Use the back door."

Waylon, who was possibly as large as Jacko, took one look, then grabbed the boy by his arm and pulled him toward the rear of the building.

Julia folded her arms and tried to appear calm as Jacko approached the forge. Waylon had mistakenly left an iron rod still heating in the fire, and Jacko slid on a glove, then picked up the rod, its tip glowing white-hot. "Pretty, isn't it? And yet so dangerous in the wrong hands."

Wanting to scream, wanting to run, Julia instead stood her ground. "Am I supposed to be terrified, Jacko?"

His eyes sparkled, looked amused, and his tone was light as he smiled at her. "That would be the general idea, Miss Carruthers, yes." He took a step toward her, and she retreated in spite of her determination to stand her ground. "Tell me about your father."

Now Julia was terrified, even as she realized she was more terrified of Chance finding out she'd lied to him—a sin of omission, but a sin nonetheless—than she was of Jacko and his menacing weapon. "You've been to Hawkhurst?"

His grin was positively delighted. "Oh, and aren't you the clever one. And a quick thinker, too. I've heard about Lieutenant Diamond's visit last evening. Not just the wound to Spence but to his horse, as well. Very clever, very quick, very credible. And, yes, Miss Carruthers, I've been to Hawkhurst."

"I can explain…"

"Really," Jacko said flatly. "Just let me safely deposit this pretty thing into the water bucket, and then the two of us can sit over there on those fine oak chairs of Waylon's…while you *explain*."

Julia quickly did as he said, for her knees were knocking together so badly she was sure she might fall down otherwise.

Jacko picked up the other chair as if it weighed no more than a feather, turned it around, straddled it, then rested his crossed arms on the carved back of the chair. "So? What do you want to tell me?"

"What you already know, I suppose. That I *am* from Hawkhurst," Julia began, untying her cloak because it was so very warm in the smithy, even though her fingers were cold and clumsy. "And my father was the vicar of Saint Bartholomew's." She looked down at her shaking fingers. "Until he was asked to step down."

"Ah, there we go—and so quickly, too. Confession is good for the soul, isn't it?" Jacko asked, leaning his large head on his crossed forearms, grinning at her. "And why was he asked to step down?"

Julia glared at him. "Although I'm at a loss as to how you found out, you obviously already know why."

"That I do, that I do. But now I want you to tell me."

"He was accused of thievery by his superiors from Rye."

"So your holy papa was a thief? Stealing from his own church? And then he died, all suddenlike, before anyone could be told and he could be carted off to trial. How'd he die, Miss Carruthers?"

Julia blinked furiously as her eyes began to sting. "I won't answer that."

"He hanged himself," Jacko said for her. "Took himself up to the attics of the vicarage that same night he was accused and hanged himself."

How dare the man push at her like this? "He did not! My father died in his bed. I found him in his bed. He died in his sleep."

"So everyone told me. Except for the man I found sweeping out the church. He told me something different."

Julia hugged herself, began to rock. "Penton? Penton's a simple man. And he drinks sometimes, poor soul. Nobody listens to Penton."

"Drinks quite a bit, in truth, when someone else is paying down the blunt," Jacko agreed.

He was still smiling. How Julia wanted him to stop smiling. But maybe Jacko was like some dogs—when the tail wagging stops, the dog bites.

Julia rushed into speech. "Why are you doing this to me? Why won't you let my father rest in peace? Yes. Yes, Penton helped me cut Papa down and put him in his bed. He helped me wash him, prepare him for burial, so no one would see him…see him as he was. And my father was wept over by his congregation and buried in the churchyard. And I came to London and met Chance and to my great surprise found myself back here. Is that all you wanted to hear?"

"He was fronting for the local smugglers, wasn't he? He'd give them money from the church coffers to buy goods across the Channel, then they'd pay him back, until the next time. Not for profit—unless you can call a cask of tea or perhaps some silk or lace for the pretty daughter *profit*—but to help his struggling congregation. How long had he been doing this? Who knows. But there was a storm or two at a bad time, and the goods had to be scuttled to save the men, so now there was no money when the officials from Rye came to call."

Julia nodded, giving up the fight, as it seemed there was nothing Jacko didn't know. "They were suspicious in Rye even before the storm. The church officials demanded answers, and Papa wouldn't give them to them, wouldn't betray our congregation, didn't even tell our people he was in trouble."

She looked at Jacko. "They *were* his people. For as long as I can remember, they were his people. And he'd rather die than betray them. There," she ended, wiping at tears with the back of her hand, "are you satisfied now?"

"I am that." Jacko got to his feet, hiked up his trousers that had a tendency to slip low on his belly. "You'll do."

"I'll *do?* Really. And precisely what does that mean?"

"Only a fool trusts the town drunkard, Miss Carruthers."

"What?"

"I needed to hear the story from you, Miss Carruthers, and you were brave enough and proud enough to tell it to me." He gave a quick tilt of his head. "And I suppose I wanted you to know that I know. You knew too much, you see, and reacted too well—on the Marsh, with that fool Diamond last night. Now I know why. Your papa may have killed himself to protect his congregation but mostly he did it to protect you. Because you were also a part of it."

Julia sighed. "Only marginally. But, yes, I was involved from the time I was a young child. I would have stood with him, Jacko, proudly. But he didn't give me the opportunity. I understand why he did what he did and have come to grips with his death and can even remember him fondly now. You'll tell the others? You'll tell Chance?"

Jacko shrugged. "Don't see the point, do you? Unless you want to one fine day. Not as if you've lied to us. You lived in Hawkhurst, your papa was the vicar and now he's dead and buried in the churchyard as the holy man he was. Oh, and Penton, his pockets full, is aboard ship and on his way to Saint Augustine in America, which he'll learn when he eventually sobers up and looks over the rail."

Julia's heart leapt in her chest. "He's gone? You did that for my father and me?"

"We protect our own here, Miss Carruthers."

"So you no longer believe me to be a danger to…to the family?"

Then Julia had to grab hold of the chair behind her as Jacko advanced on her with his lumbering walk before bending to raise her hand to his lips. "Welcome to the family, Miss Carruthers. Chance would be more the young fool than I take him for if he let you go."

"Julia," she said, her mouth so dry she could barely get out the words. She still wasn't sure quite how it had happened, but Jacko had accepted her. "Please. I'm Julia."

Jacko's smile suddenly didn't seem quite so dangerous, although she doubted she'd ever be so foolish as to consider the man harmless. "All right then," he said, nodding. And then he shouted out so unexpectedly that Julia jumped. "Waylon! Haul your singed arse back in here and fix Miss Julia's betrothal ring. What a pitiful excuse for a smithy you are, Waylon, letting a lady stand waiting on you."

Julia bit back a laugh as Jacko winked at her even as Waylon and his young assistant came scurrying back into the smithy.

But that didn't mean that her hand refused to stop shaking for the whole of the time Waylon measured her finger and refit the ring…especially when she had a sudden thought: had Morgan deliberately maneuvered for her to be alone with Jacko? Had this entire meeting been planned?

But when Morgan finally joined her at the blacksmith shop, her smile was devoid of guile as she asked Julia if she wanted a piece of rock candy she then handed to her in a twist of greased white paper.

"I saw Jacko," Julia said, accepting the sweet as the two of them waved good day to Waylon and made their way back toward the village proper.

"Did you?" Morgan remarked in seeming innocence, licking her fingers after popping a small bit of the confection into her mouth. Then she winked broadly at Julia. "Had the old warhorse come to Waylon to be re-shod?"

Julia smiled at the small joke as she wavered between two conclusions. She was overreacting to what she had romantically imagined to be a family not only rife with secrets but loyal to the death…or this *really was* a family rife with secrets and loyal above all to each other.

No matter which conclusion was correct, she knew she was very glad to be on the inside with the Beckets rather than classed as the enemy.…

CHAPTER EIGHTEEN

CHANCE SAT IMPATIENTLY, looking toward Becket Hall as he was rowed toward shore, having been told he was dressed like "too much the toff" to be handed an oar of his own. Four days since he'd seen the Hall. Three full days too many, to his way of thinking.

He was caught between anger and bemusement at how much he had missed Julia. Her voice, her smile, her dogged inquisitiveness. Her bravery. Even her stubbornness.

Her ability to draw him out of himself, make him look at his past again, at his choices, at his failings. At his newly discovered hopes.

His last sight of her had haunted him as he'd stood on deck on the *Respite,* his face turned into the wind. Her nervousness as she had complied with his wish to leave her as she'd lain half-naked and sated in her bed had stayed with him, along with the certain knowledge he had taken with him that this woman would bend, but she would not break. There was a strength in her, a quiet strength, and more than a little daring.

Being on the water again had set Chance's heart pounding, not with the hated memories he'd expected but with the desire to have Julia standing beside him, sailing ahead of the wind. Showing her the stars by night, holding her close against his side as they raced the tide, chased the moon. Lying beside her in the captain's cabin as gentle waves rocked them to sleep after an evening of loving…

It wasn't just the timing of the thing—Julia coming into his life just as he returned to Becket Hall, just as he began to make peace with his past, with his family.

Or maybe it was. Perhaps Julia had entered his life precisely when he needed her, turning it upside down, questioning his responsibilities to Alice, even questioning his loyalties. And never taking a step back.

Chance swiveled on the plank seat to look back at the *Respite,* its sails lowered and secured, riding high in the water while firmly anchored. How cannily Ainsley had crafted her, a gentle mix of the Bermuda and the Jamaican sloop.

Over sixty feet long and twenty-one feet wide, her weight had to be close to one hundred and fifteen tons, yet her draft was only eight feet. Fast, agile with its fore and aft rigs so superior to the square-rigged Waterguard vessels.

The *Respite* could be safely handled near the shore with a skeleton crew of twenty, skim shoals that would ground Waterguard vessels, yet was fitted to take to deeper water with a crew of forty-five or more.

The gun ports were so cunningly disguised by what appeared to be a rich man's penchant for costly overly ornate decoration that even Chance hadn't noticed at first that the sloop carried ten four-pounder cannon that could be readied and fired in less than a minute's notice.

Yes, the *Respite* could outrun anything the British Navy had made available for chasing down freebooters, and not only defend itself but be the aggressor in a fight.

An intriguing mix of a man, Ainsley Becket. Retired from the sea, a ship fashioned from dreams anchored within sight of his self-imposed life on the shore. Didn't he itch to take the *Respite* out, at least to put her through her paces? Or was the *Respite* actually another penance for the man?

Chance clamped his teeth together tightly and turned once more to look at Becket Hall. Ainsley's penance. But not Chance's penance. His has been removing himself to exile in London. Chance saw that now, and if he saw Ainsley's actions as overdone, what then would he call his own?

"Foolish," he said quietly as the hull of the small boat hit the sand and he and the others jumped into the shallow water to pull the boat ashore. "Thanks, mates," he said, reaching into his pocket and pulling out several gold coins. "Here you go. Have a drink or three at the *Last Voyage* to celebrate our success, why don't you." Then he grinned. "And it's up to you whether you row back for Billy and the others before you do."

"A fine idea, 'cept that Billy'd skin us alive," one of the seamen said, saluting Chance. "Good to be on the water with you again, Chance Becket. Almost like havin' the Cap'n callin' out the orders. 'Course, coulda taken her out inta the wind more, mayhap played some slap an' tickle with that there Frenchie cutter we seen off Folkestone."

Chance grinned. "Perhaps some other time, Cholly," he said, then headed along the shoreline toward Becket Hall, his mind once more concentrated on seeing Julia, even as he knew Ainsley and Court were waiting for his report. He had two, after all. A carefully worded packet to be sent off to London via one of the dragoons and the one meant only for the family.

First things first, though, as once he was alone with Julia, he had no plans that either of them would be disturbed until morning. Smiling at the thought he didn't bother to examine beyond the notion that she would welcome another "lesson" in loving, he climbed the stone steps to the terrace two at a time and headed into the house via the door to the morning room, then down the hall to Ainsley's study.

And he had been expected. Ainsley sat behind his desk, balancing a silver letter opener between his fingers, while Courtland immediately halted his pacing to stand in front of one of the windows, his hands clasped behind him, to stare at his brother.

"Well?"

"I didn't expect you to fall on my neck, weeping in joy over my safe return, Court. But not even an offer of wine?" Chance asked facetiously. "Very well, I'll pour my own. Ainsley," he said as he walked past the desk, toward the drinks table.

"You're looking particularly well-pleased with yourself," Ainsley said, putting down the letter opener and folding his hands in front of him on the desktop. "What do you think of the *Respite?*"

"She's a wonder," Chance said sincerely, holding up

his wineglass in salute to the sloop—and to Ainsley's genius at insisting he take her out, get his feet wet again, as it were. "And a bit of a wolf in sheep's clothing, I'd say."

"When your back is to the sea, a measure of prudence is only natural," Ainsley pointed out quietly. "What have you learned?"

Chance dropped onto a soft leather couch and smiled, already loosening his neck cloth. "That why the French aren't chomping down frogs and snails in Carleton House right now, with Prinney waiting on them hand and foot, is a true wonderment. That's what I discovered, to my dismay—or at least, the War Office Chance Becket would see things that way."

He slid the undone neck cloth out from around his collar, then sighed as he opened the top button of his shirt. "Ah, that's better. How quickly a man can lose any affection for starched collars. But back to business. The Waterguard, as I'm sure you know, is criminally understaffed and ill-equipped—I think you could outswim some of their ancient ships, Court. Of course, there's a war going on and the best ships are needed elsewhere. I'd say that now that the fear of imminent invasion seems gone, the coast is remarkably underprotected, with most of the hopeful deterrents reduced to land defenses. I will, naturally, suggest a readjustment of London's mind-set on that. We need double the cutters we're allotted now and ships that aren't in such a sad state of disrepair. Not that anyone will listen."

He turned to Ainsley. "Rethinking building so close to the Channel?"

"No, because I'm not concerned. If the French didn't

attempt an invasion before Nelson trounced them at Trafalgar, they aren't coming. Besides, Bonaparte would never so divide his *Grande Armée* to fight on yet another front, not when we're so willing to present ourselves to him on the other side of the Channel. I agree with the government on that head. Now other than what we already knew, what have you learned in your absence?"

"Very well. I've learned that being stationed in the Martello Towers, that make up much of the land defenses I spoke of, is somewhat akin to living at the bottom of a damp well, one that just happens to grow upward, not down. Two dozen men squashed in together in one windowless barracks room, with the officer of the tower having a similarly sized room all to himself—with windows, naturally. We heard considerable grumbling about that. The food is nearly inedible, the hours long and the pay atrocious. Such conditions don't breed loyalty—and certainly don't encourage the men to risk their skins to intercept a load of salt, soap and shoelaces."

"In other words, the common soldier, unlike our Lieutenant Diamond, can be bought," Courtland said.

"Correction, Court," Chance told him. "They *have* been bought. Or at least enough of them, including many officers, had to have been willing to turn a blind eye for smuggling to have increased at least tenfold across the board in the past year. From Hythe to Dover and to the other side of us, from just west of Rye and into Sussex and probably beyond Wexhill—and all of the operations highly organized. I was quietly taken aside and given quite a tale of woe from a few of the frustrated officers stationed at Dover Castle, although I don't think anyone expects me to return to London and effect a miracle that will change anything for the better. Most of them sounded more resigned than hopeful."

"A tenfold increase from Dover to beyond Wexhill. That's even more than I'd imagined," Ainsley said consideringly. "Quite enterprising. Extremely profitable. And with hirelings to take most of the risks as those in charge keep their hands relatively clean while pocketing the lion's share of that profit."

Chance neatly folded his neck cloth. "Exactly. Somebody, probably an entire group of powerful somebodies, are becoming very, very rich, and all that stands between them—the Red Men Gang, if you will—and even more wealth is our dominance in this area of Romney Marsh now that the Black Ghost is riding."

Ainsley pressed his lips together a moment, then asked, "And everywhere they're known as the Red Men Gang?"

Chance shook his head. "No, nothing like that, which is fairly intelligent. One gang large enough to control over forty miles of coastline would have drawn London's attention very quickly. However, in each area the gangs do wear distinctive colors—their caps, their smocks, whatever. Very clever. But when you have the opportunity to stand back, look at what's happening as parts of a single whole, you could—"

"You could," Courtland interrupted, "look at any map of Romney Marsh and realize we are completely surrounded except for the sea. And how long will they leave that avenue open to our people?"

Chance toasted his brother with his wineglass. "My thought exactly. Until I considered the thing."

Ainsley sat forward, looking intently at Chance. "And what have you considered?"

Chance sighed, put down his wineglass and lightly rubbed his palms against each other as he looked at Ainsley. "That we might be able to convince the Red Men Gang—or whatever we choose to call it—that we're simply not worth the effort it would take to destroy us. London is already nervous or else I wouldn't have been given my last-minute assignment. One good fight, one solid defeat and, if I were in charge of this string of gangs, I'd cut my losses and be content with what I had rather than continue the fight and call any more of London's attention to Romney Marsh—which could end with London paying considerable attention to this entire stretch of coastline. Hell, Ainsley, half of London doesn't even realize the Marsh is home to anything but sheep."

Ainsley began tapping the tip of the letter opener on the desktop. "Lieutenant Diamond and his men discovered some of the bodies," he said quietly. "He undoubtedly sent a report to London, which I'd considered a stroke of bad luck. But you'd say it was a stroke of good luck?"

"Definitely," Chance said, not even bothering to try to conceal his excitement. It was as if his mind had gone to sleep years ago and was now finally waking up. "A gang this huge—and it's definitely huge—must have informants everywhere, including London. When they realize that further bloodshed might bring fresh troops to the Marsh, they may just take their losses and leave."

"But you don't think so?" Courtland asked.

Chance smiled at him. "No, I don't think so. Not for one skirmish. We have to whip them, whip them soundly, just once. And it would be fortunate, indeed, if we were to capture a few of them, question them."

"So that we actually gain ammunition we could use against the rest of them? The leaders, those in London?" Ainsley asked, apparently without needing an answer. "We question the prisoners, get what bits of information we can from them, then send them back to their leaders with a message. An offer of a truce. They leave Romney Marsh alone or the next time, anyone captured will be trussed up and delivered directly to London, a list of the names of his cohorts pinned to his chest."

"And it's true that only a fool would try to navigate the Marsh without locals to guide them. The entire area is useless to them if we band together, refuse to join them. So why keep fighting, right?" Courtland said, then looked from one man to the other. "And this will actually work?"

"Ainsley?" Chance said, grinning, because three-fourths of the plan was based on a similar triumph Ainsley had managed in the islands, years ago—a triumph that had ended in actually "dividing" the sea into exclusive areas of operation. Speak certainly, act boldly, back up your words and defeat someone else very, very decisively to prove your point and discourage further argument. Fight once and well, and your reputation does the fighting for you in the future. "Do you want to answer that for the halfling?"

"Sit down, Court," Ainsley ordered quietly as Courtland took two quick steps toward Chance, his hands drawn up into fists. "Yes, Court, it could work. If we handle ourselves correctly, it *will* work. But only until the war is over and there's no longer so much official attention paid to the revenue lost due to smuggling. Then, I would guess, freebooting will go back to the accepted activity it's been for centuries. At which time all bets will be off and we'll see these Red Men again."

Chance got to his feet, still eager to see Julia, although he had rather enjoyed his meeting with Ainsley. Their minds worked so very much alike and always had. "I've one thing more for you," he said, reaching inside his jacket and pulling out a folded vellum sheet.

Ainsley took the sheet and unfolded it in front of him. "This is your handwriting, Chance."

"Yes, but not my words. I was fortunate enough to discover the original pages in the pocket of one Captain Flagg. I returned it, of course."

"You picked the fellow's pocket, you mean, copied this note and then returned the originals." Ainsley sat back, shook his head as he grinned at Chance. "A trick once well learned is never quite forgotten."

"Or once a thief, always a thief. You could have been caught. Had you thought about that?"

"Ah, but I wasn't, was I, Court? Still, thank you for worrying for me. I'm touched, really I am."

Courtland made a rather rude noise in his throat. "What's in the note?"

Ainsley employed a large magnifying glass, for Chance had transferred quite a lot of information to one easily hidden page. "The land and sea deployments of every dragoon and Waterguard up and down the coast, which Martello Towers are fully manned. Where they are, how many there are, their patrol hours." He laid down the paper. "All that's lacking is a list of pubs where the soldiers do their drinking."

"Billy has that information," Chance said, grinning and feeling like a child who has just pleased his teacher.

"And this captain carried all this information with him? Why?"

"To please me, I suppose, Court, as we met for dinner at a local inn in order to discuss just these matters. Very pleasant inn. We had a private dining room so we were quite isolated, although Captain Flagg's oysters didn't sit well with him and he had to excuse himself to the privy for a good half hour, poor man."

Now even Courtland looked impressed. "You snagged the information, slipped something into his drink, copied the information while he was puking his guts out, then returned the original to his pocket when he came back—all without him knowing?"

Chance bowed to his brother. "That's pretty much the way of it, I'd say. And if that's all for now…?"

"Is it?" Ainsley asked, raising one expressive eyebrow as he looked up at Chance.

Chance shifted from one foot to the other, eager to be out of the room. "No, it's not. Billy made himself some new friends in a few pubs along the way, along with one very interesting connection with a drab who goes by the name of Laughing Sally, who swears to know the when and where of the next large Red Men Gang operation on the Marsh."

He grinned to see Court actually looking at him with something grudgingly close to admiration. And about damn time his brother understood that a black silk cape, a willing heart and the purest of intentions weren't nearly enough to succeed in a dangerous world. Isabella had coddled Courtland, then Ainsley had ignored him. Somebody had to take the idiot in hand, and Chance had decided he'd been elected to that post.

"I'd like to hear about this Laughing Sally," Ainsley said.

Chance sighed. "I know. But if you don't mind, I'll let Billy tell you all he learned once someone pries him out of the *Last Voyage*. Which will probably be sometime tomorrow."

"Very well, I've detained you long enough. I believe Julia is in the main salon with Eleanor, embroidering," Ainsley said, already sliding one of his ever-present maps toward him. "Court, come over here. Show me where you would propose we engage the enemy. Here, perhaps—or maybe here?"

Chance smiled as he made good his escape from the study, leaving Courtland behind and in the very good hands of Cap'n Geoffrey Baskin, one of the great masters of strategy. And with the Cap'n back, Jacko would not be far behind. Add Billy to the mix, and Courtland would be very shortly whipped into shape, leaving Chance much more time to be with Julia.

"Embroidering," he muttered to himself as he made his way to the main saloon. "I'll soon put a stop to that."

CHAPTER NINETEEN

JULIA SENSED HIM BEFORE she saw him. Suddenly the air seemed charged with tension, an awareness that she was no longer alone in the main salon, that Chance Becket had returned.

She recognized his sure step on the parquet floor, felt the frisson of awareness she'd felt from their first encounter turn her body cold, then almost uncomfortably warm. Her heart beat faster, and she had to concentrate to control her breathing.

Nobody should have such an intense effect on another person. If not sinful, it was at the very least criminal.

Breathe in, she commanded herself, *breathe out.*

Should she stay bent over the pillowcase she was embroidering and force him to approach her, speak first?

Should she lift her chin and give him a bright, impersonal greeting, just to let him know she hadn't been sitting here for the past four days pining for him?

Did she dare stand up, meet him halfway, throw her arms around him, as if she assumed he had missed her, too?

Julia already knew the answer to that last question. No, she didn't dare. She wasn't sure if his absence had made her heart grow fonder, but she did know his absence had given her time to reflect, consider…and realize that her outrageous behavior with the man could neither be explained nor justified.

Although that behavior could be definitely remembered each waking moment and treasured most when she climbed into her bed at night and held tight the pillow he had lain on, the one that still held his sharp, clean scent.…

Contrary woman, Chance thought, smiling, *pretending she doesn't know I'm here. While I remind myself that it isn't gentlemanly to* pounce.

"Good afternoon, Julia," he drawled as he skirted around one of the couches and approached her. "My, my, don't you look domestic? And what have we here? The letters *C* and *J,* all daintily entwined in ivy. Very nice. Your own design? I must say I'm very flattered."

Julia sighed. He had to know she was only embroidering these silly initials under protest. Why hadn't she considered one more alternative? Boxing his ears, for instance, certainly held a great appeal.

Putting down the offending pillowcase and covering the embroidered hem with her hands, Julia glared up at him. "And to think it was so peaceful here these past few days with you gone. I imagine I—"

Julia completely forgot what she was going to say. Chance was looking at her so oddly. As if she were familiar to him and yet also a stranger. His expression seemed part knowing, part inquisitive.

She stared back. What else was there to do? She felt her blood heat even more as her heartbeat doubled. Her body was betraying her.

But Chance's intense stare wasn't the worst of it—
or the best of it. He looked…he looked so…so *alive*. His
shirt collar lay open beneath his deep green coat and
white-on-white waistcoat, the leather strip holding his
gad visible amid the tangle of golden curls on his chest.

He smelled of the sea, of the sun. His collar-length
hair hung free, with one heavy lock falling onto his
cheek, and had lightened a little, as if streaked with sunlight, while his skin had gone a golden tan. Even his
eyes looked greener.

The man. The man beneath the gentlemanly facade.
The true Chance Becket.

Julia wanted to close her eyes, burn the sight of him
this way into her brain. But all she could do was look
at him while he looked at her and the clock continued
it's steady ticktock on the mantel….

Chance realized he should say something. If he could
get any words past the sudden constriction in his chest.
"And there they are," he teased, "those incredible green
eyes. That proud chin. And, of course, one can always
depend on your sweet nature and kind words."

And then he lowered his voice and succumbed to
honesty as he held out his hand to her. "God, Julia—I
had no idea I'd miss you so much."

Julia took his hand and let him guide her to her feet,
the pillowcase slipping to the floor unnoticed. How did
the man do it? How did he always seem to know exactly
the words she would find impossible to resist? Was he
that convincing? Or was she that eager to be convinced?

He began backing toward the hallway, both her hands
in his now as he smiled down at her, drew her along with

him, not really using the hold he had on her hands but with the sheer power in his stormy eyes.

"You…you'll trip over Eleanor's footstool," Julia told him, wetting her dry lips with the tip of her tongue before she could speak. "Where are we going?"

Chance released her right hand, drew her forward so that he could turn and walk beside her, his moves graceful, like steps in a dance. "You know where we're going, Julia," he said in a low, intimate tone. "Even if you only want me half as much as I want you, you couldn't want anything else."

There was no answer to that, so Julia didn't bother to offer one, and a denial was out of the question. "It's only the middle of the day…"

Chance smiled at this feeble protest. "Yes, I know. Do you think we're going to shock everyone if we don't reappear until tomorrow morning?"

Julia was beginning to enjoy herself as they entered the hallway. After all, she was a practical woman, and there certainly was no point in playing the nervous virgin, was there? "I doubt much shocks you Beckets. Besides, I have no intentions of disappearing for any such scandalous length of time. That's ridiculous."

Chance leaned close to whisper in her ear. "Ah, sweetheart, not if you knew what I've been considering these past few days. How I would kiss you for an hour, simply kiss your mouth. How I'd nibble on your bottom lip, then draw it into my own mouth, suckle on your sweetness. How I'd trace those lovely ears of yours with my tongue and then dip inside to—"

"Well, look what the tide brought in. Hello, Chance.

Rian said you probably wouldn't be home until tomorrow. He wants to speak to you, nag you into buying him a commission now that the Frenchies have been chased back to Spain. You won't, will you? Papa says it's not to be thought of because Rian's still such a clumsy ape, but—"

"Later, Fanny," Chance said, watching as Julia seemed to swallow with some difficulty while blinking furiously. "Julia and I have something to discuss right now."

"Yes, but—"

"*Later,* Fanny," Chance growled, and Julia pushed her face into his shoulder, caught between laugher and horrid embarrassment.

Chance led her up the wide staircase, his arm around her as Julia wondered if she could ever face Fanny or any of the Beckets again after this bit of folly. Being taken off in the middle of the day—going willingly, even eagerly—to perform carnal acts with a man not her husband. She was going to be so ashamed. Later.

"I suppose I should tell Alice you're back," Fanny called up the stairs. "They're playing hide-and-seek in the greenhouse, she and Callie, so I'll just go out there and—you're not listening to me, are you, Chance Becket? Not listening to a single word!"

Chance turned at the top of the stairs and waved at his sister, who stood glaring up at him, her fists jammed against her hips, then bent to lift Julia into his arms, to carry her down the hallway to her bedchamber.

"Did she see you do that?" Julia asked, her face now buried against his chest. "I suppose you'd want Fanny to allow a man to treat her the way you're treating me?"

"I'd tan her hide and lock her in the cellars," Chance said, grinning.

"Oh!" Julia exclaimed as Chance bent his knees so that he could reach the handle of the door to her bedchamber. "If that isn't the most despicable thing you've ever said to me. All but announcing to the world that I'm your willing mistress—and, no, we will *not* consider the ring you tricked me into accepting or those wretched pillowcases Elly has me embroidering. But your sisters? Oh, no. No such fate for them. Only for me, only for the defenseless, orphaned, unprotected—"

Chance kicked the door shut, then put Julia down. "One, you are far from defenseless just as long as you have a tongue in your head, and well I know that. Two, yes, you're orphaned, but you are not unprotected. Ainsley would have my liver on a stick if I hadn't sworn to marry you, make an honest woman of you."

Julia opened her mouth to speak, then shut it again.

"What? I know you want to say something. Please, say it—" Chance coaxed, stepping closer to her to take hold of one end of the ribbon holding her hair tight at her nape and pulling on it slowly so that her hair swung free against her shoulders. "Tell me again that you plan to leave here the very moment you're sure Alice is settled, never to see me again. Never to let me do this again…"

Julia closed her eyes and mentally flayed herself for the soft moan that escaped her lips as Chance bent to whisper those last words into her ear, his sweet breath warm against her skin.

"Or this…" he continued, sliding his hands up her rib cage until he could stroke his thumbs over her nipples through the soft muslin of her gown.

"Don't…don't do that," Julia said, easing against him. *Don't stop doing that…*

"Do you mean that?" Chance asked against her throat, aware that his words sounded rather slurred, as if he were slightly foxed. And maybe he *was* drunk. Intoxicated with the sight of her, the taste of her, the feel of her. "Because, if you really mean that, Julia, I'll—"

Julia raised her hands to his face, pushed her palms tight against his cheeks. "Will you just please shut up? Isn't it embarrassing enough that you're here without making me say no, I don't want you to leave? Or are you simply mean?"

Chance's smile grew slowly as he took hold of her hands, then placed a kiss in each palm as he looked deeply into her eyes. "I do admire an honest woman," he said, then scooped her up in his arms once more and carried her to the bed.

"Wait," Julia said, pushing herself up on her elbows. "I'm not ready. The drapes are all open, for one thing. And if I have to hand over one more wrinkled gown to be pressed, I'll have to begin wearing a sack over my head to hide my blushes."

"If you'd finish embroidering that pillowcase, you could use that," Chance suggested as he watched Julia clamber from the bed, then turn her back to him. "I suppose I'm to play lady's maid and undo those buttons?"

Julia was caught between wanting to tell him to leave and grabbing Chance by the shoulders to physically toss him onto the bed. Did he know that? Of course he did. Just as he knew she would be cutting off her own nose to spite her face if she did tell him to leave. So he was teasing with her, perhaps to prove to himself how much she wanted him—or possibly to prolong the moment?

Because as she stood there, her hands drawn up into fists at her sides, breathing heavily in her need to hold him, to have him…he was slowly opening the row of buttons on the back of her gown, placing a soft kiss on each new inch of skin that was revealed.

Torture. Sweet torture.

She allowed her head to drop forward as he pushed her hair out of the way, trailed kisses across her shoulder blades as the gown sank, forgotten, to the carpet.

His hands on her shoulders. Inching away her undergarment, until she felt the cool air on her and saw that she was now naked to the waist.

Then she watched, holding her breath, as he eased against her back, slipped his arms around her. Cupped her breasts in his hands, using the pads of his thumbs to once more tease at her nipples.

Julia swallowed with some effort, then watched, amazed, as her body began to respond to him, flower beneath his touch.

Had she actually asked him to shut the heavy velvet drapes, throw her bedchamber into deep shadow, rather than stand here in the sunlight that still filtered in through the sheer white panels on the windows? How marvelous that he had ignored her…

With his lips still teasing her nape, his teeth nipping

gently at her skin, he somehow managed to push her chemise down and over her hips so that now she was standing in a puddle of sprigged muslin and lace. Entirely naked.

She felt a tightness between her legs, a gentle burning followed by the urge to move her hips, to push her legs tighter together, to savor the sensation that built there.

And still Chance was behind her. She could feel his clothing against her bare skin even as he gently insinuated his thigh slightly between her legs.

"I...I think we should..."

Whatever she'd thought to say was cut off by her gasp as Chance moved his hands lower, his fingers splayed as he slid those hands down her rib cage, her belly. She watched as he circled her navel with one finger, then dipped it inside, instantly tautening the cord of desire that had already been pulled tight between her breasts and her groin.

Her skin felt like warm silk beneath Chance's hands as his mind tumbled with tense, disjointed commands from his own body. His own hands looked so huge on her slim body. Capable of spanning her hip bones. *Touch her. Taste her. Here. Now. In the light of day. Teach her, learn her every secret.*

Chance's manhood strained almost painfully against the buttons of his breeches, but he wasn't about to give in to his own passion. Not yet. Not when Julia pressed her head back against his shoulder, moaning softly as he realized he could keep his last finger occupied in teasing her navel, even while he could span her well enough that he could travel over her taut nipples with his thumb.

And more. Holding her upper body this way with one hand, he slid the other lower to cup her soft blond mound...and then dip his fingers into that warm nest and find her very center.

Naked, against his body. Marginally opening her legs as he watched what he was doing to her, watched her reaction even as he licked at the sensitive skin behind her earlobe.

"I can't...I can't..."

"I know, sweetings, I know," Chance said, his own breathing shallow.

Reluctantly he released her, then backed her toward the bed once more, shocked into a grin when she nearly fell, as she was still ankle-deep in her clothing, then pushed her down on the bed, her legs hanging over the side of the high mattress.

He went to work on his own buttons, ripping at them like a madman, his fingers clumsy, his heart pounding as if he'd just rowed across the width of the Channel. Never. Never had he felt like this. Wanted like this. Needed to please more than he wanted to be pleased. Never...

Julia lay back, her eyes closed, lost in a sensual mist that promised to keep her senses swimming too deep for her common sense to effect a rescue. Only belatedly did she realize she was only half on the mattress, but by then Chance's hands were on her again, spreading her thighs.

Blindly she reached for him, and her fingers tangled in the thick, warm length of his hair. Julia's eyes shot open and she gasped as she realized that he was kneeling between her legs.

"No," she said, the sound of her voice coming to her as if from a distance. "Don't..."

But there was no stopping him. She could feel him parting her with his fingers. And then his mouth, warm and moist, sealing over her. Drawing on her sensitive, swollen flesh in a kiss that condensed her entire world into this most intimate union.

And then she felt his tongue, pleasantly rough, delving deeper, finding a part of her she never knew existed, rubbing her there, his tongue moving faster, faster, even as he drew all of her more closely against him.

She felt an incredible, nearly undeniable urge to raise her hips, to wrap her legs about him. But if she moved even a little, he might stop. And it was important above everything else in the entire universe that he did not stop.

Because nothing had been like this, would ever be like this. Bliss like this wasn't meant to be survived. But if this was death, she welcomed it.

Instead of tightening, yearning against him, Julia gave in to the inevitable and relaxed her body, her legs falling completely open to him to do with her whatever he wanted. Anything, everything. She was his.

She felt his finger tease at her, then slide inside. Deep. Impaling her even as he began to move his tongue in tight circles around her, so that the darkness behind her eyelids suddenly seemed bright blue and then sparkling white, then blended into all the colors of the rainbow.

His hands, his mouth. Everywhere. All she could give him, all he was giving her. Spiraling out of control, moving faster, faster, the sensations higher, tighter, better when better was impossible. And better yet.

And then, still marveling, she died....

CHAPTER Twenty

THE SUN HAD ABANDONED the windows on its daily trek west, leaving Julia's bedchamber in soft shadows. Chance lay on his back, Julia's head against his chest, stroking her hair as she told him about her father, holding nothing back, including her own involvement with the local freebooters. And then, all seemed just the just

CHAPTER TWENTY

THE SUN HAD ABANDONED the windows on its daily trek west, leaving Julia's bedchamber in soft shadows.

Chance lay on his back, Julia's head against his chest, stroking her hair as she told him about her father, holding nothing back, including her own involvement with the local freebooters.

"...and the church officials wanted everything kept quiet more than they wanted to punish a dead man, as Papa's actions could raise more questions than they wished to answer," Julia said, sighing. "I don't know why I thought I had to tell you, but I do feel better now that you know everything about me, about Papa."

"And you said Jacko knows?"

Julia smiled softly. "He's really a very sweet man, at the bottom of it."

Chance had to bite back an outright laugh. "Jacko? Have you taken up strong drink in my short absence, woman? Jacko does what Jacko does, but never tell anyone you think he's *sweet*. He'd have no other choice but to kill you."

Chance's smile faded as he looked up at the ornate ceiling, knowing that he was only avoiding the inevitable. He was now all but honor bound to share some secret with Julia. Women expected that, especially after sex. A confidence for a confidence—why, he didn't know. And yet just this once he felt a similar urge to unburden himself.

"I wasn't exactly ripped from a loving home when Ainsley found me. My mother had years earlier lost a knife fight with another wharf slut while everyone in the taproom looked on, cheering. At least I think she was my mother. I don't remember her name, just that she was Angelo's woman, the way I was Angelo's brat. I may not have belonged to either one of them."

He lowered his voice, for he knew that, in truth, Chance Becket was a nameless nobody, no matter how far he'd come in life. "God knows I don't know—and I don't care."

Julia felt tears sting her eyes at the thought of that long-ago child, the life he had led before Ainsley took him in, even as she quietly rejoiced that he was willing to tell her something so very personally painful. Because Chance was lying—to her, to himself—because he *did* care. His childhood had left wounds still not completely healed.

Julia felt an almost irrational need to heal those wounds for him. But would he let her? Would he ever let anyone that close? He shared her bed, yes, he'd even given her a ring, insisted they marry to protect her—both her safety and her reputation. As if she *had* a reputation to protect.

But never a word of love. Earlier, when he'd first seen her in the main salon, he'd even seemed surprised to realize that he'd missed her.

Marriage to Chance Becket would rescue her from penury, keep her close to Alice…keep her close to him. Still, Julia couldn't accept everything he offered, not as long as he still kept so much of himself hidden and hurting in the past.

"Ainsley's your father in all the ways that count," she said at last, looking up at him.

"I know," Chance said, then grinned, because he didn't care to feel maudlin, not with Julia lying here beside him. "And Billy's my mother."

"And don't forget dear, sweet *Uncle* Jacko," Julia said, trying to match his teasing tone.

"Jacko named me, you know. Second Chance. And I took advantage of that chance in every way I could."

"They're all very proud of you."

Chance sniffed, shook his head. "Not of all of me," he said, a trace of bitterness in his tone now. "I'm not, either." He sat up more against the pillows, pulling Julia up with him. "Do you know I often wondered if Alice is my own child? That first day, when you said she looked so much like me, I was shocked. Nearly struck speechless, because suddenly I realized that it didn't matter. None of the Beckets are Ainsley's except for Cassandra. And *it doesn't matter.* Alice is my daughter, and I love her."

Julia tried to wipe at her eyes without Chance noticing that he had brought her to tears. "Alice loves you very much."

"I know. I'm one damn lucky man. I'm simply telling you what a stupid ass I can be sometimes. A stupid, blind ass." He laid his fingers against her bare breast. "What's this?"

Julia looked down at the small cut. She'd felt it, of course, but had ignored the pain, as the pleasure had been so much more compelling. "My *gad* bit me," she said, sniffing away the last of her tears.

"Or mine. Damn stupid tooth, that's all it is," Chance said, sitting up to lift the leather cord over his head as she also removed her own—the only differences between the two being that her *gad* was on a golden chain and she'd tied the black grosgrain ribbon to it. "Were you just humoring Odette?"

Unashamed of her nakedness, Julia lay down against Chance once more. "As a clergyman's daughter, I should say yes, shouldn't I?"

"But someone's been telling you stories about Odette's powers?"

"A few," Julia said, nodding. "Callie's extremely impressed with Odette's...abilities."

"I imagine Alice has her own *gad* by now?"

"Oh, I would think so. And that's another subject for another time, if you don't mind?"

Chance cupped his hand around her breast. "Not at all, as long as you stay here," he said, watching her reaction as he lightly pinched her nipple between his fingers.

Julia drew a shaky breath. "You're trying to distract me because I'm asking too many questions."

"I'd say that was a brilliant deduction, but I think I'm being too obvious. Very well," he said, fully prepared to continue dodging her questions. He lifted a finger to his mouth, moistened it, then returned to slide the tip over her already aroused nipple. "What else do you want to know?"

"I…I'm trying to remember," Julia said, struggling to control her breathing. "Mmm." She sighed in pleasure, then pushed on. "Tell me about Becket Hall."

"Must I?" Chance asked, employing his free hand to lightly tickle the side of her neck. "Aren't you finding me irresistible?"

If he could tease, then so could she. "I'm not going to answer that. I'd prefer to convince myself that I was kidnapped this afternoon, completely against my wishes, of course, and am only hoping to keep you talking so that you don't ravish me again," Julia said, returning his touch by laying her palm flat against his lower belly. "But I don't think that's working, do you? Tell me about Becket Hall."

Chance felt himself begin to rouse as the heat of Julia's palm seemed to make his temperature rise. "Not fair, not fair. All right, I'll tell you about Becket Hall. But I fully expect a reward."

Julia moved her hand a fraction lower, delighted to see her effect on him. "That's only to be expected."

"Then I'll make this quick," Chance said, amazed yet thrilled by Julia's bold advances. "Ainsley ordered Becket Hall built long before we arrived here. We all knew he was preparing us to leave the…leave the sea. Anyway, he was forever poring over plans, shipping furniture, bits of art, fabrics and the rest here on one of his own ships, along with copious instructions for the hapless man he'd put in charge."

"He had everything planned?"

"Ainsley always has everything planned—or at least he used to. He stepped up the work once he'd brought

Morgan home as a newborn, as he believed where we were was no place to raise up a daughter. Then there was Fanny, and then Ainsley married. In fact, we were to leave for England in only a week or so when—"

She was distracting him, using her naive skills with more effect than Odette worked her magic. He'd almost told her. And he couldn't deny that he felt a strong desire to tell her, tell her everything. But he wasn't ready to allow her that deeply into his life. He might never be ready to share those last days with anyone. "That's enough for now."

Julia felt his tension and searched for something to say that would take the pain from his voice. "Does Elly know about Becket Hall? What you told me, I mean."

"That's a strange question. Of course she does. Why?"

Julia thought about the tall tale Eleanor had woven for her benefit, about how Ainsley had seen the mansion from his ship, then rowed ashore to purchase it out of hand.

Obviously Eleanor still did not trust her. Either that or she had another reason to want the world to think she was no more than a very sweet, shy, domestic and presumably uninformed creature. Except when she ruled her siblings with a soft word, a simple gesture. There was that, wasn't there?

"Oh, no reason," Julia said, pushing on to another question. "You're so very informal here. When I told Morgan I was sure she'd have to deal with quite a few more rules in London, she said then she simply wouldn't go." Julia looked up at him and winced. "I was to tell you that."

"She'll go," Chance said confidently. "Once she hears I'm planning to provide her with an entire new wardrobe. She may clomp about like a filly in a muddy field, but she does love her clothes, almost as much as she enjoys being admired." He shifted slightly onto his side, cupped her breast more fully. "Now...where were we?"

"Yes, where were we?" Julia asked, suddenly nervous again, which was silly, incredibly silly. "Oh, I know. I was just about to climb out of bed to get washed and dressed for dinner. I believe I'm famished."

She attempted to rise, and Chance grabbed her, pulled her down beside him once more. "The devil you were. In fact, I seem to remember someone saying something about a *reward* if I answered your questions. Do you remember that, Julia?"

Of course she did. Why else was she so suddenly nervous?

But then again, after he had touched her so intimately, she *had* been curious about what it would be like to...

Julia bent her head so that she could watch as she slowly brought her hand lower, slipped her fingers around him, lifting him slightly as she slid her hand up his shaft, then down again. He seemed to grow in her grasp.

Her breaths became shallow, more rapid, even as her curiosity mingled with some other, deeper emotion. "It's...you're so... My goodness, I had no idea."

"You're intimidated?" Chance asked, fairly certain he never before had been both so embarrassed and so aroused at the same time.

"Nooo," Julia said slowly, consideringly. "I...I think

I rather like it, the way you feel. So strong and yet so soft, so…silky. So clever, the way we're fashioned, isn't it? To fit together so perfectly, like two halves of the same whole." She stroked upward again, placing her finger directly on top of him. "So silky…"

"Oh, for the sweet love of heaven," Chance all but gasped out as he sat forward and grabbed her by the shoulders, turning her so that he could cover her with his body. He looked down at her. "Do you have any idea what you just did?"

Julia's heart was pounding now. "I didn't *do* anything. I was going to, but—what's that?"

Chance lifted his head, heard it, too. "Someone's coming," he said, quickly pulling up the covers to hide their bare bodies. "And calling your name."

"Alice?" Julia said, her eyes widening. "Oh, God, it's Alice." She pushed at Chance's shoulder. "Quickly, get yourself out of my bed."

"And do what, sweetings, scurry beneath it? And then there's the small matter of my clothing strewn everywhere and—ah, too late."

They both lay on their backs now, propped against the pillows, the coverlet drawn up beneath their chins, as Alice burst into the bedchamber.

"Julia! Julia, come quickly! Callie is lost! Maybe someone bad took her! She was hiding, we were playing a game, and now she's gone and—Papa? What are you doing in Julia's bed, Papa? It's not time for bed."

"Oh, God," Julia said, wishing she could just pull the covers over her head and stay there until she was old and gray.

"Never mind that, Alice," Chance said. "How long has Callie been gone? Maybe you simply couldn't find her? Maybe she hid herself too well?"

Alice shook her head violently. "I *looked*, Papa, I looked forever. And I called and called, but she didn't answer. She's lost. Papa Ainsley has gone looking. Everyone has gone looking. And *they've* been looking forever."

"Damn and blast," Chance muttered under his breath. "All right, Alice, Julia and I will look, too. You…you just go downstairs and wait for us, all right?"

"All right. But why are you in Julia's—"

"Later, Alice. *Go*."

Alice nodded, sniffling, then left, closing the door behind her.

Chance was out of the bed even before the door closed. "Ainsley must be half out of his mind. His sun rises and sets on Callie. Jacko told me Ainsley's let her run wild, probably because she looks so much like her mother. And this is the reward he gets for such indulgence. Please remind me to beat Alice on a regular basis, all right?"

Julia was out of the bed an instant later. "Do you think Callie may have hidden herself near the sands? The grasses are so deep, the rushes—but you said she knows not to go on the sands."

Chance pulled on his clothing, cursing again when he saw that his shirt was now missing two buttons. "She's teasing Alice, that's all, and scaring the wits out of Ainsley, who probably deserves it. And when Court or I get our hands on her—"

"You're already assuming Callie's playing a trick on Alice?" Julia asked, turning her back to him so that he could button her gown. "Isn't that assuming too much?"

"With that little hellion, a person can never assume too much. Even Elly can't control her, and Odette threw up her hands years ago," Chance told her, taking her hand in order to head downstairs, only to have her break free because she still hadn't found her second shoe. "Good thing the house isn't on fire or you'd burn to a crisp. Although I suppose you should probably comb your hair?"

"You can be exceedingly annoying, you know," Julia told him truthfully and then raced to her dressing table to drag a brush through her hair before turning on him, eying him up and down. "And you, Mr. Ready, might want to consider buttoning your breeches."

Chance looked down at himself. "Damn."

"Indeed. And what are we going to tell Alice?"

"Nothing, unless she asks again. Then you can take care of it."

"*Me?* Why me?"

Chance smiled quickly. "It wasn't *my* bed."

"No, it wasn't, was it?" Julia stamped her foot more firmly into her shoe. "And you won't be back in that bed again, Chance Becket. You coward!"

"Guilty as charged," he said, pushing his arms into the sleeves of his coat. "Turn around once more, let me see if you're entirely decent."

"More decent than you," Julia said through gritted teeth, then did as he said before returning the favor.

Once satisfied that neither of them would embarrass

themselves or frighten Alice with their appearance, they headed down the front staircase just in time to see Ainsley hobbling in from the outside, leaning heavily on Rian.

"What in the hell—?"

"He stepped into a hole on the beach and injured his ankle. We don't think it's broken, though," Rian said, holding on to Ainsley's wrist, as Ainsley's arm was draped across his son's shoulders. "You want to stand there and watch or do you want to help?"

Chance immediately went to Ainsley's other side, offering his support. "Callie?"

"Found her, over in the village, perched fine as you please on Judah's counter, eating rock candy. Court's got her outside now, tearing a strip off her hide."

Julia came to attention. She'd thought Chance had been teasing her with all that talk of beatings, his hint at what he or Courtland would do when they found Callie. What, after all, did she know about this curious family and their customs? "He's—is he *beating* her?"

"She deserves a good hiding, don't you think?" Chance said, both surprised and angry that Julia would immediately believe they were some sort of savages, the kind that would physically harm a child. Especially Courtland, who knew firsthand what it felt like to have the strap against his back.

But if that's what she wanted to think, then he'd leave her to her rash conclusions and her damning expression. He turned his back on that damning expression to help Ainsley into the main salon, where Eleanor waited, calmly giving out orders to one of the maids to fetch hot water, bandages and Odette, and not in that order.

"She was only playing a trick on Alice," Julia argued, following after them. "She never could have realized that her little prank would have such…such consequences."

Ainsley winced as his sons lowered him into a chair, and Eleanor rushed to install a footstool beneath his left ankle.

"Actions have consequences, Julia," Ainsley said. "Callie's reckless decision has consequences. My foolish panic for my daughter's safety had its consequences. We will have both of us learned a lesson in consequences today."

"But…but surely you aren't going to let Court punish her like that, make her—"

"Julia, this is none of your concern," Chance said, knowing now was not the time to explain the rules of survival to her. "We have to be able to depend on each other here. Callie has to learn that. Now why don't you and your delicate sensibilities take yourselves off upstairs?"

Eleanor looked up at Julia. "Callie will be fine," she assured Julia, who quickly decided that the Beckets were all bordering on the edge of madness. All of them.

"I will *not* stand by while Court hits that child. I'm going to put a stop to this right now."

"Julia!" Chance called out, before Ainsley grabbed his arm.

"Let her go, son. She's already drawn her own conclusions. And Cassandra must be punished."

Julia heard Ainsley and was tempted to stop, turn

around, and give him a piece of her mind. But there was no time for that. Punishing a child for being a child? Ludicrous!

She pulled open the heavy front door and raced out onto the stone porch, looking to her left, then her right, hoping to see Cassandra and Courtland. And there they were, sitting with their backs to her just on the bottom step, talking quietly.

"So you'll apologize to Alice," Courtland was saying to her, looking toward the horizon, as was Cassandra.

"I said I would, yes. And to Papa, too. Why did he go running like that, Court?"

"Your papa loves you very much and he couldn't bear losing you."

"I wasn't lost. I was hiding from Alice. It was a *game.*"

"Really? And does it still feel like a game?"

Cassandra shook her head, her windblown curls bouncing. "I didn't think Papa would be so upset. I didn't think anyone would be so upset." She turned to look up at Courtland. "Are you upset?"

"No, I'm disappointed. I thought you were growing up, Cassandra, that you understood the rules, but now I know you're still a child."

Julia closed her hands into tight fists. Of course Cassandra was a child. Only thirteen! What did he expect from her?

Julia noticed that Cassandra hadn't answered Courtland. And then she saw Courtland sigh and hand the child his handkerchief.

Cassandra buried her face in the fine white linen.

"I won't do anything so silly again, Court, I promise."

"Not silly, Cassandra. Dangerous."

"Yes, yes, whatever you say. I don't ever want you to be disappointed in me. Not ever." She lowered the handkerchief and looked at him, her young heart painfully visible in her eyes. "I love you, Court. You know I love you."

Julia watched as Courtland's spine seemed to stiffen. *Oh yes, Callie,* she thought, *he knows that.*

"God's teeth," Courtland said, a man on the verge of losing control. "Just what I don't need—your silly love. Now go apologize to your papa and Alice and everyone else. And be in the scullery straight after dinner to scrub the pots. For two weeks, Cassandra, that's your punishment. You're in the scullery for a full fortnight, and remember that Bumble expects no half measures or you'll feel the back of his spoon across the back of your head."

"I hate you," Cassandra said, jumping to her feet as she threw the handkerchief at him. "I hate, hate, *hate* you and I'm never going to speak to you again!"

"If only that were true," Courtland called after her, then slammed his palms hard against either side of his head. *"Damn it."*

Julia stepped against the wall as Cassandra raced up the steps, sobbing wildly as she disappeared into the house.

"That couldn't have been easy. I'm sorry I was here to overhear you, but I thought you were going to beat her," Julia said when Courtland slowly got to his feet and saw her, at which time his tormented expression went perfectly blank.

"Did you now, Julia? Maybe I should have. A good spanking would have been less painful—for both of us," he said as he climbed toward her.

"So her *consequences* are a few apologies and two weeks as scullery maid?"

He stopped to look at her. "A paltry punishment, isn't it? But we're not at sea, so I couldn't order her keelhauled," he said with a faint smile.

"I think Chance would have spanked her," Julia told him as he paused on the step just below hers. "Ainsley, too."

"Chance? Oh, I doubt that. Chance is more likely to ring a long, loud peal over her head, I'd think, and Ainsley has a way of speaking quietly and reasonably that makes a person feel lower than barnacles on the hull of a sunken ship."

"But they seemed to think that's what you were going to do. Spank her, I mean." She frowned, thinking back. "Or at least I thought they meant that...."

"And maybe I would have swatted her behind a few times if I believed it would help. Unfortunately withdrawing my...my affection seems to work best with Cassandra. She won't do anything so potentially dangerously again. Do you realize how many treacherous places there are around here, not to mention the possibility of strangers in the area? She knew her boundaries, where she's allowed without one of us with her, and she deliberately went outside them. And now, Julia, if you'll excuse me, I think I'd like a full decanter and a deep glass. Playing the heartless bastard is thirsty work."

Julia remained leaning against the wall of the immense mansion, considering the relationship between Courtland and the young Cassandra. That it was a complicated relationship was obvious to her. Was it obvious to anyone else?

Becket Hall was a household of individuals, each with their own past, their own secrets, and all of them banded together to turn as one against anyone or anything that threatened the whole—even if that someone was one of them.

Cassandra's innocent prank had caused an unforeseen accident to Ainsley Becket, as well as badly frightening Alice, and for that Cassandra had to be punished. She'd weakened the "whole."

And Chance? One moment they had been so close, so intimate, so in tune with each other. He had begun to talk to her, to tell her some things about his past, just as if he trusted her. And the next moment? The next moment she had been the outsider again, told to take herself off as the Beckets closed ranks.

And she'd expected it. Perhaps even helped separate herself from, again, that "whole." Because as much as she wanted them all to trust her, how sure was she that she could trust *them?*

Trust Chance.

No matter how close the two of them became physically, he still didn't trust her enough, care for her enough, to truly let her into his life. Yes, he had begun to tell her some things. But he always monitored what he said and then stopped when he came close to revealing more.

If she wasn't allowed into his life, how could she ever believe she'd be welcomed into his heart? How could she fully welcome him into hers?

And that realization hurt. That hurt quite a lot.

CHAPTER TWENTY-ONE

"HOW'S THE CRIPPLE feeling today?" Chance asked, gesturing toward Ainsley's wrapped ankle as he lowered himself onto one of the leather couches in the study. "Still that swollen? It's been four days."

"I can count, Chance, and the swelling had been going down. Odette said the god-awful grease she smeared on me this morning would mean the last of it, but I'm beginning to think the woman's cursed me instead, because it's worse," Ainsley said, shifting slightly in his chair as he readjusted his foot on the tapestry footstool.

"Not you, Cap'n. You're her favorite," Chance said, grinning. "She'd never find a way to punish you for carelessly running across that stretch of shingle."

"I wish you sounded more convincing—and less amused. Oh, and Cassandra has asked Odette to make a *caprelata* especially fashioned from straw, some of Court's hair from his brushes, his ruby stickpin and several rather nasty herbs and other ingredients I really don't want to dwell on, frankly. Tell me, have you seen Court this morning? Is he looking at all sickly? I believe the idea was that his nose and ears should turn blue and drop off."

"Her mother's child," Chance said with a smile before he could stop himself. His smile faded. "I'm sorry."

"No, don't be. It's time, well past time, that everyone stops tiptoeing around me, leaving me free to selfishly wallow in my guilt and grief. For Isabella, for everyone hurt by my stupid, *stupid* misjudgment. Too many wasted years, Chance. For both of us. It's time to move on." He smiled up at his son. "Or do you really enjoy seeing Court and the others so abominably ill-suited for anything save standing on the shore, tossing stones into the Channel?"

"And hoping they won't miss?" Chance sat forward, resting his elbows on his knees. "Seriously, Cap'n, they can all ride and shoot tolerably well, although I'll agree they're more spirit and fire than common sense. They all seem to think with their hearts, not their heads. So you're serious? You're really going to take charge again?"

"I don't believe I have a choice. Jacko's been doing what he can with them, but he loses interest quickly when the rum calls him. Not that I'd ever want any of them depending on their wits and pistols. We've made a new life here, a different one. Safer. I foolishly believed that if they weren't raised as you were, didn't put themselves in danger, then they'd avoid danger. But sometimes danger comes to us whether we want it or not."

"This Red Men Gang."

"Yes. They worry me. Court's heartfelt but dangerous action has brought them too close to Becket Hall for any of us to be comfortable."

"You could leave, go somewhere else. Or do you still think you need to keep everyone here, in the back of beyond? I mean, it's been more than a dozen years. Even if some were to talk, brag in some pub about having sailed with the Black Ghost, especially on that last enterprise, no one would listen."

"Perhaps not. England has more to worry about than hunting down Geoffrey Baskin and his men. But we're settled here and have been safe. The problem, however, is that the girls will soon be ready to marry, and I'm selfish enough to want them to be able to choose from more than a few local dragoons. I understand you've invited Morgan to London for next year's season?"

"I'd take Elly, too, but she won't go."

"No, Eleanor and I have come to an agreement about that. She's much happier here."

"Because of her leg."

"I'm sure that plays a part in her decision, yes," Ainsley said, his tone mild, but Chance knew he wouldn't say anything more on the subject, just as they both knew there was much to say.

"Julia isn't speaking to me," Chance said, surprised to hear his own voice, because he certainly hadn't planned to say anything about his most vexing problem. "She's hiding behind Alice—and I'm allowing her to, which is fairly pathetic. But I don't know what else to do."

"Apologizing would, I imagine, be completely out of the question?"

Chance shoved his fingers through his hair, then pulled off the black grosgrain ribbon, holding it in his palm to look at it. He'd found the thing on his dresser two days ago. "I could do that, I suppose, if I knew what in blazes she was so angry about. But I don't."

Ainsley raised one expressive eyebrow as he looked at his oldest son. "Haven't the ghost of a notion, have you? I wonder, would that make you deaf, dumb and blind…or just thick as a post when it comes to females? And here I thought you were an educated gentleman, traveling about in London society."

"Julia's not like any woman I've met in London." Chance got to his feet, began to pace. "I gave her the ring. She has my word that I'll marry her. She could be very reasonably upset that I compromised her the way I did, but she doesn't exactly avoid my touch—at least she hadn't been." He spread his hands as he looked at Ainsley. "What else does she need?"

"Thick as a post," Ainsley said as if coming to a decision. He steepled his fingers in front of him and lightly tapped them against his chin. "Could it be, Chance, that Miss Carruthers wants more from you than your ring and your offer? Oh, and your *touch?*"

Chance knew where this conversation was heading. "I'm not ready for that, Ainsley. I've told her a few things, more than I've ever told anyone else—mostly because she plagues a man out of his mind with her questions. Besides, you just said we should forget the past."

"Did I? I don't think so. I said we need to move on with our lives. We'll never, none of us save the youngest ones, be able to forget the past, but we can forgive that time if we are to have any hope for the future.

That's why I'm so very pleased that you've come back, that we've been able to make amends. Why I'm so eager to take the boys in hand—the young men, for they are young men now. And most definitely why I want the girls settled, happy. You do believe you deserve to be happy, don't you, Chance?"

Chance folded his arms over his chest, began rubbing his hands on his upper arms as he looked toward the window, toward the Channel, the deep blue alive with small whitecaps from the wind as sunlight glittered on the surface. "I miss the sea. I tried to convince myself that I didn't, but going out on the *Respite* brought it all back. The wind, the smells, the deck under my feet. Even the creak of the rigging when I'm below deck, rocking in my hammock. That's the true siren song, you know."

"So is that it? Why you refuse to allow Julia too close? You want to return to the sea? Leave England?"

Chance turned to face Ainsley. Leave Julia? That thought had never occurred to him. And, he realized in some shock, never would. Never. "No, that's not what I meant. I turned my back on all of my former life. It's time to get some of that life back. I'm thinking of commissioning a sloop of my own, if you'll allow me to keep it anchored here."

"I see. Then perhaps in the meantime you'd be willing to go out on the *Respite* again?"

Chance waited for more, but nothing seemed to be forthcoming. "You have a particular time and place in mind?"

"I do, yes," Ainsley said, reaching for his wineglass,

his movement sure, subtly elegant, as Ainsley had always been elegant. The tall, slim body, the long, straight fingers. The quiet air of command. The man Chance had always so admired was very much in evidence again, even with his bandaged ankle on a pillow. The spirit was back, the *heart*. God, how Chance had missed him.

"I've overlooked something that's been happening under my nose, haven't I?"

"While mooning over that young woman of yours? Yes, I think you have. Billy's made another visit to this Laughing Sally person. I hesitate to say that he's indulging in a game of April and May, but I've been told he did endure a bath before he left yesterday."

"I suppose I should have taken the time to meet this woman who could be toying with Billy's affections. Not that Billy can't find himself a woman. I don't mean that. But not one he didn't have to pay for."

"Poor Billy, but a babe in arms when it comes to romance." Ainsley took a sip of wine, replaced the glass on the table. "In any event, Laughing Sally, who apparently entertains other suitors upon occasion, was eager to tell him she'd learned that the Red Men Gang is planning a rather daring adventure."

Chance retook his seat, not bothering to disguise his interest. If he couldn't make heads or tails of what he should be doing about Julia—and groveling like some lovesick puppy had yet to occur to him in any serious way—he would be more than relieved to have something else to occupy his mind. "Surely they're not planning a run before the new moon. Not with Diamond and his men making such a point of patrolling the area."

Ainsley sighed theatrically. "You do have your head in the clouds, don't you, Chance? Still, better we settle our problem with the Red Men Gang before you make more of a fool of yourself with Julia. The Red Men Gang, Chance, doesn't worry about the phases of the moon. Full moon, new moon—nothing impacts their plans or their arrogance. Certainly not the ineffective and inept Waterguard."

"And this Laughing Sally knows these plans?"

"So it would seem. The plan, as Billy heard it, is for a very large shipment to be off-loaded near the shore from some nameless sloop or cutter—possibly French—then moved overland that same night through territory we have always claimed as our own. To the tune of two hundred landsmen, most of them quite unhappy to be there. An insult, a dare and a large haul—one the local freebooters might covet, especially since they lost most of their last run to that same Red Men Gang. In any event, the Red Men are out for revenge for the men we killed, that's simple to see, and dangling this run as bait. Fetch me that map, if you please."

"Is this all striking you as too perfect?" But Chance did as he was told, then stood behind Ainsley's chair, leaning forward to look at the map.

"What Billy heard is that the landing will be about here," Ainsley said, putting a finger on the map, "Saint Mary's Bay, with the goods immediately moved overland, straight through the heart of the village. Very bold, very ambitious."

"And extremely obvious. This is too easy."

"Very good, Chance. Which is why I've decided the

real landing will be here," Ainsley said, pointing to a spot some distance from Saint Mary's Bay and closer to Becket Hall.

"There's better cover there, I agree, and less beach. And only two ways to travel to the spot—along the beach itself or the much more dangerous marsh in that area. We'd ride straight into them, believing them somewhere else."

"And if I were planning this battle, they'll have their sloop running in close, then luring any waiting boats out into the Channel to destroy them. They can't know they'll be facing the *Respite,* as she's never been used before. What *we* can't know is if they're running a sloop or a cutter—or both."

"We could be badly outmanned." Chance straightened. "Why not just alert Lieutenant Diamond? Lord knows he's itching to be a hero."

Ainsley shook his head. "Odette doesn't like him."

Chance rolled his eyes. "Oh, well, if Odette doesn't like him—"

"She didn't care for the way he goaded Spencer into reopening his wound." Refolding the map, Ainsley said, "For what it's worth, Jacko shares her opinion, although I've yet to see him fond of any man wearing the king's uniform. Besides, since when do we send someone else to do our fighting for us? If Laughing Sally's information has been bought and paid for, the leaders of this Red Men Gang—God, I loathe that insipid name— have come to the same conclusion we've come to."

"That there needs to be one decisive win, and the loser will have no choice but to abandon the field to the victor. In this case, the shoreline of Romney Marsh between Dungeness and Dymchurch," Chance said, taking the map and spreading it open again on the table so he could study it.

"So they intend to draw us out. This Laughing Sally couldn't have been the only one spoon-fed the story. I imagine every doxy from here to Dymchurch has been paid to whisper the same tale, to be sure it reaches us."

"Yes. Gautier brought back much the same story from his visit to New Romney to fetch the mail and, obviously, amuse himself. Poor Billy. Do we tell him he's just another unfortunate pawn in the game of love?"

"Better than letting Jacko tell him." Chance grinned, then returned his attention to the map, his palms pressed against the table. "Two hundred landsmen, you said. I doubt that, especially if they've been forced to cooperate. The Red Men Gang couldn't count on such men to stand and fight or even be sure they wouldn't turn and attack them."

"You may not be any more perceptive in matters of the heart than Billy, but you can still manage to think your way around a battle plan. At any rate, I concur. Their vessel will be heavily armed and manned, that's for certain, sans cargo and riding high and fast in the water—prepared to attack what they believe will be no more than ancient luggers—with another ambush planned on shore. And our part in all of this is to charge ignorantly to the slaughter."

Still with his palms pressed on the tabletop, Chance looked at Ainsley. "Or we simply remain here, do nothing, and then they can have their fine battle without us.

This way, we're fighting on their terms, especially if we're wrong about the point of ambush."

"Yes, I thought of that, too. But we'd only be prolonging the inevitable. Only one gang can control Romney Marsh, and for our own protection there's no choice but to have the Black Ghost in charge. We don't need to bring any more of London's attention to this area, to Becket Hall, no matter that my son is a part of the war effort."

"How many men can we count on? I'll need at least forty of our best on the *Respite,* and Court can't be left shorthanded on shore. Oh, and one other detail, the very first question I asked, I believe. *When?"*

"Did you have plans for this evening? Possibly something including Julia and a few words of contrition and affection?"

Chance looked at Ainsley. "Tonight? Why didn't you wait until after dinner to tell me about this?"

Ainsley lifted his wineglass once more. "Because I only had corroboration on Gautier's information from Billy a few hours ago. Clearly we were meant to have little time to prepare. And if you must know, I had planned to take charge of the *Respite* myself and hope you and Court wouldn't kill each other as you waited on shore for the land battle."

"And would Odette know that?" Chance asked. "That you planned to be on the *Respite?"*

"She seems to know most things. Why?"

"Well, Cap'n, I can't be sure. But I think, were I you, I'd leave off letting her smear any more of that grease on my ankle."

Ainsley frowned for a moment, then gave out a short, rueful chuckle as he collapsed against the back of the chair. "Well, I'll be damned. And the woman dares to claim she is a good *mambo*."

"She probably thinks she's saving your life, old man." Chance rang for someone to come help Ainsley remove his bandages, then said, "I'll have to hunt down Court. Jacko and Billy, too. It's going to be a long day and night."

"Yes. But you might want to also find time to speak to Julia at some point. I want your head fully in the battle tonight."

Now it was Chance's turn for a rueful chuckle. "In that case, I believe I need to stay as far from Julia as possible, because if she learns what we're about, I won't have a head left to take into battle."

"And do you perhaps wonder *why* she would be so upset to learn you were about to put yourself in danger?"

"I know why, Cap'n. I just don't know what in blazes to do about it. And before you offer, this is one lesson I have to learn on my own."

CHAPTER TWENTY-TWO

JULIA TOOK A STEADYING breath, then knocked on the heavy wooden door before depressing the latch and entering, just as Fanny had instructed her.

The room was located in the very back of the house, reached only after passing through what looked to be a deserted storage room, as there was nothing of note inside it other than a small rug and several crates of differing shapes and sizes stacked along the walls.

That, and a mixture of not-quite-pleasant yet rather evocative smells that had grown stronger as she'd approached the second door.

The room she entered now was full of eerie shadows dancing on the walls, floor and ceiling, the windows covered with black cloth, both light and shadow the result of the glow of dozens and dozens of candles. Thick candles on china plates. Tapers. Stubby candles stuck into bottles covered in what looked like the wax from generations of previously burned candles. Red candles, white. Blue, green. Black.

Julia advanced toward the brightest concentration of light and realized she was approaching a rude altar. The thick wooden cross surprised her, as did small paintings clearly meant to represent the Madonna and Child and several gilt halo-topped saints, all arrayed amid several odd-shaped and multicolored, corked bottles. Was that a grasshopper floating in the yellow one?

At the back of the altar, tacked to the wall, was a yellowed piece of parchment with the name Isabella crudely printed on it in red paint.

In the very center of the altar, directly in front of the cross, sat a crystal bowl filled with bits of this and that, nothing easily recognizable except for a few feathers and shells and a delicate circlet of carefully braided, nearly black hair....

"You don't be touching that," Odette said from so close behind Julia that she gave an involuntary yelp of surprise. "That be none of your business."

Julia had quickly withdrawn her hand, folding it with her other hand in front of her as she turned to face Odette. "Of course not. Forgive me." And then, as was her greatest curse, she gave in to curiosity. "Isabella. Is she...she's Cassandra's mother?"

"You've seen enough for now. Here, put this in your pocket."

Julia automatically held out her hand, surprised to feel heat inside the small black cloth bag tied with red ribbon. "But what is—"

"So many questions. Now you act for me. Come. You're needed."

"What?" Julia blinked as Odette turned and began shuffling toward the door in her ancient slippers. "Odette, wait, please. I'm needed where? For what?"

"I have the answer for that, for the questions. I could conjure me up a bad *loa* to keep your tongue silent."

"Well," Julia said, stung. "There's no need to be nasty, Odette."

The woman chuckled and kept moving, passing into the other room, where she began rummaging through a dark wooden chest, coming out with a large, curiously bulging cloth bag. The woman seemed to live surrounded by bags, bottles. And crosses? "A bad *loa?* Or perhaps you'd pray to a saint instead? I had no idea you know anything about saints. Are you a Catholic *and* a...a voodoo?"

Odette straightened, one hand to the base of her spine, and held out the bag. "Here. You carry this for an old woman. Be useful."

Julia wanted to say no, but Odette's dark brown eyes had widened so that Julia could see a ring of stark white completely encircling her irises, and she realized she'd just thought better of that idea.

Odette, with her back once more to Julia, pressed on an area of the wall, and a part of that wall seemed to slide back on itself. She then padded toward a steep, narrow flight of stairs that twisted around on itself twice and seemed to go all the way down into nothingness. Julia followed, her curiosity surfacing again as she realized this could be nothing else save a secret way to exit and enter Becket Hall.

And Ainsley had ordered it built, because he had ordered Becket Hall built. How many other passages like this were there? Surely where there was one, there were more. And why did Ainsley feel they were needed?

Once at the bottom of the staircase, Odette patted her hand along the stone wall, located a large iron key and slid it in the lock of a door Julia hadn't even noticed in the darkness.

And then they were outside, in the darkness beneath the terrace, and Odette closed the door behind them, locking it once more. There was no latch, Julia noticed. Indeed, the door had been neatly covered with stone that matched the other stone that made up Becket Hall.

"Very clever," Julia said, then followed Odette toward a very ordinary wooden door that brought them out from beneath the terrace and into the bright morning sun. They turned and headed toward the stables and the village beyond.

After a few minutes Odette spoke again. "I saw the way you bandaged that foolish boy who was shot. The daughter of the priest, you learned to nurse the sick and the hurt?"

Julia hastened to keep up, for Odette might shuffle in her slippers, but the tall, long-legged woman covered ground amazingly quickly. Clearly they were headed toward the village. "My father was not a priest, Odette. He was a minister. A vicar. But no matter. Is someone injured?"

"One was, a week ago, in a fall down his own stairs in the dark, in order to save his candle. But he's mending, his head only cracked a little bit. It's the other you will treat."

Julia stopped quickly, as if she'd run into a wall. "Treat? You want me to *treat* someone? Why can't you treat this person? You treated Spencer—and Ainsley. And surely there's a doctor in the village?"

Odette paused a moment to turn her white-toothed

grin on Julia. "And he'll doctor again once his head isn't cracked no more."

"Oh, God," Julia said, her heart pounding as they continued on their way. Had Fanny known this when she'd sent Julia to Odette's room? Silly question. Of course she had. This was a test, another test. What did she have to do to prove herself to these people?

And what did that matter anyway, since she had no intention of staying at Becket Hall now that she and Chance were no longer…no, she wouldn't think about that. "But what about you, Odette? Surely you can help?" she asked as she hopped up onto the wooden flagway.

"Again, so many questions," Odette scolded, clucking her tongue. They passed two buildings, then turned to climb some rickety steps that ran along the side of the shoemaker's shop. The woman stopped, huffing and puffing, on the small landing and banged hard on the door with the side of her fist. "Stand where Ollie can see you when the door opens. Now we see how much the fool this man be."

"Yes," Julia groused, also out of breath. "We'll see if he's even more the fool than I am, chasing after you like a ninny."

The door opened and the older man Julia had spied through the window of his shop the day she and Morgan had come to the village stepped out onto the now-crowded landing.

"You!" he shouted, pointing one dye-stained finger at Odette. "What you doin' here? I told 'em, don't none of you bring her, we don't want her here! You were so smart, you and your mumbo jumbo. You said we were protected. Safe! My woman gone, my kiddies gone. You won't lay those bloody black hands on this one— God as my witness, you won't!"

Julia looked from Ollie to Odette, saw the woman flinch at the words as if she'd been physically attacked.

"I won't touch. I brought Chance's woman. Stupid Odette will only watch and learn from the English lady. Now go away, foolish man. Go drink yourself drunk."

And with that, she gave Ollie a hard push on the shoulder and Julia had to grab the handrail as he went stumbling past her down the stairs…just as a woman's scream pierced the air inside the building.

"What was—?" And then Julia understood. "Oh, no. No!" she protested as Odette grabbed her arm and dragged her inside to where a large-bellied woman writhed on a rude, rope-strung bed. "You can't honestly expect *me* to—"

Odette's grin was back. "Ollie knows no one else here can help her no more, save me. He been bringing in everyone and nobody does nothing. He waits, and now I may be too late, foolish man. So many foolish men! This one, she been screaming for two days now. He don't know you, but he knows you're Chance's woman. Don't know what you can do, but he hears how you helped that boy on the Marsh."

The entire time Odette had been speaking, she'd also been stripping off her rather frayed sweater, before yanking the bag from Julia's nerveless fingers and spreading its contents on a scarred wooden table.

"So…so I'm just here as a part of some subterfuge

on your part? I don't have to *do* anything?" As the woman on the bed moved, screaming once more, Julia, although horribly ashamed of her reaction, began to relax.

Odette's bright smile flashed in the dim room. "Oh, you'll help. That baby's turned round sideways, I'm betting, ain't never coming out without Odette calling to him, putting her hands on him. Another foolish man for the world, this one stubborn, too, like his papa."

She picked up an evil-looking iron contraption that resembled a huge shears with wide, rather spooned ends, held it up as she took a cloth-wrapped packet from the pile on the table and shook it in the direction of the metal as she chanted a few words that may have been French— Julia was trembling too much to pay close attention.

Now the woman on the bed spotted Odette. If she'd screamed before, it was nothing to the terrified shriek that came out of her mouth as she tried to shift her bulk higher on the bed, her swollen bare belly now visible above the wrinkled blanket.

Grabbing an enormous wooden knitting needle in her free hand, Odette advanced upon the bed. "Come. You get on the bed and sit her chest the way the men they sit a horse. Facing me. We push her legs high, you hold them high and wide and we get this done."

"What!" Julia shot a panicky look toward the woman to see her huge belly begin to move, seem to come to a point as the woman grabbed on to the iron headboard and screamed yet again.

"You look here to me! You listen here to me! You do as Odette says or they both die!"

"I'm sorry. I'm so sorry," Julia then told the woman on the bed, whose eyes had now rolled back in her head. "Dear God, Odette," she said as she hiked up her skirts, prepared to climb onto the woman's chest, "I think she's fainted."

"Good. Better for her, better for us," Odette said, placing her hand on the rather pink, wet sheet. "Her waters are gone," she said, tossing the knitting needle away, much to Julia's relief.

Then Odette worked herself onto the mattress on her knees, placed the horrible iron contraption on the bed and reached beneath the woman, grabbing the underside of the pale thighs with her large black, pink-palmed hands. With a grunt, she spread, then lifted the woman's thin legs, ordering Julia to grab them, pull them toward the woman's chest.

"Go to your knees, girl," she ordered Julia. "Else you want to take her breath."

Julia was beyond so much as a consideration of disobeying this intimidating, clearly confident woman, and only did as Odette said, then watched, marveling, as Odette spit on her palms, then, unbelievably, plunged one hand into the woman's body. "Oh, God. Sweet, merciful God, hear our prayer. The Lord is my shepherd, I shall not want...."

With one hand on the woman's tight belly, the other inside her past the wrist, Odette began chanting again. A soothing, almost melodic chant that blended with Julia's fervently whispered prayer, her words a gentle, encouraging mix of English, French and something else.

"Yea, though I walk through the valley of the shadow of death, I will fear no evil…"

"I move him now," Odette said quietly as Julia could see the woman's contraction easing. "You come to me now, little one. You don't want no big, ugly dents in your foolish head, so you come to Odette now. You know what I have and you don't want me to touch you with it, hmm? You do as Odette commands. Ah, yes, little one. And now Odette, she leaves before your sweet mama she bites my hand off."

Julia's eyes went wide when the woman's belly seemed to grow into a point once more, then slowly empty of its burden.

"I see him!" Julia shouted, filled with sudden joy, nearly losing her grip on the woman's thighs. "I can see his head!" Then she fell silent as nothing else happened, and panic returned. "Get him out, Odette! He's not coming out!"

"So anxious. We need one more pain to help with the push, don't we, sweet baby? Just one more…"

CHAPTER TWENTY-THREE

IF IT WEREN'T THAT HER clothing was still in her bed-chamber and that everyone he'd questioned had denied helping her escape—no, not escape; she didn't need to escape, did she?—Chance's panic would have been even worse.

As it was, he was unnerved enough to chase Julia down when he at last spied her on the beach stretching away from Becket Hall and the village, grabbing her shoulders to rudely stop her, turn her around to face him. "Where in blue blazes have you been all day, woman? Do you have any idea the worry you've put me—Julia?"

She was looking at him rather blankly. Dreamingly. Her cheeks were wet with tears, yet she was smiling.

She scared the living hell out of him.

"She named her Julia," she told him, sighing. "Odette isn't always right. But, oh, she is remarkable." She blinked rapidly. "I'm tired. I think I'm going to sit down now."

And she did, much to Chance's dismay, right there on the damp sand, still smiling and sniffling.

He went down onto his haunches to look at her more closely. There was something on the front of her gown.

Something wet. He touched it. Wet and sticky. Blood? "Are you hurt? Julia, for the love of Christ, look at me. Are you hurt?"

"Hurt?" Julia laughed at this foolishness. How could she be hurt? She felt *wonderful*. Awed. Blessed. "No, I'm not hurt," she said, finally realizing that she was acting strangely. But then, how many times did a person have the opportunity to take part in a miracle?

"You're not hurt," Chance said soothingly, pulling her to her feet. "All right, Julia. I'm glad you're not hurt, really. So now let's the two of us head back to Becket Hall and you can have a nice hot bath and—"

"Oh, Chance, stop coddling me as if I'm two steps away from Bedlam," Julia said, dancing away from him, her arms wide. "I'm fine. I'm glorious! And she named her Julia. I washed her. I *held* her."

Drinking? No, not Julia. Then what in hell was wrong with her? What was she saying? Chance tried to sift through everything she'd said since he'd found her. Odette's name had been in there somewhere. Had Odette done something to her? Miserable, meddling woman!

"Julia. Julia, stop spinning around like that," Chance ordered. "Julia, listen to me. Did…did Odette give you anything?"

Julia stopped dancing and looked at Chance again. He looked so concerned. *Poor foolish man.* "And a good thing she did, I think, or I may have fainted myself. Wait!" she added quickly, as Chance looked ready to commit mayhem. "It's not like that. I helped Odette bring a baby into the world today, Chance, and she's the most *beautiful* baby in the entire world and her mama is going to be just fine and her papa is passed out drunk and doesn't even know he's papa to this perfect little baby." She sighed. "Baby Julia."

She walked toward him, her eyes shining. "You really should take Odette's powers more seriously, Chance. She's a true wonder. She will be there for me for all of my babies, she promised." Julia giggled. "But I don't think I want her to spit on her hands."

Chance reconsidered his earlier conclusion. Julia *was* drunk—drunk with excitement. Her green eyes were shining, her wide smile nearly beatific. He'd never seen her look quite so beautiful. He gently stroked her warm, windblown blond hair, smiled at the new sprinkling of freckles across her cheeks. "You plan to have a lot of babies, sweetings?"

"Oh, yes."

"I see," he said, taking her hand and guiding her back along the beach, toward Becket Hall. "If I can be of any assistance in the matter?"

Julia sobered immediately. "That…that wasn't what I was saying. Suggesting." She shook her head to clear it, looked up to see that the sun had traveled quite a distance since she'd last noticed it. "What time is it?"

"Nearly six."

"Six! I've been gone forever," Julia said, pulling him along with her as she walked faster. "Alice will be wondering where I am."

"We've all been wondering where you were," Chance informed her.

"But Fanny knew. Fanny sent me to Odette."

"Really. I never learned the purpose of sisters. But I imagine she was enjoying watching me run around like a fool. I'll have a few choice words for that girl later. Julia, stop a moment. I have something important to tell you."

He also had much to do, but all of that had been pushed to one side when he'd realized that he couldn't go out on the *Respite* tonight without seeing Julia, talking to her.

"Can't it wait until later?" she asked, for she was nervous now that her euphoria was fading. She had been avoiding this man for several days, and now here they were, alone together on the beach, and he wanted to talk to her. "Really, Chance. I'm a sorry mess. I'm famished and I need a bath."

"We're heading out tonight, Julia, to face down the Red Men Gang in one great contest to decide who rules the shores of Romney Marsh. There. I've said it. Now will you stop?"

Julia shook her head again, sure she had misunderstood. But, no, she hadn't. He was looking entirely too serious. "You...you're—no! You can't do that!"

"You'll worry about me?" Chance asked, knowing he should be ashamed of how good it made him feel to see the sudden panic in her eyes.

"I couldn't care a snap about you, Chance Becket," Julia lied with desperate heat. "But what about Alice? Is she to remember her papa as the traitorous freebooter who was hanged in chains at Dover Castle for his crimes? And what about Elly? Fanny? Morgan and Callie? Baby Julia, all the women and children? What happens to them when you men bring Lieutenant Diamond down on Becket Hall? And…and what if you *lose?* Will these Red Men come here?"

Chance rubbed at the side of his head, hiding his expression as a painful mental flash of what they'd found on the beach all those years ago when the Black Ghost had come back from her last foray stabbed his mind.

"Well, thank you for that, Julia. Your confidence in our expectations for success and our ability to take care of our women and children is just what I need to send me on my way full of hope for my mission."

Julia knew she'd hurt him, hurt his manly pride, probably. But she wasn't going to apologize. "Your mission, is it? Your mission, as I recall the thing, is to serve your country, not…not break the king's laws."

"That mission, Julia, was abandoned the moment you talked me into bringing those boys to Becket Hall. I'm a part of this now."

She couldn't believe what she was hearing. "So now it's *my* fault?"

"No, no, damn it, I didn't mean it that way. That was coincidence. Besides, if anything, finding that dead boy opened my eyes." He stabbed his fingers through his hair that, like Julia's, was blowing free in the wind coming in off the Channel. "But you're still the most confounding woman."

"And you're a liar. I know why you're doing this." Julia's fear for him was overcoming her common sense and most definitely her control of her tongue. And as for womanly pride? When it came to this man, she had none.

He had to listen to her, he just had to! "You're risking your life because your family is a part of this. I've realized that I don't care about your past anymore, it's not important. You *escaped*, Chance. You went to London, you built your life there. Don't you see? You're not like them anymore. We can go. We can go now. Take Alice. Take all the girls. You've done enough. Please, Chance!"

Chance narrowed his eyelids as he looked at her. "You really mean that? You really think I'd abandon my family?"

"You did once—oh! Oh, Chance, forgive me," Julia said, horrified at what she'd said, knowing she'd gone too far, that her fears for him had taken her past the point of reason. "I'm sorry. I'm so sorry. I didn't mean that."

"Which doesn't make what you said untrue, unfortunately. But not again, Julia, whether or not you understand why. Not ever again. Not for Alice, not for you. Not if I'm to be able to live with myself, live with you, live for anyone or anything ever again."

"I love you," Julia said quietly, because there was nothing else to say.

At her words, Chance pulled back from the brink but refused to waver. "Do you, Julia? Do you now? And I suppose that's what I most wanted to hear, fool that I am, tardy as those words are."

He then turned, left her where she stood, and she didn't immediately follow after him. She needed to collect herself, marshal her emotions, time to convince herself it didn't matter that he hadn't said he loved her, too.

Which was wise, because Chance was looking for a fight, someone or something to punch, punish, destroy.

And he found that someone when he climbed back up the steps to the terrace, where Courtland was waiting for him, his arms akimbo, a scowl on his bearded face and unknowingly just about to say exactly the wrong thing.

"I saw you two on the beach. Did you really think you had time to sneak off and diddle your woman? Ainsley says you're in charge, and this is how you take charge? We've got important things to do."

Chance's fist connected with Courtland's jaw even before he realized that he'd moved, and his brother went down hard on the stones, to be quickly followed by Chance himself, the two locked together and rolling around the terrace, intent on destroying each other.

Julia saw the punch from her place on the beach, saw Courtland go down, then realized Chance had disappeared below the thick stone balustrades, as well. She hiked up her skirts and broke into a run, stumbling twice as she crossed the uneven shore, then ran up the steps, calling out, "Stop it! Stop that at once!"

"Let them go, my dear."

She whirled about to see Ainsley Becket standing just outside one of the pairs of French doors, leaning lightly on a cane, his foot and ankle still heavily bandaged.

"But…but they're killing each other!"

"Oh, not quite that terrible, I'm sure," Ainsley said, watching the two men roll about on the stones, hitting, kicking, cursing. "I've been waiting for this from the moment Chance came home."

"You've been—but that's ridiculous. They're brothers!"

"They were—and they will be again once this hurdle has been cleared. Besides, I've already asked Billy to bring us a pail of water."

Julia looked toward Courtland and Chance once more, then back to Ainsley, who was smiling. "Oh, well, in that case," she said, joining him, "I suppose it's all right."

Ainsley laughed. "And you a vicar's daughter."

"Not an ordinary vicar, sir."

"And not an ordinary daughter. Have you and Chance settled things between you now?"

Julia winced as Courtland managed to roll on top and began pummeling Chance around the shoulders and head. "Will Billy be coming soon? But, no, Chance and I haven't...we aren't...that is ..."

Ainsley leaned more heavily on the head of his cane. "I know what he's done, child, all of it, from its not-very-laudable beginning. If you demand marriage, I'll see to it."

"I *don't* demand marriage."

"Spoken much too quickly and vehemently to be believed. He loves you, you know."

"Really," Julia said, her tone bitter. "And I suppose, just to prove himself worthy of me, he's about to get himself killed." She turned when Billy appeared, to take the heavy wooden bucket from him, nearly staggering under its weight. "If you'll both excuse me?"

"With pleasure," Ainsley said. "Just be mindful of thrashing limbs."

Julia approached carefully, secretly pleased to see that Chance had regained the upper hand, then poured the contents of the bucket over both their heads before flinging the bucket to the stones. "I'm only sorry it wasn't enough to drown the pair of you! Now get up!"

Chance had already leapt to his feet, for the water had mostly hit him and it was damn cold. He shook himself all over, like a dog after a plunge in a pond, then pushed his sopping-wet hair back from his face. "What in hell do you think you're doing, woman?"

"Thoroughly enjoying myself," Julia said from between clenched teeth. "Court—get up. And the two of you shake hands."

"The devil I will," Courtland said, still sitting on the stones, wiping his hands over his face as he blinked away the water. "Can't you even control *her,* brother?"

Chance grinned. God, but he felt better. Except for his left cheek and eye that he was fairly certain would be sporting a mass of bruises by tomorrow. "Apparently not," he said, looking at Julia. "I think those may be real sparks shooting out of your eyes, sweetings."

"Just a moment," Courtland said, getting to his feet, nearly losing his footing on the wet stones. "We're not done here."

"I think we are," Chance said, moving his jaw back and forth, checking for soreness and glad to find none. "When did you learn to punch like that?"

"If you'd come home sooner, you would have found out sooner," Courtland said, then touched his fingers to his nostrils, coming away with blood. "Damn. I'm not the only one who knows how to punch."

"I was just lucky," Chance said, feeling the tension easing between he and his brother—or at least on his side. "You probably would have killed me if Julia hadn't thrown that water. Right, Cap'n?"

"You seemed fairly evenly matched to me," Ainsley said. "Billy?"

"Yeah," Billy agreed glumly. "Both dumb as shrimps. We've things to talk over, Cap'n."

Bowing to Julia, Ainsley turned, still leaning on his cane, and reentered Becket Hall.

"Now," she said, turning back to the two very wet men. "Exactly what was all this nonsense in aid of, hmm? Has it anything to do with this ridiculousness you're planning for those Red Men?"

Chance hesitated, and Courtland stepped into the breach. "It does, if you must know. You see, Julia, we've only the one black silk cape, and he wanted it."

"So you *fought* for it?" Julia asked, glaring at Chance, who was having some difficulty holding back his laughter. "I should have just let you kill each other."

"Julia, wait," Chance said as she flounced away, heading indoors. He turned back to Courtland. "That was fast thinking, brother. We fought over a cape?"

"We've got two or three, as a matter of fact. But better that lie than to admit I'm a jackass who'd insulted my brother's beloved."

"We're not... She's not... Oh, bloody hell. Go change, you look like you fell overboard—and so do I. *Julia!*"

Inside the house, Julia heard Chance call her name and hastened her steps, hoping to safely lock herself in her bedchamber before he could catch up with her. A vain hope as it turned out, because she'd barely made it to the top of the staircase before he was there, taking her arm, pulling her into an alcove.

"Out there, on the beach. You said you love me."

"I did not. You misheard me," Julia shot back, longing to push his wet hair back from his face, rain kisses all over him. "In truth, I've developed quite a fondness for Jacko. He...he does have quite a lovely smile."

"Really. You'll pardon me if I've never noticed," Chance drawled, stepping closer to her. "Julia, we don't have time for this now."

"I...I suppose not." She looked down at the floor. "Please don't go. Please don't do this. You've nothing to prove."

"I have everything to *protect,*" he told her sincerely. "We didn't start this fight, we didn't cause that boy's death on the Marsh, among others, but it's our fight now and we have no choice but to win it. Do you understand? Please tell me you understand."

Julia's gaze met his, and she sighed, knowing it was useless to continue struggling against the inevitable. "Where? Where does this happen?"

"I won't tell you that. It's enough that Morgan and the others have noticed all the activity without having any of you chasing out after us. But it's nowhere you can interfere, in any case. I'll be on the *Respite,* and Court and the rest on shore. We have every hope of destroying the Red Men's ship—or at least driving it straight toward the Waterguard's guns and boats."

"Will Ainsley be in charge on the *Respite?*"

"I'll be in charge," Chance told her, then quickly

added, "Look, Julia, you have no reason to worry. We know what we're doing. I know what I'm doing."

"Because you've done it before," Julia said, sighing again. "And I don't need to know about that, either. When do you leave? When will you return?"

"We sail after dark, but there's much to do before then, and we'll be safely anchored back here when the sun rises tomorrow."

Julia put her hands on his chest, fussing with his clothes as if smoothing the wet wrinkles could possibly improve their condition. "Very well then. I'll sit with the others while you're gone, embroider more pillowcases. And run quietly out of my mind."

Chance eased himself even closer, tilting his head as he smiled. "Because you can't help yourself—you love me."

Julia blinked back tears she refused to let fall and kept plucking at the collar of his shirt. "It's amazing, isn't it, that I never knew what I was missing, not all of these years, and yet I already know that I would now miss you very much if you were not in my life anymore. I'd miss you very much indeed. So, yes, I must love you." She lifted her chin. "And if you don't come back tomorrow morning, I will hate you forever."

"Then I'll be sure to come back, my love," Chance said and then he kissed her, held her tightly for a moment, clinging to the promise of the new life he might at last have within his grasp, then left her there before he was tempted never to go.

CHAPTER TWENTY-FOUR

CHANCE HAD ONE FOOT in the catboat when he heard Julia call his name, and turned to see her running toward him in the near dark, her long hair flying behind her in the breeze.

"Got to train her up better'n that, boy," Billy said from his seat at the stern, then spit into the water. "Men sail, women wait and work their beads."

"Stow it, Billy," Chance said, then stepped back into the water, sure that, otherwise, Julia wouldn't stop running until she was wet to her knees.

"You...you can't go without this," Julia said, trying to catch her breath as she held out her hand. He looked down to see his *gad*. She lowered her voice. "You left it in my bedchamber, remember?"

Chance took the thing and lowered it over his head, tucked it beneath his black silk shirt. "You're a constant amazement to me, Julia. The vicar's daughter, putting her faith in voodoo amulets? Still, I've been feeling rather naked without it. Thank you."

"You're welcome." Julia wanted to hold him, yearned to hold him, keep him close. "By the time sun rises?"

Chance looked at her, his expression intense. "I

swear it." Not caring that the beach was filled with his crew, he slipped one arm around Julia's waist and pulled her toward him, pressing a hard, claiming kiss on her mouth. He broke the kiss and pulled her closer, whispered in her ear. "I've never had anything to come back to before you."

And then he was gone, his over-the-knee boots protecting his legs as he walked back into the water, then gracefully hefted himself into the catboat once more. Dressed in black from neck to toe, he seemed to carry with him an air of confidence, and competence...along with a hint of barely contained wildness that both intrigued and frightened Julia. At his signal, the crew began rowing toward the *Respite*.

He didn't look back.

Julia watched with the other women from the village, some of them waving, some of them openly weeping, until the catboat reached the *Respite* and Chance had climbed the ropes to the deck. He was met there by Jacko, who immediately clapped one beefy arm around his shoulders, pulled his head down against his chest, and planted a rough kiss on the top of Chance's head before going toward the bow.

Julia could barely see Chance now, but his voice carried clearly over the water as he barked out orders. She was so proud of him. She was so frightened for him.

The last catboat was returning to shore when Ainsley pressed a heavy brass spyglass into her hand and she used it to locate Chance on the deck, his dark blond hair blowing loose and wild around his face and shoulders. Billy was helping him settle a black silk cape over his shoulders, the silk immediately filling with the breeze, and giving Chance a dangerous look that curled something deep in her belly.

A pirate. Her Chance made a fine pirate. And it was time to stop denying that fact. As long as she didn't have to deny that he was her Chance.

"A touch of the dramatic instills courage, my dear," Ainsley seemed eager to explain, lowering the glass he'd been using. "Anchors are up and stowed," he added. "Bring down your glass, Julia, and watch. It's time to be impressed with more of that odd mix of romance and pageantry of war that has lured us since the beginning of time, making otherwise rational men willing and eager to believe they are invincible. Or do you not believe that both the enemy and those who wore the scarlet cape of the Roman Centurian were not equally awed by the spectacle?"

And then, as Julia watched, several men swiftly climbed into the rigging. She could hear snatches of Chance's orders before there were sudden snaps as the sails came down, filled with wind.

The sails had been refitted, were no longer white. They were black, pitch black.

"The Black Ghost," Julia said, her chest tight with realization. "I...I think I finally understand. Not a person at all, but a ship."

"Every piece is a part of the whole, Julia." Ainsley smiled down at her. "Not everything, or everyone, it would appear, was dismantled and rebuilt," he said, standing tall, his handsome face looking proud and yet sad at the same time. A leader, Julia knew. A man born to lead. A man who, for whatever reasons, had abdicated that post of leadership.

"They'll be all right? Chance. Everyone. I saw Ollie rowing out there, his new daughter just born today. Ollie, and Waylon, young Jacob and the rest."

"With God's grace and Chance's skill they'll all return safely, yes," Ainsley assured her as the *Respite* moved silently along and then away from the shore, disappearing into the darkness as the light cast by the waning moon could find no reflection on the black sails. "Now, how would you like to help this hapless cripple sneak away to the ponycart Jacko readied for me, so we can both go hide ourselves and watch the proceedings?"

"But…but we won't be able to see Chance, will we?"

"No, my dear, but Court, Spencer, Rian and the rest have their own mission to accomplish. And, like a mother hen with too few chicks, I am determined to be on hand, one way or another. Not that Court can ever know, or he might go into a sad decline, believing I don't have my full faith in his abilities."

"And you trust me to go with you?"

Ainsley smiled down at her. "More than I would Morgan, who would disobey me the moment she felt the excitement rushing through her veins, and the rest are too young. So? Are you willing?"

Looking first to her left, then to her right, and realizing that the women and children were slowly returning to either Becket Hall or their homes in the village, Julia nodded. "Which way will we go?"

Within minutes they were driving along a narrow track through the Marsh, the cleverly-fashioned lantern

Jacko had provided opened halfway, providing sufficient light for them to see the path, but still shuttered enough that few others on the Marsh could see the lantern itself.

Julia pulled the ends of her cloak closer around her body, fearful that her teeth would soon chatter audibly, not really with the damp of the evening, but with fear. "Can you tell me what's going to happen?"

"Certainly. Court and his men have already positioned themselves on either side of a well-worn track leading to the shore, hours before anyone is expected to move on the Marsh. They're awaiting the arrival of the Red Men Gang, who are hoping to ambush us as we ride along the shore on our way to Saint Mary's Bay, where we have been led to believe they are to be. Complicated, I'm afraid. You won't be able to see them, but they are there."

"How many?"

"Sixty-three, all well trained and well armed. In the meantime, the *Respite* will be waiting offshore for the expected cutter or cutters to swoop out of the night to surprise our smaller boats, those we would have naturally sent out to intercept the Red Men's haul before it can reach the shore."

Julia thought about this for a few moments. "So neither the Red Men Gang nor, um, nor our people are expected to be using anything save small boats?"

"Ancient luggers at best," Ainsley agreed. "Fore-and-aft rigged, able to run close to the shore, and not slow-moving, but certainly unable to outrun a sloop or fore-and-aft rigged cutter. So much easier when the opponent is running square-sail. Square-sail, you see, can only run with the wind behind the sails, never across the wind, as the *Respite* does so well. Another way I hope the Red Men have seriously underestimated us."

"I don't understand," Julia said, but quietly, because Ainsley had drawn the pony cart to a halt beside a wide scrub tree that should hide the cart, and set the brake.

"If, for instance, the Red Men are using square-sail, and are forced to take cover in some nearby estuary, it cannot come about, escape again, until the wind changes. We'd have them trapped, have them at our mercy."

"So we're hoping for square-sails," Julia said as Ainsley helped her down from the seat, still using his cane as they began walking along the track.

"Yes. As long as the breeze blows inland from the Channel, as it is right now. Chance would immediately see his advantage, and herd the square-sail along in front of him, straight toward Court, who should have dispatched the landsmen by then. But never put all your eggs in Hope's basket, my dear," he told her. "A silent prayer or two that Lieutenant Diamond and his men are sailing along the coast tonight would probably not come amiss. That is, if he got that anonymous note telling him a few of his men and boats hovering near Saint Mary's Bay tonight could gain him a real coup."

"You alerted the lieutenant?"

"To the area, Julia, not the exact spot. We don't want him shooting at the wrong people, now do we? But it would be nice to have someone else around to clean up once we're done."

"You like this, don't you?" Julia couldn't hide her amazement. "You and Chance, Court—all you men. You *like* this. The danger—all of it."

"Guilty as charged, yes. A man needs to feel his blood thrumming through his veins from time to time, to know that he is alive." He stopped, stepped off the path, motioned for her to follow, then couched down in the tall grasses. "Now, we must be quiet, I'm afraid."

And silent they were from that point on, for two long hours. Julia's feet were damp through the thin soles of her shoes. Her muscles had begun to cramp, her body felt chilled to the bone, and something was biting at her—sand fleas, Ainsley had whispered as she'd smacked at her neck and the sound of the slap had caused him to frown at her.

If going into battle was exhilarating, waiting for others to go into battle was mind-numbing and uncomfortable.

Just as she felt she could crouch there no longer, Julia heard a quick jingle of harness, followed by an abrupt curse, then more silence. She tapped on Ainsley's shoulder and he nodded to her, acknowledging that he, too, had heard it.

He put his arms forward, his palms on the ground, and lay flat on his belly. Julia did the same.

She held her breath, sure her rapidly beating heart could be overheard by the men, both on horseback and on foot, who appeared out of the darkness single-file, heading toward the shore…toward Court and the rest.

She counted as well as she could in the moonlight,

and became dismayed when that count went to fifty, and then beyond. To sixty. To seventy. And more.

Julia squeezed Ainsley's upper arm, not considering the intimate gesture, and he smiled at her and shook his head, clearly not worried.

"We can move now," he whispered after a few minutes. "Not too far, and staying low as we go. Are you up for this, Julia?"

She answered by getting to her feet, then bending herself nearly in half as she waited for him to lead the way. As they moved along, she occasionally lifted her head slightly, hoping for a glimpse of the Channel, of Court's ship.

How had she believed the Marsh to be one long, flat land with no hills? This track led upward, then finally downward again, nothing near a towering hill, but the way slippery, her view more and more obscured because of the ground mist that had begun to rise.

There was a shout, then another, and Ainsley pushed her to the ground so unexpectedly that Julia's face landed in stagnant, foul-smelling water. Coughing, spitting, she struggled to rise again, but Ainsley held her tight as the shouts increased, along with the sound of gunshot, the clash of metal against metal.

Which was worse? Chance, out on the water, possibly being fired on by several ships? Or Court and the rest on land, standing toe-to-toe with men as intent on killing them as they were on destroying their opponents?

The first man stumbled over Julia's legs a few moments later, fell, picked himself up, and began running wildly again, leaving an ancient, evil-looking cutlass behind on the ground.

"Are you all right?"

Julia nodded her answer to Ainsley just before he pushed into her, rolling the two of them off the track and into the tangle of vegetation that bordered it in time to avoid being trampled by more wild-eyed men who were fleeing the battle.

Ainsley was breathing heavily now, too, but he smiled down at Julia as he lay protectively on top of her. "You can't buy loyalty, Julia," he said, "and you can't threaten people into giving it. We counted on that."

Feet pounded on the ground on either side of them, another man stumbling over them as they lay there, until at last Julia felt sure the entire world had just stampeded across the Marsh.

"Is that it? Is it over now? Or will Court follow them?"

"Court's still too busy with the Red Men to worry his head about their timid hirelings," Ainsley told her, helping her to her feet. "Where's my damn cane? Oh—my apologies, Julia."

"None needed, sir," Julia told him as she scanned the area for his cane, then quickly retrieved it for him. "Do we move closer now?"

"Yes, we do, if you're up to it," he told her, stepping out into the track once more, then holding out his hand to assist her. "Listen."

Julia frowned, then tried to concentrate. There was still fighting farther along the track, but there was no more shouting, no more gunshots. Just the sound of metal against metal and, more than once, a scream that chilled her to the bone.

Then a new sound came to her ears, from across the water, and she flinched. Rumble after rumble following hard on each other. She looked to Ainsley, gripping his hand tightly.

"Four pounders. That's the *Respite*."

Julia clapped her hands to her mouth. "Oh, God."

There were more rumbles.

"Ah, not the *Respite*. But only three pounders, I'd say, and not fired in tight precision. Brute force and threats may have worked when we were not yet joined in the battle, but they'll have to do better than that to best us. Come along, Julia. You have your spyglass?"

"Yes," she said, fighting the urge to run ahead of him along the track. Chance was out there, locked in battle. But with whom? The Red Men Gang? Or the Waterguard? And did it matter?

No. It did not. What mattered was that Chance was out there...

"Can't we go closer?"

Ainsley was holding his spyglass to his eye, although it was so dark, she couldn't imagine what he expected to see. "No need. I don't know how he's done it, but he's managed to both acquire one of the Waterguard cutters and herd the Red Men toward the shore." He chuckled softly. "Not that they can come closer. Look, Julia. Can you see? The Red Men seem to have lost their fore mast." He pumped one fist into the air. "Fine shooting, boys!"

"What does that mean? That they lost their fore mast?"

He was once more searching the horizon with his spyglass. "It means, my dear, that even the inept Waterguard will have no trouble boarding the ship and relieving us of our problem. Ah, and there's no sign of the *Respite*. She's already drawn away offshore. Now you, Court. Show us that— Ah, and there it is. Come along, my dear, or else Chance will have beaten us back to Becket Hall. I don't think he'd be best pleased to know I've brought you along tonight."

"But what about Court and the others?"

"Court? The old hen's fears have been ill-founded, I should say. He knows his orders."

"But aren't they still—"

"Julia, look up, into the sky. Quickly, or you'll miss it."

She did as she was told, and saw what seemed to be a trailing ball of bright yellow fire racing toward the water. "What is that?"

"Court's signal. Had it been blue, Chance would have known to come to his aid. Yellow tells us all is secure. Two yellow would have meant secure, but with injuries. Now I suggest we return to Becket Hall before Chance beats us there and knows what we've been about."

Julia turned away from the water and followed after Ainsley. "No injuries? But how is that possible?"

"It's not," Ainsley told her, taking her hand as the path had become slippery with damp. "But at least we know no one is dead. The rest we'll know when Court returns."

"And you're so calm," Julia said, pressing him, because she had begun to shake very badly as reaction to the night's events became more real to her. His sons had been in danger, his friends, his crew, in danger. Men had died tonight, she was sure of that. "How can you be so calm?"

"Calm? Far from that, my dear." Ainsley turned to her, just a hint of his smile visible in the dark as he said, "The first thing a man who wishes to lead others learns, Julia, is to deceive with confidence."

CHAPTER TWENTY-FIVE

JULIA AND AINSLEY RODE together in companionable silence, Ainsley pretty much giving the old mare her head, which meant they moved along the narrow track at a slow plod. No clouds obscured the waning moon, so there was enough light to see the darker shadows, the flatter Marsh to their right, enormous grasses and wind-stunted bushes and scrub trees dividing them from any view of the Channel.

Julia, exhausted from the excitement, the worry, had begun to nod off, when Ainsley pulled the mare to a halt and cursed, not bothering to apologize this time as she looked at him curiously. He reached for the half-shuttered lantern and closed the metal door completely.

"Is something wrong? What's wrong?" she asked, then shifted on her seat to look toward the Channel, thinking she might see the *Respite* on its way back to Becket Hall. But all she saw was wild vegetation and darkness. So she looked right, over the flat expanse of the Marsh, and sharply drew in her breath at the shadowy sight of a small group of horsemen silhouetted against the horizon. "Lieutenant Diamond?"

"I think so, yes. Their progress is too orderly to be the Red Men Gang," Ainsley said, helping her down from the plank seat. "Distances can be deceiving out here, but I believe they're a good mile away."

"They won't see us?"

"They haven't seen us yet, thank God, with this brush to our back to hide us among the shadows, so I think we're safe. Besides, he's much too intent on riding toward Becket Hall. A man on a mission, I believe. You'd think the idiot would stay where he belongs. I have to warn Chance or he'll be bringing in the *Respite* with Diamond watching him."

"But how can you warn him?"

"The lantern. If I can just get down to the beach, into the clear, I can signal him."

"But…but you can't do that, at least not quickly enough," Julia told him, desperately holding on to her calm with both hands, when she felt such a strong need to scream, to cry, to deny this new danger. "I'll have to do it." She reached for the lantern. "Quickly, sir. What's the signal?"

"Julia, I can't ask you to do this. Damn! This will teach me to be arrogant. The note was to be enough to keep him where we wanted him. I didn't set up sentries, anyone to warn Chance." He rubbed at the back of his neck. "But Chance will remember. He'll be watching and he'll remember the signal, take the *Respite* back out to deep water."

"Yes, yes, he will, I know he will," Julia said as she reached down between her legs to catch on to the back hem of her gown. Then she stood again, pulling the back of her skirt through her legs, tying the bunched material fast to the ribbons that hung from the high waist of her gown, as she'd seen women in Hawkhurst do when they scrubbed their floors.

"Julia, if Diamond sees you, if he catches you out while you're down there warning the *Respite* away, you'll be hanged right along with them."

"I know that. Dear God, I know that. Please, Ainsley, the signal." She stole another look toward the lieutenant and the troop of dragoons making their way slowly through the dark night. "Ainsley. Tell me the damn signal! Oh! I'm so sorry."

"No need to be sorry. Open and shut the door quickly three times. Then once, holding it open to the count of three. Wait, then repeat the process until Chance returns the signal. Watch closely, as he'll only do that once, because anyone on shore will be able to see. And then he'll be gone."

Ainsley handed her the lantern. "As soon as he answers, Julia, you are to leave the beach, come back to me. I have a way to get us back inside Becket Hall."

"You have the key to the door under the terrace?" Julia asked before she could think to deny her knowledge.

Ainsley managed a smile. "It's a very good thing, Julia, that you've aligned yourself with us and not the good lieutenant. Now, three short, one long, repeat until Chance answers you."

"I understand. Say a prayer, Ainsley."

"I will if you wish, but my son has you. You're as good as a prayer. Now go."

Keeping low, Julia slipped and slid her way through reeds, taller than her head, that slapped at her skin, stung her bare legs and cheeks as she ran. Oblivious to the scratches, some that had already drawn blood, she kept on toward the beach, no more than one hundred yards away…although it felt like miles and miles.

Out on the water, Chance stood with both hands on the wheel as he grinned at Jacko and Billy, who had been doing a little celebratory jig on deck, their elbows locked together as they swung each other in circles. "A fine example you two set for my authority," he told them, shaking his head.

The men stopped their foolery, Jacko laying one beefy arm over the slighter Billy's shoulder. "It's wrong to feel alive, boy?" he asked, his eyes twinkling as he smiled. "And here we two were, worrying if you'd remember fore from aft."

"Very amusing," Chance said, looking toward the shore, because he was anxious to be back at Becket Hall. Anxious to be with Julia. "I suppose you both want me to take her out, swing her wide before we take her in. Maybe find us that Frenchie who's been hanging out there, taunting us."

Billy pushed Jacko's arm off his shoulders and stepped forward. "Cap'n wouldn't want that."

"No, I suppose he wouldn't. It is, after all, his ship. A man can be pretty particular about what goes on aboard his own ship. All right then, men," he called out, "we're taking her in now. Everyone—"

Jacko hitched up his breeches. "Everyone what, son? You forget the words? Pitiful, that's what that is. Billy, I don't know what we're going to tell the cap'n. The boy is rusty, that's what it is."

"Look to the shore, Jacko," Chance commanded tersely, his blood running cold. "Tell me you see what I see."

Both Jacko and Billy had already turned to squint into the night. "Jesus," Billy whispered. "I'll fetch a lantern."

"Yes. Do that," Chance said quietly, then looked to Jacko. "Hand signals from now on. Pass the word, Jacko. Not another sound from anybody. Where the Christ is Billy?"

"Here," the seaman said, returning to the deck at a run.

"Give the signal—and watch your head for the mainsail," Chance ordered. "We're coming about now."

"That we are—but the wrong way. Last thing we want is to get closer to shore. What are you doing, boy?"

Chance was already stripping off the black cape with one hand as he gripped the wheel tight with the other. Damn cape, all it did was get in a man's way. "Just take the helm, Jacko. *Do it.*"

Jacko sprung to, and Chance dropped to the deck, Billy already helping him out of his tight, high boots.

Billy tugged with all his might. "You think there's trouble on shore, boy?"

"I don't know, Billy, but I'm about to find out." He got to his feet, hesitating with one hand on the rail, waiting for the *Respite* to draw a little closer to the shore. "Take her out now, Jacko, and keep her out until the crew has switched sails. Get it done before dawn, Jacko, or the *Respite* will be defenseless if the Frenchie shows up again."

"Don't tell me my job, boy," Jacko said. "It's not me abandoning my ship."

"Haven't used your brain in a while, have you, Jacko?" Chance wanted to be gone, and it didn't occur to him that any awe he'd ever had of Jacko had disappeared, that he was now truly, at last, the one in command. He kept his gaze on the spot where he'd seen the signal, waiting for the *Respite* to draw closer to the shore. "Who else knows that signal, Jacko? Who else would risk his skin to give it?"

"The cap'n," Billy said, whirling to look at Chance. "Should have known he couldn't stay out of this." He took an evil-looking knife from his waist sash and handed it to Chance. "Go, son."

Chance slipped the knife into his own waistband, climbed onto the railing, held on to a bit of rigging for a moment to steady himself, then dived into the inky-black water.

He broke the surface again, gasping at the cold that was so unlike the warm waters surrounding the island, then struck out for the shore and whatever he might find there, the strength of both his strokes and his fears moving him swiftly forward.

Julia had seen the signal, then left the shuttered lantern on the shingle beach before heading back through the brush and grasses, stopping only when she heard voices. She dropped to the ground, praying no one had heard her mad scrambling.

"…and so I say again, sir, what would a man be doing out alone on the Marsh in the middle of the night if it was not in aid of something nefarious."

Lieutenant Diamond. Julia bit her bottom lip to keep from saying the man's name aloud. He'd seen them. Ainsley had been wrong, their cover had not been sufficient, and the lieutenant had seen them.

Seen Ainsley. Not her.

"Lieutenant, I am a man of peace," she could hear Ainsley reply evenly. "A quiet man, retired to the country with my family. But it would appear that I will have to be firm here. This is my property, Lieutenant. What I do on my property and when I choose to do it is my own prerogative. And you and your men are trespassing."

That won't work, Julia thought wildly. *He'll just say he's on the king's business What should I do? What should I do?*

"Mr. Becket, I apologize yet again, sir," Lieutenant Diamond said, the edge in his voice even more apparent now. "But I am about the king's business this night and I go where I go in the commission of that business. Your son would understand."

"Really. And what, may I ask, is the king's business tonight?"

"Freebooters, sir, if you must know. If you don't already know."

"I'll ignore the insult, as it's late and you and your men look as if you've been riding hard. But freebooters? Tonight? Really? I've heard or seen nothing. Have you caught anyone, Lieutenant?"

"My men have taken charge of quite a few of them, yes, about two miles east of here. The losers, I would think, in some falling-out among them."

"Is that so? Then I must consider myself lucky I

didn't stumble into the middle of any such bloody fracas, shouldn't I?" Ainsley said, a slight nervous tremor in his voice now, just as if the thought had terrified him. "That will teach me to drive out at night."

"Yes, sir. To do what?"

Should I get up? Should I join them? Would that make things better or worse? Julia didn't know what to do.

"Again, Lieutenant, I owe you no explanations. However, since I see you don't plan to go away on your own, I will give you one. I had the headache, Lieutenant. I often have the headache and I find that a solitary drive up behind this tired old mare often helps to clear my head."

"With no accompaniment? No lanterns?"

"Beulah knows the way, and the light hurts my eyes. You will pardon me for not first alerting you when I choose to drive on my own land. Now if we're done here, shouldn't you and your men be out looking for the victors?"

"Pardon?"

"The victors, Lieutenant. You already said you've located and contained the losers."

"Yes, sir, we did. Unfortunately anyone else has managed to elude us."

Julia closed her eyes, sighed in relief. Courtland and the others were safe. Hopefully Chance was safe. But she and Ainsley most definitely were not. And she didn't know what to do about that.

"Which is why I've decided it necessary to search Becket Village, sir. It is possible, sir, that they've taken refuge there, putting your villagers in danger. The king's business, you see, includes protecting the safety of his subjects. Therefore, with or without your permission, sir, and much as it pains me to do so, my men and I are going to search the village."

A village peopled only by women, children and those too old to fight or sail. That's what Lieutenant Diamond and his men would find, Julia knew. She had to do something—anything—to keep the lieutenant here until at least the men with Courtland had made it safely back to Becket Hall.

Loosening the ribbons she'd knotted around her skirts, Julia was just about to rise—to do what, she didn't know—when a hand clapped over her mouth and Chance's face was inches from hers.

"Shh, sweetings," he whispered, smiling into her wide eyes. "He's handling it. But even Ainsley couldn't hope to explain *you*."

Julia pulled his hand away from her face as they lay side by side on the damp ground. "How…?"

"So helpful of you to leave the lantern behind," he told her. "I'm only glad I got here before you martyred yourself."

"I was not going to—listen. They're leaving."

Chance kept his arm around her until the sound of hoofbeats faded, retrieved the lantern he'd brought with him from the beach, then helped her to her feet. He pushed back her hair, frowned as the thin moonlight hit her face. "You're bleeding."

"I am?" Julia touched her cheek, her fingertips coming away wet. "I don't feel anything."

"You won't, not for a while," he said, dropping a quick kiss on her forehead, wanting to hold her tight but knowing there was no time. "Come on. Ainsley is going to tell me what the hell he was thinking, bringing you into this, and by the time I'm done with him, he'll wish Diamond was asking the questions again."

CHAPTER TWENTY-SIX

IT WAS LATE THE NEXT morning before Julia awoke in her bed, coming instantly awake. "Chance," she blurted out, sitting up, then winced as she realized she felt as if she'd been beaten from head to foot by someone who most definitely knew what he'd been about.

She moved her legs, and the sheet rubbing across her bare skin reminded her of the myriad angry scratches on her lower legs. Which served to remind her of the scratches on her face. Odette had promised they'd heal without leaving scars, but Odette had also said Ollie's baby was a boy.

Pushing back the covers, Julia went to look in the mirror overtop her dressing table, assured herself that her face hadn't been turned into a mass of ugly welts, then raced through her toilette, eager to be downstairs, more than eager to see Chance.

He'd been so wonderful last night, once they'd finally been back at Becket Hall and Lieutenant Diamond had gone on his way unhappy and empty-handed.

She hadn't realized that Courtland and his men had traveled by way of small boats they'd then hidden along the shore or that they'd returned so swiftly to Becket

Hall, reaching there long before Lieutenant Diamond had even thought to search the village.

But what of the others? Jacko and Billy and Ollie and the rest hadn't reappeared by the time Eleanor had ordered Julia to bed.

She raced to the window, pushed back the heavy velvet draperies and sighed in relief when she saw the *Respite* riding at anchor offshore.

"Yes, sweetings, as Ainsley told me to tell you, all the chickies are safely back in their nests," Chance said, closing her bedchamber door behind him. "And what are you doing out of bed and dressed? Heroines are supposed to keep to their beds for at least one day, where they recline in splendor, receiving their impressed and dazzled admirers."

"Chance!" Julia had exclaimed halfway through his silliness and had launched herself at him, her arms now clinging around his neck. "I have never been so frightened in my life."

"Or so invigorated?" he asked, whispering the words into her ear.

She pushed her hands against his shoulders so that she could move back, look up into his face. "Are you insane? There was absolutely nothing invigorating about anything that went on here last night. Please tell me it's over now, that the Red Men Gang is gone."

"We can't know that for sure, Julia, but with many of them dead and the rest already in Dover Castle, it will be some time before they'll dare to venture this way again. Not when they've much more lucrative, less dangerous areas for their activities."

"I suppose that will have to do," Julia said, resting her head on his shoulder. "How many injured are there? Does Odette want my help?"

"You're all done helping," Chance told her, kissing the top of her head. "Do you have any idea what I thought when I saw you lying facedown on the ground last night? I couldn't move, couldn't even call out your name—not until you tried to get up and I could be sure you were alive. I spent an hour last night yelling at Ainsley, and he let me."

"You were really frightened?" Julia asked him, her heart leaping with joy, which should have embarrassed her but didn't. "Now you know how I felt, watching you sail off on the *Respite*."

"So we're even," Chance said, smiling as he pressed his forehead against hers. "It's strange, isn't it, how many emotions there are wrapped in that single word, *love*. Desire, fear, even anger. God, Julia, I can't imagine life without you."

Julia reached up to lightly brush a misbehaving lock of hair behind his ear. "I've imagined life without you. Last night. I don't ever want to imagine that again."

He covered his mouth with hers, slipping his arms more fully around her, and knew he held his world.

"Chance! You're needed! *Now!*"

Julia buried her head against his chest as Chance looked at his brother. "Spencer, you need to be taught some manners. Knock next time, damn you."

"Right," Spencer said, nearly dancing in place, his face flushed. "Next time. Right now, *Romeo,* you're needed. It's trouble that's knocking now."

Julia lifted her head. "Spence? What's wrong?"

Spencer kept his attention on Chance, ignoring her question. "Chance, come on—move. He's talking, and you're not going to like what he's saying."

"Who's talking?" Julia asked, grabbing Chance by the elbow as he went to follow Spencer, who had already turned and left the bedchamber.

"The leader of the Red Men Gang. Courtland carried him here last night. We've been...we've been questioning him."

Julia swallowed painfully. "You've been torturing him?"

Chance's expression closed. "Spence was right not to tell you. This one isn't for women, Julia."

And then he was leaving her—again—and she was left alone. Again.

He'd promised it was over. How could he have made a promise like that, knowing they were torturing someone for information that could only continue the fight?

How she wanted this madness to be over!

Since having a good cry didn't really appeal to her at the moment, Julia went in search of some breakfast, as being a heroine had turned out to be hungry work. But when she realized that it was nearly time for luncheon, she decided instead to take a walk on the terrace.

That's when she saw Cassandra running up one of the flights of stone steps. "Well, aren't you in a rush. Good morning, Callie. Or should I say good aftern—"

"He's got her," Cassandra said, hanging on Julia's arm, bent over, trying to catch her breath. "He's got Alice. She was hiding. We were playing. We weren't doing anything wrong, we didn't go too far. And I saw him. I told her not to go to him, but she did and she wouldn't come back, and he—where's Papa? I was to bring Papa."

Julia grabbed Cassandra's arm and gave her a small shake. "Callie, wait. Is this another game? Because if it is—"

"He's got her!" Cassandra shouted, her eyes wild. "Oh, never mind! Nobody believes me! Find Papa! I've got to go help her!"

Julia put a hand to her mouth as she watched Cassandra run down the steps once more and out onto the beach, turning to her right, heading toward—

"The sands," Julia said quietly. "Oh, sweet Jesus. Alice, what have you done...?"

Julia ran toward the last set of French doors, the ones that led directly into Ainsley's study, and damn them all if they didn't care for the interruption!

But when she opened the door and stepped inside, she stopped dead at the sight of the bloody-faced man slumped in one of the leather chairs. "My God, what are you doing?"

Ainsley stepped in front of the unconscious man, blocking her view. "We're finished, actually, Julia. Chance, stop growling. What is it, my dear?"

Julia shifted her gaze from Ainsley to Chance to his brothers, all of them looking at her as if she should be anywhere but there. And she should be, because she had not wanted to see this, not needed to see this. The barbarity of men...

"Julia!"

She pressed her hands to her chest. "It's Alice. Callie says someone has her. On...on the beach somewhere. A man. I didn't believe her at first, but I don't think she's making up stories, I really don't. She ran, Callie did, toward the sands."

Chance was the first one past her and on his way down the stone steps, with the others in quick pursuit, except for Rian, who Ainsley held on to by one arm.

"Cassandra went after her?"

"Yes, sir. I...I'll go get her, bring her to you."

"Not necessary, my dear," he said, walking around his desk and pulling open a drawer, revealing a pair of nasty-looking pistols. "These might be needed."

"I want to go," Rian argued. "Damn it, this is my fight, too!"

"Someone has to watch this one," Ainsley said, inclining his head toward their captive. "Get someone to do that for you and you can join us."

His cane left behind, Ainsley quickly walked outside, Julia right behind him. Together they made their way to the beach, just as Spencer came running toward them.

"It took too long to break that bastard. He's got her. He's got Alice and he wants to talk terms."

"I don't...I don't understand," Julia said, looking to Ainsley, who handed one of the pistols to Spencer.

"Give it to Chance. Hell, here, give this one to Court. Go!"

Spencer ran back toward the curve in the shoreline, toward the sands.

"What's happening?" Julia asked, all but begged, as

she and Ainsley continued along the shore at a near trot. "Who's broken?"

Ainsley kept moving, limping badly. "The smuggler Court brought back with him last night. He was…reluctant to give us information until only a few minutes ago. And before you ask, that information had to do with who *his* leader is in this area. That's who has Alice, I'm sure of it. He wants to use her to force us to cooperate with him. But how he knew we're the ones…?"

"Perhaps we weren't as clever last night on the Marsh as we thought we were?"

Ainsley actually stopped for a moment to look down at her. "You mean that *I* wasn't as convincing as I wished to believe. Yes, that's probably it in a nutshell, considering who has Alice."

They'd rounded the bend in the shoreline now, and Julia could see Cassandra standing well back of Courtland, Spencer and Chance.

Then she looked farther, across the treacherous sands…and saw Alice.

And Lieutenant Diamond.

"Oh, God," she said nervously, trembling where she stood. "It's him? It's Lieutenant Diamond? Look how tightly he's holding Alice against him."

"And with that pistol cocked. It would appear we're at *point non plus,*" Ainsley said as they approached Chance. "What does he want?"

"Out," Chance said, not taking his attention away from Diamond or from his terrified child. "He wants out of England and the money to keep him comfortable when he gets where he's going."

"He must have counted noses last night and realized our new friend had gone missing, realized who had to have him," Courtland added, motioning for Cassandra to stay where she was, as the child was approaching, her fists to her mouth to stifle her sobs. "Callie said Alice went to him willingly when he called to her. Why would she do that?"

"Alice has no fear of strangers," Julia heard herself say, then she winced.

"She does now," Chance growled, hefting the pistol he held, knowing he couldn't use it. "We have to give him what he wants."

"Until we get what we want, yes," Ainsley agreed.

"No, damn it! I won't play with my daughter's life. We give him what he wants. No tricks."

"He'll want to take her with him, as hostage. But he won't keep her with him, and we both know that, Chance. He'll kill her."

The sun was shining. Julia knew that was a horribly silly thing to notice at a time like this, but the sun was shining. It was a beautiful day, warm, with a sweet breeze coming off the water. The sky was a gorgeous blue, with only a few lovely white clouds.

Nothing could be more beautiful, more peaceful.

So how could any of this horror be happening? She and Chance had finally found each other, found happiness. Last night had been a complete success, and there would be no more threat of exposure by the Red Men Gang bringing London down on them all. Everything was perfect. More than perfect.

How could this be happening!

"He'd really kill her?" Julia asked as all eyes were once more trained on Lieutenant Diamond and Alice, thirty feet away. So close but as unreachable as if there were a bottomless chasm between them.

As it was, the sands were between them, a fact Courtland pointed out at that moment. "He has to know the sands. This is all my fault. I'm the one who started this...."

"The button I found," Chance said, cutting him off. "We've all been blind, Court. Completely blind. I thought we were playing him, and all along he was playing us."

"He's standing where it's safe," Spencer pointed out tersely. "But if we threaten him, if he moves the wrong way, if the sand shifts..."

"Well?" Diamond shouted across the sands. "I'm not going to stand here all day!"

"How much does he want?" Ainsley asked calmly, seeming to have come to a decision.

"Does it matter?" Chance stabbed his fingers into his hair, angrily getting it out of his way. "I won't let him take Alice."

Julia had listened to every word, as they all seemed to have forgotten her, forgotten she was there. She blinked, looked past Diamond. *Rian.* Had anyone else seen him? He must have circled around, thinking to come up from behind the lieutenant. To do what?

"Rian!" Chance yelled, having also seen him. "Back off, damn it! You're only making things worse!"

The lieutenant turned, turning Alice with him, to look at Rian. Everyone was looking at Rian.

And Julia began to run.

She didn't think about the sands. She didn't think about the danger she was putting herself in. She simply ran, out onto the sands, toward Alice.

"Julia!" Chance made to follow her, but both Courtland and Spencer grabbed him, held him back. "What in Christ's name does she think she's doing?"

But he already knew. Julia was going to offer her life in exchange for Alice's life. Chance would have done the same, but Diamond wasn't stupid enough to trade a helpless child for a grown man. But Julia? A woman? Yes, that Diamond might do, might see the advantage in doing.

The man had to die. Slowly, with Chance's hands around his neck, squeezing, his face the last sight Diamond had before he met the devil....

Julia stopped a good ten feet away from Lieutenant Diamond, the only clear thought in her head now being Ainsley's words of last night: *Calm? Far from that, my dear. The first thing a man who wishes to lead others learns, Julia, is to deceive with confidence.*

Could she do it? Could she, a mere woman, deceive Lieutenant Diamond with confidence? She didn't know, couldn't know until she tried.

Alice, whose sobs had already nearly torn Julia in two, began to cry louder, so that the lieutenant tightened his hold around her neck and shoulders.

Julia's fears turned to cold, hard rage.

"Stop that, you big bully!" she commanded as if she were addressing the Hawkhurst child she'd caught out throwing rocks at a village dog. "Shame on you!"

"Shame on me? Shame on them—they send a woman to do a man's job? Miss Carruthers, you will oblige me by going back where you were."

"Or what?" Julia wasn't even a little bit afraid anymore. Her fears for Alice had taken all her other fears away. "Or you'll shoot me, Lieutenant Diamond? But that would leave you with an empty pistol, wouldn't it. Much better you allow me to take Alice's place and you let her return to her father."

Chance heard Julia's words carried to him on the breeze and cursed both her bravery and his impotence. "She can't do this," he muttered as Ainsley put a reassuring hand on his back. "I can't let her do this."

"But she is doing this," Ainsley pointed out soothingly. "And she's right. She has a much better chance than Alice would have. She'll obey our orders without question when we see an opening and give the man fits in the meantime. What's Diamond doing now?"

Chance fought to get himself back under control— no easy feat when everything he loved in this world was in danger—and realized that Julia was speaking again.

"Hush, sweetheart, no more crying," she was saying, crooning, to Alice. "Buttercup wouldn't want you to cry, now, would she? Buttercup would think you a silly thing indeed. Besides, you've got your *gad*, don't you? Nothing can hurt you when you've got your *gad*. Callie told you that—and Callie wouldn't lie, would she?"

Amazingly Alice stopped sobbing. "I don't want to be here anymore," she said, her small chest heaving, her bottom lip trembling as she hiccuped a few more sobs. "I'm so scared, Julia."

"Of course you are, darling. But you're going to come to me now, aren't you? Lieutenant Diamond is going to let you go, and you're going to come to me, and I'm going to take your place, aren't I?"

"He...he'll hurt you," Alice said, showing a wisdom beyond her years nobody was happy to see at the moment. "I won't let him hurt you."

Chance saw that Rian, who had retreated from the sands, had somehow made his way through the tall marsh grasses and was now no more than ten feet away from Diamond. God bless the boy! When in danger, the Beckets thought and acted as one, all their differences forgotten. "Wait until Alice is free, wait until Alice is free," Chance chanted quietly beneath his breath, and Ainsley's grip tightened on his shoulder.

"Why do you hesitate, Lieutenant?" Julia asked when he released his tight hold on Alice's body but still kept possession of her arm. "Surely one hostage is as good as another. And Alice barely protects you, she's too small. I will make a much better shield."

She thought she had him. She believed she had him. *Deceive with confidence.* Now all she needed was for him to let go of Alice.

And then he did.

"Go to Papa, Alice!" Julia shouted. "This way, straight past me! *Run!*"

His pistol trained on Julia now, she didn't dare hesitate more than a second or two to watch as Alice ran past her, but when she turned once more, it was not at Diamond's command but at the loud bark of a pistol shot.

A bright red flower of blood had somehow blossomed on the lieutenant's shoulder, and he had whirled toward the marsh grasses, firing toward them wildly.

Everything happened seemingly at once then: Rian's head and shoulders popping up above the grasses; the boy shouting for Julia to run; Chance grabbing her roughly, pushing her behind him, also ordering her to run.

But it was Lieutenant Diamond who ran, as they all watched.

Holding on to his injured shoulder, the panic of a man who knew he'd made a fatal blunder vivid in his eyes, he turned and ran, stumbling as he tried to escape the inevitable.

And then he stopped running, his arms pinwheeling now as he nearly lost his balance.

And he began to scream.

"Oh, my God, the sands!" Julia yelled, grabbing at Chance's arm. "The sands have him. *Do something!*"

"I am doing something, Julia," Chance said, a muscle working in his cheek. "I'm watching."

"No! Chance," Julia begged, grabbing his face between her hands, "look at me. Listen to me. He'll hang. You can watch him hang if you want to. But you cannot do this. None of you. I don't care who you were, who you think you were. It doesn't matter. You're Beckets now. You fought so hard to be who you are now. All of you. Don't let this man destroy what you've gained. For your sisters. For Alice. For me! Please, Chance!"

He covered her hands with his own and felt himself drawing back from the brink. Julia was right. He'd fought too hard—they all had—to go back to the sort of violence that had brought them there. "At the end of the day, sweetings, I don't know if Diamond will thank you or not."

Then he yelled to his brothers and the others who had now joined them on the shore to help him make up a human chain that would reach out to where the lieutenant was slowly sinking into the sands....

EPILOGUE

CHANCE HAD TRIED, they'd all tried, especially as they realized that the lieutenant might be able to give them much more information about the real leader of the Red Men Gang—the head of the hydra that controlled all the new gangs up and down the coast—but Diamond, in the end, had not cooperated.

"Your hand! Give me your hand!" Chance had ordered when he knew he could go no closer without being trapped himself, but Diamond, who had stopped screaming, only smiled and shook his head.

"Why? So you can torture me into telling you what you want to know? So the Crown can hang me, put me on display? If they don't get to me first. And they would. They're everywhere, Becket, you can't stop them. I'm a dead man, no matter what, so I'll choose how I die."

"Don't listen to him, Chance," Julia yelled to him, even as she felt herself being dragged farther from the sands; she, along with Alice and Cassandra.

"There's nothing we can do, if he won't help." Chance spoke quietly to Spencer and Courtland, telling them to take the women back to Becket Hall.

"And you, brother?" Courtland had asked as the two of them watched the lieutenant, who was now in the sands up to his thighs, his injured arm still bleeding profusely.

"I'll stay with Diamond. Somebody has to, Court. We have to be sure. Just get them out of here. *Now.*"

"He may change his mind. We could use any information he has," Courtland said, handing Chance the thick rope someone had produced. "It's a hell of a death."

"It's a hell of a life, if we pull him out of there," Chance said, watching Diamond as the man began to move his arms across the top of the sands, as if he could push the sand out of his way. "I'm not sure which I'd choose."

"What?" Diamond yelled from his sandy prison, not ten feet from them. "Deciding which of you is going to watch? Hoping I'll scream? Hoping I'll beg? Well, the devil with you all!"

And then, as Ainsley and the rest walked away, turning their backs on the man, Lieutenant Diamond began to sing. A sailor's song, a distinctly bawdy song. A song of defiance.

After a few moments, Chance joined in.

Julia pulled free of Ainsley's hand, and turned to look back at the sands. Saw Courtland walking toward them, shaking his head. "Madness," he said, lifting Alice into his arms, pushing the girl's head against his shoulder. "Here. Anywhere. We live in an insane world."

Julia's bottom lip trembled as she nodded her head, then took hold of Cassandra's hand and headed for Becket Hall, Chance's voice, and Diamond's voice, finally fading in the distance, blown away by the warm, soft sea breeze. She turned her back on death, and prayed for a better life.

Sometimes the sands were greedy. Sometimes they were agonizingly slow. It could have been minutes, it might have been hours. Chance would never be sure.

Diamond's show of bravado hadn't lasted long, and Chance had sat down on the sands, to wait, to watch, to offer, one last time, a way out.

Chance's face had been the last thing the lieutenant had seen before he disappeared beneath the shifting sands, one last curse on his lips, a curse that had ended in a scream.

And then, silence. The sun shone brightly, the sky was a brilliant, cloudless blue. A fresh breeze off the Channel blew strands of Chance's hair across his tear-wet eyes. The lieutenant was gone, and the world had moved on....

For a long time after that, there was nothing but the sound of the water slapping at the shore, the cry of a few circling gulls, before Chance slowly got to his feet and walked away.

He'd be haunted now, by the memory of Diamond's terrified expression as he sank into Hell; haunted, yet not sorry the man was dead. Just one more dead man on his soul, one more hurdle for him to overcome if he was ever to be a civilized gentleman.

But he had hope now, because he had Julia.

She was waiting for him on the stairs leading up to the terrace, the wind catching at her long blond hair, the skirts of her gown. He approached slowly, searching her face for condemnation, for disappointment, for disgust.

And none of those emotions were there.

She stood proudly, her chin high, watching him as he put a booted foot on the first stone step, then began walking up toward her, the weight of the world on his shoulders, the pain of the world evident in his eyes.

"Julia…"

This was her man, the man she had chosen, the man who had chosen her. Together, they could face anything. They would be each other's sanity in this insane world and, together, they would find a place of love and safety for themselves, for their children.

Julia held out her hand to him as he continued to climb toward her, and when he took it firmly in his, they both knew they'd sealed a bond that would never be broken.

"Alice is waiting for us," she said as they mounted the last few steps together, arm-in-arm.

Chance scrubbed at his face with his hand, feeling fresh tears on his cheeks. Cleansing tears. Freeing tears. He turned, took one last look at the innocent-looking sands, before pulling Julia closer. "Then let's not keep her waiting," he said.

Hours later, Julia lay cradled in Chance's arms in her bedchamber, content in the aftermath of loving, that age-old reaffirmation that the world, that life, still moves on.

He kissed the top of her head, then said, "Julia. There's something I want to tell you. No, something I *need* to tell you. A long, often sad story. About the island, about Isabella and Ainsley and everything that happened there, everything that made me what I am, just as you make me what I want to be."

Julia shifted against him, smiled up at him as Odette's words came back to her: *The day he tells you, his heart is yours for the keeping. Do you want his heart?*

"I'd like that," she said simply.

* * * * *

*Here's an exciting preview from the next book
in Kasey Michaels's
The Beckets of Romney Marsh saga,
THE DANGEROUS DEBUTANTE,
available this April from HQN Books.*

CHAPTER ONE

MORGAN BEGAN TO STROLL around the country inn yard. Perhaps someone would see her in her lovely new riding habit and be impressed all hollow. She'd like that, and it would be a good omen perhaps, a hint of how she and her wonderful new wardrobe would be received in London society.

Except, she realized, frowning, she was very much alone, save for a man just now leading his mount into the yard. No, not leading the stallion, for the reins were loosely tied up on the saddle. The horse was following him like a faithful hound, not looking at all subservient but more as if he followed, yes, but only because it pleased him to do so.

Morgan laughed out loud at the sight, then concentrated her attention on the animal.

The stallion was magnificent. Beyond magnificent. Nearly white in the sunlight, its hindquarters dappled gray, with a thick silvery mane that flowed to its shoulder and a proud tail that nearly skimmed the ground.

Not a huge stallion, although the chest was fairly massive for its size, which had to be between fifteen and sixteen hands. Probably closer to fifteen. The ears were small and perfect, and when the horse turned toward her, as if aware she was admiring him, Morgan saw huge, intelligent eyes on a finely shaped head with a slightly convex nose.

Without a thought to convention—something she was definitely unaccustomed to considering at the best of times—Morgan set out across the yard, calling out to the man as she neared: "What a beauty!"

ETHAN TANNER LOOKED to his right at the sound of the female voice and was quick to agree. A definite beauty. He watched, caught between amusement and fascination, as the young woman advanced toward him, walking with the confident, long-legged stride of a man, except that she was most amazingly female.

Lush. Tall but far from angular. The breeze whipping through the inn yard all but plastered her divided skirt against her long thighs with each step she took, clearly delineating them, and Ethan unexpectedly felt a familiar stirring in his own.

He continued his inspection of this exotic beauty whose appearance was so at odds with the current fashion that centered on petite, blue-eyed blondes. Her nearly black hair was brushed sleekly back from her head, probably twisted into a knot at her nape. God, he hoped so, because a man should be able to see that dark silk tumbled over her bare breasts and back before he lowered her onto his bed. The green shako hat was set at a provocative tilt on her forehead, while a thick, sleekly curved lock of almost shoulder-length hair caressed the creamy ivory skin of her flawlessly beautiful face.

She came closer, and Ethan's inspection continued unchecked by any thought he might be staring like some starving fool with his nose pressed against the pastry shop windowpane.

Dark winglike brows over unusual gray, smoky eyes that seemed to hint at all the sensuous mysteries of the ages. High cheekbones that gave her that slightly exotic look. A wide, full mouth that lifted faintly at the corners. Her riding habit was of the first stare, although it was doubtful any modiste had ever dreamed any of her creations could be so flattered or look so circumspect and so wanton at one and the same time.

As a package, taken altogether, Ethan decided this woman was Original Sin. And Adam had his full empathy. He amazed himself at his almost embarrassingly poetical mental impression of the female, although he was not surprised to feel eminently attracted to her face and form. This female was fashioned to be alluring. This female who, he finally realized, was so blatantly ignoring him.

"Alejandro, you're being admired, you lucky bastard," he drawled quietly. "Bow to the lady."

Morgan, still fairly oblivious to anything save the magnificent horse, stopped short when the stallion turned toward her, then slowly, gracefully, bent his left knee to the ground as he extended his right leg and lowered his head.

"Oh, you brilliant, handsome boy!" Morgan walked straight up to the horse and placed her gloved hands on either side of its muzzle before planting a kiss between its ears. "What's his name?" she asked, looking adoringly at the stallion.

"Alejandro," Ethan answered. "And damn me if I don't find myself jealous of a horse. Here now, up, you toad-eating sycophant."

Alejandro smoothly stood up once more and swung his handsome head toward Ethan, showing his teeth in a horsey smile.

Morgan laughed in genuine delight, neither seriously considering the hinted flattery nor insulted by the swearword. After all, she knew who she was, how she looked, and she had grown up at Becket Hall, with brothers who rarely watched their words around her. "It's as if he understand you," she said.

"If so, he's got the advantage of me," Ethan said, his gaze still drinking in the sight of this gorgeous woman. This gorgeous, well-dressed, unchaperoned woman who didn't seem to entertain the slightest hesitation to speak with an unknown man.

"Is he Andalusian? I've seen a few drawings, but this is the first time I've ever—"

Morgan had at last drawn her attention away from Alejandro to speak with his owner. Whatever she'd planned to say—had she planned to say anything?—became lost as she looked at him.

Simply looked at him. As if she'd never seen a male of the species until that moment.

His eyes attracted her first. Nearly straight brows, low over long, green eyes, with the whites accentuated by thick, dark lashes, those eyes seemed amused and unreadable at one and the same time, as if the laugh lines that fanned from the outside corners could be genuine or were just a clever facade meant to keep anyone from looking any deeper.

His nose was magnificent. She'd never thought a nose could be described that way, but this one could be—so wonderfully straight, the nostrils slightly flared above a most…a most intriguing mouth. Even his ears seemed perfect, lying flat against his head and visible because his darkly blond hair had been ruthlessly combed straight back off his only slightly lined forehead to brush at the collar of his shirt.

His long, leanly muscled body was clad seemingly carelessly in that open-necked white shirt, a dark leather vest, fawn buckskins and high-topped riding boots.

Her brothers dressed much the same way at Becket Hall. But this was different. This was…this was dangerous. Personally dangerous. And she was being silly! She wasn't intimidated by a man. Why would she be? Men were intimidated by her.

But not this one. He was the most man she'd ever seen.

A dangerous man. Definitely dangerous; a clear warning positively radiated from him. She could all but see it, an aura of deep red ringed with yellow that surrounded him that could be some trick of the sun but she was certain was not.

Years earlier, Odette had told her about such things, how certain creatures, human or beast, stood apart from others merely by being alive. Their power was stronger, for good or for evil, and a wise person who encountered one of these creatures recognized that and made their choices, their decisions, accordingly.

Odette had told her that Ainsley Becket was one of the dangerous ones. Odette had seen that in an instant and she had followed him because to be with him was much preferred to being against him, as she had also sensed his good heart.

"But he's only Papa, he's not dangerous to me, not at all. What should I do, Odette?" Morgan remembered asking the voodoo woman. "If I ever see one of the dangerous ones, I mean? What should I do?"

Odette had laughed that deep, rich laugh that came from somewhere deep inside her. "Child, you already know the answer. You are one of them, one of the dangerous ones. You do not pick the danger, it chooses you, and only a foolish woman would deny that truth. But, inquisitive child, to answer your question…the good Virgin only knows what would happen if you ever came up against one of your own kind, your own powerful will."

He had waited, watching her look at him, enjoying the luxury of looking at her, then finally broke the silence. "You were about to say something?"

Morgan raised her chin slightly, refusing to be embarrassed that she had been staring, and only said, "And who, sir, are you?"

"Me?" His grin was boyish, unaffected, carving long, slashing dimples into his lean, tanned cheeks—which made him seem even more dangerous than before. "Why, I'm abashed," he drawled, slowly advancing toward her. "Bedazzled. Enchanted. And, for my sins," he added, bowing from the waist while keeping his amused green gaze on her, "I am also Ethan Tanner, Earl of

Aylesford, at your service and your every command, madam."

"Really," Morgan said, wishing her heart would show some sympathy for her and slow from its furious gallop. She'd already half expected him to be somebody important, as he was dressed well, if casually, and his horse was not the possession of a simple country squire.

She schooled herself to calmly raise one hand to stroke Alejandro's strong neck as the stallion nuzzled her shoulder, never realizing how striking woman and animal looked together. "How wonderful for you."

Ethan tipped his head slightly to one side, looking at her quizzically. How wonderful for him? Harriette Wilson wouldn't be so bold, and she was a practiced courtesan. And damn Alejandro for the traitor he was.

Who did this luscious woman belong to? And how much would it cost him to take her away from any fool so stupid as to let her roam free? Half his fortune didn't seem too much to pay.

"Yes, thank you," Ethan said, "I am rather pleased my mother had the good sense to marry well. And, if I may be so bold, as no one else seems to be present to do the honors, may I ask your name, beautiful lady?"

Should he have called her a beautiful lady? Morgan doubted that he should. She more than doubted it after enduring long hours of Eleanor's lessons on how one behaves in society. Still, he intrigued her, and she'd never backed either away or down from anything or anyone that intrigued her.

She'd play his game to see where it might take her, but she'd be damned if she'd curtsy. "I suppose turnabout is only fair. I am Morgan Becket of Becket Hall. That's in Romney Marsh, so you probably won't have heard of us or it." And then, before she could bite her tongue, she added, "I'm on my way to London for the season."

"Is that so," Ethan said, hastily attempting to reshuffle his initial conclusion that she was a kept woman. "Unaccompanied, Miss Becket? How…very original."

Morgan blinked at this, at the earl's tone that suddenly seemed entirely too familiar, as if in the blink of an eye the game had turned serious. She suddenly wished the six outriders back. She looked toward the stables just in time to see Jacob leading Berengaria out into the yard.

Yes, there he was. Her remaining "accompaniment." And here she was, having disobeyed her papa's strict orders to stay as private as possible and for God's sake not cause any disasters between Becket Hall and Upper Brook Street. *I can rely on you to do this one thing,* Ainsley Becket had asked her, *can't I?*

Obviously her papa had overestimated both her limits of obedience and Jacob's power to control her.

But if she was in a pickle now it was through her own fault, and she couldn't allow Jacob to become involved, try to defend her honor or any such nonsense. Not with a man like the earl, who could easily chew up Jacob and spit him out again before the younger man could count to three.

She quickly looked at the earl once more.

He was still smiling at her. As if he knew something she didn't know and delighted in that fact.

Damn. This was no longer even in the least amusing. Now she truly understood why she was supposed to stay in the coach or in her private dining room when they stopped for meals and in her private bedchamber at the inn when she'd passed the single night they needed to be on the road.

Bringing a maid from Becket Hall had been out of the question, partly because Morgan didn't actually have a personal maid there, partly because no one at Becket Hall had the faintest idea of how to properly dress a lady's hair or such things...and mostly because the fewer tongues hanging about and liable to flap, the better.

Careful. Through years of practice, the Beckets had learned how to be careful. Too careful, Morgan had always believed, which was one reason she'd always tugged so hard on the reins. After all, the island had been so many years ago...

Yet now here she was, alone and seemingly unprotected, strutting about as if she had an army at her back when Jacob was her only soldier—and with no reason for the earl to believe her better than it had to appear she was. How different from Becket Hall, where everyone knew her and every last man there would stand in her defense against any danger. Why, if Jacko or any of the others had heard the earl's words, even seen the unnervingly familiar way he was now smiling at her, Ethan Tanner's life wouldn't be worth a bucket of warm spit.

But Jacko wasn't there. The outriders weren't there. Nobody was there. And Morgan couldn't simply stand there and brazenly stare back at the earl while waiting for Jacob to do something that would probably get his nose broken. She had to talk her way out of the predicament she'd created.

"My maid has taken ill, my lord," she improvised quickly, "and therefore is on her way back to Becket Hall in the company of my outriders. I know my position to be precarious at the moment, except for the fact that my groom, Jacob, along with my coachman, would skewer anyone who dared to so much as look at me crookedly or take insulting notions into their heads. You wouldn't be addlepated enough to do either of those things, would you, my lord?"

Ethan bowed again, amused by her sudden vehemence and very much pleased that he would appear to be without competition. Miss Morgan Becket wasn't a kept woman, a high-flying concubine. She was simply badly managed by her keepers and more accustomed to free and easy country ways. In short, she was marvelously unencumbered—and his for the taking if he played his cards correctly.

Until she showed her face—and that body—in London society. After that, she would set her own style, and he could end up as one of many vying for her favor.

The devil he would. He'd noted the way she'd looked at him. He knew how he'd felt when he'd first caught sight of her, would not easily forget that figurative punch to the gut that had all but bowled him over. The attraction had been instant and definitely mutual. Even Alejandro seemed to know, for God's sake. The horse also appeared to be smitten, which simply showed how a man can never quite trust other males when a beautiful female was added to the mix. In fact, there was now only one new problem to supplant what he'd believed his previous problems. Miss Morgan Becket, if truly a hopeful debutante, was also most certainly a virgin. He'd always made it a point not to come within ten yards of a virgin.

Then again, in exceptional circumstances, exceptions could be made. In this case, the exceptional circumstance was that he felt reasonably sure he'd never want another woman until he'd first had this one beneath him.

If you enjoyed what you just read,
then we've got an offer you can't resist!

Take 2 bestselling love stories FREE!
Plus get a FREE surprise gift!

KASEY MICHAELS

77038-3	SHALL WE DANCE	___ $6.99 U.S.	___ $8.50 CAN.
77006-5	THE BUTLER DID IT	___ $6.50 U.S.	___ $7.99 CAN.

(limited quantities available)

TOTAL AMOUNT	$ _____
POSTAGE & HANDLING	$ _____
($1.00 FOR 1 BOOK, 50¢ for each additional)	
APPLICABLE TAXES*	$ _____
TOTAL PAYABLE	$ _____

(check or money order—please do not send cash)

To order, complete this form and send it, along with a check or money order for the total above, payable to HQN Books, to: **In the U.S.:** 3010 Walden Avenue, P.O. Box 9077, Buffalo, NY 14269-9077; **In Canada:** P.O. Box 636, Fort Erie, Ontario, L2A 5X3.

Name: _____
Address: _____ City: _____
State/Prov.: _____ Zip/Postal Code: _____
Account Number (if applicable): _____
075 CSAS

*New York residents remit applicable sales taxes.
*Canadian residents remit applicable GST and provincial taxes.

HQN™

We *are* romance™